BRIGHT HEART

ALSO BY EMMA HAMM

The Otherworld

Heart of the Fae

Veins of Magic

The Faceless Woman

The Raven's Ballad

Bride of the Sea

Curse of the Troll

Of Goblin Kings

Of Goblins and Gold

Of Shadows and Elves

Of Pixies and Spells

Of Werewolves and Curses

Of Fairytales and Magic

Once Upon a Monster

Bleeding Hearts

Binding Moon

Ragged Lungs

and many more...

BRIGHT HEART

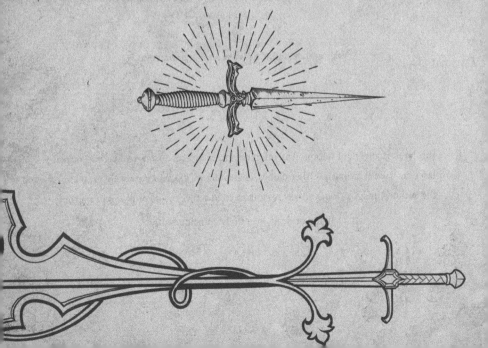

For the little dog who kept me company
while I wrote, but didn't get to see his namesake in a book.

We miss you a thousand times every day Zephyr.
Can't wait to see you over the rainbow bridge, bud.

MALIS

KINGDOM OF
UMBRA

STYGIAN PEAKS

FIELD OF SOMBER

CITY OF TENEBROUS

CHAPTER 1

An icy wind howled through the empty great hall. Tattered crimson banners waved, their tails snapping like whips. Glass shards littered the floor and crunched underneath Lorelei's feet as she strode through what had once been the most impressive building in all of Umbra.

No longer.

Crouching, Lore picked up a shard of mirror and met her own tired gaze. Dark circles ringed her eyes. Her usually sunshine bright hair hung lank around her face, but baths hadn't been frequent while she tried to convince the rebellion not to loose their members in the castle and destroy everything that had once been the King's. She'd failed in that argument. The exhaustion of her continued battles showed on her features all too well.

1

Lore turned the mirror piece in her hand. A small inscription on the back revealed a single word. Vanity.

How appropriate. Considering the entire world had seemingly lost their minds, and here she was, standing in the rubble of what she'd created. Sure, it wasn't entirely her fault. Margaret had planned this for years, and the tricky elf hadn't given Lore a chance to say she wanted nothing to do with this.

Still. It felt like the crumbling castle and the destruction of history rested on her shoulders.

The wind brushed against the back of her neck, stirring the hairs at her nape. This time, no howl accompanied the breeze. Only the complete and utter feeling of being alone.

She'd forgotten that war turned a lively haven into a barren graveyard.

Only a few weeks ago, the castle had glowed with grandeur. Sure, it had also been the home of a tyrant king who should never have control over others. But the plants that were now brittle skeletons had once hung over a golden throne without the obvious dents of hammers wielded with anger.

Sighing, she stood, mirror shard still held in her hand. Lore had known it would come to this. No sane magical creature would walk into this castle and not feel the effects of so many years dedicated to cruelty. She should destroy everything she could get her fists on.

Lore simply... couldn't. Instead of the symbolism built by the King, she saw all the hands that touched every opulent piece and the hours it had taken to build them. She saw the artist who made the stained glass window, which now was little more than decorative dust on the floor. The mason who spent a lifetime on the carvings of mortal men in battle. Even the florist who came twice a week to feed and water the plants.

Too many years had gone into building this castle, and so many hands had placed their dreams and dedication into every expression of beauty.

That wind pricked her neck again. But this time, she recognized the feeling. She wasn't alone anymore, although the presence had become slightly more familiar than before.

Abraxas's deep voice broke through the silence of the great hall. "They're meeting. I thought you'd like to go."

She didn't want to.

Margaret had been trying to get all the "heroes" from the sacking of the Umbral Castle together so they could all plan their future. She wanted Lorelei to be the face of all that, considering she was the person who had killed the King.

But she wasn't, now was she? Even Margaret knew the spurt of blood from the King's neck hadn't been a mortal wound. And yet, here she was, still lying through her teeth, saying that Lorelei had done what no one else had managed.

Lore found it was rather difficult to trust a liar.

She stared at the broken throne and the mess the rebellion had made, then let out a long, low sigh.

A broad, warm hand pressed against her back. She hadn't realized how cold she was until the heat of his skin sank through the thin white shirt she wore. The instant she recognized the chill was the moment she shivered. The shakes violently traveled from her shoulders to her fingertips. Her hands spasmed.

That wouldn't do. She had to be stronger than that.

Lorelei tamped down on the shaking, forcing her body to stop moving before she stepped out of his reach. "I suppose I have to go, now don't I?"

3

"Everything's a choice. If you don't want to go, I'll make excuses for you."

Like he'd been doing for two weeks. As though he knew the inner workings of her mind and everyone else trusted him to tell the truth. They wouldn't trust him with any serious matters within the rebellion, but when it came to Lorelei's thoughts, they took his word as law.

Why? They weren't all that close. Adrenaline had certainly pushed them together, but the moment that had drained from her body was the moment that...

Her eyes trailed up the length of him, and she had to swallow the anxiety that leapt into her throat. He was so handsome. Tall and wide, enough so that he made every other mortal she'd seen look tiny. But of course he did. He was a dragon in the form of a man, and no one could match him.

Yet her heart screamed when she looked at him now. Common sense had finally squeezed through the adrenaline and connection she'd felt with him. Abraxas was the sole person who had made the largest impact in taking down the King. And with that common sense trailed the reality that this man had killed her mother. Yes, he wasn't the one who had ordered it. No, he hadn't wanted to kill anyone on the orders of the King.

But he'd still done it.

She remembered the flames that had erupted from his reptilian mouth. She remembered the single scream of rage that her mother had blasted at a nightmarish monster before the fire had consumed her. This was the man who had taken everything from Lore with a single flick of his power.

Forgetting that took a little longer than a few weeks at the hands of an evil King. Only a mad woman would brush that aside so easily.

Abraxas tilted his head to the side, likely watching the thoughts play across her features. "That look isn't about meeting Margaret."

"No, it's not."

"Care to share what's going on in that mind of yours, Lady of Starlight?"

Even the nickname made her wince. It was a name for friends, or people who were moving toward becoming far more than that. And she couldn't afford to be more than that with him. Not now. Not when her head was so fuzzy with memories and dark, lonely nights.

Lorelei denied him, though she knew his opinion may help. "No. I'm not interested in sharing."

His brows drew down in a deep frown, but he still nodded.

Discomfort stretched between them like a string ready to snap under the pressure. She shouldn't feel guilty for causing this, but she did. How could she not? They had kissed in the forest, and she'd have done a lot more if Beauty hadn't interrupted them with the horrible news that the King had survived. Lore would have thrown all reason to the wind simply because they had done the impossible.

She'd gotten caught up in all of this... nonsense. She wasn't a hero anymore than the man in front of her was a monster. They'd both committed unforgivable acts against the kingdom and its people, and in the end, they would always have to bear those marks on their souls.

"I'm sorry," she whispered, the words slipping unbidden off her tongue. "Things are just... different now."

"Are they?" Abraxas moved closer to her, his throat working in a heavy swallow. "We're still the same people we were in the forest."

"I don't think I am." And that knowledge terrified her. "I don't know how to be the woman you want me to be, Abraxas. I don't know how to step back into the footsteps of the woman who killed the King. I never

5

wanted to be her in the first place."

If she'd drawn a knife across his throat, she thought he might look less surprised. Abraxas moved away from her then, as though even he needed more space between them. "My opinion of you hasn't changed."

"I wish I could say the same."

He winced. The slightest of movements. But she saw the way his lips twisted and how his right shoulder rose toward his ear. Maybe she'd been too harsh. Maybe she was pushing him away because all of this terrified her a little too much, but... How was she supposed to deal with all this?

The madness of battle had passed. And in its wake, all that remained was a silence like a never ending scream in her ears. She touched a hand to the side of her head as though that might stop the horrible ringing. "Where are they meeting?"

"What?" he asked, before he understood what she meant. "Ah, right? Margaret and them. They're in the King's quarters this time, I believe. Something about reclaiming the room where the King had cooked up all his plans to destroy those who now hold the castle."

Of course, that was the first place Margaret would wish to leave her mark. The woman thought everything was a pissing contest and acted more like a werewolf than she did an elf.

"Fine," Lore muttered as she walked around him. "I'll head that way, then."

The last area of the castle she wanted to visit was Zander's private quarters. What horrible place had he made it? Had he filled it with the heads of his enemies? She wouldn't be surprised if he had.

But then she remembered that Zander had been remarkably normal when he wanted to be. And that even though he'd done terrible things to her people and to anyone who wasn't human, he also had been more like a child than a man.

She stopped at the door to the great hall and placed her hand on the frame. Looking over her shoulder, she cast her eyes to the vision of the dragon standing in the hall.

The last time they'd been in here, he'd thrown himself on top of her. Wings spread wide. Glass shards and balls of acid falling on his back. He'd done everything he could to protect her, and it was because of him that she stood here now. And as thanks, she'd reject all that had brought them together.

Her fingers curled into a fist on the door frame.

"I haven't forgotten any of it, you know," she said quietly, though her voice rang too loud in the empty room.

"Oh, I never questioned that." He tucked his hands behind his back and lifted his chin. He looked every inch the imperial dragon who had helped run this country for multiple generations. "You've never struck me as someone who didn't see every situation from multiple angles. I know you've remembered I'm the villain."

"I don't enjoy thinking of you as that," she whispered. Which was the problem, really. Her entire body hurt to think ill of him. Then her mind screamed that he'd killed her mother and that she should hate him.

But she couldn't.

All those thoughts tangled around each other, twisting and coiling into knots she couldn't untangle, even though she tried. She wanted to. Of course she did. Maybe if she pulled at least one of those threads free, then she wouldn't feel like her soul was ripping apart.

"No one enjoys thinking of another as a villain. I know what I've done, Lore. My memory is better than most, and I know it will take time to win your trust and that of the others." A muscle in his jaw jumped.

"I'm working on that. All I ask is that you see me taking the steps in the right direction."

Lore didn't even try to stop her snort. "You helped kill the King, Abraxas. I don't think any of us question where your loyalty lies."

"But we didn't kill him, now did we?" He looked her in the eyes until guilt burned in her stomach. "None of this will be over until he's dead."

Right.

Because the only answer they had ever come up with was killing Zander.

Lorelei touched her still broken nose and hated that she agreed with him. She'd love to put her fist through Zander's black heart and rip it out of the King's chest. He deserved worse for what he'd done to her and to so many others.

Tracking him down wouldn't be easy, however, and that was the problem. Margaret had made it very clear she wanted no one leaving the castle just yet. She wanted the rumors to run throughout the entire kingdom. Those were far more powerful than sending out any other news, apparently.

Lorelei didn't know she agreed. Rumors distorted into stories. And then legends. She wasn't a legend, nor did she want to become some hero in a story that children listened to at night.

She was an elf who existed. People could ask her what had really happened, and she would tell them without hesitation. They should want to do that rather than believe in made up stories.

Of course, she also knew they'd prefer the tall tale.

Who wouldn't fall in love with the story of an elf who captured the attention of a dragon? A dragon who was enslaved by an evil mortal, but who wanted to protect his people. And the love that bloomed between them that would eventually save a kingdom.

She could already see the paintings that people would make. The little paper cutouts that children would place in front of candles while they told the story in their own way. This could so easily get out of hand. And then where would she be? Who would she be?

Sighing one last time, she rapped her knuckles against the wooden frame, narrowly missing slivers of wood that might have impaled her skin. "This is bigger than the two of us, Abraxas. I'm afraid killing him might not stop what is coming for us. Does that make sense?"

"I thought you said you weren't interested in there being an 'us'." There it was. The fire that ignited in his eyes whenever he talked about her. As though she were something to be won. Or hunted.

She swallowed hard and then left the room. What else could she do? She couldn't stand so close to him when he looked at her like that. All that heat would call out to the icy shards in her very soul, and she'd wrap herself in him again. She'd try to melt the painful icicles that wriggled through her heart.

Lore couldn't afford to melt right now. She had to be the hardened version of herself, the one her mother would have urged her to become.

After all, a hero couldn't fall for the dragon.

CHAPTER 2

He let her get a few steps ahead of him. The little elf needed time to herself and her thoughts, which he was more than happy to give her. He had all the time in the world. Abraxas had learned long ago that trying to rush women usually ended in heartbreak.

If she needed him to wait a century for the ache in her soul to ease, then he would. And gladly.

He'd do anything to bask in the rays of her starlight once again.

Abraxas tucked his hands into his pockets as he trailed down the same hallway she'd fled down. It made sense that she would return to fearing him. After all, they had a tumultuous past. He still didn't understand why she'd been so angry when he told her that her mother had a good death, but there was likely some difference in their cultures that he hadn't factored in.

This was difficult. Dragons didn't have to justify themselves to anyone. Let alone an elf. He remembered their kind being kidnapped and placed in his homeland. Those who were more similar to Lorelei had always gone off on their own.

He'd been too young back then to even consider having an elf as a mate. Dragons were useful to each other for prolonging their species, but they rarely ended up together forever. Dragons enjoyed a little more variety in their life than that.

His boots clicked down the hall like the sound of a clock. The ticking rushed his thoughts and urged him to understand what was going on in her mind. Did she remember the old days? Had someone once told her that the dragons kidnapped her kind?

They hadn't only kidnapped elves; he reasoned with himself. Dragons found their mates in all manner of people and all kinds of creatures. They'd always taken pride in that. Bringing in others who had unique experiences, who had seen different worlds, that was what made the dragons so strong. They were able to understand those they didn't know.

He could roll the thoughts over in his thoughts until they became smooth as river stones and he still wouldn't change her mind. She'd have to come to that conclusion on her own.

And he hoped she would realize that he was a good man at his core. That he'd never wanted to hurt anyone, but would do so again if it meant he would save his people.

Or her. Now she was just as important as those eggs. And shouldn't that bother him? Perhaps it did.

He paused in front of the meeting room, staring at the door that now held scratches from swords and countless people who had run through the halls, destroying everything Zander had built.

Even now, the ghost of the King still taunted him. Abraxas could almost see the man's spirit standing outside the door.

The last time he'd been here, the King had leaned against the frame and teased Abraxas about how he never seemed to want any of the prostitutes he brought back. "Are you not interested in women, my friend?" he'd asked. "You can tell me if you'd rather I find more interesting men to bring."

Abraxas hadn't wanted to tell Zander anything about his people or his kind, so he'd kept his mouth shut. It didn't matter that dragons cared little for what gender their partner was. Zander wouldn't have understood what he meant. The King would have pulled and pried at every detail until he made Abraxas feel even less of a man.

Those ghosts had to die, or he'd never make it out of this castle. He planted his hand flat against the door and shoved it open.

True to her nature, Margaret had remade the bedroom. It should have been full of crimson draperies, a large mirror where Zander liked to stare at himself, and platforms all around the room. Sometimes the King used those to see outfits at different angles, other times he ordered lovely women from across his kingdom to dance on each tiny stage that he'd created in his own private rooms.

Now, those had all been removed. Only a few remnants of the draperies remained where someone had clearly cut them with a knife or sword. They dangled like hanging guts from the ceiling. Margaret had dragged one of the larger tables from the dining hall into the room and sat at the head of it.

Eight other people were seated in rows down the sides, some of them he recognized, others he didn't. Lore looked up when he walked in, and her cheeks turned a bright red before she refocused on Margaret's face.

He'd expected a better reaction, but if she wanted to ignore that he existed, then he wouldn't force her to look at him. She would on her own, anyway.

Rather than irritate the elf any further, Abraxas settled himself next to Beauty. He pulled the chair out beside her slowly, then sank down without looking anywhere other than Lore. How could he? Those eyes drew him like a flame attracted moths, and he would gladly cast himself into the angry fire of her rage if that meant she'd talk to him again. Or at least look at him with the passion she had in the forest.

"Abraxas," Beauty murmured. "You've made yourself scarce lately."

"So have you." He turned toward the human, then eyed her clothing. "I still think you look better in that gold dress."

She blushed, and he chuckled at her reaction. That dress would forever be his favorite outfit, simply because she had captivated him like no other while wearing it. He was still getting used to this version of her. The one who wore leather armor and unapologetically gave orders to people twice her age.

Although... He noticed when the man on her right shifted in his chair, Beauty moved to give him more room. As though she were taking up far too much space.

They'd have to work on that.

Margaret struck her fist to the table, and the solid thump was apparently a warning to them all that it was time for the meeting to begin. "Now that everyone is here, shall we? I think we've all waited long enough."

Every single person in the room sat at attention. Just from the power in the elf's voice.

Abraxas didn't understand it. Margaret paled in comparison to

Lore, quite literally. Where Lorelei was gold and ochre, Margaret lacked any color at all. Her white hair was pulled back from her too pale face, so ashen that even her lips weren't the normal pink he'd seen in elves for centuries.

The older elf wore her customary black armor that plastered to her like a second skin. He'd smelled the magic on that leather from a mile away when he first met the woman. Margaret wanted no one getting close enough to her to take a shot at her life. She'd enchanted her armor to make sure that no one ever tried it.

He'd found it strange then and still did. If she was such an impressive fighter, and had so many people who believed in her cause, what reason did she have to think that someone might try to kill her?

"The King is our top priority," Margaret said while reclining in her chair. "Our first and only mission is his death. I'm sure all of you realize how important it is that no detail leaves this room. To the people of Umbra, the King must remain dead until we find him."

He cleared his throat. "I hate to be the bearer of bad news, but if the King doesn't want you to find him, you won't."

"I think we have enough skills sitting at this table that we'll find him if we want to." She cocked her head to the side as though she were challenging him. "Or do you doubt your peers?"

Ah. Of course. She would pit the others against him if he didn't follow along with this plan that would get them all killed. Or worse, waste enough time for the King to return to health.

What was Margaret's game here? She had to know the clock spun faster when it came to finding the King. Zander would either die of that wound, unlikely, or he would come back with more power than before.

He licked his lips, tempted to keep arguing but knowing that

Margaret didn't want him to speak. Was he stepping on her toes? Looking at the others in the room, he realized that he held everyone's attention. Effortlessly. No pounding on the table required.

Perhaps that was why she had gotten so angry. Everyone here wanted to know what the dragon had to say, and they were more likely to listen to him rather than to her.

He had a unique power. The question was if he wanted to use it.

He glanced across the table and caught Lore's gaze. Most of the time, she glared at him as though he had killed her mother yesterday. But right now? Now she arched a delicate brow and gave him the slightest nod.

Time to speak, then.

"I don't doubt the people in this room are talented. This is clearly the best we could get, but you have to know that the King didn't die because Lore's blade wasn't true. Dark magic kept me bound to him, which means it's only more likely that same magic kept him alive. The Umbral Knights didn't exist before the King's father found that damned warlock, so... I can only assume that there is more at work here than we know."

Margaret's usually pale cheeks turned red with anger. He knew she wanted to argue with him, but her pride wouldn't let her lose this battle. "This is good information, Abraxas. Although why you've kept it to yourself for so long, I will never understand."

"We're here now, Margaret. This is the time to share what we know." He opened his hands wide, spreading his fingers as though he were innocent in this situation. "I tell you only what I must. There are secrets even dragons keep to themselves."

"If I remember right, there are a lot of secrets dragons keep. Helpful mysteries." Her gaze narrowed. "I find it hard to trust someone who willingly worked with the King."

The accusation hung between them. He had done the dirty work of the King for years and the others wouldn't forgive that. He wouldn't blame them, either.

Just as he opened his mouth, ready to argue with her that he had done enough to be washed of those sins, a hand came down on his. Silencing him.

Beauty squeezed his fingers two times before she jumped into the conversation. "While I understand the King should be our largest focus right now, Margaret, I'd like to bring up another situation."

The elf pinched the bridge of her nose. "What else, Beauty? Really, is there anything more important than tracking down the man who held us all by the throat for so long?"

She hadn't let go of his fingers. He could almost feel the burning spear of Lore's gaze where she looked at their connection. Why had Beauty not released his hand?

As he watched the expression on the mortal woman's face change, he knew in his gut that whatever she said would wreck him. He would have to leave this room because he already knew what she was going to say.

"You tasked myself and a team of people to go through Abraxas's hoard and find the eggs." She coughed slightly, as though her lungs had frozen in her chest. "The eggs are gone, Margaret."

His stomach dropped out of his body.

Beauty looked over at him again, and there was that damned squeeze of her fingers. Comfort when she had no idea what the words had done to him. "I'm sorry, Abraxas. I know how much they mean to you. Considering the King was already summoning the eggs before Lore got there, we thought maybe they had made their way out of the cave. We searched for a week and a half now, in every direction we could figure that they'd have traveled, but they're... They're not near the castle."

Voice ragged, he whispered, "You didn't look in the right place for them. They could be underground."

"We had a witch cast a spell for any magical objects around the castle. We found quite a few useful things, but no dragon eggs."

He should have known. He should have guessed this would be the King's final jab at him. No murder. No eggs. Nothing had changed other than the fact that Abraxas was now on the wrong side.

What was he going to do now?

His heart tried to beat its way out of his chest and suddenly the air felt thick. A cold sweat broke out over his body and a drop of liquid slid down the back of his neck. All at once, he thought he might throw up.

Everything he'd worked so hard for, and everything he'd risked, it was all in vain. He hadn't done all the good he'd thought he had.

Margaret's voice barely split through the panic attack. "We cannot focus on the dragon eggs right now. Once we have the King in our hands again, we can force him to tell us what he did with them. But until then, we cannot split our focus. We have to do what is right."

He interrupted her and he sounded like he'd already shattered into a thousand pieces. "They're the last of my kind."

Silence filled the room. No one would even look at him now.

He tried to catch the gaze of anyone, but they all kept their attention on Margaret as though his words had never captivated them. "They're just babies," he added.

Still, no one would budge. No one even tried to comfort him. Even Beauty slid her hand away from his and settled her shaking fingers into her lap.

Finally, he looked back at Margaret. Those fierce eyes refused to give in. "We're all losing people, Abraxas. This is not just for dragons or for your own kind to flourish. This is about bringing an entire kingdom back to its former glory."

No. He refused to sit here and listen to someone tell him that the deaths of innocents were worth a throne. He stood abruptly, his chair screeching along the stone floor. "Then you won't need my help. My only purpose here was to ensure that my lineage and kind remained out of his hands. If you're not willing to help me ensure that, then there is no reason for me to stay."

Margaret's left eye ticked. "You'll come back. They always do."

He bared his teeth in a snarl and whirled away from that table full of people who refused to see reason. Those heartless individuals could hunt down the ghost of a man who had harmed them. He didn't care. But they had no right to refuse their assistance.

Abraxas slammed the door behind him and paused in the hallway as his heart flipped in his chest. He pressed a fist to his ribs that suddenly weren't big enough to hold the ache of his soul. The thundering of his heartbeat raced in his ears.

The eggs.

How could they be gone?

CHAPTER 3

Lorelei watched Abraxas as he blustered out of the room. The door slammed hard behind him, and every inch of her soul wanted to rush after him.

She hadn't known the eggs were missing. Her heart broke, knowing that he must be reliving all the fear and anguish he'd felt for so long. He had lived only for those eggs for centuries now, and the thought that he would never get them back? It must tear him up inside.

Her hands gripped the arms of her chair, ready to leap up and rush down the halls to him. But the chair creaked at the last moment. Everyone fell silent, and she felt their gazes on her as if they were physically pressing down on her shoulders. She couldn't get up. She shouldn't comfort him in his time of need because he was the dragon who had killed her mother.

He was also the dragon who had saved her life multiple times. Abraxas had made it very clear that he valued her life and her words, so was she throwing that all in his face by not offering her help when he needed it?

Margaret tapped her fingernails against the table. The rhythm grew angrier the longer Lore looked like she might stand.

Finally, the other elf snarled, "By all means, Lorelei of Silverfell, run after him. If you agree the eggs are far more important than saving this kingdom, then I will not be the person to change your mind."

Damn it.

She couldn't go anywhere now that the rest of the rebellion leaders were looking at her. They'd made a figurehead out of Lore. She was the elf who had killed the King. Whatever she did had more meaning than any other in this room.

One by one, she peeled her fingers off the chair and forced her body to settle back onto the plush cushion. It took more effort than she wanted to admit to smile.

"Of course not," she replied through her teeth. "I'm here with you, Margaret. That's been the plan all along."

Although that didn't mean she had to listen. Lore sat in that conference room with the others because that was what they expected of her. But her mind raced through the possibilities of what she might have lost.

Abraxas could be leaving the castle even now. He'd turn back into the terrifying dragon and fly through the night sky. Off to find the King and the eggs the man had stolen. What would that mean for them?

If Abraxas fell back under Zander's spell, then the rebellion had surrendered one of their most important bargaining chips. They needed the dragon so that the rest of Umbra would see that they had power. Otherwise, they would return to a group of misfit creatures who had no idea how to run a kingdom. No one was afraid of a couple of elves who had gotten themselves a few weapons.

Margaret had forgotten just how little everyone in this kingdom thought of them. Sure, the King had been the one to order that they all be exterminated. But the humans were all too happy to comply with the rules.

She still remembered being given up to the authorities by a neighbor who had seen her ears. The incident had happened a few months after her mother died, and Lore had been careless in her grief. All it took was for a single person to see those pointed ears and the Umbral Knights had been called. She'd been in hiding for three months before the search had finally ended.

"And that's it, then. We all know the plan and we all agree with it. Yes?" Margaret's voice cut through her thoughts.

Lorelei blinked, and everything else came back into view. The table. The people who were looking at her as though she had all the answers to their problems, even though she knew less than they did.

None of them cared about her experience or knowledge. They didn't want to know what her personal opinions were. They wanted to hear her say that Margaret knew what she was doing, so they could all go back to trusting their esteemed leader.

But if she tried to lead them? They would all end up in Margaret's claws.

So all Lore could do was nod like the good little doll she was. "Of course. Whatever you say, Margaret."

The Darkveil elf smiled, but the sight was eerily similar to looking into the mouth of a shark. "Perfect. Lorelei, I want you to see me again tomorrow, just to be sure you're on board with everything else. And I have a few other things for you to do. The rest of you stay on your guard. We cannot have any of this slipping out into the public. Do I make myself clear?"

They all agreed, and everyone stood as one. Lore trailed them as they left, slowly making her way through the corridors that had once been beautiful.

Some inner workings of her mind needed to be released. She couldn't be free here. She couldn't be herself and... and...

She somehow lost a few hours. Lorelei caught herself staring at the wreckage of the castle, and suddenly another hour had passed by. Someone would ask her a question, and that would snap her out of it. But not enough to leave her feeling like herself.

She missed the girl from Tenebrous. The wild creature who had evaded so many people who wanted her dead.

By the time the moon rose, she found herself with her hands on a latch that would lead her out onto the roof of the castle. Few people knew this existed, but she'd discovered it back when they were all tasked to search for the castle's secrets. This one had been harmless, so she kept it a secret.

Hand over hand, she hauled herself outside. She didn't know why. Maybe to return to her favorite pastime in Tenebrous, but another part of her heart knew what she'd find out there.

A full moon traced the clouds with a silver thread. They glittered beyond the dark silhouette of a dragon who rode the wind currents like he floated on a river. Perhaps this was why she'd come up here.

Even though she couldn't show her support for him in the war room, at least she could be here with him now.

Lore sat on the roof's curved tiles and wrapped her arms around her knees. She stared up at the dragon, who wasn't running. He hadn't left. But she could only imagine that way up there, he felt very much alone.

The moonlight sank into her skin, and her body drank the power, though she had no need of it. Even as she tried to stop herself, Lore already saw the sparkling of magic rising to the surface. Apparently, even her magic refused to listen to her these days.

"I thought you might come out here." The familiar voice was one she had difficulty hearing. After all, Beauty had lied to her for a very long time.

"What are you doing out so late, Beauty?" she asked, turning her head so her cheek pressed against her arms.

Her friend struggled through the small hatch. And here Lore was, thinking that she had lied about being a little klutzy. Apparently, Beauty couldn't lie about some things.

The human nearly fell off the edge a couple of times before she plopped down beside Lore with a heavy breath. "Goodness, I have no idea why you'd want to come out here to be alone. You realize there is a garden maze, don't you? I'd imagine that would be easier to avoid people in rather than a roof."

The smile crossed Lore's lips before she could stop herself. "I know where it is."

"So you thought it was necessary to risk your neck out here when there were other options?"

"I feel safer when I'm up high." Lore shrugged. "Besides, if you're on a roof, it's very unlikely anyone will interrupt your thoughts."

The hint was there for Beauty to pick up on, and yet, the mortal woman had no intention of listening. Beauty rolled her eyes and shook her head. "Elves. Always trying to be so sneaky."

"Of course. Being sneaky was the first reason why I came out here." Not because she wanted some time to herself and with her dragon, albeit from afar.

A companionable silence fell between them. Lore hated how easy it was to be friends with Beauty again. They'd created a bond throughout all the bridal affairs. But it still should have been difficult to forgive the other woman for lying to her.

Lore had wasted so much time trying to train Beauty to take care of herself. How to fight. And here she was, a rather high up member of the rebellion, who knew how to fight very well. It didn't feel fair that everyone in her life was dead set on deceiving her.

Still. This was the young woman who had giggled with her over dinners and who had snuck into her room late at night to talk with her and the pixie she'd saved. There were few people in the world who were born human and would do that.

Beauty was a hard person not to love.

Said human sighed and leaned back on her hands. "Wasn't this how it all started?"

"Excuse me?"

Beauty nodded up to the sky. "Sitting on your roof, or in my case, in a drawing room. Looking up at the sky and seeing that damned silhouette and knowing someone had to do something about it."

She supposed so. They'd all felt the continued presence of the dragon as though he had their throats in his claws.

"The King's guard," she murmured. "Everyone was afraid of him because the King controlled him. A dragon. Who wanted to fight a dragon?"

"I always find it so curious how little things change. Here we are, in the same place we'd always have been, looking up at the same dragon with the same thoughts." Beauty turned toward Lore, her eyes wide and questioning. "I know I wasn't the only one in that room thinking about Abraxas. Margaret might assume we can run this place without him, but you and I both know differently."

"The dragon cannot be controlled by anyone other than himself," she replied. "Thinking otherwise is foolish, Beauty."

"We both know that's not true. Abraxas is his own man, of course. But he has lived his life in servitude to someone. And now I think that power has crossed over to you." Beauty reached out and put a hand on Lore's arm. "In a different way, of course. I don't mean to say that he thinks you're like the King. But he is dedicated to you, Lore."

What did Beauty want from her? An admission that she'd recognized the same thing? Of course she had. She knew exactly how much Abraxas felt for her and how strong that bond could be if she let it. But that didn't mean her mother's ghost wasn't screaming her dying breath in her ear.

"I don't know what you want from me," she said. "Everyone wants something, don't they? The elf who killed the King must have more to offer. Well, I don't. I want to go back home, and then I want to smoke a ridiculous amount of elfweed and sleep for a week."

"You can do that, eventually. But right now, I think we both know who we need to focus on." Beauty pointed up into the sky. "If we lose him, then we lose everything."

"Right." Lore rubbed her arms, a sudden chill causing her skin to ache. "Another job to do, I suppose. Keep Abraxas around without making Margaret want to slit my throat in the middle of the night."

Beauty shook her head as though the mere thought terrified her. "No, no. I don't think you're understanding. Lore... We both know that

Margaret is a planner. She has something else up her sleeve and I've known her long enough to realize she won't tell us what that is. I know you don't trust her, and even though I do… I think we need to make the right choice for ourselves. Even if that means we will do something that Margaret won't like."

Lorelei stilled. She froze in place, staring at this little human who thought she had everything figured out.

And maybe she did. Beauty was the risk taker, after all. And she had known Margaret for a lot longer than Lore had. Still, it was strange to even consider that a rebellion leader, or at least someone who Margaret admired, would want her to go directly against Margaret's orders.

"Are you trying to trick me?" she asked. "Is this some test that Margaret sent you to perform? Because I don't know how I feel about you lying to me again, Beauty."

"It's not a lie." Beauty scooted even closer. "We know Abraxas will not stick around when those dragon eggs are still out there. And we know we need him. Margaret refuses to see reason and I don't think… All I'm saying is that it might be more prudent for us to take matters into our own hands. I want you to agree with me on this, Lore. I want to work together again."

Lore couldn't believe Beauty was saying this. Beauty didn't go against the wishes of Margaret. She couldn't. No one could.

A Darkveil elf was a dangerous creature and no one should ever try to test them. And yet… If they could make a difference, choose a path that would change the course of the rebellion when Margaret refused to see reason…

"How do I know you'll go through with it?" she asked, looking Beauty in the eyes. "You lied to me the entire time we were here, Beauty. You played me for a fool while we were here, and you plotted with Margaret to keep me in the dark. How am I supposed to trust that you won't do that again?"

Beauty's eyes widened with every word and then filled with tears. She pressed a hand against her heart with a firm thud. "It killed me to lie to you like that, and it kills me to think that you can't trust me. I want to make this up to you, Lore. In any way that I can."

With a sigh, Lore looked up at Abraxas, so far out of their reach. "A lot of people have been saying that to me lately."

"Then let's make a difference. Right here, right now. Together, we can do what is reasonable and we won't let anyone else stand in our way. I know we can do this, Lore."

"And just what are we going to be doing?" she asked, pulling her attention away from the dragon.

Beauty grinned through the tears. "Finding the dragon eggs, of course."

CHAPTER 4

Abraxas tucked his wings tight against his sides and crawled underneath the waterfall into what had once been his hoard. There wasn't much that remained, really. Nothing of importance. Without the ever present warmth of the eggs, this place seemed cold and vacant.

Still, he had to be here. He had to see with his own eyes what the King had done.

Strangely enough, most of the gold was where he'd left it. The coins still jingled as he crawled through the mounds that he'd left behind. But he didn't care for the coins or jewels or crowns that tumbled around his feet as he crept toward the one place that did matter.

The pool of melted metal was smooth as the surface of a mirror. The center had been peeled open, cracked like one of the eggs. This was where he had healed himself, trying desperately to be well enough to fight the King and ensure that Lore didn't die. And there, in the far corner, was a hole where the eggs had once been.

The King's magic was stronger than he'd expected. Even molten gold, hardened by the beats of his wings, hadn't been able to prevent the eggs from being stolen from right underneath his nose.

Swallowing hard, he wiggled through the coins until he stood on the flattened metal. Once there, he peered down into the darkness of the hole. Even though he knew they wouldn't be there.

Ah, the anxiety returned with a vengeance as emptiness stared back at him. His heart thundered in his chest. His mouth went dry. And every thought in his mind screamed that he had failed. Not just them, but himself, the memory of his people, and the legacy he'd given up so much to preserve.

Wings shaking, breath rattling in his long neck, he placed his head down on the gold and tried to calm himself. He couldn't afford to lose his iron will, not when there was still a chance he could find them. He could bring them home or take them far away from this cursed place.

And yet... There would always be the haunting sound of her voice. The whispers in his soul that he had left something behind. If he didn't stay, he would forever wonder what might have happened if he did.

Why would the King even want the eggs? It wasn't like he could hatch them. The first king had tried himself far more times than Abraxas could count. No mortal flame could get hot enough to birth a dragon. Bonfires lacked what dragon fire contained.

So the King didn't want to wake the babies. He would know that his own father had failed at that. Even mage fire wasn't the same. The only logical conclusion was that Zander still felt he could manipulate

Abraxas. And the more he thought about it, the more Abraxas leaned toward thinking that the King might be right. Those eggs could control him, especially now that Lore had taken a step back from him.

"I know a secret." The starlight tone eased through the angry pain in his chest. It banished all the anxiety, as the mere sound of her voice was a cool breeze to douse the flames of fear.

He lifted his head, glancing up to find her.

Lore sat on the edge of the cliff, as she had done when trying to steal from him. Her legs dangled over the abyss, leather leggings hugging tight to her stunning form. The honey gold of her hair tumbled over her shoulders that were lifted high to her ears as she braced herself against the stone.

What he wouldn't give to go back to the first moment he'd seen her like this. Before all the complications of emotions and history had turned her gaze from him. Even now, all he saw was her.

His Lore.

"What secret?" he asked. His voice was rough and ragged with emotion, deeper than normal in this dragon form.

"Beauty let it slip. It's a long shot, and I don't know if you're going to be all that interested in hearing it." She tucked a strand of hair behind her ear. How he loved it when she did that.

"Anything you have to say I will listen to," he replied, stretching his wings. "But considering how tightly you are wrapped around Margaret's fingers, I didn't think it was likely you would want to help me."

"Oh, there are a lot of things I wanted to say in that meeting, but she has her claws in me just as deeply as she does in you." Lore kicked her feet in the air. "We've both got chains these days. I assume you're aware that we're becoming heroes."

"Heroes?" He meandered closer to the cliff, eyeing the best way to climb up to her. The talons at the ends of his wings had healed enough for him to move lithely through his hoard. "I doubt anyone would consider a dragon to be a hero."

"Oh, but they are. Already, the rumors are flying about the elf and the dragon who defied all the odds. The two of us are becoming an idea of who we are, rather than what the truth is." She shrugged. "Margaret wants to control what the stories become. I think, in her mind, we're her way of controlling legends."

"Or gods," he added. Abraxas climbed up the cliff, using his talons to dig deep into the rocks and earth. He made his way to her side until his head crested the edge and he could look at her with one giant eye. "I would think that might appeal to one such as yourself."

"Do you believe I want to be viewed as a god?" she asked with a snort. "I just want to go home, Abraxas."

Home? She must know that word had little meaning now that she'd stepped through the doors of the castle. He found it so endearing that she still believed there was a chance for either of them to return to the lives they once lived. Even if it was a childish dream of hers.

He crawled over the edge and then returned to his mortal form. The change took time and though it was painfully rushed, he eventually stood before her as the powerful, if a little foolish, man at her side.

Lore didn't even look at him. She stared down into his hoard, her eyebrows drawn down in tight, angry little furrows. "You didn't have to change, you know."

"I know." He let out a tiny groan as he sat down beside her. "But I am getting older and being in the dragon form always makes my back hurt. Besides, it would be hard to maintain a conversation with you without lips."

She snorted, and that was when he knew he could fix everything. If he kept this up, perhaps she would forgive him sooner rather than later. That was all he wanted, anyway. Just to see her smile and laugh at the stupid things he said.

His hand ached to hold hers. His fingers reached for her without him even realizing it, although he set his hand down on the stones instead of her skin. So close he could feel the icy waves coming off her.

Gods, he wanted to touch her. Even just to put his arm around her shoulders when he could see she was struggling. But that was the very last thing she wanted. Clearly.

He sighed. "A secret, you say?"

"One that Beauty knows, but apparently no one else does. Other than Margaret, of course, and she didn't want us to find out." Lore bit her lip, and he felt that all the way into his bones. "She said I shouldn't tell you until we were on the road, but I think... Well, I think you should hear this."

"Ominous." He doubted she could tell him anything worse than the missing eggs. "Beauty rarely keeps things from me these days."

"Really?" That got her to look at him. Lorelei stared at him with those bright ocean eyes. "She talks to you?"

"She doesn't talk to you?"

He frowned and watched all the blood drain out of Lore's face. She muttered something that sounded like, "Not really," before she cleared her throat. "Anyway, Margaret has been hiding a report that the King has a half brother. His father had some affair after Zander was born. Beauty seems to think it's a rather romantic story, but..."

Abraxas shook his head. "No. I promise you, it wasn't that."

He remembered the woman, although the memory was one of

tragedy. Zander's father had taken a liking to one of the young maids, and he had pursued her relentlessly. He didn't know if the feelings were mutual, or if the woman had understood that if a king wanted her, then she had no other choice.

"Their relationship was swift," he murmured. "I remember she left the castle less than a month after she'd caught the King's attention. The poor thing fled in the middle of the night as though she'd seen a ghost."

"You let her go," Lorelei correctly mused.

"I did."

"Why?"

He rubbed the back of his neck, not sure how comfortable he was with her seeing this side of him. But finally, he cleared his throat and said, "She needed to leave. Who am I to stand in her way?"

"It's just..." She ducked her head, looking away from him once more. "I forget you are kind sometimes."

"Sometimes," he agreed. "But I didn't know there was a child from that union. The boy could follow in his father's footsteps. That bloodline is..." He paused.

"Corrupt." Apparently, they were finishing each other's sentences now.

He hoped that was a good sign. "Right. Well, Beauty must want to find this boy for some reason."

"She thinks he can give the eggs back to you. That it just takes the bloodline to transfer the ownership. So if we can find the eggs, steal them, and then have him open the box, we won't have to find the King at all."

It was a theory, but he knew better than to get too excited over the theoretical. How many times had he tried to break those eggs away from the King? More times than Beauty had seen the sun. So he couldn't imagine it would be that easy.

Still, Lore was willing to try, and that meant she had to believe in it. She must believe in Beauty too, and that belief meant something to him. More than it really should.

He sighed and nodded. "If you think that will work, then we will try. I'm not so sure that the King would leave his half brother alive if the bloodline was strong enough in the boy."

"What if he couldn't find his brother?" She spread her hands wide. "We have to try something, Abraxas. I can't sit here and think that those eggs are going to be pawns for the rest of their lives. You were right. The time of dragons has come again, and I want to help see that in my lifetime."

He stood, dusting his hands off on his pants before he reached out a hand for her to take. "Then it would be my honor to work with you, Lorelei of Silverfell. The elves have come to help the dragons again, it seems."

She eyed his hand as if it might bite her. He'd be lying if he didn't at least admit to himself that he'd thought about biting her before. And in many ways. However, right now they were working together, and he had no plans to harm her in any way. Even pleasurable ones.

Wiggling his fingers, he added, "I won't hurt you, Lorelei. We're a team."

"Are we?" she asked, those ocean eyes widening a bit with the question.

"Always."

She slipped her hand into his and it felt as though the sun had come out from behind clouds. Finally, she'd forgiven him enough to trust him. Or at least touch him. And that shouldn't have been the balm to his aching soul.

Tugging gently, Abraxas drew her to her feet. But when she stood, it was a little too close to him. He could feel her breath fanning across his collarbone where the ties of his collar had come undone. Her fingers curled into a fist around his, her grip too tight for someone who didn't want him to touch her. And when she looked at him, really looked at him, he saw how dilated her pupils were.

"Abraxas," she whispered. "I don't... I don't know how to..."

Oh, damn it all. He kept telling himself he was a good man, but she'd already labeled him as the villain in her story. Maybe it was time for him to be a little evil.

He tugged her sharply into his arms, so her hands spread wide against the rapid beat of his heart. Abraxas palmed the back of her head and promised himself that he wouldn't go too far. He wouldn't do anything that he regretted tomorrow.

And yet, the moment his lips met hers, he was lost.

He dove into the depths of her mouth, plunged deep and savored the honey sweet taste of her tongue. Every second of the kiss was one he used to brand himself into her skin because how dare she deny herself what they had? He'd felt nothing like this connection in his life, and she sought to withhold that from him?

Once he was certain he had relit the fires of passion in her chest, he released her. Lorelei stumbled away from him, her lips berry red and her eyes wide.

"What was that?" she asked, but she didn't seem angry at him for at least trying.

"I just wanted to make sure," he replied. Abraxas wiped his mouth on the back of his hand, knowing the grin on his face was one of a true villain.

"Make sure of what?" Lorelei stammered the question, her mind not working fast enough to keep up with his words. If she had been thinking straight, she might have already known what he'd say.

Instead, he smiled wider, the smile of a real dragon, and replied, "To make sure it was real. And it was Lore. Every bit of it was real."

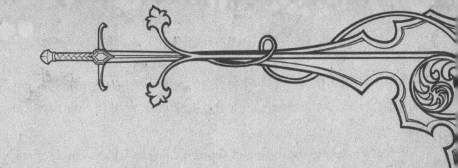

CHAPTER 5

Lorelei wanted to press her fingers against the warmth on her lips. She still remembered that kiss, which had seared through her entire being, even though it had been hours ago now. What right did he have to kiss her like he would die if he didn't get the taste of her one more time?

Although, she supposed it was kind of nice to have someone want her so badly. She'd forgotten how powerful their connection was.

She couldn't afford to think about this when there was so much left for them to do. Beauty had the bare bones of the idea in place, but that didn't mean any of them had a clue where to start. Abraxas had to meet with them first, hear their ideas, listen to them even though it might sound crazy. And then all three of them had to figure out the best way to go about this.

Which led them all back to Lorelei's bedroom, even though her cheeks burned at the mere knowledge that Abraxas was so close to where she slept.

She strode into the room and hoped it didn't look like a family of rats lived within the walls. Lore had never been organized, and considering how strange her state of mind had been lately, she couldn't remember the last time she'd cleaned. No maids had remained after the King disappeared.

"Beauty should be here any minute," she said to the dragon as her eyes moved anywhere but him.

The room wasn't quite as messy as it could have been. Small blessings. Her clothing was still tossed over every furniture piece that existed within the four walls, but at least the floors weren't covered. She hadn't made the bed. At least the two plush chairs near the fireplace were free of clothing, although the worn leather had been snagged a couple times by knives she'd forgotten about. And damn it, her weapons were strewn all over the vanity table where she should have been making herself presentable for the meetings and gatherings. Instead, she'd been cleaning all her weapons.

"Excuse the mess," Lore muttered as she rushed over to the table. "I didn't think we'd be having a meeting of a second rebellion in here."

"Let's not call it that," Abraxas replied, his voice little more than a grumble. "Might bring bad luck."

He had a point, she supposed. Lore glanced over her shoulder only to catch her breath at the sight.

The dragon stood next to her side of the bed that she slept on. He stared down at the indent with an intensity that stole the air from her lungs. He didn't seem to notice her staring at him, or if he did, he didn't care. Abraxas reached out and ghosted the back of his fingers over her pillow. The touch was so infinitely delicate, as though he only wanted to see if heat lingered from the morning.

Once, twice, her heart thudded hard in her chest. It woke her from the deeply intimate moment and shook her out of the daze. He shouldn't be touching her bed. He shouldn't...

Beauty cleared her throat from where she leaned against the doorframe. "What are you two doing in here?"

"Nothing," they both snapped at the same time.

Beauty lifted her hands in a peace offering. "I can always come back later if there's something the two of you need to work out. I don't think we have to rush this."

If she didn't like the human so much, Lore might have slapped her across the face. "We do have to rush this, and you are withholding information again, so I'm sure there is a lot for the three of us to talk about. Now get in here and close the door before someone hears you."

"It's not as if they won't put their ear to the wood if they want to eavesdrop," Beauty muttered. But at least she closed them into the room.

Gritting her teeth, Lore strode up behind the mortal girl and lifted her hands. "You do realize you're around magical creatures now, right? If I don't want anyone to eavesdrop, then no one will."

She'd had enough time to gather the moonlight last night. She could weave a web so tight it would muffle any sounds that they might make, as long as none of them started screaming.

Though the spell made people a little uncomfortable to watch. Lorelei already knew that her skin would glow, glittering like it always did when she tried to use magic from the moon. Then those pieces would pull off her flesh and float through the air. They'd stretch until they pressed against the walls and floor. Each tiny patchwork web of magic would weave together until there was a net of light that surrounded them.

She felt the last bit stitch into the others, then dropped her hands from the door. "There we are," she muttered. "Let's see anyone try to listen through that."

Both Abraxas and Beauty wore matching, shocked expressions when she turned. Beauty's mouth had even opened and her eyes were so wide, Lore could see the whites entirely around her irises.

"What?" Lore asked. "Why are you two looking at me like that?"

"You can do that?" Beauty asked.

Abraxas cleared his throat and swallowed hard. "I had forgotten what a Silverfell elf looks like when they use magic."

Well, now she was self conscious. They could stop staring at her any time. It wasn't as if she'd done anything all that surprising. Elves could use magic. Little spells, mostly, warding a room or casting a net into the sea and always coming up with fish.

"People still know elves can cast spells, don't they?" Lore pressed her lips together in a firm line. "I didn't think that was news to anyone."

Of course, the King had spread a lot of rumors about her kind, considering people were apt to trust an elf. They were similar enough to humans to blend in, after all. And if the King wasn't careful, the humans might have liked the elves. Surely a friendship would have mucked up his plans.

Beauty shook her head. "No. People think elves are just good at fighting, and that they're dangerous because they can beguile a man with their looks."

"Beguile a man?" Lore repeated. Oh, that wasn't something she could manage without sitting down. She strode past the two of them and sat at the end of her bed, then waved a hand for them to sit in the chairs near the fireplace. "We can't beguile anyone unless they're attracted to us, but that's hardly magic."

Beauty stumbled over the chair and fell down into it. "Well, that'll be useful later on, I'm sure."

She supposed it might. Power wasn't the easiest thing to control, and most people didn't want to use it all the time. It would only make her weaker, and Lore much preferred to fight with her hands. Sure, there had been elves in history that used curses in battle. But those stories always ended tragically with that magic burning out the user. Power couldn't be contained even in magical bodies. Not all the time, at least.

Steepling her fingers, she pressed them against her lips and tried to think through what they would have to do. "So you're planning that we just leave? Was that the thought?"

Beauty shrugged and moved her legs so Abraxas could step over her and sit down in the other chair. "I don't really see another way. I think Margaret will know what's happening if we all sneak out of the castle at the same time. And I don't think she'd be all that willing to listen to our plan if we ask to speak with her. She's already planned our future out in her head."

"Doesn't mean it's the right future," Lore muttered.

"No, but she doesn't see it like that. This is her baby. This is the entire plan she's had the whole time, and suddenly, it worked. She will not let us tell her that she was wrong." Beauty's face paled at the thought. "I don't know what else to do other than leave in the shadows, one by one, and run."

"But wouldn't that mean Margaret would send her own people after us?" She shook her head in disbelief, but knew that's what she would do. Margaret wouldn't let the three of them leave.

She'd hunt them down throughout the entire kingdom if she had to. The same way she planned on hunting down the King.

A small squeak interrupted them and the tiny pixie she'd released flew through the air. The little woman landed on Beauty's knee and frantically gestured with her hands.

Beauty watched the movement for a few heartbeats, then lifted the tiny creature up to her ear. "Uh, huh. Really? Well, that's helpful."

Lore waited for the human to at least tell her what the pixie said, but Beauty merely put the pixie back onto her leg, crossed her arms, and reclined in her chair.

Ah, so she'd learned from Margaret all this time. Beauty wouldn't give anyone any details without being asked for it. Lore hated these games that everyone insisted on playing.

She sighed and rolled her eyes up to the ceiling. "Beauty, would you care to share the information you just received?"

"I'm so glad you asked. Apparently there are plenty of servants' corridors that will help lead us out of the castle if we'd like to go that way." Beauty nodded at the pixie. "She can guide us, although she says she can't leave the castle with us. She's decided to take this place back as her home now that the other pixies are released."

Good. The pixie wouldn't do well on the trip, Lorelei was afraid. Even rain could hurt the little one, and the last thing she wanted was the death of another magical creature on her conscience.

Lorelei nodded, then licked her lips. "All right, I suppose it's settled then. We leave at midnight, through the servant's corridors, and then we try to stay out of the way of Margaret's goons. It probably won't be as easy as we're thinking, but... I guess we don't have another choice?"

After all this talk, Abraxas interrupting her felt like someone had rung a gong in the middle of the room. The deep tones startled her so much that Lorelei actually flinched.

"I don't think we're going about this the right way at all," he grumbled. "You two seem to think the only means to get out of this situation is to sneak off as though we're all fugitives? I thought you two had better reason than that."

Lore lifted a brow. "You've been oddly silent throughout this entire conversation and then surface to say that? What's your great plan then, dragon? Give me something better."

"Tell Margaret what we're going to do." He mimicked her expression, arching a brow of his own. "What is so wrong with that?"

Beauty leaned forward, bracing her forearms on her knees. "Margaret won't let us leave. She definitely won't approve of this plan, because she already said it at the meeting. Getting the eggs back is at the very bottom of her list. And in case you hadn't noticed, we're her best bet at killing the King. We got close last time."

If looks could have seared, Beauty would be burning right now. Abraxas looked at her with more fire in his eyes than Lore had ever seen.

He bared his teeth in a snarl. "Do you think she could stop a dragon from doing what he wants?"

"I think she could very easily tell everyone in the rebellion that Lore cannot leave the castle without escorts. That you should be chained in your hoard with magical bindings. And then she'd send me back to my father with my tail between my legs because I couldn't listen to orders." Beauty's voice grew more acidic with every word. "You can't throw around that you're a dragon and expect everyone in this world to bow to your wishes. That's exactly what chases people away."

"Oh, now you're trying to tell me how to make more friends? That's rich coming from you."

The two of them were going to keep fighting until they were purple in the face and Lore would have to do all the work on her own. If she let them continue being idiots, then nothing would ever get decided.

She heaved a sigh and stood up. "The two of you stop talking."

Beauty hissed, "I'm tired of him telling us all what to do because he's some ancient dragon."

"I've lived at least ten of your lifetimes, little girl!" Abraxas snarled in reply.

"If neither of you don't stop talking now, I will sink a dagger into each of your hands and tip your chairs back into the fireplace." Lore looked down at her nails for a brief moment before making eye contact with both of their shocked expressions. "I know you think that's harsh, but I absolutely will do it. You're both wasting my time."

Beauty crossed her arms over her chest and rolled her eyes, but at least she stopped talking. That was the first step.

Now she had to focus on the stubborn dragon who met her gaze head on. He clearly did not care at all that she had threatened him. If anything, the threat had only made the fire in his eyes burn hotter. And that wasn't what she'd wanted, damn it.

"Abraxas?" she bit out through her teeth. "You aren't going to argue anymore, are you?"

"I will argue until the very last breath in my lungs leaves my body," he replied, but at least then he inclined his head. "However, I do understand that there are two differing opinions here. I'm asking you both to trust me. We need to tell Margaret what we're doing. Otherwise, we'll be fighting against her every step of the way."

He had a point. If they were going to find the King's brother at all, they needed to be secretive. They couldn't afford to have more people trying to hunt them down.

Sighing, she chewed on the inside of her lip until she finally gave in. "Fine, okay. You're right. We can't fight against Margaret and everyone else at the same time. But I do agree with Beauty and don't think she's going to let us go so easily."

At least he nodded in agreement with that. "I don't think she will let us go without a quarrel. That much is true. Leave Margaret to me, Lorelei. I promise, after we're done talking, she won't try to stop us."

Why did that sound so ominous?

She stared into his eyes, looking for any sign of aggression within them, and could find nothing. All she saw was the confidence of a dragon who would get his way and no one would survive if they tried to stop him.

So, she supposed, this was now their best option.

"Fine," she said, tossing her hands up in the air. "We'll try it your way first. But if Margaret even flinches toward keeping us all on lock down, we're sneaking away at night. Deal?"

"Deal," Abraxas replied.

Although Beauty remained rather sullenly silent.

CHAPTER 6

Abraxas had to admit, he might have been a little overconfident. Elves were notoriously difficult to compromise with, and he knew very well that Margaret followed the old ways more than most. However, he also had to believe she could see reason. Finding the King's brother would have multiple benefits, not just that the man might be able to give the eggs back to Abraxas.

It took their second rebellion three days to settle on a plan of attack for how to convince her. Namely because Beauty wanted to argue her case even further and somehow persuade Abraxas to change his mind.

She'd have a better chance of yelling at a wall until it fell over. If her anxiety eased after ordering him around, then he supposed he might entertain her. At least for a little while.

Still, she had to know he wasn't listening to anything she said. He could actively take part in a conversation without changing his mind.

And by the end of the week, he'd had enough. Abraxas asked to meet with Margaret himself, without the other two women who would accompany him on this journey.

The Darkveil elf had surrounded herself with more than a few soldiers. All the time. Abraxas never saw her without at least three men who were armed to the teeth and seemed quite happy to glare at anyone who came near Margaret. He could only assume they were among the original rebellion members, but he thought he would remember their faces. Many of them had fought against the King and thus had fought against Abraxas.

He stood in front of a glaring man now, ignoring the mortal who thought he could intimidate a dragon. Instead, Abraxas stared at the door and waited for it to open. It would, eventually, and he would free himself from this man's ridiculous gaze.

"Enter." Margaret's voice floated from beyond.

She still remained within the King's old rooms, and he had to guess that was a power play. As he pushed the door open, Abraxas knew she'd set herself here so others would automatically see her as the leader. She'd put Lorelei into harm's way because she didn't want to do it herself, but she was the one with all the authority in this castle.

He hated her for that.

Abraxas strode into the room and ignored all the papers Margaret had strewn about the table. He already knew what they were. Maps with small markers for rumors where someone had claimed to see the King.

She chased a shadow of a man. And though he knew there were better ways to hunt, he wouldn't share them with the likes of her. Let her struggle to find Zander. They would only find the King when he was ready for them to find him.

"Thank you for meeting with me," he said, trying hard not to wince through the lies that slipped off his tongue. "I appreciate your time."

"You know I'll make whatever time I can for you, Abraxas. You're a great asset to us all."

She wore her usual leather armor, although Abraxas was surprised to see that her top had no sleeves. Her wiry arms were muscular to a point of unhealthy. She'd lost weight, or perhaps she didn't want anyone to see just how thin she'd become. The pale skin showed vibrant blue veins that struggled to pump blood through her body. And when he took a deep inhalation, there was the thick scent of healing potions oozing from her flesh.

Was she injured? No. He'd seen her moving far too easily for an injury. He couldn't even hazard a guess at why she'd need a healing potion, however.

"Don't analyze me too hard, Abraxas, you'll hurt yourself." She arched a pale brow, then pointed to a seat at the table. "Sit down. I imagine this will be a long conversation if you're meeting with me privately."

He didn't enjoy following orders, but this wasn't the battle he wanted to pick. "I'd like it to be short, but no. I highly doubt it will be."

Margaret cleared her throat and sat down herself. This time, he could see how tired she looked. She settled into her chair like a woman twice her age. He hated to pity her, considering all the lies and deceit. Honestly, he didn't trust her, and he wasn't sure that he ever should.

Margaret was dangerous. She held secrets in her palm and then crushed them into a dust that no one could ever piece together again.

Margaret waved an imperious hand in the air, ordering him to begin. "You seem troubled. I don't like it when a troubled dragon is sitting in my drawing room."

"This was not a drawing room," he corrected. "It was a fitting room, actually. Most of the time the King had countless seamstresses ensuring that every outfit was more stunning than the last. He liked to make an impression."

Her expression pinched. "I don't care what it was for the previous leader of this kingdom. It's my drawing room, and therefore, it is only a drawing room."

Right, because she wanted to erase the past rather than face history. He supposed that was easier for her.

He leaned back in his chair, trying his best to appear calm. "I want to take Lorelei and Beauty to find the King's bastard brother."

Margaret remained silent, watching him with a narrowed gaze that threatened violence. Maybe cracking her over the head with that information hadn't been the finest plan, but he wasn't expecting her to say yes. Abraxas had, of course, expected her to argue with him.

What he hadn't expected was this silence. He didn't know what to do with it.

She looked at him with clear anger in her eyes, but didn't move a muscle. She didn't even blink. The elf before him had turned completely to stone and watched him with an unimpressed stare.

"Did you hear me?" he finally asked.

"I did. I am waiting for you to laugh and tell me you were joking." She frowned even harder at him. "You understand that girl is more important to this mission than anyone else? That without the symbolism of her face, we are all finished?"

"Beauty is a wonderful addition to your team, but I think you're exaggerating her importance." He tried to lighten the mood, considering they both knew they weren't talking about Beauty.

Lorelei was the biggest pawn in Margaret's game. He'd have to be blind not to realize that.

He could have cut through the silence with a knife. Obviously, this woman was not interested in his jokes. Not in the slightest.

Margaret leaned forward and braced her elbows on the table. Brows furrowed and eyes flinty with rage, she asked, "Why do you think this is the smart approach?"

"There are more than a few reasons to bring in another of the bloodline. You know it as well as I. Even if we find the King and murder him again, which I will remind you that the last attempt didn't go as planned, there will always be this brother who may surface to take the throne." He spread his fingers wide as if that might help convince her. "It's a good idea. Even you cannot disagree."

"The boy hasn't been seen in years. Allow me to repeat that. Years. It's a rumor to begin with that the King ever had a half sibling, and if they try to come to light, then I will inform them that the previous king wasn't strong enough to defeat us. What would a half blood little whelp hope to do?"

Margaret's eyes grew even more feral as she spoke. He could see the wild need for the hunt in the set of her shoulders and the snap of her jaw. She wanted the young man to show himself. She wanted the bloodshed and battle that would come with him.

Abraxas chose his next words carefully, realizing that he could only win this fight with words. "And yet it was a half blood who defeated the last king. Your insults would only give him more power."

"You think you're so smart, don't you?" She shook her head, disbelief written all over her features. "Has it ever occurred to you that you're very old, Abraxas? Perhaps even out of touch."

He would have taken any other insult on the chin, but his age? He wasn't an old fool who hadn't ever seen the world beyond his farm. Abraxas had seen kingdoms fall, men die, kings become ill with dark magic. And she thought she could use that against him? That knowledge made him who he was. It gave him power.

Drawing himself up straight, he narrowed his gaze at her. His voice deepened to a growl. "Just what are you implying, Margaret?"

"That perhaps you don't have the capabilities to see beyond your nose." She didn't back down, he gave her that. The woman had pride. "You see only a pretty little elf which you haven't seen in a very long time. Her beauty is unmatched, I'll give you that. She's captivating in more than just looks, but in her history and the wrongs you could right by allowing her to fall in love with you. I am not so selfish. I can see beyond a lovely face and recognize what else she's capable of."

"Of course you know what she's capable of. Or more what she can do for you." Abraxas ground his teeth together, hating this woman all the more. "You see her as a pawn in this game you're playing. What I can't figure out is your plans for her."

"I will not tell you that."

"No, I knew that you'd keep all your information close to your chest. You want her to suffer for you. And then the kingdom will see how their legend declined and they will think you are their savior. I'm old, Margaret. Like you said. I've seen this play out before."

She lifted a pale brow and looked for all the world as though she were unconvinced. "You forget that I have lived many years as well, dear dragon. Elves are nearly as long lived as your kind."

"And you think that makes you qualified to know how to handle this? You're going to get her killed."

It was his greatest fear. This woman played a game that was bigger than a single elf. And he remembered her clan. They were bloodthirsty at best, mad at the worst. She saw only darkness, and so she fed the world even more of that bitter venom.

Already he could see how easily Lorelei could get caught up in Margaret's plan. And the kingdom would only see that a half elf was the cause of all their problems. The humans would rise against Lore, not against Margaret. No one had even seen the Darkveil elf in years. They'd likely forgotten she ever lived.

So she would use Lore. She would tell the others that the half elf was the one who had done everything and spread her stories until everyone believed her. Until there was no one in the tale other than Lore.

He watched Margaret's eyes, and for a brief second, she flinched.

"You've been planning to let her die," he whispered. "That's been your plan all alone, hasn't it?"

She swallowed hard. And he knew. He knew the truth without her ever having to open her mouth.

Still, Margaret at least had the guts to confirm his fear. "You said it yourself, Abraxas. Every good story, every real hero, has to become a martyr. So you see why I cannot let you take her away from the castle? I have bigger plans for her."

All the blood in his veins went cold. She'd even admit it so easily, as though Lore weren't a person, only a game piece. Lore's death meant nothing to her. Not in the slightest. And he could do nothing to stop it.

Except he could.

Unlike all the people in this castle, he didn't report to Margaret. He didn't even believe in the cause that she had built up around herself.

Sure, she wanted the magical creatures to flourish, but her ideas weren't the only way to do that. And if her only plan was to take away the one person who meant the world to him, the one person who had made him feel like he was more than just a dragon?

He would stop her.

Abraxas stood from his chair before his thoughts had even finished. He'd made it halfway across the room before his mind caught up with his body and then they linked together. Dragon and man. Both protecting what was theirs.

His hand closed around Margaret's throat before she could wiggle free. The elf was sly, but she wasn't quick enough to escape him. His fingernails lengthened into claws that dug into her skin. Tiny beads of blood welled up from where he touched until she stopped moving. The thick ooze dripped to her collarbone.

"I can end all this now," he growled. "It would be so easy, so quick, to break your neck."

"You wouldn't," she wheezed. "Then you'd have the humans and the rebellion after you."

"I have wings, Margaret. I can fly all the way back to my homeland, dead as it is, and I would live out the rest of my long life remembering that your eyes grew so wide when you realized I would actually kill you." He leaned closer, opening his mouth and letting out a long hiss that sounded eerily close to what he would make in his dragon form. "I want you to listen to me now. You're going to let us go of your own accord. You're going to let us find the King's half brother, and you're going to say this was all your idea."

"Why would I do that?" she asked, her voice little more than a thready breath.

"Because you're losing the approval of your own people. Because the longer Lore is here, the more they will look to her for what she wants to do. You already saw it at the council meeting. They wanted her opinion. They looked at Lore before they looked at you. Margaret, you said it yourself. You need to create a hero, and that means that people will begin to worship her. Wouldn't it be easier to control that devotion if you're her mouthpiece?"

Abraxas knew she thought he had forgotten about these games. She was under the impression that the dragon had stayed on the sidelines while the King worked, but he knew how everyone played this game of nobility.

All he had to do was convince her that his words were her own thoughts. That she'd already feared what he said, and he was only confirming the dread that lived in the pit of her stomach.

Her expression changed, slipping from the usual mask and revealing her terror. She had thought Lore would unseat her in her position of power. She'd been so afraid, and he knew it.

Swallowing hard, she nodded once. Just enough of a jerk for him to release his hold on her neck.

The moment he removed his hand, Margaret pressed her own to where his had been. She massaged the skin there, glaring at him with so much hatred in her gaze. He knew she'd hate him for that. Honestly, he would have thought less of her if she didn't. But now it was up to her to decide what to do with that hatred.

Would she see reason? Would she believe the lies he had spewed, or would she stick to her own story?

"Fine," Margaret spat. "Waste your time running after a ghost. The bastard son of a maid means little to me, but if you think it will work, then run after your dreams. Take the girl. Keep her out of my way. But if she dies, dragon, I will cut your throat in your sleep."

"I have no doubt you will try," he replied with a sly smile. "You would fail, but your dedication is admirable."

"I mean it, Abraxas. She's important to all of us. Not just you."

"Oh, I know." He stepped away from her, letting the fire drain from his body and sink into the floor in a wave of heat. "I know you want to use her. To take away her freedom just like everyone else. I'll return her alive, Margaret. You have little to fear."

CHAPTER 7

"That was your plan this whole time?" Lorelei snapped as she threw clothing into a small pack. "Threaten Margaret until she feared for her life and then gave you what you wanted? Abraxas, you absolute idiot."

She could have breathed fire at him, she was so angry. He thought it was hilarious, obviously. He couldn't stop chuckling and that stupid, prideful expression on his face only made her want to slap him.

Margaret was not the person to threaten. Not like that. The mad elf could do literally anything to keep them in the castle and yet, he walked into her bedroom, grabbed her by the throat, and that changed everything?

Lore seized one of her knives from the vanity and pointed it at his heart. "You're not telling me the whole story, are you? What else was said that made her cave so easily?"

Unbothered by the knife pointing at a vital organ, Abraxas shrugged. "There's nothing else to say. She wants us all to stay out of her way. I gave her the opportunity to let us go, and now we're going. Why do you think this is all some grand plot?"

Because it had been. Everything on this journey so far had been a grand plot to get her to do what other people wanted. She had been played with, toyed, forced to do things she never chose to do. All because Margaret had told her this was the only way for their dream of the future to come true.

She trusted nothing that came out of that elf's mouth. Especially not when Margaret agreed with Lore's desires.

"It makes little sense," she muttered while waving the knife in the air. "She wouldn't agree to let us go. Even Beauty didn't think that Margaret would ever see reason."

"You don't know how to trust other people, do you?" He reached out and wrapped his hand around the knife's hilt. Just over hers. The heat of his skin sank into her flesh and, oh, how she wanted to release the deadly weapon into his care. He could take the weight of it.

No. She wouldn't. That wasn't who Lore was and nothing could or would change that.

"No, I don't trust anyone," she snarled, pulling her hand away from his, but at least setting the knife in its place. "Though I think I could trust you, and that bothers me more than I care to admit."

"Really?" He sat down on the edge of her bed, leaning back on his hands and looking like he hadn't a worry in the world. "Why does that bother you? Dragons are quite loyal."

She turned her attention to her pack. They didn't have time for this conversation, and frankly, she'd hoped to avoid it for a little while longer. But if he wanted to know then... Well.

"My mother," she replied. "I can't stop thinking about my mother."

"I thought I had explained that to you." His gaze softened and the wrinkles around his mouth deepened. "I'm sorry for what I did, but I didn't have a choice. Your mother was the one person the King demanded to see dead more than anyone else. She was that generation's Margaret. I gave her the quickest death I could without raising suspicion. Such was the best I could offer her."

"I know," Lore whispered. And she did. Really, she didn't blame him any more than she could blame herself.

Yet that guilt still lived inside her. So, she supposed, she was blaming him a bit.

"I miss her," she allowed herself to say. The words ripped through her entire being, tearing at her lungs, leaving her throat raw and aching.

She wanted to see her mother again. She wanted to hold the delicate hands that had rubbed her back through nightmares. She wanted to watch her mother's head tilt with laughter so much that she started snorting with glee. All these moments were taken from her in an instant, and she craved to have them.

And yes, she should blame the King. She did. She hated the man for all he'd done to her and countless other little girls who had grown up lacking something so important.

Hands touched her back, smoothed up between her shoulder blades and down her spine. "Breathe, Lore," Abraxas murmured in her ear. "You have to breathe."

How could she when everything seemed to ride on her shoulders? Her heart wouldn't stop pounding in her chest and her ribs felt like they might crack with the pressure.

"I feel like there are more chains around my neck than ever before. I can't sleep. I can't eat. All I know is that so many people are counting on me to do the right thing for them, but I have no idea what they expect." She swallowed hard, staring at her fireplace but not recognizing anything in front of her. "I dream of a light that bounces just out of my reach, and no matter how many times I try to catch it, it always slips through my fingers. And then I'm left alone in the dark. Terrifying shadows nip and claw at my skin. And I can't do anything about it because I'm not smart enough, nor fast enough, to reach the light."

The heat of his palms slid down her back again, curving over her ribs until both his arms wrapped firmly around her. Abraxas drew her into the safety of his body. Into the haven that only his embrace had ever created.

He rested his chin on the top of her head and simply held her. He didn't expect anything in return, or if he did, he never made a move other than to clasp her to his heart.

Lore stayed stiff for all of a minute before she let herself relax into him. She set her hands on top of his muscular forearms, feeling them flex underneath her fingertips as she traced the worn wool sleeves. The fibers reminded her of home. Of homespun fabrics that were made by hand, not ordered from some far off place that used magic to create pretty clothing.

His chest lifted and rose, gently, steadily. He wasn't overwhelmed by any of the emotions that ate at her. Instead, Abraxas was a steady tide on a clear evening. The sails of his soul did not whip with storms. Not like hers. His journey was silent and calm.

Her heartbeat eased and then matched his. It slowed from its wild thunder, calming to a steady thud.

Taking a deep breath, she let it out with one long sigh. "Thank you."

"It is easy to feel as though your legacy might pull you under the tide, but you are not alone. Never alone." For the briefest of moments, she swore he pressed his lips to her hair.

But then he released her and stepped back, his arms limp at his sides and his fingers curled into fists. As though he wanted to hold on to the memory of touching her.

"I suppose I'm not alone," she replied, turning around to watch him. "You're going through the same thing I am."

"Ah, but they have always looked at dragons as monsters and villains." His lips twitched. "You're a god or a hero to them. I don't know which one I'd prefer to be."

Grumbling, she returned to pulling out whatever clothing she could bring that would be easy to carry. She didn't know if she preferred to be a hero, either. But it seemed like people left gods alone.

A knock at the door warned that they were about to have a visitor. At least Lore was almost packed. Beauty would have nothing to scold her about.

Her friend entered like a thunderclap. The door slammed open, and she stalked into the room with a pack on her back that could have carried a human. Quite literally. The bag that Beauty had strapped onto herself poked out over her head and Lore swore the bottom was somewhere near the woman's knees.

"Are you ready?" Beauty asked, casting her gaze about the room to make sure they were alone. "I don't want to wait until Margaret changes her mind to get out of here."

"Almost." Lore took her time packing up her knives. Though it might seem a little extravagant to the untrained eye, the knives had to be properly cleaned and put away or they would dull. Chip. Warp. All manner of horrible things could happen to a knife that made it a much less effective weapon.

Beauty turned her attention to the dragon standing in the middle of the room. "You don't have a pack."

"I do not," Abraxas replied.

"Why don't you have a pack?"

Abraxas didn't reply. Instead, he just stared at the little human like she had to say more for him to understand her question.

As Lore watched, Beauty's face turned more and more red. It started at the base of her throat, or likely deeper in her clothing, where Lore couldn't see. Then it spread up her neck, to her chin, her cheeks, then all the way to her forehead before it finally burst out yet again.

Beauty ground her teeth and flipped the straps off her shoulders. Her bag hit the ground with a clank of pots, pans, and who knows what else. "Are you trying to tell me that you have not packed at all, dragon?"

Oh no. There was a look on Beauty's face of madness. Like she might attack at any moment.

Lore paused and planted a hand on her hip. "Do you see steam coming out her nose, or am I hallucinating?"

Her dragon tilted his head to the side and bit his lip. "You know, I think I see it too. I didn't know humans could do that, did you?"

"I was under the impression they lacked all talent in magic." Lore shrugged. "Apparently we were wrong."

Beauty balled her hands into fists. "I knew traveling with the two of you was the worst decision I could make. I said we needed to pack for this trip and I said we needed to do it quickly. What part of that did neither of you understand?"

Oh, she was packing. Lore wasn't taking the fall for Abraxas on this one.

She waved the shirt in her hand and then shoved it into her own bag. "I'm done. I don't know what you're talking about. I took your order very seriously, and I have completed my task."

Beauty pointed to the dragon, jabbing the air with a sharp finger. "That one is still standing around like he doesn't have to bring anything at all. He doesn't even look apologetic for making us wait!"

No, he didn't. Abraxas leaned against a post of her bed, ankles crossed, arms crossed, looking for all the world like he was relaxed and comfortable. In her bedroom.

Had it gotten hot all of a sudden?

Lore pulled her shirt away from her chest, fanning her face before replying. "I'm not sure we can force him to do anything, Beauty."

To his credit, Abraxas did at least look between the two of them as if he were searching for the answer to this argument. He broke down and replied, "I'm not bringing a bag, pack, or knapsack. There's nothing a dragon needs to carry on a journey like this. All I need is my teeth and my claws. The rest will come naturally."

Oh, there was the real steam. Beauty was going to punch a dragon square in the face and Lore would have to pull them off each other before they'd even left.

Beauty pulled herself together, though. Instead of hitting the man as she clearly wanted to do, she sucked her teeth before growling, "Clothing?"

"When I change into this form, I need only summon clothing to mind. It's part of the magic. Otherwise, I would change and be entirely naked in front of the two of you."

That was news to Lore. She remembered him nude in the great hall after the first attack. It was one of her fondest memories of him, although she refused to admit it to anyone but herself.

This time, she was the one who frowned at the dragon. Had he lied to her? Or had he changed so quickly that he'd forgotten clothing?

Beauty continued on her list. "Food?"

"We all know I'll be hunting while we're on this journey. Dragons eat far too much for me to bring food with us. I'll need to hunt to sustain myself, and whatever is left I'll bring to you both."

"Water?"

"Again, I'll find it wherever we go."

"Armor? Weapons? Anything to protect us with?" She threw her hands up in the air.

"Again, dragon." He flashed a sharp toothed smile. "I'm not sure what you aren't understanding here, Beauty. Everything I need is right with me wherever I go. I don't need to bring a bag like the other mortals you are so used to. The body I live in is more than enough."

All the wind blew out of Beauty's sails at that moment. With a fierce grunt, she stomped her foot on the ground and turned to pick up her own pack. "Well, it must be nice to be a dragon, then."

"It is," he replied with a snort. "Until humans try to hunt you down because all the legends claim dragons steal virgins for their personal hoards. As if any of us would want a little farm girl in our hoard."

Poor Beauty looked so dejected that Lore couldn't let Abraxas win. After all, he was the stronger creature, and he didn't have any right to make her feel worthless. Beauty had more power in her than any mortal she'd ever met. All because she was brave and kind.

So Lore arched a brow, popped her hip to the side, and crossed her arms over her chest. "Oh, I don't know about that, Abraxas. Rumors and legends come from somewhere. So you dragons must have a taste for the farm girl, after all. I'd imagine one of those would be much better than a princess locked away in a tower somewhere."

Beauty giggled, snorted, and then fell into a pile of laughter on top of her own pack.

There, that was better.

With a soft smile on her own face, Lore picked up her backpack and threw it over her shoulders. The pack was light, the weight comfortable on her shoulders. She'd packed enough to get them through a week. That was all she needed, after all.

Once Beauty stopped laughing and hauled herself to standing, bag included, she asked, "Where are we going, anyway? Do we have an idea of where to look?"

Lore did. Of course she did. There was only one place in all the Umbral Kingdom to go when one was searching for someone.

"I know where we're going," she replied, checking her straps one more time.

"Where to?" Beauty asked, now a little too chipper.

"Home," Lore replied. "We're going home."

CHAPTER 8

Was this how humans traveled? Abraxas hated it. His feet and ankles ached, his thighs burned after a long, hard day of walking all the way across Umbra. The two women with him were still breathing heavily, sweat sticking their shirts to their chests.

He understood that he couldn't turn into a dragon. Their reasoning was sound. The people of Tenebrous would see him flying over their city once again and they would either assume the King was back, or they would start looking for Lorelei in the crowd. None of them could afford any of that.

So he'd walked. Like a mortal. And he didn't think he'd ever traveled that way before, nor would he ever travel like this again. If they tried to make him, then he would simply take the choice away and fly before they could tell him he couldn't.

Yanking off one of the stiff boots, he tossed it onto the ground with a grunt. "This is ridiculous. We couldn't have at least rode horses?"

"Tenebrous doesn't have a lot of horses, in case you missed that." Lorelei pulled her own shoes off and shoved her fingers hard into the arch of her foot. "They're too expensive. We ride in on stallions and everyone will start asking questions."

"Ah." He should have remembered that, but he wasn't thinking straight. "Should I light a fire, then?"

It took him only a short amount of time to gather all the wood and sticks together. Then, with a puff of his breath, he set the entire pile ablaze. That would keep them warm overnight, and he looked forward to a good night's sleep.

Lore rubbed the back of her neck, staring into the flames, then sighed. "I'll take first watch. I want to let my mind settle a bit, anyway."

Beauty pulled a roll off her bag and laid it out near the fire. She flopped down hard onto the mat, didn't say a word, and then appeared to fall asleep. Deeply. Was she snoring?

"There's light and flame," he said, returning his attention to Lore. "We don't need someone to keep watch."

"Maybe not if you were in your dragon form," Lore replied with a slight laugh. "But anyone walking through here with ill intent will think we're just two women with a single man to protect us. And that's very easy to overpower. I'll keep you two safe, and I'll wake you when I need someone else to take the next watch. Sleep well, Abraxas."

None of this settled well with him, but he knew he couldn't argue with her. If someone walked by, they would think they were vulnerable. They had no way of knowing he was a dragon and that Lore could cut their throat with the mere flick of her hand. They'd take advantage and then where would he be? With more blood on his hands and Lore telling him that she'd told him so.

Sighing, he laid down on the opposite side of the fire.

Maybe Beauty had been right. He should have brought a pack with him. The ground was hard and stiff against his spine, and would only make tomorrow's journey much harder. At least they should be in Tenebrous by nightfall, as long as they kept the same pace.

The mere idea of the torment made him want to groan. His body hurt. Everything ached. Another day of vigorous walking and rushing through the fields would only make tomorrow night worse. Hopefully, there would be a hot bath waiting for them in Tenebrous, even though he doubted that would be the case.

"Here," Lore's voice whispered through the darkness. Her hand touched his shoulder, gently rolling him onto his side.

The firelight caught on the sides of her face, coiling around the curves and arches of her cheekbones and the sharp edges of her jaw. Her hair turned from gold to pure fire that outlined her lovely face. He'd never seen a woman like her before, or if he had, his mind had wiped away the memory so he'd never forget how beautiful she was. How stunning.

She held a bedroll in her hands, unfurling it beside him. "You're going to get a cramp if you sleep on the ground like that."

"Taking care of me?" he asked, though he pulled the roll into position. "I thought you said we weren't going to pursue anything between us."

"We aren't. You'll slow us all down if you're a fool who sleeps with a rock in his back all night." But she hesitated for a moment, still crouched on the ground as he settled. Watching him.

Those ocean eyes saw everything, but he would never tell her how much they revealed. She wanted to touch him again. He could see that need in the way her gaze lingered on his collarbone that likely had been set ablaze by the fire. Just as her own skin had been.

He took peace in the fact that they both still felt this way. They both burned to touch each other, even when it was wrong. Even when they knew that there were so many obstacles standing in the way.

He wouldn't let her force herself, though. They didn't need to rush.

"Good night, Lore." Even saying the words felt like he'd ripped something out of his own chest and handed it to her, raw and bleeding. "Wake me for the next watch. We'll let Beauty sleep tonight."

"All right." She swallowed hard, then stood and walked away into the night.

Abraxas didn't have the heart to tell her that he wouldn't sleep a wink tonight. Not with the memory of her hand on his shoulder, turning him around so that he could see the pure darkness in her gaze. The night sky reflected in the still pools of her eyes. Twinkling starlight with a hint of cruel hope.

No, sleep would not be easy.

He staggered the last few steps through the marsh and out onto the road beyond. Finally, his feet touched solid ground. Firm ground.

Abraxas stretched his spine and pressed the palms of his hands into his lower back. "I never want to travel like this again. The fact that humans do it regularly is horrible. I pity the lot of you."

Though the women chuckled, Beauty was quick to remind him, "Stop talking about mortals and humans. You are one right now, remember? No one can know who we are or why we're here."

Of course. He had to watch what he said and now that they were out of the damned marsh, he could think straight. He'd flown over Tenebrous more times than he could count. The place was as familiar to him as the castle. He knew where to search.

Except, as they strode down the road toward the town, he lost that confidence. Tenebrous was a mish-mash of homes all built haphazardly upon uneven ground and sometimes even over the remains of buildings that should have been condemned. This led to walls that listed to the side, roofs that were ominously tilted, and shattered windows covered by cloth. The gray tinge over the city never disappeared and a faint fog always crawled along the street as though it were a living, breathing thing.

They caught up to a group of people who staggered toward Tenebrous, and he'd forgotten what the families here looked like. Their clothing was ripped and moth eaten. Dark circles under their eyes. Some of them were even skeletal, although he never had seen that from the King's carriage.

"A little different when you're walking through them, isn't it?" Lorelei asked, stepping a little closer to him. "They aren't the beloved people the King visited on a regular basis."

"No, they seem…" Tired? Ill? He didn't know the right word to describe these poor people who had been forgotten by their king and country.

"They're the citizens of Tenebrous," she replied. "They've always looked like this. It's just hard to tell when you're sitting in the lap of luxury."

His stomach turned, and he thought for a moment he might vomit. The scent rolling out of the city and down the street was… was… Human waste, years of refuse and garbage tossed out of back doors, and the faint hint of rotting meat.

He'd breathe through his mouth from now on.

Beauty shifted her pack on her shoulders and gave them a nod. "This is where we split up, I'm afraid. My father will want to see me and I have too much of a recognizable face in these parts. I have to visit him first, and make some excuses for why we're here. Then at least no one will ask questions when they see us together."

Really? He thought that might make more of a problem than if Beauty just stayed hidden. Except Lore nodded and replied before he could speak.

"That's fine. I already know where we're heading, anyway. I'll send a messenger to you when we're finished and tell you where to meet up with us next."

"You know the place to send it?"

"Your father's home is well known, Beauty. The bird will find it, don't you worry."

Bird?

He felt as though he were the child they dragged behind them. Abraxas didn't know the plan at all, nor did he understand where to go or what to do now. This entire journey had rather firmly put him in his place, and it had only been a couple of days.

What a humbling experience. And also one that reminded him how lucky he was to be a dragon while all the other individuals in the world struggled far more than he did. Perhaps they were stronger than him, because he was certain he'd have folded like a stack of cards long ago.

He watched Beauty trail away from them, waving to individuals as she went. They all knew her, although she looked much healthier than the others. He'd have thought that would create some resentment for the lovely girl. Instead, the crowd watched her walk by them with fond expressions and soft smiles.

"She always makes people feel comfortable around her, doesn't she?" he asked, belatedly realizing he'd given the question a sound rather than thinking it.

"Always," Lore replied. "I never knew her when we lived here, but I'd heard of her. The Lord's daughter with a heart of gold and a smile that could chase away the clouds. I didn't recognize her when we arrived at the castle, likely never would have. But now I see they were always talking about her."

Yes, that was a fitting description.

Abraxas was so caught up in his thoughts, he almost didn't notice Lore walking away from him. She ducked through the crowd with her head down and hair over her ears. Never catching the attention of a single person, even when she had to move them out of her way. What a stark contrast to the other young woman who had lived in this town.

He frowned and marched after her. "Were you going to tell me we were heading out?"

"No," she muttered. "This would be easier if you weren't with me."

"So you want to leave me to my own devices in the middle of Tenebrous?" He already knew her answer.

"Also no." Lore ducked underneath a strand of laundry and suddenly she was gone. Completely out of his sight, and he had no idea which way she'd gone.

"Lore?" he called out. "Where did you go?"

They couldn't afford to lose each other. Not while they were in Tenebrous. Namely because he didn't know where to go and if his guide disappeared, then he would find himself on the wrong side of town. They'd have to save a gang from his teeth or risk him revealing that they'd traveled with a dragon.

"Lore?" he tried one more time before he planned on turning back into his normal form. Abraxas looked forward to hearing the screams as the people of Tenebrous realized they'd been walking alongside a monster this entire time.

"Oh, for all the Light, you could just look up. Dolt."

He looked straight up and there she was. Hanging onto a very flimsy looking shutter, leaning over him like a spider clinging to a wall. Her thighs flexed and biceps bulged as she held herself perfectly still.

"Look at you," he marveled. "You just have to be stunning at all times, don't you?"

She rolled her eyes and held out her free hand for him to take. "I've never liked walking on the streets of Tenebrous. Too many people and too many eyes. Care to join me?"

"Where?" Of course he would join her. He'd reached for her hand before he even had any idea what she might want from him. And that was all right. He wanted to experience her life the way she'd lived it here. He wanted to know everything he could about her.

She closed her hand around his with surprising strength, then tugged him up the wall toward the other shutter. "It's a quick climb, but then we can walk across the roofs. I think it's faster."

It was certainly more risky. He could already see his foot going through a roof and a young woman screaming in terror that a full grown man had fallen through her ceiling. Yet, if Lore seemed to think they could travel this way without fear, then he would do whatever it took.

Abraxas closed his hand around the shutter and hauled himself up the wall.

She moved far more gracefully than he did. If she were a spider weaving her web, then he was the clunky grasshopper who had yet to learn how to walk. He banged his boot a few times against the rotten wood planks, hard enough that he heard a man ask, "What was that?"

But finally they crawled onto the roof of the building and he rolled to his back. Staring up at the gray skies, he heaved in the first deep breath he'd taken in a while. "You used to do that all the time?"

"Still do." Her face appeared over him, the smile curving her lips quite possibly the prettiest thing he'd seen all day. "You're breathing rather hard, Abraxas. Was that a tough climb for you?"

"Absolutely." He didn't mind admitting it to her. "Now, where are we going? You never answered that question."

"I already told you we're going home." She glanced down at the rooftops, then pointed to their right. "I used to live over there. Most of my things are probably still in the attic. I don't think they were all collected before I headed out to the King's castle, so there might be a few useful items to collect."

"I thought we were supposed to be finding the King's brother?" He rolled onto his hands and knees, then shoved himself upright. "How is stopping at your old apartment going to give us any information?"

"Oh, you'll see." She shook her head with a wry grin, then wrapped an arm around her waist. Almost as though she were uncomfortable. "It's less about the things in the apartment and more about who will visit us while we're there."

Now that was an odd thing to say. And he had always been a sucker for a mystery.

"Lead on, then," he said, his voice low and interest piqued. "I'm curious to see where you spent your days."

Was he imagining it, or did she wince?

CHAPTER 9

Lorelei's heart beat faster the closer they got to her old apartment. Or at least, the one that she'd sheltered in. The owner of the building didn't have a clue that a half elf had lived above them, but she was quiet most of the time. No one had ever been the wiser.

What would Abraxas think of the little rundown home she'd made for herself like a mouse in the walls? She knew what it looked like through her own eyes. Dust covered. Moth eaten. Ragged. It was safe, though, and that was good enough for her. This apartment was better than sleeping in a garbage pile on the street.

Lore hoped he would realize that in Tenebrous, she'd gotten a pretty decent pick of the abandoned attics in the area. But she also knew he'd lived in the castle for a hundred years. And before that, she had no idea what the dragons thought of as a suitable home. They were wild creatures, flourishing in the mountains and by riverbeds. Surely he'd seen worse living conditions than her little abode?

Maybe not, though. And that was terrifying.

She hopped over the last roof, making sure to step carefully over the loose tile that always tripped her up. And then they were there. Right on the shingles with the tiny square addition at the top with a single window.

She'd never known what it was for. Maybe just to add meager light and air into the attic. At the very least, it had given her an easy in and out of the location in case she had to run. Though there hadn't been a reason for a quick escape, it was helpful to know that she'd had the opportunity.

What a life. Always wondering when and where she was going to be attacked. Eventually giving up on the idea of saving herself.

Lore had forgotten how tired Tenebrous made her.

She put her hand on the cold window covered in grime and gently pushed it open. If it were locked, then she'd know the owners had figured her out. They were an elderly couple who never went up into their attic. Maybe their children had inherited the house.

Her heartbeat thudded in her throat and then the window opened. The dirt hadn't sealed it shut, and no one had locked it at all. It was like she hadn't disappeared for a few months, only to return empty-handed. Well, other than a dragon at her side.

"Come on," she muttered. "This is where I lived. You'll have to fit through here."

She shoved it as far open as it could go and then slid through the opening. She was pretty sure he'd be able to fit. Or at the very least, squeeze through.

Lore landed in a crouch, hands raised to fight just in case. But no one was in the room at all. And it was just how she'd left it. Stacks of odd objects from the owners, some furniture, some books, others just large stacks of paper that had fallen out of a box. Her tiny cot in the corner, covered in scraps of fabric because she hadn't been able to afford a real comforter. So she'd sewn together the pieces she could find to create some kind of warm nest.

Bird feathers floated through the air and dust covered every surface. It was clear no one had been here in a very long time.

Lore straightened and listened to Abraxas struggle through the window. But she wasn't paying attention to him. Not when she could see a tiny rat sitting in the center of her bed, gnawing at the blanket. It was gathering its own supplies for the upcoming winter.

A crop of dead elfweed in the corner had started to stink. The whole place always smelled musty, though. She supposed elfweed didn't make any difference.

Damn, she hadn't thought about what it would be like to see her old living quarters.

Her room in the castle had been so much nicer. And that wasn't even the most opulent of rooms there.

She'd changed. In just a couple months, she looked at this room with different eyes. It wasn't safe for her anymore. It didn't even feel good to be here. Not in the slightest.

Abraxas walked up to her side, dusting his hands off on his thighs. "This is the place? Cozy."

"Is it?" She shook her head in disbelief that he could ever think that while looking at all this. "I can't believe I used to live here. This was nice to me. And it wasn't that long ago that I believed this was a suitable home."

His hand pressed against her back, rubbing in tiny circles like he always did when he sensed her discomfort. "It was a safe place for you to rest your head, Lorelei. We all need somewhere to sleep. Some it's a castle, others it's an attic. And for dragons, that happens to be a cold, damp cave deep within the earth."

That broke through her horror. With a snort, she turned toward him and let the anxiety leak out of her body. He continued to rub in those captivating circles, and that helped. It really, really did. "How do you always know the right thing to say?"

He must have sensed that she was ready for more. That she was fine with him touching her, holding her as he had what felt like months ago. Abraxas palmed her hips, slid his arms around her and tugged her against his chest. He propped his chin on top of her head and chuckled. The deep sound vibrated through his throat.

"I am hundreds of years old, Lorelei. An ancient being. If I didn't learn how to say the right thing at the right moment after all those centuries of life, then I really would be a fool."

"Ah, so you have a lot of experience with women." Her face was smashed against his chest, so the words were garbled.

He understood, though. "Enough to know that you're struggling to connect the person you've become with the one you were before. Our lives change. We change. And there's nothing to be ashamed of in that growth. Where we came from molded who we are today. The good, the bad, the ugly. All of it. You must honor the memories of who you were so that you never forget to be proud of how far you've come."

Tears pricking in her eyes, she pulled away from him with a deep sigh. "Right. Of course. Well, this is the place. I have some things underneath the cot that might be helpful. Just some magical items I pilfered along the way."

She thought there could still be a few amulets under there. She didn't know what they did or what spell had been put on them, but she could only imagine they would be useful in the long run. And then there were the potions. A few of those could help.

Before she could move, Abraxas had already walked over to the cot. He leaned against it, hand nearly squashing the poor rat, who raced away from him. "Under here?"

"Ah..." She didn't know if she should let him paw through in her things or not. "Yes, but be careful. I have no idea what magic was placed on them, and they might be a little volatile."

"I think I know how to touch magical objects, Lorelei. I've dealt with them many times."

Sure, but he also was a rather cocky bastard and considering their history...

A hand closed around her arm and jerked her toward the window. "I wondered when you'd be coming back."

Though she should have recognized the voice, her immediate reaction lacked any recognition at all. Lore jabbed her elbow into the gut of the fool who dared grab onto her. And when she heard the "oof" that always came from losing the air in their lungs, she whipped around, grabbed ahold of their hair, and then kneed them in the face.

"Lorelei!" The shout was followed by an answering groan. "What was that for?"

The short man in front of her didn't deserve a knee to the face for so many reasons. Namely because he was a member of the rebellion, but also because he'd been her neighbor for a very long time.

"Goliath!" she gasped.

Then Lore did the only thing she could think to do.

She wrapped him up in her arms and hugged him so tight she heard his ribs crack.

"Stop," he moaned in her ear. "Why are you trying to kill me? I didn't do nothing!"

"I'm not trying to kill you, you dolt. I'm hugging you because I missed you." She sank down onto her knees so she was eye level with him, then grabbed him by the shoulders to get a good look. "Are you all right? I know things must have gotten crazy here when everyone heard the King was dead."

"Yeah, I'm fine." He touched a hand to his nose, then eyed the blood on his fingertips. "Or well, I was fine until you kneed me in the face. Is it broken?"

It was decidedly crooked, but if she remembered correctly, his nose had always been a little bent. Lorelei bit her lip and shook her head. "I think it's fine."

"You're lying."

"I'm definitely lying. I'd have someone look at that pretty quick if I were you." She released her hold on him so she didn't hug him again. "It's good to see you though, old friend."

"I wish I could say the same." Goliath touched his nose one more time, but then sighed. "At least I won't be any less handsome. I've heard the ladies like a dwarf who looks a little rough around the edges. Think that's true?"

She had no way of knowing, but Lorelei was glad Goliath still lived. She'd dreamt he hadn't made it after riots broke out in Tenebrous and the mere idea... No. She couldn't think of it again.

Standing, she took a few steps back and thudded hard into a

warm, broad chest.

Ah, right. She'd brought a dragon with her and Goliath likely had no idea who the hulking man was. At least the dwarf didn't pull a weapon on him.

"Lorelei," Abraxas said in her ear, the rumble sending shivers down her spine. "Who is this?"

"Goliath. A good friend of mine and one of the rebellion members," she responded. Hopefully that would be enough to cool the temperature of the room, which had risen since she'd noticed Abraxas.

Considering she had kneed a man in the face and then hugged him, she could only assume the dragon wasn't sure if he should kill Goliath or not.

"Ah." Abraxas didn't move or say anything else.

Goliath had paled as he looked up at the other man. His usually rosy cheeks were white as parchment paper, and that color sank even through the dark curls of his beard. He still wore vibrant colors. His yellow suit made her eyes burn. That should have been her very first clue that a thief wasn't trying to attack her. He hadn't been quiet about any part of his entrance.

"Lore, who's this?" Goliath asked. His beard trembled. "He looks like a big man."

"He is a big man, but he's... uh." She glanced over her shoulder, wondering how much she should reveal about who Abraxas was. In her experience, the dragon was a very secretive man and he wouldn't take kindly to her revealing everything about him.

He was a dragon, but that wasn't knowledge everyone needed to know. And he didn't like telling people that he worked for the King.

Abraxas stepped out from behind her, leaving a gust of cold air in his wake. He walked up to her dwarven friend and bent at the waist with a grin. "My name is Abraxas. You've likely seen me flying at night over your city, a reminder of who takes the King's orders and who is… no longer necessary. We'll call it that in honor of those who have lost their lives to my fire."

Oh, so Goliath could turn even paler. "You're the King's dragon?"

"I'm no one's dragon," Abraxas replied with a snarl. "But you may have known me as that once, yes."

This was getting out of hand. Lore leapt between the two of them and planted her hands on Abraxas's chest. "Right, well. Lovely introduction. I think maybe you should take those magical objects and put them outside for the night? They're elf made, so I assume the moonlight will charge them up and we'll be ready to use them in a jiffy. Sound good?"

Abraxas glowered at her.

She gave him a little shove back toward the bed. "Just do this for me, will you? Obviously, no one has filled Goliath in on what's happening and you're going to make him have a heart attack."

"I don't see how that would be bad."

"Abraxas," she snarled, hopefully as intimidating as him.

He stepped up to her, nose to nose, glaring into her very soul. She could see the fire burning in his eyes. He wanted to tear something apart because he'd seen her fight, and that meant his hands were already turning into claws and his teeth had sharpened into hard points. But if he were there for her when she grew anxious, then she would be there for him when he needed to get his powers under control. With a snarl that sounded a little too animal-like, he backed away, gathered up her things, and slipped out the window to bring them outside.

The breath in her lungs all whooshed out at once. She'd never had to make a dragon stand down, and frankly, she was surprised it had worked.

Goliath watched her with a shocked expression.

"What?" she asked, although she already knew what he was going to say.

"You're the one handling the King's dragon now?"

Oh, that terminology brought a lot of thoughts to mind. She wouldn't mind handling him if he'd let her, but that was the wrong thing to even think. She shouldn't. Couldn't.

Yet...

No. She had to get her mind off of that pathway or she wouldn't ever surface again.

Lore shrugged. "I'll tell you the story once he comes back inside. It might do him some good to hear another person repeat it."

"Lore, it's just..." Goliath rubbed the back of his neck, color returning to his cheeks. "Just be careful, would you? Dragons collect things. They build a hoard and they protect it with everything they have. But sometimes that can become possessive."

"All right." She had no idea where he was going with this.

Goliath listened for Abraxas, who must have finished setting everything outside. "Don't become part of his hoard, or heaven's forbid, all of it. I don't think you understand just how far a dragon will go to protect what it views as treasure."

Abraxas slipped back in through the window, and she eyed him with a renewed interest.

Was she part of his hoard already? And if she was, did that bother her?

CHAPTER 10

Abraxas couldn't sleep, so he poked around the attic while Lore slept. She didn't even move when he stood up, nor when his footsteps rang a little too loudly. Though she thought herself to be a huntress in every way, she lacked the ability to hear in her slumber. Or at least, she did while he was nearby.

He liked to think that was because she was so comfortable with him. That his mere presence let her sleep deeply when she never got the chance to do so.

It was a fanciful thought, considering he knew that wasn't the case. She slept because she was home, and he couldn't rest because... well...

He'd never been free. Not for a very long time, and all this space threatened to swallow him whole. One moment he'd been the slave to a King, knowing where he stood and what he should do, and without that structure he drowned in possibilities.

Now that he'd been forced into this tiny attic room, so different from anything he'd ever experienced, Abraxas realized he had thrown himself into yet another slavery. He'd trailed along behind Margaret, then Lore, hoping one of them would tell him what to do. He needed orders. Structure. A heavy hand to tell him where to go, who to kill, who to protect.

That wasn't just because of his history, he knew that. Crimson dragons always searched for a mate or a queen to serve. Their personalities required for someone else to guide them. But he feared that he'd chosen wrong.

Not Lore. He trusted her. He knew that her intentions were pure, and that she wanted the best for all, even the humans. But Margaret? He didn't trust that elf. Not in the slightest.

A miniature jar rested on one of the many stacks in the attic. He smoothed his thumb over the dust covered glass, revealing a small skull inside it. Obviously, a child had made it. Placing the macabre treasure deep within the jar, but having dropped it at the last second and cracking it. The tiny fangs suggested it might have once been a lizard, and he just couldn't stop staring at it.

A lizard. Like him.

Perhaps the child had found the dead creature and wanted to preserve it. Or perhaps this had once been the home of a warlock who used the carcasses as a conduit for spells. He didn't know. But he felt some connection to the poor critter locked inside the glass.

Abraxas didn't know how long he stood in front of the morbid art piece in the middle of the attic. He just knew that the next time he blinked, daylight spilled through the single window and his thumb was still on the dusty jar.

He blinked again, pulling himself out of the fog in his mind and the horrible realization that he had no idea where time had gone. He turned in time to see Lore stir.

The sunlight cast rays upon her form. She was still dirty, her pale shirt still clung to her skin from the hard days of labor they'd had to get here. But she was beautiful. Arching her back into the sunlight and stretching her arms over her head as though she weren't so sore, she could barely move.

It had been a long hike. And he could only imagine it would get harder the longer they were away from the castle.

He let his touch slip away from the jar and made his way to her side. Kneeling beside the bed, he gently started untangling the wild knots of hair surrounding her head like a puff of dandelion. "Good morning," he murmured.

"Good morning." She caught a yawn with her hand. "This is rather domestic of us. I thought you'd still be sleeping and I might have time to slip out to get the best breakfast sandwiches in the kingdom to surprise you with."

"Ah, and what are they?"

"Probably made with rat," Lore chuckled. "But they aren't half bad."

Right, well, he would not be eating those. But if she wanted him to run out and buy one for her, then he supposed he'd do it.

Maybe a little later. He'd rather stay here and untangle her hair. The strands slipped through his fingers, soft as silk even though they both desperately needed a bath.

This moment felt like they'd done it a thousand times. It was so easy to be domestic with her, as she liked to call it. He didn't mind waking up with her at the crack of dawn, with splashes of sunlight playing across her face. He wanted to spend countless mornings with her. Especially when her expression finally relaxed and he could see how truly beautiful she was. At ease. Comfortable.

"I told Goliath we'd meet him in the marketplace," she whispered, her eyes searching his. "He said he might know someone who could point us in the direction of the King's half brother, although it's a long shot. It's always a long shot in these parts."

"Do you want to wait until we see Beauty again?"

"I think she'll have her hands full with her father and we might as well get going on our own." Tension wrinkled her face. It started in the corners of her eyes, drawing the edges in. Then it moved over her brows that furrowed in concentration, all the way to her chin that she drew up slightly. All that tension never left her unless it was first thing in the morning and she was lying on a moth eaten cot.

Strange woman.

"We don't have to go just yet," he said. "We could stay here for another hour or so. You could move over a bit and let me get comfortable, then you could tell me stories from the time you lived here. I'm sure you have more than a few that would take up the better part of an hour."

She chuckled. "Oh, I could tell you about the time a bird flew in here and Goliath and I spent hours trying to get it out. He refused to kill the poor thing, and I wouldn't have let him, anyway. So we had plans to tame it just so that we could set it free again."

He could see how she'd do that. She had a way about her that made many creatures want to fall under her spell. He should know. She had eased the dragon's needs and desires. Instead of burning, he had wanted to hold her.

"That sounds like a hilarious story, and I would love to hear it."

One last knot remained, although it was the largest at the base of her skull. He'd spend an hour working at it until he could massage the back of her neck. If he was lucky, maybe he'd see that relaxed expression one more time.

Except he wouldn't get that chance.

She shook her head, groaning a little, and then sitting up. Out of his reach, yet again. "No, we can't do that. We have to get going or Goliath will leave and we'll lose our chance to talk with him."

"Why can't he come here like he did last night?"

"Goliath is a bit of an enigma, and most people are unfortunately looking for him in the city. If it wasn't the Umbral Knights, then it was a gang he owed money to." She shrugged. "He's not the best person to hang around if you want to keep all your fingers and toes, but he knows more people than anyone else."

"What company you keep," he muttered. Right now, he wanted to throw the dwarf over a bridge just for a few more moments with her.

But he knew that expression on her face. No matter how much he argued, he would not slow her down. Lore wanted to leave this attic. And that was exactly what they were going to do.

He stood with her and waited until she gathered the rest of her things. She'd already stuffed her bag full, but there were amulets and potions outside that they'd need to bring with them. As much as he hated even saying the words, he sighed and pointed to a leather bag in the corner.

"Grab that," he grumbled.

"Why?"

"Because you aren't going to fit all the things we need in that tiny bag you brought. I might as well carry some of the heavier items." He hated that he'd stooped so low. Dragons didn't lug around bags of materials. They had a hoard, and that was where everything went. If he needed to gather something, it wouldn't take him very long to fly back to his hoard and gather supplies.

For her, he would allow this small moment of losing his mind. And credibility.

"Are you sure?" Lore asked, with one brow lifted. "I thought you said dragons didn't need to carry anything."

"I don't." He held out his hand and waggled his fingers. "You need to carry many things, however, and I don't like the idea of you wandering around with explosive potions on your back. I would survive such a blast. You, I think, would not be so lucky. Let me have them, Lore."

Though she had a strange expression on her face, she handed it over to him without complaint. Abraxas had to get out of this small space where they were too close together. He'd do something foolish. Like try to kiss her again when he knew she didn't need that right now. At least not yet.

He clambered out the window and filled the bag with all her stolen magical objects. And he didn't question that they were stolen. The bottles had someone else's name written on them when he'd wiped away the dust.

"Ready?" she called out as she yanked herself through the window.

"Sure. Are we traveling on rooftops again?" He glanced over his shoulder at her while he pulled the pack on.

"Goliath hates heights. We will unfortunately walk on the streets today." She made a face. "Come on, I know the fastest way."

She took off across the mix of tiles and shingles, light and delicate where he was heavy and clunky. Abraxas hadn't thought it would be possible for her to impress him more than she already had, and yet, here she was. Sprinting across the roofs of Tenebrous like she'd been born to run across them.

He feared a collapse every time he stepped.

The gray mist trailed along his arms, leaving behind a wet slime that made his skin crawl. He'd never once realized how horrible it was to live in Tenebrous, and he'd flown over the city for years now. Up in the sky, it was easier to think that this was simply another crumbling town full of people the rest of the kingdom didn't want to see.

Finally, she paused and dropped into a low crouch on the edge of a roof. His heart jumped in fear that the molding would give way and send her tumbling onto the streets below, but it held.

"Here we are," she said. "How are you with heights?"

He refused to respond to that. Abraxas waited until she looked at him before he slowly arched a brow.

"What?" she asked.

"Ask that question again."

"How are you with heights?" Her face blushing bright red. "Oh, right. Dragon."

"I have spent my entire life much higher than this. I don't think a building will be all that different," he grumbled. It was insulting to think he would fear heights.

She flashed him a radiant grin, then turned so her back was to the street. "Good. Follow my lead, and you'll be just fine."

Lore took a step into thin air and then plummeted to the ground below. Damn woman! He rushed to the edge, trying his best to catch her arm only to see that she'd fallen into a very thick canopy of what he assumed was part of the market.

She laid on her back, looking up at him with her limbs loose and akimbo. The grin on her face, however, was one of utter happiness. He didn't know that he'd ever seen her look like that before, and he intended to remember this moment forever.

"Did you think I would just leap into thin air?" she called out. Apparently, she didn't care at all that people had seen her or that the busy street below was full of bystanders. "Come on! You said you weren't afraid of heights!"

He wasn't. That didn't mean he wanted to throw himself onto a very fragile sheet. But it had held her so...

What a life he would lead if he lived it like her. Without fear. On a whim.

So he turned around and let gravity take him to her. Although, he was careful that he didn't land on top of the poor elf, or he'd crush her. He hit the fabric with a harsh smack, laughter bubbling in his chest before the worst happened. He heard the snap and creak of the tent poles holding it upright before he felt them both fall yet again. Although it was only six feet this time.

They struck the ground hard, both wheezing air into their lungs that was filled with dust and who knew what else from the crates they'd smashed below them. He turned over, arms reaching for her through the rubble.

"Are you all right?" he asked, frantically running his fingers over her sides. "You didn't break anything, did you?"

Lore grabbed onto his hands with a laugh, holding his fists tight to her heart as she shook with mirth. "I'm fine, Abraxas, I'm fine!"

Still panting, he stared down at her and felt heat bloom throughout his body. She had shards of wood in her hair and dust covering her cheeks, but her eyes twinkled with starlight and laughter. He couldn't breathe, and not because of the fall, but because of how much he wanted to kiss her.

Her bubbling giggles died down as she stared back at him. "Abraxas?" she asked.

He didn't know what question she wanted to ask. All he knew was that his gaze refused to move from her lips. And then she tilted her head just so, as though preparing herself for a kiss.

Oh, what he would give to do that. Right now. And why not? She obviously wanted him to kiss her, and he was dying to do so. Abraxas scooped his hand under her neck, tilting her even further and the breathless way her lungs caught only spurred him on more.

"Hey! That's my shop!"

The two of them stiffened before she shoved his chest and muttered, "Up. Run. Now. Quickly!"

They both scrambled to their feet and Lore took off in the opposite direction. He sprinted after her as laughter trailed along behind her like the long tails of a dress. He would have followed that sound to the very end of the earth.

The crowd parted before them. No one wanted to get in the way of a chase like this. The angry shopkeeper ran after them, cursing the entire way. Lore was quick, though. And Abraxas kept up with her well enough. They raced through the streets, skidding around corners and grabbing onto pipes so they could throw themselves ahead even further. Finally, Lore turned one last corner and stopped running.

She grabbed onto his arm, pressing his back against the wall and holding her hand over his mouth. "Quiet," she whispered, still giggling.

"Let him run by."

And he did. The shopkeeper angrily blustered past, his bright red hair glowing in the distance as he ran the wrong way. The moment he was out of sight, Abraxas pressed a kiss to the center of her palm, then flicked her skin with his tongue.

Lore dropped her hand, but not without her eyes widening with a secret message for him.

They burst into laughter again, relief flooding through his chest as they sagged against the wall. "That was more adventurous than I thought it would be," he chuckled.

"You and me both," she said, her eyes crinkled at the edges with mirth.

This was nice. Perhaps he had found someone who he could follow with complete trust and she wouldn't lead him wrong.

But then her joyous expression fell as she looked at where they were. Her brows furrowed and a darkness spread over her face until her shoulders curved in on themselves.

"What?" he asked, looking for yet another threat. But all he saw was a town square. People milling around. No one even stared at them. "What is it? What's wrong?"

"You don't remember where we are?" she breathed.

"No." His stomach twisted in fear.

"This is where she died," Lore muttered, shoving herself off the wall and tucking her hands into her pockets. "I was on the other side of the square when it happened. I saw all the fire and ash, that nothing of her had remained, no matter how much I screamed. They wouldn't even let me touch her ashes. The Umbral Knights threw me out onto the next street and refused to let me go to her. I never knew why."

He did, but he wouldn't tell her that the Knights were told to play with the victims of the families. He wouldn't let her know that the King enjoyed knowing more than just the burned had suffered.

Instead, he wrapped an arm around her shoulder and tucked her against his chest. "I'm sorry, Lore. I'm so sorry for everything that I did and have done. I cannot tell you that enough."

"I know," she pressed the words against his heart, whispering them against his shirt. "I know you are."

But she didn't linger in his arms. Instead, she shoved him back and wiped her eyes on her sleeve. "We have to find Goliath. Come on."

He watched her leave for a moment, empty hands hanging by his sides. Then sighed and trailed after her through the crowd.

CHAPTER 11

She shouldn't be so upset. Abraxas was right. Killing her mother had been an order, and they'd gone over this time and time again. He'd apologized. He'd worked so hard to ease her mind and allow her to understand what had really happened.

She just couldn't let it go. The thoughts were stuck in her head like an arrow in her side, and every time she started to let them go; they dug in deeper.

Sighing, she strode through the crowd without worrying if Abraxas kept up. She could feel him, no matter where he was. He put off so much heat it was like a wave that followed after her, followed by the burning sensation of his eyes in the center of her back.

Goliath hadn't told her where to meet him, but she knew where to go. The same ol' tavern that had started all of this. She paused in front of the door, staring at the worn wood with the worst déjà vu she'd ever had.

"Right," she muttered. "Why is it constantly this place?"

"What do you mean by that?" the dragon asked behind her.

"It always starts here," she replied. "Every adventure that changes my life forever." Lore didn't have it in her to explain anything else, though.

She put her hand against the door and shoved it open, expecting to be blasted in the face with noise and chatter from all the people who ended up here. The mead was good, the beer was better, and the bartender didn't mind when unsavory sorts shuffled into the back. It was the perfect place for the magical people of Tenebrous.

But there were only a couple stragglers in the tavern and everything she remembered had changed in such a short amount of time. The posters on the walls had all been ripped off. White shreds of paper and glue remained where there should be drawings of magical creatures and lovely women on bottles of absinthe. The merry golden light of candles and the fireplace were replaced with gloomy shadows and dark corners. Only three people were visible in the tavern, and they all hunched over their mugs with a protective glare, as though she were going to take the alcohol from them.

"What happened here?" she murmured. Lore took another step into the large room, then flinched as the door slammed shut behind her.

Even Abraxas lifted a brow and looked at the offending door, as if someone might stand there ready to attack them. Apparently not.

Goliath's voice cut through the quiet. "It just does that now. You can come in, Lore. No one plans to hurt you here."

"Again, what happened?" She sought him out in the darkness. He stood far in the back, near where she'd met with Margaret all those months ago. He didn't have a drink in his hand. However, it might have been difficult to tell, considering his dark clothing blended into the gray floor and the dusty walls.

"The Umbral Knights found out that a lot of magical creatures came here." He shrugged. "It was only a week or two after you left, so that might have had something to do with it, I suppose. They raided the entire place."

Oh, that poor bartender. All he'd ever wanted was to create a space for people like her where they could breathe. Where they could feel safe and just enjoy being alive.

"Right," she muttered. "Then why is it still like this?"

"The owner ended up in one of the King's many dungeons. Margaret hasn't found out where he is yet." Goliath's gaze slanted to the side and she knew the words he had left unsaid.

Margaret hadn't even looked at getting people out of the prisons. She was so deep into her own work, her own opinion of what was important, that she likely hadn't thought of the bartender. Or anyone else that didn't provide any immediate use for her.

Lore bit her lip and refused to say more on the matter. If she could get the man out later, she would. But right now, she wasn't even at the castle. There was nothing else she could do.

And she hated that. Oh, how she hated it.

"Have a seat, Lore," Goliath said, trying his best to twist his face up into a smile. "You said you wanted to get information, right?"

She looked up at Abraxas and saw that his gaze remained on the other people in the bar. One by one, he glared at them until they stood up and left. The last one hunched stalwart in his seat, clutching his hands around his mug and glaring right back.

As she watched, Abraxas's eyes glowed bright gold, the power inside them revealing the fire that burned in his very soul.

The man stood up and left.

"Was that necessary?" she asked, sitting down at the table and crossing her arms over her chest.

"What we're about to talk about cannot be overheard by any ears other than ours." He turned that glare on her, and she felt a shiver travel down her spine. He was right, of course, but he didn't have to be quite so aggressive.

"Fine."

"Do what you did in your room."

The order startled her. Since when had he become so... so... surly?

"Do you want to ask me to do that, or are you going to tell me what to do?" She tilted her head to the side, daring him to say the words again. Lore was not some lackey that he could order around like that. He needed a partner, and she was the one who had gotten him into this! How dare he?

A muscle in his jaw jumped while he audibly ground his teeth. Finally, he grunted, "Will you please ensure no one can hear us in this room where we could be cornered and killed?"

She forced her mouth into a pleasant smile. "Was that so hard?"

"Yes," he growled in response.

"You'll get used to it."

Lore stood back up, though. She lifted her hands and took a deep breath. Moon magic fluttered off her skin like she'd let out a butterfly that burst forth. Even behind her closed eyes, she could see the bright lights of her glittering power. It took only a few heartbeats to create a bubble around them. She didn't need the whole room this time.

When she opened her eyes, the magic had encased them in an orb that looked eerily like ice. Rainbows reflected off the surface where the faint light caught on the edges.

She arched a brow at Abraxas. "Good enough?"

The expression on his face was dangerously close to pride. She couldn't have him feeling like that about her. Not when it was so... nice. It felt good to know that someone was proud of what she could do, other than embarrassed or fearful that she'd shown her true colors.

Goliath, on the other hand, had turned green. "You're doing magic out in the open now?" he asked.

"Yes. The King has fallen. The Umbral Knights have left with him, and that means we're free to be who we are." She hoped, at least. That was the plan.

Lore had only gone along with this mad journey because she wanted to see her own people exist without fear. She wanted to see them all using magic out in the streets. Her dream of seeing all magical creatures walking amongst mortals without fear was so close now that she might touch it if she but took another step forward.

"The King might be gone," Goliath replied, licking his lips and choosing his words carefully. "But that doesn't mean the humans accept us."

Of course. The wind fled from her sails in one giant sigh that sat her back in her chair with a firm thud. "What do you mean?"

"We tried to rejoice when the news came here. The King is dead. We all rushed out of our homes and cheered at the top of our lungs. But then the humans descended and so many of us were beaten and left in the streets to die." He lifted his beard to reveal a new pink scar across his neck. "A healer got to me early on. I was lucky. Others were not."

Her heart shredded at the words. Why hadn't she thought the

humans would be part of the problem?

Lore had always assumed that things would change the moment they removed the figurehead from the game. The King had always encouraged the other mortals to ruthless measures. He had spread the rumors that her kind were dangerous and should be feared. His voice was the one in their heads.

But she hadn't thought the humans would continue that fear simply because they'd been told to feel it. For their entire lives.

"We're all fools," she groaned, running a hand over her face. "Why didn't we think about the mortals? Of course, they would still be afraid of us. That's all they know."

"Margaret knew." Goliath corrected, his frown growing ever deeper. "She can lie to you and the others all she wants, but I know that woman. She knew what would happen here in Tenebrous when the news reached us, and she still told the others to rejoice. To enjoy their new found freedom once they heard that we had succeeded. She caused a lot of deaths that way."

"Why?" Lore couldn't stop herself from asking. "Margaret wanted to free us. She's just like us as well. She shares the freedom that we gained. There's no reason to risk everyone's lives."

"I don't know." He braced his elbows on the table and held his head in his hands. "But I intend to find out. That's part of the reason I brought you here today, Lore. I want to know what your plan is and if you're under her thumb."

Was she?

Lore hadn't spoken up when Margaret had verbally attacked Abraxas. She had gone along with all of Margaret's plans and hadn't complained the entire time. She'd been a good follower who had done what she'd been told to do.

"I don't know who I am anymore," she replied, her voice a little higher than a whisper. "I did what I had to do to kill the King. But I didn't... I didn't manage it."

Abraxas shifted forward, his hand outstretched as though to silence her.

"No," she said. "I'm going to tell him, and I'm not letting you stop me. He deserves to know. I trust him, Abraxas. We have to trust someone other than her."

The dragon opened his mouth, closed it, and then gave her a sharp nod. He crossed his arms over his chest and instead glared at the dwarf as though his mere look would warn the man. Maybe he succeeded. Goliath turned white as a bone the moment that gaze turned upon him.

With a gulp, Goliath looked at her and asked, "What are you about to tell me, and is it going to get me killed?"

"I don't think so." She paused, then winced. "I don't know. So much seems to have changed in just a few months. I can't promise no one will kill you for knowing, but you deserve to know it all. The whole truth."

He sighed and flexed his hands on the table. "I really wish I had a drink for this."

"Me too." Lore opened her mouth and let the entire story spill out. Every bit of it. All the details, good and bad, all the things that she knew he might judge her for. None of it mattered. She wanted him to know everything that had happened so he could make his own decisions and know what to expect. Or perhaps he might get up and leave when she finished her tale. Either way, he needed to know.

She took a deep breath once she was done, filling her lungs with air for the first time in the better part of an hour. Her throat stung with the words, raw from speaking for such a long time. But it was out now. Purged from her body like poison she'd had to vomit up.

"Well," Goliath said, his hands flexing one more time. "That's quite the tale."

"I wish it were just a story, and that you didn't have to believe me." She really did. The words were as true as they could get. "I hate knowing that all of this happened. And that... well. I don't know if we changed anything. Not really."

"You changed something. I can tell you that much." Though he didn't look like he believed the words. "Let me just get this straight. That dragon sitting there glaring at me like he's never tasted dwarf needs those eggs to keep the dragon kind alive?"

"Correct."

"We've all been lied to that he's the last dragon?"

Abraxas stirred. He lifted a single hand with a raised finger and said, "I am the last dragon. Those eggs can only be hatched by a dragon, but as of right now, they are not alive. Technically. And if I don't do it, then none will ever wake."

"That's a hard one to swallow, ain't it?" Goliath shook his head. "Dragons. Back in Umbra."

"I can't promise it'll work, but there will at least be three of us then." Abraxas shrugged. "With other dragons, I might find more eggs. They should be able to sense the unborn of their own kind, where I can only find broods with crimson dragons like myself. It's hope, Goliath. The first hope any of us have had in a very long time."

"Oh, I feel it." Goliath cleared his throat. "I hate that I feel it. I'd given up on that emotion a long time ago, but damn. That would change everything. And you think this half brother might be able to get rid of the curse on the eggs?"

"It's a start," she replied. "We don't know anything for certain, but we have hope."

"Dangerous emotion."

"Everything is dangerous, Goliath." She leaned forward over the table, holding out her hands for him to take. "Live wildly with me."

His hands shook, but he reached across wood and took her hands in his. "For you, my darling half elf, I would do anything. Even take part in this mad plan where you seem to think you can hunt down the half brother of a king. You know the young man is nothing more than a rumor, don't you?"

"Rumors always come from somewhere. I need to know what the truth is, and if he can help us." She squeezed Goliath's fingers. "What do you think? How marvelous would this adventure be if it works out? A way to find the truth."

"You walk back into my life after not killing the King, and then you expect me to help you chase a ghost through all of Umbra. That might, maybe, give us hope for a future?" His eyes widened with every word.

"A hope of a future where we don't have to hide anymore."

He groaned and ripped his hands away from hers. "You always get me in the worst trouble. It's in your nature as an elf, isn't it?"

She felt more than saw Abraxas tense. Lore suspected he would get involved if he thought Goliath was insulting her, but she needed him to stay still. They were so close, and she knew she already had Goliath on their side.

Underneath the table, she shifted her hand and gripped Abraxas's thigh with her hand. Shockingly, the muscles tensed at her touch. He was warm and broad and she sent a prayer to her ancestors because his thigh was massive.

At least he stopped moving.

Goliath sighed, unaware of the tension that sparked between the other two people at the table. "Damn it. I want to see where this goes. You'll need Madame Blanchet on your side, though. She's the only one who might know where that boy ended up."

"Ah." Lore ripped her hand away from that tempting, muscular thigh and smacked her forehead. "Why didn't I think of Madame Blanchet?"

"Because she wouldn't talk to you, anyway. She only talks to handsome young men." He pointedly stared at Abraxas.

The dragon gulped, looking between the two of them with a hesitant expression. "Why are you looking at me like that?"

Goliath had a point. Abraxas was a stately specimen, and it was no secret that Madame Blanchet had her own... preferences. At least with men. She was more likely to talk to the pretty ones than she was to anyone else.

Time was running out, after all.

"She won't talk to him like that," she muttered. "He could use a bath."

"Why do you think I brought you to this part of town?" Goliath grinned. "The baths are open. The market is full of clothing items to steal. We could make her a dream man entering her self made underground realm. Then we just have to trap her."

It was as solid a plan as they were going to get. Lore nodded sharply. "You leave the trapping to me."

Abraxas rolled his eyes up to the ceiling. "What are you two getting me into?"

CHAPTER 12

Lore held up a brightly colored red tunic and tried very hard not to laugh at the expression on Abraxas's face. After all, the last thing he wanted was to wear clothing that was quite so...

"Garish," he said.

"Listen, she won't tell us anything if you don't catch her eye. I know this all seems like a lot, but trust me when I say this is her style." Lore put it away though and tapped her lip while she looked for the perfect outfit for him.

Madame Blanchet was an old creature in these parts. Technically speaking, she was a hag. But she hated that word almost as much as she hated ugly things.

She was mostly known for her beauty and charm, although Lore had only heard men talk about her. Maybe that was why there were only pleasant stories about the hag.

"Who is this woman again?" Abraxas asked as he perused the stall they were in.

"She's the eyes and ears of Tenebrous. She knows everyone and everything that happens here, and if you want information, you go to her." Well, men did. Lore still wasn't all that confident that Madame Blanchet would know anything about a forgotten child.

The King's sibling being younger upped their chances of the Madame knowing where he was, though.

"So the plan is to use me as bait, and then try your very best to see if you can trap her while I..." He paused in the middle of the stall, opening and closing his mouth. "Lorelei, you know me well enough by now to realize I cannot seduce a woman."

"I was told to seduce a lot of people for our cause, and now it's your turn to do some seducing as well." She picked up an emerald green tunic that barely had any fabric in the middle. "What about this one?"

He had stopped talking, however. She waited to see if he'd respond, but when he didn't, all she could do was ask, "What?"

"Were you told to seduce me?"

Shit.

She should have told him about that sooner than this. Or maybe she had thought it would never come up. Either way, the last thing she wanted to do was talk about that painful truth while dressing him for another woman. Lore didn't know if she'd survive.

"I... Um..." She closed her eyes and sighed. "If you asked Margaret, the answer would be yes. She asked me to seduce you to get closer to the King and to bring you to our side."

Without opening her eyes, she heard him take another step toward her. The waves of heat coming off his body blasted hers, searing her to the very bone.

"And if I asked you?" His deep voice sent a shiver down her spine.

"Then I would say I'd already felt a connection to you, and being asked to seduce you by Margaret didn't change my plans in the slightest." She finally opened her eyes to meet his gaze. "I never intended to use you, Abraxas. I just wanted you."

"Selfish," he muttered, though he lifted his hand and traced a line down her jaw to her mouth. "You should have told me."

"I know."

"But I will forgive you." He ran his fingertip along the outline of her lip and her cheeks burned. "If I don't have to wear that god awful tunic in your hand."

Was she still holding it? Lore wasn't all that sure she could feel her hands.

She let the fabric slip between her fingers and heard it hit the ground. "You don't have to if you don't want to. I just think you should try your best to catch her eye."

All she could focus on were the flat planes of his chest and the white hot fires burning in his eyes.

His voice rumbled. "Then let me do this the dragon way, Lore. If you want me to catch her eye, I can promise you, I will."

Oh, he turned her into a moth. She fluttered at the flame he'd set for her and soon she would burn her wings on it. But maybe, if she was lucky, she'd still be able to fly.

Lore shook herself. Those kinds of thoughts were stupid. She had no right to even think them. They weren't even sure what they were, or if they would ever become something. They had so much to do before she could think of him and him alone.

And she promised herself here and now, when all this was said and done, he would be the only thing she thought about.

Lorelei took a step away from him and gestured. "All this could be yours. What would you like?"

"Considering what you were choosing, you believe this Madame Blanchet likes men to be wearing very little when they want her attention. Is that right?" he said.

None of the passion in his gaze had died down, and that made her nervous. He was looking at her like a dragon ready to feast, and she was the only thing on the table.

Gulping, she nodded. "That's right. The few times I've seen her favorites, they were always in outfits that revealed... Well. Everything."

He pointed to an article of clothing next to her. "Then buy that. It's more traditional to my people."

The item he'd indicated was surprisingly a floor length black skirt. Though, when she picked it up, she realized it parted on either side and would reveal his legs as he moved. Gold threading ringed the edges of the black silk.

"Pretty," she said, lifting it up and holding it to his waist. "What else?"

"Nothing else."

Lore's mouth went dry. "Excuse me?" she asked, staring up into his bemused expression. "Won't you get cold?"

"I'm a dragon, Lore. I rarely get cold." He took the silk from her hands, although his fingertips lingered on hers for a few moments too long. "Besides, I'll still need you for a little something extra. Dragons always loved it when elves helped them with this."

"With what?"

He winked. "You'll see. Let me get changed first."

She blew a breath out of her mouth as he strode toward the back of the tent. This was going to take every bit of her strength to not climb him like a tree, and that was so damned confusing.

Being around him made her feel like she wasn't herself. Or maybe she was more herself than she was without. Either way, all she knew was that in the castle, she had wanted to create space between them. Now, out in the open, all this distance felt like a chasm she couldn't crawl out of. She wanted him. More than she'd ever wanted anyone.

She shook her hands out at her sides, jumping up and down a bit to get back into her own body. This wasn't her. She didn't pine after any man and she didn't make herself feel sick over one.

She was fine.

Everything was fine.

They would go to Madame Blanchet's. He'd get the woman's attention because what woman wouldn't fall head over heels for a nearly seven foot tall man with a broad chest and eyes that looked like they were constantly on fire? Sure, he didn't have the prettiest face in the world, but that body...

"Lore?"

She turned to look at him and forgot how to breathe again. He wore nothing but that stupid, ridiculously good looking skirt that hung low on his hips. She'd seen him naked before, although that was hardly in a circumstance like this. Now she could see all those muscles and lean lines that drew her eyes back to the damned waistband of that skirt one more time. The gold complimented his warm skin tone. He looked a bit like the dragons of old in the stories. The ones that seduced women from their husbands rather than stole them away.

"Lore," he said again, the word filled with mirth. "Are you ready to help with the second part, or do you need a minute?"

She needed more than a minute. Looking at him like this, seeing the bulge of his biceps and the way his collar bone dipped low on his shoulders... She'd need a lot more than a minute.

Clearing her throat, she tried to shake herself out of it. "Right. What do you need?"

Damn it, he was smiling again. Like he knew what she was thinking, and he enjoyed torturing her. "The old legends claim elves can leave marks on those they wish. Temporary ones, of course, but ones that look like metal on the skin."

It took her a second to remember what he meant, and then it startled her so much that she let out a ridiculously loud gasp. "A soulmark? No. Definitely not. I can't do that to you."

"I think that would be the most eye-catching part of the entire outfit. Cover my chest and arms in them." He gestured, muscles flexing as he pointed all over himself. "It's the only way we can be sure she won't take her eyes off me. After all, we both know I'm already at a disadvantage."

Because of his face? That made her chest ache to hear.

But worse, he asked for her to put her mark on him. A soulmark was more than symbols or signatures. They were everything to an elf, and not to be used on a whim. Yet, she supposed, it was rather important that this all fall into place the way they needed it to.

Sighing, she shrugged and resolved to let it go. "All right, I suppose I can."

He frowned and took a step closer. "I'm sorry, I didn't know they were... special. We can do something else if you shouldn't use the marks. I don't want to make you—"

Lore put a hand over his mouth and smiled. "It's okay. I wouldn't do it if I couldn't. Or... shouldn't."

She lied. Any other elf who knew what she was doing right now would box her ears for it. They'd tell her that a soulmark was only for the person who was the other half of their soul. The one who had earned the marks through time and effort.

The age of the elves had ended long ago. Changing the use of the soulmark was the first step toward a new life. And if it got them where they needed to go, then that was what needed to happen.

She warmed her hands up, rubbing them together vigorously before nodding. "Come a little closer. I need to touch you."

He could have made so many jokes, but instead, he got that dark look in his eyes and took another step. So close, all she had to do was lift her hands between them.

His chest was warm, but then, he was always warm. She spread her fingers wide over his heartbeat and stilled her mind. She reached deep inside herself, beyond the well of magic like starlight inside her. Deep into the power that gave her life. Breath. She soaked in it for a few moments before drawing it to the surface of her skin.

When she opened her eyes, the magic glowed at the very tips of her fingers. Gold, like the sun. The light soaked through her nails and to the first knuckle. Unusual coloring for a Silverfell elf, but the soulmark was always the same no matter what elf summoned it.

Lore whispered as she traced patterns on his skin. "The old elves would only do this for their most beloved. They sketched light and magic into their skin, words that were meant for protection and runes to heal their soul should life become too difficult. This was a sacred ritual once."

"Who's to say it's no longer sacred?" He watched her fingers as they moved over his shoulders and chest.

"I'm defiling it by using it to seduce another woman," she muttered, adding a dot at the top of a rune. "My mother must be rolling in her grave at the thought."

He let her work for a few heartbeats before mumbling, "That's the first time you've mentioned her without bringing up her death."

"I suppose it is." Her mother had been the one to teach her how to do this, though. Every elf parent made sure their child knew the responsibility that came with these marks. They were runes like any other, but to trace them on the skin of a beloved? There was no greater honor.

Unlike this situation.

She finished up and all the light faded from her fingertips. She'd covered him with stunning metallic runes and small geometric patterns. He was a walking work of art now, and if anyone knew how to read the ancient elven language, they would also know that he was hers.

Abraxas caught her fingers as she let them fall from his side and pressed them against his heart once more. "You are not defiling her memory or your people. You have no idea how I feel, Lorelei of Silverfell. And I have no intent on revealing the depth of my madness regarding you. But know this. You honor me with these marks, and I wear them with pride."

Her heart swelled in her chest until she couldn't breathe. He had to know those were the only words she'd wanted to hear, and that terrified her.

These marks meant something. More than just a passing infatuation, they were the end all be all of elven dedication. They were...

He squeezed her fingers again, looking deep into her eyes. "Lore."

"I heard you," she whispered, then gave him a slight nod. "I'm glad they aren't wasted on you."

"Never." He let her hand fall from his chest.

She wondered if he wanted to kiss her. He looked like he did. She was getting used to the expression he always wore when his thoughts turned heated. Heavy lids, pliant lips, and his cheeks turned a bright, ruddy red. Like his own notions embarrassed him, or perhaps startled him.

She felt the same way and didn't know how to tell him that. Not while they were on this quest to give themselves a chance. And their people a chance.

Swallowing hard, she pointed out at the street. "It's dark enough now for her to be awake in the underground. We have to go now."

Like a gust of wind, he approached her with single minded intent. Abraxas swept her up in his arms with a band of muscle around her waist. He tugged her up against him and kissed her until she forgot all the worries in her head. It was just him and his taste and the all consuming tangle of his tongue with hers.

When he finally drew back, he stared down at her with a faint snarl echoing in his throat. "I'll be thinking of you every step of the way. No woman could ever compare, Lorelei. Not a single one."

She stumbled as he released her to stride down the street as though he knew where they were going. Lore touched a finger to her puffy lips and let out a surprised little chuckle.

And he thought he didn't know how to seduce a woman.

CHAPTER 13

Abraxas touched a hand to his bare chest and tried to remind himself this was for Lorelei. He could walk into this underground playhouse of magical creatures, find the hag to bring him into a back room, and then they could all leave this behind them.

But his stomach twisted at the mere thought of touching another woman. He didn't know how far this would go or what the hag would ask him to do. But his very soul screamed that he would only make a few steps into the territory of seducing before he would vomit on the poor soul. He couldn't... the idea of...

He shook himself. They had no choice.

He needed to find this half brother to give himself the potential to find the eggs. To save his kind. That was how he had lived for such a long time, knowing that all the people he loved were dead. He could continue living like this if there was still a chance.

Lorelei paused in front of him, standing before the door to the hag's realm with a quizzical expression on her face. She wore an outfit that was much more demure than his. Though he had argued it would get her more attention than she wanted.

The leather corset tightened around her tiny waist, accentuating how small she could squeeze those ribs. Her black skirt touched the ground, but the slits up the sides revealed long, powerful legs. She'd pulled her hair back from her face, and the tightness of her ponytail made her eyes seem even more winged.

But the most stunning part, the things that captivated him most, were the points of her ears, which were now proudly on display for all to see. She'd wrapped metal around the pointed ends, and chains hung from the tips then weaved through her ears in loops that ended in tiny knives.

He wanted to touch those sharp tips. He wanted to let those weapons draw blood and then slowly suck away the crimson drops while she watched.

"Abraxas?" she asked, and her tone suggested it might be the second time she'd spoken.

He needed to pay attention, damn it. If he stared at her all night, then the hag would know he wasn't interested. His mooning would lose them all the chance to move forward in this mission.

"I'm listening," he replied.

"Now you are." Lorelei rolled her eyes, hand still on the door. "Remember, all you have to do is get her to take you somewhere private. I'm going to bribe one of the guards to let me into the forbidden section. They won't even know I snuck into her private quarters and then they'll be sent away the moment she wants free time with you. It's going to be fine."

Why did she add that last bit? Of course, it would be fine. If anyone put their hands on her, then he would burn the entire building to the ground. Even the impressive amount of rubble that would fall on them wouldn't harm his dragon form. She had to know he wouldn't let anything harm her.

"Lore—"He gently cupped her cheek in his hand. "You have nothing to worry about."

The shadows in her eyes flickered, and for a moment, he wondered if she was nervous for the same reasons he was. He had to pay attention to another woman. Another magical creature who was supposedly rather charming and considered beautiful by most men. She must feel many strange emotions.

Of course, they were still nothing to each other. Perhaps friends, though he'd like it to be a lot more than that. But he could, at the very least, say that they were people who had gone through so much together. Obviously, there was a closeness between them.

A closeness he refused to lose.

She tilted her cheek into the palm of his hand, just a little, but he knew that was her way of letting him know that she understood his hesitation. That she shared the same emotions that he did and they would work through them.

Words didn't come to mind that would ease her fears. A searing kiss wasn't a good idea because he feared he wouldn't stop there. Not when he already shook with the need to brand himself into her body.

Hand gripping her jaw, he drew her forward and pressed his lips to her forehead. His hand slid along the back of her neck and he brought her closer. So close that he could feel her breath fan across the base of his throat.

It was all he could offer. The most he could give without falling into pieces himself, but he hoped... Well, he could only hope it would be enough.

Abraxas released her and walked up to the door himself. "Come in after me. I don't want to take any chances, in case she thinks we were together. I'll find you afterwards, Lore."

"I know you will," she whispered. "Stay safe."

He glanced over his shoulder, surprised she'd say that to him. "I'm not the one to worry about, Lady of Starlight. Keep yourself safe, or I will tear this building into pieces smaller than dust."

He tried very hard not to notice the shudder that rippled through her. Abraxas could only hope that it was a shudder of interest, rather than fear.

Abraxas turned before he walked right back to her and plunged himself into the crowd of people. The sights, smells, colors, all assaulted his senses until he got his bearings. Everything was so... dark.

There were only a few lights in the entire basement of this building, although all the lights appeared to point in the same direction. The crowd was barely visible, though they all wandered toward the lights at the end of a tunnel like moths to a flame. So many of the people were already chattering excitedly.

"Did you hear what happened last time? I heard she roasted an entire pig with her breath of fire and then she fucked a man behind it while everyone else ate," a nymph said beside him, shouting to her friend over the din of talking.

The nymph wore little more than a few leaves covering important bits of her body. Abraxas looked down at her form for a brief second, eyes widening with all the more skin he saw before he snapped his gaze away and swallowed hard. There were people here wearing so much less than him.

"That sounds awful," the nymph's friend replied. He had leaves in his hair and glowing emerald eyes that could only mark him as another of the green folk. "I prefer my meat not to taste like Madame Blanchet's sweat. And you ate it?"

"Of course I did! I wanted to be invited again, didn't I?"

He pushed his way through the crowd ahead of those two, not wanting to know any more of what he might find. Abraxas used his body to move through the waves of people, and easily, considering most of the magical creatures were shorter than him by at least a foot. His height was a problem in most situations, but tonight, he'd use it to his advantage.

Eventually, the crowd all poured out of the tunnel and into what appeared to be a meadow. Except everything was big.

He looked over their heads, following the line of what he had assumed were tree trunks, only to realize they were the stems of tulips. Giant tulips the size of buildings that moved over their heads.

"Would you look at that?" a satyr exclaimed next to him.

The dwarven woman who he could only assume was the man's companion covered her mouth in shock and then pointed ahead. "Look! Everyone, look!"

Farther down the clearing stood at least fourteen mushrooms that were slightly taller than Abraxas himself. On top of each one were several men and women in nothing but what looked like glitter. They all beckoned for the crowd, who took very little time in running over to see what secrets those glowing beings might hold.

What was this place?

No, actually, he didn't want to know. He didn't care what might reveal itself even further here. All he needed to find was Madame Blanchet and get all this over with. Abraxas tried to weave through the crowd again, going in the opposite direction, like everyone else.

A tall woman with butterfly wings spread wide behind her sighed and pressed her hands to her chest. "Oh, it's a garden party. I love her garden parties!"

It would have been nice if Lorelei had at least warned him what to expect. Abraxas's heart already pounded in his chest with discomfort. This wasn't... He didn't do things like this.

Zander, however, would have very much appreciated being in the moment. He'd have loved every single second and certainly would have been the very first to reach those glittering creatures.

Why was he even thinking about the bastard?

Shaking his head, he broke free from the crowd and wandered down a tiny hill that led toward what looked like an overgrown hedge maze. Strange, he hadn't expected to find a labyrinth here. There were a few other people who walked with him. Most appeared to be in better condition than the others.

In fact, looking around, he realized the magical creatures surrounding him appeared wealthy. They were well fed and wore clothing that dripped gemstones and jewels. None of them were here for the food or the promise of bodily satisfaction. Instead, they all wandered with intent in their gaze.

How strange.

He hung at the back of the crowd and trailed behind them until everyone paused in front of an overgrown rose garden. Each bloom was larger than his bed had been in the castle, the petals as tall as he was. It appeared this hag had a rose in every color, waiting for her audience.

A fairy in front of him touched her partner's arm. "Oh, you know Madame Blanchet always likes to put on a show. Darling, which rose do you think she's in?"

The white one.

Obviously.

Abraxas frowned and watched the people hem and haw. Their voices were loud enough that the hag could hear what they were saying. Honestly, though, did they think she'd show herself when they guessed the correct one?

He didn't have that time to sit and wait around for someone to impress her.

"Excuse me," he murmured to the fairy couple and strode through the crowd. He thought he heard a few of them ask, "Who's that?"

No one needed to know who he was. Let them think him a mystery rather than know the truth. Most of these creatures had probably lost family to his flame. If they found out who he was, they'd run him out of this building before they would give him a chance to see Madame Blanchet.

It was now or never for him.

Abraxas reached for the white rose and rapped his knuckles against it, as though the petals were the door to her private room. "Madame Blanchet? You have an audience awaiting your presence."

"Is that so?" The voice floated through the flowers. "And just who thinks they can disturb me?"

Should he tell her his name? He wasn't quick enough to think up a fake one, at least not now that his heart raced, knowing what he might have to do to get her into the back room.

He swallowed hard. "Abraxas."

"What a terrible name."

The venom in the hissed words made him chuckle unbidden. "You wouldn't be the first to claim that, Madame, but I assure you. Once you see me, you'll understand why that name was given to me."

"Oh, a curious little mystery."

The rose shook and shuddered. Abraxas took four quick steps back and then the petals began to fall. The rose unfurled into full bloom and revealed an incredibly stunning woman lying within.

Madame Blanchet had golden skin that shimmered like she'd covered herself with metallic dust. Her dark hair spilled down over her shoulders, pin straight and reaching almost to her calves. Winged kohl outlined her eyes, which were the only things he was looking at considering she stretched her arms over her head and he realized very quickly that she only wore a tiny golden chain around her waist.

Madame Blanchet shook herself as though waking from a nap, then cast a blistering smile over the crowd. "Look at you all. Dressed up for me?"

The crowd cheered. The woman had done nothing, and they all reacted like she'd pulled off some impressive bit of magic.

Oh, right. He was supposed to be seducing her.

Taking a deep breath, he reached out a hand for Madame Blanchet to take. "Allow me."

She looked down at him from her perch, and he could see the moment she deemed him attractive enough for her time. Her eyes lit up, too bright, and she licked her lips like a cat who had caught its prey.

"You weren't joking about them giving you the right name. With a face like that, you were born a blunt weapon, weren't you?" Her gaze traveled down his decorated chest, lingering on the marks before dipping low to the muscles of his stomach. "But a body like yours is not meant to be blunted. Not at all."

His skin crawled with her perusal. Abraxas wanted to cover himself from her gaze and search for Lorelei. He'd need to scrub for days to get the oily sensation of her eyes off his skin.

But he had a job to do, and Abraxas was good at denying himself any form of comfort. He'd always done his job the right way, the first time, so that he never had to do it again.

So he kept his arm raised, willing her to put her hand in his. Which she did.

Madame Blanchet stood, languidly stretching one more time before she laced their fingers and allowed him to help her drift down onto the grassy floor. She tangled her arm through his, and he realized whatever made her skin glittery also made her entire body slick.

The crowd watched them, seeming to hold their breath for something.

Or, he supposed, for Madame Blanchet to say what they were expecting.

She trailed her fingers over his chest, digging her gold tipped nails into his skin and letting out a sound like a purr. "My goodness, you are a big man. Larger than I've had in a very long time." She looked up at him through her lashes and grinned. "You're coming with me first. I think I'd enjoy conquering a giant and then seeing who else could measure up."

Good. He'd done it right then.

No, not good. When she gave him that horrible grin, it made him realize he was the prey. He didn't want to go anywhere with her, especially not now that her claws were latched onto him.

But Madame Blanchet apparently wasted little time. She'd already slid her hand down his stomach and... Was she trying to put her hand under the waistband of his outfit?

Abraxas grabbed onto her wrist with a punishing grip, forcing her to stay still. He could feel the bones creaking as he snarled, "Not here."

"Oh?" she gasped, but the pain didn't seem to startle her. "You're shy?"

Shy? No one had ever accused him of such a foolish emotion. Abraxas let his eyes heat and turn molten with anger, then growled, "I don't share."

Perhaps she recognized the creature who held her in his grip. Perhaps she had once seen a dragon and knew just how true that statement was. Whatever the reason, Madame Blanchet grew even more excited with his words.

"Then why don't we go somewhere a little more private?" she mewled.

No.

"Yes," he hissed through his teeth, hoping she would assume he was in the throes of passion and not that he hated every second of her touch. "Lead the way, Madame."

"Oh, you're going to be so much fun. I cannot imagine how you came into my garden party, but I do know one thing." She winked. "I don't think you'll ever forget tonight."

He was going to vomit on her pretty grass floor.

CHAPTER 14

Lore only had a couple of minutes watching Abraxas wander through the crowd before she had to force herself away. He'd be fine. She knew he would do what they needed him to do because he was good at following orders. Particularly her orders, although she wasn't sure what to think of that.

Shaking her head, she weaved through the throng with quiet murmurs that set others at ease. She'd learned a long time ago that if her ears were out, the other magical creatures trusted her. They didn't ask questions of the elves. Never had.

Her people still put a lot of weight into history. They were foolish to trust her like that. After all, her kind weren't what they used to be, and Margaret was a perfect example of that.

She weaved past the crowd circling mushrooms as men and women tried to grab onto the hands of the performers covered in magical dust. Right, she should have warned Abraxas that Madame Blanchet's parties got a little... out of hand.

Beyond them were the corridors that led away from the center of the room like burrows in a rabbit's hole. She knew they only circled around to the basement of the building that Madame Blanchet lived in, but no one else cared enough to look.

A single guard stood at the head of a tunnel with his arms crossed over his ridiculously enormous chest. He wore a metal armored plate and a scowl that could sear the flesh from someone's bones if he turned it on them. Considering the man was made of rock, she had expected his facial expressions to be a little less noticeable.

They'd never met before, but she knew this particular guard had a history with her mother. And she also knew that her mother had worn this outfit a few times in her life. Probably here, if Lorelei was being honest with herself.

She just didn't want to think of painful memories at one of the largest magical orgies in Umbra.

Walking straight up to the guard, she smoothed her hands over the side of her head to make sure every hair lay perfectly in place. No blonde curls or coils could escape her tight ponytail if she wanted this to work. Her mother's hairstyle had always been perfect.

"What's a girl got to do to get past you?" she murmured, twisting her hips so they were more rounded and less boxy.

"Vespera?" The guard's eyes widened and his voice dipped so low it sounded like gravel crunching. But then he remembered her mother was dead.

She couldn't keep up the pretense when he looked as though he'd seen a ghost. "I do that a lot too," she replied. "I look in the mirror sometimes and then turn to check behind me. Like she'll be standing there again. As if no time has passed at all."

He scrubbed a gray hand over his chest where his heart should be, as though there was pain beneath the stone. "Sorry. I just... You look exactly like her."

"I know." She did and hated it sometimes. Sometimes she wanted to scream that it wasn't fair. The only time she got to see her mother was when she looked in the mirror. And the woman in the mirror's advice was shit compared to her mother's.

The guard appeared even more uncomfortable than she felt. He cleared his throat a few times, then shook his head with a firm grunt. "What can I do for you, girl?"

"There's something I need down that way." She nodded at the corridor behind him. "I'm not going to hurt anyone. I also promise not to steal anything."

"Then what is it?"

"Information." None of it was untrue, and she knew that rock giants could always taste a lie in the air. "You know I'm not lying, and I'd hate to use Mum's name, but..."

He narrowed his eyes at her. "But what?"

"I can't tell you what I'm doing, only that she would want this." That was true as well. Vespera would have done everything she could to get those dragon eggs back because it was the right thing to do. Dragons were the hope of a kingdom, and the promise of a future.

The guard looked her over up and down as though he didn't quite believe her. He had to know she was telling the truth, which would only mean he thought she had bent the truth.

He was smarter than she'd expected.

"Aren't you the girl that killed the King?" he asked.

Her eyebrows couldn't have shot up higher if she tried. "How do you know that?"

"Word travels fast in these communities, and I know a couple of folks who like to think themselves more important to the rebellion than they are." He sniffed and crossed his arms over his chest. "So? Did you?"

She couldn't lie to him. Lorelei knew she couldn't tell him that she'd killed the King without him knowing that she hadn't. Then he would tell everyone that the King was alive, and Margaret would recall them back to the castle.

As she struggled with her thoughts and plans on how to lie to a fucking rock giant, he sighed and shook his head. "I knew it. You don't have to say anything, daughter of Vespera. I can see it on your face."

Her breath blew out of her mouth in a great gust of wind. She didn't have to say a word apparently, thank the heavens. But she was curious... "What can you see?"

"Guilt." He stepped to the side and waved at her with an arm. "Quickly, now. If Madame Blanchet sees that I let you through, she'll turn me into a pile of rubble. Be quick about it, and don't get caught, whatever you do."

On a whim, Lore paused beside him and pressed a kiss to his cheek. "Thank you."

The rock giant's eyes widened, and he touched a single gray hand to his cheek with a clink of stone on stone. "Your mother used to do that to me," he murmured. "She was the only person who I could feel the heat of her touch. Same as you, apparently."

Oh.

Tears welled in her eyes, but the only thing she could offer the poor man was a nod before she rushed down the tunnel. Dirt crunched underneath her feet, roots caught at her hair, and her skirts tangled in her legs, but she didn't stop running until she smelled the metallic scent of a hag's den.

Madame Blanchet had tried her best to hide the smell. The entire corridor reeked of earth and botanicals. But Lore had spent enough time around blood and gore to know the scent of dead bodies and rotting things.

She opened the door to her right and revealed the disgusting mess beyond. Hags always played with their magical ingredients, which also happened to be the cadavers. Or recently dead, as it was in Madame Blanchet's case.

There were three deceased women on a table at the back of the room. She had flayed each of them open, ribs cracked, and internal organs pulled out with rough hands. Though the bodies were in remarkably good condition, considering what she had done to them. Two men hung by their heels to Lorelei's right, blood dripping from the wounds at their necks.

She swallowed hard and batted at a fly that fluttered in front of her face. Madame Blanchet played with darker magic than most, but knowing how old she was, nothing surprised Lorelei.

A pile of sticks and twigs in the back right served as the hag's bed. It looked like an overgrown eagle's nest, but some of the straw was mixed with the bones of those who tried to cross the Madame.

"You've been busy," Lorelei muttered before walking over to the three women. "She'll try to hide you ladies first, so let's hope I get caught up in the magic that prevents him from seeing you."

Now she hoped Abraxas made quick work of convincing the hag. The smell of the room already turned her stomach and staying in here for hours with five dead bodies only made her want to vomit all the more.

It didn't take long. Unsurprisingly, Madame Blanchet must have taken one look at Abraxas and knew he was the very first man she would convince to bed her. After all, Abraxas was unlike anyone they'd ever seen. Literally no one had seen a dragon in his mortal form in centuries. The uniqueness of him would have tempted a creature as old as the hag.

And also the signatures all over his body that screamed he was owned by an elf, but still arrived at her doorstep. That alone would arouse Madame Blanchet's curiosity.

Lorelei stepped back behind the last table as power seeped into the room. The dark fog sparkled with gray magic and sluggishly crawled over the floor. Everything it touched changed. The dried blood on the stones melted and gave way to plush navy carpeting. The hanging bodies disappeared altogether, although Lore knew they were still there.

The magic finally reached the tables, but instead of hiding them, it built a wall. Lore could see through the shimmering edges of it, as though she were behind a mirror and everything else remained on the other side. She touched a hand to it and was relieved to find she could walk through if she wanted. The mirage was solely a smokescreen.

"Madame Blanchet," she muttered. "You're one wily old hag."

The door burst open seconds later, with a stunning naked woman clinging onto Abraxas like a leech. She'd already climbed halfway up his body, and Abraxas walked them both into the room with his hands at his sides, curled into fists.

His eyes were too wide. He frantically looked around the hag den, which had now turned into a very luxurious bedroom with a black silk covered bed in one corner and too many plush handcuffs hanging from the ceiling. She knew he wouldn't see her anywhere at all, and that was when panic set in.

Every muscle in his body locked up tight. His eyes glowed bright yellow and smoke trailed out of his nose as though he exhaled elfweed.

Oh, no. He was going to pop because he thought Lore hadn't made it to the room.

"Sweetheart," Madame Blanchet crooned, dragging her nails across his chest hard enough to leave welts in their wake. "You and I will have so much fun. You have no idea."

His deep voice rumbled in his chest long before he spoke. "I think you'll be surprised at just how much fun I'm going to have."

"Oh," she growled back. "Look at you. So gruff. I can't even guess what kind of creature you are, but that's part of the fun. How rough are you in bed, darling?"

Lorelei stepped through the illusion of the wall with her hand in her pocket. She pulled out a tiny vial, unstoppered it, and then interrupted them. "He's probably very rough. He is a dragon, after all."

Madame Blanchet turned toward her with a twisted, angry expression. Lore enjoyed this far too much. She splashed the contents of the vial directly in that perfect, golden face.

The searing sound erupted before the smoke cascaded up from where it had handed all over her body. And then the screaming. Oh, the hag screamed as though she were dying.

Abraxas stumbled away from the woman, hands raised. "What did you throw on her? Acid? I thought we weren't going to kill her!"

"It's not acid," she muttered. Lore grabbed Madame Blanchet's arms that were pinwheeling around and held them down at the other woman's side. "It was hagweed residue. Just enough to put this lying witch in her place."

Madame Blanchet stopped screaming, and the eerie silence was almost worse than the screams.

Lore looked the hag in the eyes and took her time perusing the face that yet another illusion had hidden. Hags only had half a human face. The eyes were the same, but a mottled beak stood in place of a nose. No lips. No chin. Just a beak with folded skin at the edges taking up half her face. All that golden flesh lost its luster and faded into a sickly yellow. Loose skin hung from her arms, not quite hidden by tangled strands of oily gray hair.

"There you are," Lorelei said with a smirk. "And here I thought that you had gotten that glamour locked in place for good."

"Where did you find hagweed in Tenebrous?" the hag snarled.

"My mother had some remaining from the last war," Lorelei replied, releasing her hold on the hag's shoulders. "And a daughter always knows the right time to use what her mother left her."

Madame Blanchet looked her up and down, chest heaving with angry breaths. "Ah. I thought you looked familiar." She spat on the ground. "Vespera's daughter, lost child of Silverfell, with all her powers leaking out of her pores every time she steps into the moon. Cursed child."

"Don't speak in riddles, hag."

"Your mother was the Evening Star of Silverfell and what are you, half blood?" Madame Blanchet chuckled. "Dragon tamer? Is that what you want to be known as? You will fail at that. Just like you failed to save your mother."

A wall of heat slammed against her back, and it took every ounce of Lore's strength to hold Abraxas behind her. "Stop it," she snarled. "We need her to work with us."

"Work with you?" Madame Blanchet waved a hand in the air and shattered the illusion.

Lore took a step back, slamming her spine against Abraxas's chest as the wall of scent struck her again. Rotting meat. Metallic blood. The sound of flies buzzing in her ears and all those poor dead creatures who had fallen prey to the hag's spell.

Even Abraxas hissed out a long breath in her ear and wrapped an arm around her waist.

The movement did not go unnoticed.

Madame Blanchet pointed a curved finger at the point where they were connected. "You've already fallen so far, little elf. How much farther are you willing to go down the rabbit hole?"

She choked down the vomit in her throat. "The King has a half brother. You know where he is."

Like that would work. Lore didn't know why she always thought magical creatures knew how to be direct. They didn't, and they weren't interested in such conversation. If there wasn't a game, then she would get no information.

Madame Blanchet cackled and pointed at the two of them. "You think I'm going to tell you anything? After ruining my party and my face?"

Well, she had hoped it wouldn't get more difficult than that. "I thought you'd want to help all of our kind seek freedom."

"I am free." The hag backed up to the tables with the dead women and plunged her hand into the chest cavity of the nearest one. Muttering, she yanked out what looked like a kidney and clutched it in her bloody fist. "Now, you two are going to die. And I'm going to return to my party. Such a pity. I would dearly love to enjoy your friend's company before I go." She looked at Abraxas with a calculating stare. "Maybe I still will."

All right, that was it. Lore had thought they could deal with this as adults, but she'd clearly been wrong. Even as Abraxas snarled something that sounded like, "I'd like to see you try," Lore's temper got the better of her.

She reached underneath the folds of her skirt and grabbed onto the weapon she'd strapped to her inner thigh. Dangerous, that, but she'd taken the calculated risk. With two long strides, she planted her foot on a stool and leapt into the air. She came down hard on the hag as the other creature dropped the kidney into her mouth.

The glamour shimmered back into place just as the two women fell onto the ground. Lore crouched over Madame Blanchet with a knife at her throat, a boot on one side of her head, and the other grinding between Madame Blanchet's perfect breasts.

"Go ahead," Madame Blanchet hissed. "I've already cast a spell that if you succeed in killing me, the magic will bounce back on you."

"I think you forget just how talented elves can be." Lore bared her teeth in a smile. "And you've definitely forgotten what the knife in my hand can do."

The hag sneered until her eyes traveled down the hilt of the dagger to the black blade she could barely see from her angle. Then her demeanor changed. The stunning hag pinned beneath her shuddered and quaked in fear.

"Where did you get that?" she whispered in both fear and awe. "You shouldn't have that."

"But I do. And I will let it feed if you don't tell me what I want to know. You know I will. You know what its magic already whispers and begs for."

The hag stared up at her with wide, horrified eyes. And she was right. Lore shouldn't have the grimdag that whispered every time she touched it. She should have thrown it away or left it with Margaret, but the truth was that she didn't trust the other elf with something so powerful and dark.

She dug the blade closer to the hag's throat. Not enough to break skin, but only a breath away from doing so. "You know what this is," she muttered. "You know what it can do. Save your own hide, Madame. You don't have to die today. Not like this."

"And if that information could kill me, anyway?"

"It won't." Lore stared down into the other woman's eyes and willed her to see the truth. "If I wanted to hurt him, I wouldn't come to you. Where is the boy hiding?"

"He's not a boy." Madame Blanchet swallowed, and the knife made a shaving sound against her skin. "His mother hid him in the Fields of Somber last I knew, but that might have changed."

"Are you lying to me?" Lore hoped she wasn't. She couldn't stand another liar.

"No." Madame Blanchet's eyes widened. "I'm not lying. He's there, and if he isn't there any longer, then there will be some hint of him there."

Lore leaned as close as she dared to the dangerous hag's lips and breathed her threat into Madame Blanchet's lungs. "If you're lying to me, I will come back here and I will feast on your soul."

Another swallow, another tiny movement of a nod, and that was enough.

Lore stood and slipped the chortling grimdag back into its holster against her thigh, then turned back to Abraxas. "Come on," she muttered while grabbing onto his arm. "We're leaving."

The heat in his eyes still burned. "That was... incredible."

"All I did was pin the woman to the ground and threaten to kill her. Anyone can do that." She dragged him from that haunting room and out into the corridor beyond. Rather than returning to the party, she intended to sneak through the basement and out onto the street.

Abraxas tugged her back to him, reeling her into his arms until he cupped the back of her head with one hand and ringed her waist with the other. "You did more than that. You got us the information we needed without spilling a drop of blood."

"I did what I had to."

She let out a tiny sound as he captured her mouth with his. He devoured her, sipping her cool anger until he burned it away with his heat. She came alive underneath his hands, returning to herself. No longer the cold huntress, but a living, breathing woman.

And when he pulled back, he traced the line of her jaw with a sigh. "Bloodthirsty woman, you wouldn't need a knife to have me begging at your feet."

As if she knew how to respond to that.

CHAPTER 15

Lorelei led her dragon out onto the dark streets and found she didn't know what to say to him. Not yet, at least. They'd been in one of the worst places in the city and he'd managed well enough. He'd let her handle the entire situation with the hag, even though she had known he wanted to rip the woman to shreds.

But now he wasn't saying anything.

Not even a little.

She glanced over her shoulder when they were halfway to her old apartment and noted how he had crossed his arms over his chest. He wasn't cold. Dragons didn't get cold, so...

Ah.

Right.

Abraxas hadn't been one of the many people at the castle who had flaunted his body. He'd always worn armor and more clothing than she'd seen anyone else wear. Unfortunately, that had translated into a discomfort with so much skin showing.

She was a horrible guide and an even worse friend, wasn't she? And they had to be friends. That's all she could think of them as right now, although a part of her soul declared that he was hers. Friend or not, it had killed her inside to see the hag touching him like that.

She paused at a line of laundry and ripped a cloak off it. The owner would be livid in the morning, but who still left their laundry outside these days?

"Here," she muttered, holding it out to him. "Put this on."

His movements were strange. Even as he reached for the cloak, she realized with sudden clarity that he was trying to hide the scratch marks on his chest. Why? She'd seen the damn hag make them. The wounds were rather garish at the moment, but she hadn't broken skin.

They wouldn't amount to visible scars, really. It would just take a couple of weeks for them to disappear.

Stepping closer, Lorelei swatted his hand away. "Here, let me."

She lifted the cloak up and over his shoulders. The man was so damn wide and big. She wrapped it around him, then drew the tails of the fabric tight to his front. Her touch lingered on the fabric, though, holding it slightly open while she stared at the faint red marks on his skin.

Abraxas spread his fingers a little wider, hiding more of it from her sight. "They'll fade."

"I know they will." She met his gaze, forcing him to hold it when she knew he'd rather look away. "Why are you so upset about them?"

"Dragons..." He frowned, then let his hand fall from the marks. "These are common among dragons, especially while in our mortal form.

They're signs of ownership, of... mates. It's a disgrace to have them made by anyone but our chosen partner."

Ah, so he was embarrassed and slighted by the hag.

Lore held her breath and hoped she wouldn't insult him even more by what she was about to do. She gently set her fingertips on his chest, tracing just above the scratches along her own glittering gold runes. "You wear many marks tonight, then."

"Only one that matters."

His deep voice sent a shiver down her spine and, oh, how she wished that were true. She wished he'd give up being so sweet and romantic, or her heart would fall for him and she didn't want that.

Or did she?

Damn her thoughts. Damn her traitorous mind that so desperately wanted to wipe away the past so she could focus only on him and her standing in the middle of a damp cobblestone street.

Swallowing hard, she flattened her palm against the rune she'd etched over his collarbone. The one that meant her own name, and thus, was more important than all the rest. "This is me, you know."

"What is?" He glanced down at her hand, then eased it out of the way. "This rune?"

She nodded, staring at the tiny four-pointed star. The north and south points were longer than the other two, with a hollow center that held a single straight horizontal line. It was a lovely mark and one that her mother claimed meant enchantress. If only she had become that. Instead, she'd leaned more toward a disappointment and a young elf who knew nothing of her own magic or abilities. She'd never even tried more difficult magic.

Silverfell elves could do anything, her mother used to say. But there weren't any of them left now, so how would Lore ever know her own potential?

She tried to take a step away from him. This closeness became too much. Abraxas captured her hand in his, however, and held her to his heart. "Then when you remove the others, leave this one."

"I can't do that," she replied with a scoff. "Magic doesn't last that long. Besides, you don't want to walk around with my name on your chest."

He opened his mouth, then closed it, but she saw the words in his eyes.

He did. He wanted to proudly keep her name on his skin. That desire burned through her and she almost said she'd do it. She'd turn it into the mark of a Silverfell, not just some pretty golden bauble but etched with gray and diamond dust.

No.

The voice of reason in her head scolded her for daring to think such a thing. Leaving him with that mark set a precedent that she wasn't sure she wanted. And besides, it was wrong. He didn't deserve that. He wasn't a piece of meat for her to mark, so that other women wouldn't try anything while she figured out what she wanted from him.

With a slight wince, she waved a hand over the marks and watched them fade from his skin. He must have felt the loss of them. Disappointment marred his usually handsome face.

Abraxas sighed, the gust of his breath teasing her cheeks. "Let's go home, Lore."

"And where is home?" She met his gaze again, and a chilly breeze played with the ends of her ponytail. "Not here. Not anymore."

The sorrow in his eyes spoke of a man who knew what she meant. "I've lived for a very long time without a home, Lore. You make one inside yourself, or you find one in another. Homes are fragile things. They can change so easily."

Grinding her teeth, she forced all her emotions back into her stomach with a hard swallow. She turned around and led him back to the apartment building, then climbed up the side with her feet on the windowsills. Perhaps no one even lived in the home anymore. It certainly was buttoned up. The shutters locked tight against the cold, but at least made it easier for her to climb onto the roof.

Once there, that stiff wind blew even harsher. It stole underneath her skirts and through the leather of her corset. Gooseflesh rose all along her arms and her ponytail lashed like a whip behind her. She stared up at the gray sky as the clouds parted to reveal a bright full moon.

The light tangled around her skin, giving her just enough magic to hold out her hand and willed a tiny wood finch to life in her hand. It glittered as though covered in diamonds.

"Go find Beauty," she said. "Tell her we're ready for her."

The finch took off into the night, spears of moonlight guiding its way. And without even looking back at the dragon, who was likely shocked by her display of magic, she slipped back into the dusty attic.

Lore landed in a crouch, then surveyed her old home. Fragile, Abraxas had said, and he was right. She'd once felt so safe here.

He clambered in behind her, and Lore gathered up a half-burned candle. The pooled wax at the base would hold it up for her, and she lit it with the sharp strike of a match.

"What's that for?" he asked, wandering over to her cot and taking a seat.

"Goliath. He'll see the light and know I'm home. Hopefully he'll get here at the same time as Beauty, but we might have to wait a few days for her. I've heard her father's business is... difficult. The man oversees what the King should have. He's busy."

Where did this awkwardness come from? She just wanted to be in a room with him without feeling like she was either going to climb on top of him or strangle him or have a mental breakdown about his part in her mother's death.

"Lore." It was like he knew. He said her name and all the tension in her chest faded.

She turned toward him with a sigh, and saw that he felt the same thing. Of course he did. They were going through this together, weren't they? Two opposite sides of the spectrum. He suffered with guilt for what he'd done to not just her mother, but so many others. And she agonized over knowing neither of them could bury this.

Abraxas held the cloak tightly around his shoulders, as though he were trying to hide from her gaze. He sat curved forward on himself, hunching over his knees. And his eyes... Oh, his eyes burned with fires for her and only her.

"Just tonight," he murmured, his voice floating through the air with so much temptation in it. "We can pretend, just for tonight."

"What are we pretending?" Her voice was a harsh snap. "That you didn't kill my mother? That we didn't try to murder a king together and erase an entire dynasty? That we aren't hunting down the King's half brother and both of us know we might have to kill him in the end?"

The words kept going. She couldn't stop the rant as it ripped out of her very soul. It was like the pressure had made her violently ill and the word vomit had to erupt.

Lore lifted her hands in the air and stared at her palms. Her fingers were shaking. "Are we supposed to pretend that I haven't been made into a weapon? And that you haven't killed hundreds of people like me simply because someone told you to do it?"

Large hands covered hers. He laced their fingers together, weaving his larger ones through hers and then lifting them all to his mouth. Abraxas blew a warm breath over her shaking hands, holding them with such care that it made tears spark in her eyes.

"Yes," he admitted without hesitation. "Yes, tonight we are going to pretend none of that happened. Tonight, you are a woman I met at a party I shouldn't have been at. A woman who saved my life, or at least my honor, from a very talented but terrifying hag."

Lore chuckled, unbidden. The hag's den had felt like a nightmare induced fever dream.

"I'm not asking you to forget." He pressed his lips to the back of her hand. "All I'm asking is for one night to not think about the past. It will heal on its own, or it will fester. I know that. I know I cannot expect you to ever fully forgive me for what I did, nor can I expect you to give me what I desire most."

What did he mean by that? What did he desire?

She searched his features for the answer. His worried, furrowed brows. The way tiny wrinkles had appeared around his mouth when he tightened his lips like that. The bouncing muscle of his jaw. None of it gave her the answer she wanted.

"Lore," he whispered again. "Have I ever told you how dragons used to kidnap elves?"

Well, that caught her attention. "No, you haven't. I had no idea that dragons used to attack our kind."

"It was never an attack." Still holding her hands, he drew her toward the cot and sat down on the edge with her. "Usually such circumstances were more of a bribe. Dragons always found themselves fascinated with the elves."

"Everyone is fascinated with the elves," she corrected.

"Indeed. But dragons are more so than most. Very few creatures in the world connect with dragons. We're ambitious, horribly jealous, and we protect what is ours to a fault." He squeezed her fingers, perhaps a little too tightly. "Elves are similar enough, and if I remember right, your kind gets very testy if they are not allowed to protect themselves."

Well, he had her pegged. She cleared her throat and wiggled a hand out of his. "Yes, yes, go on. We all know the flaws of my kind and yours. You said you used to kidnap elves?"

"I never did. I was too young back when there were still dragons flying about. But I knew many elves who allowed themselves to be kidnapped." He launched into a fantastic tale of magic and power. How dragons used to soar through the sky and find elves that captivated them so thoroughly that the two would agree to a deal.

The elf would leave his or her home and the dragon would make a rather large show of forcing the elf to return with them. In exchange, the two would live out their lives in the famed Dracomaquia. The home of the dragons.

He told her how beautiful his home country was. How the lands rolled with emerald hills, mountains, and deserts that met the sea for every type of dragon that wished to live there. He filled her mind with glorious memories of emerald dragons sleeping in moss, while elves gently watered the flowers that surrounded them. He laughed at stories of sapphire dragons that floated along the riverbeds and their stolen partners who steered their rafts with long poles. She could almost see them. Like some part of her soul still remembered what they once were, and what they once could have been.

At some point during the story, she'd leaned against his shoulder, toying with the fingers of his closest hand. His story had paused with a slight hitch, but then he continued and let her touch the callouses along his fingertips and palm.

Then she'd shifted again as her eyelids grew heavy and dreams begged to take her to a land of dragons and elves who lived side by side. Lore's head listed to the side, and she was lifted into powerful arms.

She hardly had a chance to complain before Abraxas had shifted them both. He braced his back against the wall and settled her against his chest. His muscular thighs bracketed either side of her, and the massive expanse of his chest cushioned her head surprisingly well.

Casually, he threw an arm around her and continued telling her about the desert dragons, the crimson ones that were his family. As though he hadn't just cuddled her close with surprising ease.

She shouldn't let him do this. She should wrestle her way out of his touch and scoot to the end of the bed.

But he was warm and comforting. The strength of his body ensured that no one would disturb her dreams. Without threats, she felt certain she might sleep through the night.

And what had he said, anyway?

One night. Just one night where they pretended that there was nothing outside of these four walls. Nothing else existed but the rising and falling of his chest in steady, deep breaths that she mimicked. His stories guttural in her ear, easing her off into a deep sleep full of happy dreams.

Dreams of hope and light, where there was a place for them in this world.

And if his arm tightened around her a little more when she went limp in his grasp, she pretended not to notice. Just as she didn't notice how he slid her hair away from her face and draped the ponytail over her shoulder. Nor the way he traced a line down her cheek, and adjusted her head so her neck wouldn't hurt in the morning.

CHAPTER 16

L et the sun rise. Would you look at what we have here?"

The voice cut through a rather wonderful dream of holding Lorelei in his arms while he told her stories about his people. Abraxas had liked it quite a bit, and that sound sure resonated through the room like the dwarf Lorelei had introduced him to.

"I can eat you in a single bite," he snarled without opening his eyes. "Go away."

"Sorry, mate. It's morning time and there's a journey to prepare for, I reckon." The dwarf knocked into jars that clanked against each other. "So if you wouldn't mind waking the sleeping beauty in your arms, I'd very much appreciate it. I think if anyone else wakes her up right now that she'll probably take off a finger."

He blearily blinked in the dim light shining directly on his face. It felt as though someone had thrown sand in his eyes and damned if he wouldn't eat that dwarf for daring to wake him.

Except then he realized he hadn't been dreaming at all. He had told Lore stories in the middle of the night to ease her into sleep. And somehow she'd ended up curled up against his chest like a kitten he'd picked up off the streets. At some point, Abraxas had slid down the wall even further and his upper back burned as soon as he shifted.

Worth it. Every ounce of pain was worth it.

Sunlight gleamed from the window, a rare sunny day in Tenebrous when most of the time clouds covered the sky. If they were going to prepare for the journey to the Fields of Somber, then they should use this unusual opportunity.

He still planned on taking a bite out of Goliath the first chance he got. Grumbling, he stretched just enough to bounce the woman on his chest.

Every muscle in her body seized as she woke, surely not knowing where she was, and then relaxed as though she were asleep again.

"I know you're awake," he chuckled. "Goliath wants us to get up and start preparing. I assume that means he needs your attention."

Maybe she was embarrassed to be caught in such a position. He was... less so. He'd love to wake up like this every morning, but last night was the night for pretending. They'd done what they could.

This morning, all the memories that stood between them came rushing back and there was nothing he could do to stop them. Only time would help, or maybe it wouldn't. Maybe he'd suffer like this for centuries until she finally ran from him.

Ah, they had to get up or his mind would bury him.

Abraxas lifted her and set her on the other side of the cot. Getting up, he stretched his arms overhead as though his stiffness was the reason for him to move. Not that he was trying to put some space between them before his own guilt swallowed him whole.

"The Fields of Somber," he said with a grunt. "That's where we're going."

Goliath's eyebrows lifted into the considerable length of his hairline. "Excuse me? I hate that place. Why would we go there?"

Without looking at Abraxas, Lore stood up and strode toward the window. "Because that's where Madame Blanchet said the King's half brother is. I'll start getting food for the journey, and I'll see if I can steal some packs to take with us. You coming or not, Goliath?"

And then she slipped out onto the roof. Without looking at Abraxas at all.

Goliath frowned and stared at him. "What did you do, dragon?"

"I haven't the faintest idea."

Apparently, he wasn't allowed to go on the supply run. Nor was he allowed to leave the attic. Lorelei made it very clear that she didn't think the risk of him walking around unsupervised was smart for any of them. Stay here, she'd said. Don't move and don't let anyone find you.

He spent an entire week in that tiny space, only seeing the other two for brief moments before Beauty stuck her head in the window and waved at him.

"Hello, again!" she said. Her voice was a bright chirp and a wonderful change, considering it had been a week since anyone had talked to him. "Are you ready to go?"

"I've been ready for ages," he snarled.

Abraxas had even gotten dressed every morning as though they were traveling that day. Comfortable black pants. A black shirt that tied in the front and was loose enough to not impede his movements. Lore had tossed the outfit at him one of the times she'd come back to pass out on the cot and then forget he existed.

He'd have to make sure she never got it in her head to punish him like this again. If that were possible. He slipped out of the window and into the gray twilight beyond.

Beauty stood with her hands on her hips and a bright grin on her face. She wore clothing very similar to his, although hers fit her better. Goliath and Lore stood behind her, both of them in equally dark clothing, although they didn't share Beauty's cheerful smile.

"At least someone is happy to see me," he muttered.

Lorelei threw a pack at him, and he caught it with a slight oof.

"No one has to be happy to see you, Abraxas," she said, though a grin broke through that icy exterior. "We're walking, by the way."

"Again?" He glared at the leather bag in his hands and resented how heavy it was. "You realize we could get just out of sight of Tenebrous and then fly to the Fields of Somber?"

"Not without a ridiculous amount of people following us. The King is supposed to be dead and the entire kingdom knows it. Don't you think they're curious where his pet dragon ended up?"

The wind played with the ends of her hair, and his fingers itched to tuck the strands behind her ear. He should pay attention to what she said, but... Well. That was growing more difficult by the day.

He sighed and hauled the straps over his shoulders. "Fine. We're walking. I understand that you don't want me to fly. And I won't."

Maybe.

It took them a few hours to get out of the city. Apparently, Tenebrous had a lot of fixing to do, and Beauty's father was at the head of all that. She chattered while they walked, and Abraxas found he was grateful to have someone break the silence between him and Lore.

"My father's plan is to build up everything that Zander broke. He intends to create a council of elders from every community, and together they will make decisions for the city. Of course, he has to get Margaret's blessing, but I can't imagine she'd complain all that much. If he succeeds, then that's just one less city she has to worry about. You know how she gets when she's stressed."

He hated it that she still referred to Margaret as if the elf was a good person. Time, he reminded himself. Time revealed all.

Goliath snorted. "A council with a member of every magical community? You realize some of the magical communities consider elders to be retired, right? Not all of them will want to send someone old. I know the dwarves would prefer a younger representation. Someone more attuned to the needs of the present rather than the past."

His words almost made Beauty fall. She stumbled through a rather deep puddle, then back onto the road. "They do? But I thought everyone would want someone wise and... and... well, a person they can listen to!"

"What about a gray beard is easy to listen to? All they'll do is tell very long, detailed stories when they get back and none of us will understand a word of it." Goliath forced her back onto the road again before she soaked her shoes any more. "Your father could just ask, you know."

"I suppose." She tapped a hand to her lip, eyes not even remotely on the dirt path they followed. "Do you think anyone would talk with us, though?"

Abraxas wanted to interject that the creatures likely were still angry that her father even ran the city. They wanted a magical creature at the forefront of the one place that the King continually sent those he didn't want to kill. He kept them there so he could find them later. When he'd gotten a thirst for blood.

Clearing his mind of those dark memories, he hurried to catch up with the rest of his companions. And then, like the gentleman he sometimes was, he held out his arm for Beauty to take.

"Walk with me," he said.

She looked up at him with glittering eyes. "Why?"

"Because apparently when you think, you wander in every direction and I, for one, would like to get to the camp before nightfall." He patted the hand she set on his arm. "And also because I have a few ideas for you. I'm ancient, remember? I've seen things done like this before."

He thought that might be the first time Goliath smiled at him. The dwarf listened to their entire conversation, but Abraxas was the one who talked Beauty through every stage of frustration that the magical creatures felt.

They were woefully under represented in the leadership. Elders might work, but preferably people who were passionate about helping others.

Sure, they would then have positions of power. But they'd never had such influence before, and that meant they were uneducated about any processes.

Furthermore, they would have a significant amount of fear in even stepping into these roles. Fear of it being a trick, fear of failure, fear of losing their lives to the humans who had convinced them to give a damn when nothing had ever given them reason to do so.

At least the conversation helped pass the time. They made it significantly further than they had in traveling toward Tenebrous, and when he looked up, Abraxas could see the white tips of the Stygian Peaks in the distance.

"There they are," he said, and something inside his very soul took flight. He wanted nothing more than to soar through that icy air. To feel the clouds touching his wings and caressing his aching shoulders.

The need to disappear rose into his throat and stole his very breath away.

"Would you look at that?" Goliath said, popping his fists onto his hips. "Sure looks like mountains to me."

"How many mountains have you climbed?" Lore asked from the front of the pack.

"Many. Or at least my ancestors did. Mountains are for dwarves." He pounded a fist on his chest. "That's where I come from. My homeland."

Abraxas didn't have it in him to tell the poor dwarf that his ancestors weren't all that fond of the tall ridges. Dwarves had a talent for mining, that's for sure. But it was a job. They were more likely to be found in the valleys at the base of the peaks, mostly by lakes. He hadn't met a dwarf who didn't like to fish. Not in five hundred years.

Lorelei paused them with a sharply said order. "Stop."

They all did.

"I think we can stay here and rest," she said, glancing around the marsh that seemingly ended right at the forest's edge. "We're close enough to the mountains that it feels safe."

"You sure about that?" Abraxas wanted to poke at her, and maybe the words were a little rough. But she'd ignored him for a week after spending the night in his arms, and he wasn't too ashamed to admit his pride stung.

"Do you see anything wrong with it?" She arched her brow while looking him over.

And no, of course he didn't. She had eyes as good as he did, but that didn't mean he had to go along with every plan she thought up. Abraxas made a show of looking around the marsh, taking his time to assess any potential dangers.

Finally, he sighed and shrugged. "Just tell me where to put the bag down."

"Good, because it's the heaviest one."

They set up camp, all working well together, if he did say so himself. But he'd be lying if he said he didn't struggle with the guilt running through his soul.

Every time he looked at the mountains, he felt a tug deep inside himself. A pull that whispered to his dragon that he hadn't been himself in a long time. He needed to be free, and this journey wasn't allowing him to be so. He had to fly. The dragon needed to be let out.

Goliath lit a fire and Beauty started cooking dinner. But the dragon refused to be appeased. No matter what they did, no matter how many times he told himself that he had to travel with them, the voice whispered in his ear.

By the time they were all settling down to sleep, the whisper had become a scream.

Get out.

Fly.

You are not a tamed beast.

He had to do something about this or he wouldn't make it to the morning. The magic inside him would burst forth in the middle of a trail and damn it, he'd get stuck between trees because he couldn't control himself.

He waited until they all laid down before he wandered over to Lore. She'd snuggled down underneath a thin blanket, but her eyes were open and staring at the fire.

"I'm not interested in a repeat of the last night we shared together," she muttered.

"Good, neither am I. You've been insufferable for a week now." He crouched down beside her and stared into the flames. "I cannot continue this journey with you, Lorelei."

A silence fell between them as she processed what he said. "Do you... Do you not trust that we'll be able to find the eggs?"

"I trust it. I know you will and I'll be there when you find them." Damn it, he was mangling this. "I only meant to say this part of the journey, this long walk, is not something I can do."

"I told you to bring different shoes." She still wouldn't look at him.

"The mountains call to me." More than called. They screamed. They raged in his ears until he could think of nothing else. "I have to answer them."

Lore sat up, bracing herself on an elbow while glaring at him. "So you're leaving? Because of some bullshit that the mountains are calling you?"

Anger flared in his chest, though he knew it wasn't entirely at her, but at everyone. "You have yet to realize that I'm not a man, Lore. Just because this form is one you prefer doesn't mean it's my natural state. I've been like this for too long. My skin itches and splits. I'm not meant to stay in this form indefinitely. You're asking me to be something I'm not."

Her eyes widened with every word, horror growing at his proclamation. He knew it wasn't fair to put that on her. She'd done nothing wrong, or at least, nothing that others wouldn't have done. Or had done.

He couldn't think straight like this. Already he felt the writhing of scales and wings underneath his skin.

"Forgive me," he growled, and the words were hardly human.

Abraxas scooped a hand beneath her neck and lifted her. He inhaled her lush scent of salt and earth, flowers and brine. He filled his lungs with her so that he wouldn't forget he had to return. That someone waited for him here and the dragon had to come back from the mountains.

The mountains did not own him. The caves that begged to be packed with gold were not worth more than the soul he left behind.

"I will join you in the Fields of Somber," he muttered. "Wait for me there."

Releasing her felt as though he cut off a part of himself. But he couldn't ask her to fly with him. He certainly couldn't ask her to sit astride his neck and... and...

No. He sprinted from the camp at the edge of the forest and felt his body dissolve with every step. In seconds, the man he was had disappeared.

A dragon unfurled its wings, shook its massive head, and then rose into the air. Toward the silver light of the moon and the mountains beyond.

CHAPTER 17

One week. A whole week since she'd seen that stupid idiot dragon.

She shouldn't think of him with such venom. He'd laid out a decent reason for abandoning them. The guilt still ate at her heart because she hadn't realized that she was forcing him to be something he wasn't. Lore had left her old life behind so that no one would have to feel like that, and here she was, the hypocrite.

Stomping over the fallen leaves and brush in the forest, she told herself that she was okay with him leaving. She couldn't expect to control a dragon.

Abraxas had not lied to her. He'd explained where he was going and then he'd even informed her of his reasoning. He'd done all he could do for her to be comfortable with his absence.

She was still angry.

Goliath's chuckle sliced through her tumultuous thoughts. "Are you planning to keep muttering all day, or are you going to let us help with those concerns tumbling through in that head of yours?"

Lore whipped around with a retort on her tongue. But then she saw the surrounding forest glowing with bright emerald hues and the heated words stuck in her throat. How had she missed how lovely it was here?

They'd been traveling through the forest for days. The marshes of Tenebrous long behind them, they had moved through thin barked birch trees that waved in the wind. Then they'd traipsed through an oak forest and the trunks had gotten thicker every step of the way. She hadn't noticed until now that they were in an older part of the wood. Much older.

And oh, these trees were beautiful. They glowed with the sunlight bouncing through those green leaves. Every time the wind brushed through them, light filtered through the veins and cast shadows on the forest floor. The mossy beds they walked upon had likely been here for centuries. Even the logs that had fallen in her way were dotted with pale white mushrooms perfectly crafted by nature.

The magical part of her soul stretched out its arms and sighed for the very first time in her life. Like another knot had loosened in her chest.

"There she is," Goliath said with a smirk. "Welcome back, elf."

At his side, Beauty adjusted the straps on her shoulders and grinned. "Or should we say, welcome home?"

It felt like that, even though it shouldn't. She spun around in a circle once, just looking at all the splendor and how wonderful the sights made her feel. The clean, crisp air filled her lungs, and that felt as though it were magic.

She knew it wasn't. It couldn't be. The forests in these areas weren't any more magical than any other forests. But... Well, it did feel like home.

Goliath tramped over a particularly loud bundle of fallen tree limbs before stopping in front of her and planting his fists on his hips. "So are you going to tell us what's gotten a bee stuck up that bonnet of yours?"

"Excuse me?"

"You've been stomping around like someone told you elves didn't know how to write their own names." He arched a fuzzy brow. "It's pretty obvious you're upset, Lore."

Everything upset her right now. Traveling through the forest with few supplies, Abraxas leaving, her own confusion with literally everything that was happening. She hated every minute of it and wanted nothing more than to go back to her old life. She wanted to sleep in a bed!

But that wasn't really what was upsetting her. Was it? She missed Abraxas. The damned dragon had made her feel a lot more comfortable each night just knowing he was around the campfire with them, and now he was gone.

And she hated that she missed the man who had killed her mother.

"I don't... I can't..." Angrily, she ran a hand through her hair. "I don't know what you want me to say, Goliath."

He shrugged. "The truth is a good start."

Beauty strode up to her other side and offered her another small smile. "It's not as if we have anything else to talk about. Besides, we're both aware your anger is directed at the person who is obviously not here."

Damn it, was she that easy to read? Abraxas always said he could see her thoughts on her face as clear as an open book, but she hadn't thought everyone else could as well.

She didn't want to talk about the dragon. She didn't want to talk about any of this.

Slapping a branch out of her way, she grumbled, "There's nothing to say."

"Sure seems there's a lot to talk about if you ask me," the dwarf replied. "Let's see, I found you two all curled up together on the cot like long lost lovers. Let's start there."

"We aren't lovers," she hissed.

"Well, clearly not because as soon as you realized I could see you, you took off like I'd lit your hair on fire. And then you stopped talking to him for a week. Which was rather childish, Lore. And then we ended up on this adventure where he disappears in the middle of the night." Goliath tossed his hands in the air. "It's all a rather intriguing mystery. Wouldn't you agree, Beauty?"

"I would," the traitorous human replied. "In fact, I think it's one that a long walk might be able to solve if the mystery was perhaps voiced to those who wanted to help."

They were incorrigible. She refused to believe for a second that they wanted to help more than they wanted to hear the gossip between the King Killer and the King's pet dragon.

"Like I said, there's nothing between us." Even the trees seemed to groan at her words.

Goliath snorted. "Right. I'd have to be blind not to see how he looks at you, Lore. He stares like you're the only thing that matters in this realm and he'd rip his own wings off if it meant you'd give him more attention. Come off it and just tell us."

"Fine!" she snapped, her shout echoing through the forest. A flock of birds mimicked her sound in anger and they flew off through the trees. "There's a connection between the two of us. I cannot deny it. But he killed my mother, Goliath, and a thousand of our kind before I ever met him. If I hadn't shown up, we all know he would have continued killing, and murdering, and burning everything to the ground. How am I supposed to reconcile having any sort of attachment to a monster like that?"

She hated purging her feelings. She always said too much.

Even the wind had stopped, holding its breath to hear what the dwarf had to say.

To his credit, Goliath didn't agree with her or bark at her with instructions. He watched her eyes, her movements, and he stayed eerily still while doing so. Then he took his pack off and looked at Beauty with a stern frown.

"We're staying here for the night," he informed them both. "Beauty, if you don't mind finding some sticks, I think Lore and I need to have a talk."

Beauty wasted very little time heaving her backpack off her own shoulders and then rushing off into the woods. At least she didn't question that the dwarf might be better help in this situation, although Lore could see the questions in the other woman's eyes. She'd wanted to know what was said, most likely.

When they were alone, Goliath sat on a fallen log and patted the space beside him. "Come sit."

"I'm going to stand."

"Suit yourself, but you'll want to sit after I'm done with you. I'm sure of that." He crossed his arms over his chest. "So you think you cannot be with this man because he was the weapon that brought about your mother's death? Is that it?"

"Obviously." She mimicked his posture and crossed her arms over her own chest. "Are you saying I shouldn't consider that a factor in how I feel about him?"

"I wouldn't ever say that, Lore, but I do think you need to realize that it was a war. We all did terrible things, your mother included. She knew the risk when she got involved with all of it. She likely even knew that she'd die at some point, although I'm sure she didn't think she'd die to dragon fire." He ran a hand over his beard. "But the way he looks at you? That's not a look to be ignored."

"You've got to be joking. After everything he's done. Everything you and I know about him, and you want me to forgive that?" She couldn't believe what she was hearing. Surely he didn't believe that nonsense. This wasn't the Goliath she knew, otherwise, he'd be raging that she should burn the dragon like he'd done to so many others.

"I'm not telling you to forgive him, and I'm definitely not telling you to forget. But I am telling you to give the poor man a chance for redemption." He leaned forward, staring down at his open hands as though they held some kind of secret. "I saw him holding you and I realized that man has more to him than just being a murderer. He's not just a weapon. He held you like I used to hold my Lily, and that's saying something."

She'd never heard the name before. Goliath rarely talked about his personal life, and most of the time, that was for good reason in her experience. If he didn't want to tell her about his past, then he didn't have to.

"I didn't know," she whispered. Her face burned with embarrassment. "You never... Well. You didn't have to, I suppose."

"She wasn't part of the rebellion. Didn't believe in any of it like the rest of us did. When I got involved, she told me it would get me killed."

His hands flexed, then curled into fists. "Ended up killing her instead."

Her heart broke for her friend. She could see now that he stared at his shaking hands because he knew they should hold another's hand, and they weren't. The lack of the woman he loved had given him a sense of emptiness that she wasn't so sure he had fixed yet.

"I'm sorry," she whispered. "Was it..."

He looked up at her fiercely. "Not everything is about him, you know. There were so many of us who killed. The war made monsters out of men and villains out of heroes. Mark my words, the only reason you think we're all the good guys is because we eventually won. History would have written us into terrible beasts, otherwise."

"Goliath—"

"I'm not done," he interrupted. "Now, I'm not sure I can ever forgive him for what he did to all of us, but I know the look on his face when he was holding you. I've only seen that expression on someone who genuinely cares. So don't you tell me that he's a monster or a villain, Lorelei of Silverfell. He's a man, and he doesn't deserve your judgment like that. Not when he'd tear down the stars to see you smile."

She didn't know what to say. One minute she knew she should leave Abraxas alone, the next, she still had that horrible feeling that she couldn't survive without him. All she wanted was to make up her mind, but the two sides of her soul wouldn't stop arguing in her mind.

"Lore," Goliath said. "You don't have to save him. Just give him a chance at redemption."

But how?

How was she supposed to do that when every part of her soul screamed just looking at him, for very different reasons?

She opened her mouth to ask the question, then paused. A shadow darted between the trees. For a moment, she thought perhaps Beauty spied on them, wanting to know what Goliath had to say. She wouldn't put it past the sneaky little twit. Then the shadow moved again.

Tall and lithe, it moved between the trunks with unnatural grace. That was no mortal, and if it were, then she'd eat her own tongue.

"Goliath," she said. "We're not alone."

He craned his neck to look behind him. Idiot.

"Don't look," she hissed. "Keep talking to me like I'm here. I'll go look."

"You will go nowhere without me, woman. What if that person has kidnapped Beauty? What if we're being hunted?" He reached for his pockets, where he always kept a couple of knives. Just in case.

"None of us are being hunted just yet, but I need to know who is following us. So stay where you are, keep talking, and if Beauty comes back, then you have to get her out of here. This is home, remember?" She winked at him. "The mountains are yours, but the forest is mine."

She waited until the shadow moved again before she left Goliath's side. Thankfully, the dwarf did what he was told. Goliath kept talking loudly, as if he were arguing with Lore still. That would give her the cover she needed to approach whoever thought it was smart to spy on unknown strangers in the woods.

She held her knives close to her chest, wrists loose and ready to fight if she had to. Although she hoped it wouldn't come to that. There were still a lot of creatures trying to hide in the lesser known places of the world. Perhaps this one was one of those.

She didn't hear any twigs cracking as the shadow moved. She didn't even hear birds chirping the further she got from Goliath's side. Shadows didn't move like that. She'd never seen magic like that other than the...

The Umbral Knights.

Lore pressed her back against a tree and took a single, deep inhalation. If the shadows were corporal Umbral Knights, then that meant the King was nearby. She couldn't imagine that he'd have tracked them down, but her heart still ticked an angry beat in her throat. If it were him, then she would put a knife through his heart this time. No need to slice through a jugular when she could twist metal through that evil, black heart.

With a leap, she strode out between the trees and brandished her knives. Eyes wide, she stared at the person who had followed them with more than a little horror.

"No," she whispered. "It's not possible. You're dead."

The shadow lunged for her and she knew that fighting would get her nowhere other than an early grave. So as the person tackled her and magic wrapped itself around her like chains, she let loose a single scream.

"Goliath! Run!"

CHAPTER 18

The wind rustled across the leather membranes of his wings. The holes in them didn't help, although they were almost healed now. Nothing more than memories of pain that had ached when the rebellion attacked the castle and he had to save Lore from the burning acid.

Abraxas tilted his body, angling himself so that he circled over the highest of the Stygian Peaks. If he remembered right, this was once called Umanor Esari, ancient elvish for Castle in the Clouds. He remembered it well.

Once a magnificent building had stood here. The high spires were made entirely out of a glass that blinded the closer one got to it. He had flown around it when he was a dragonling, watching the elves wave to him and then go about their business. They had worn spider silk clothing, and some had dyed the clothing pale blue. Like the deepest part of ice.

Those years had been good, long ago. He missed those times more than he cared to admit.

Abraxas stretched his neck, tilting his chin back, so the wind itched underneath the thick plates of scales that covered his throat. This was what he'd missed so desperately. The sensation of freedom and the breeze touching all parts of his body. The trust that the gales would never let him drop, no matter how they raged or stormed. He soared through the air currents with confidence and power.

He couldn't do this as a human. That mortal form was weak and small. Limited in what it could do. Sometimes, if he were being honest with himself, being a man made him feel trapped. Like he couldn't quite get enough of an inhale, no matter how much he breathed.

There was a name for that, he felt certain. Someone would tell him the obvious answer was anxiety and that he had struggled with panic attacks his entire life. But it couldn't be that.

He was a dragon.

Dragons didn't feel stress or anxiety. They were powerful. Stalwart. And he was a crimson dragon! The protector of all he deemed worthy, and that meant something. He couldn't, wouldn't, admit to such feelings.

But that twist in his gut threatened otherwise. Once again, he smelled saltwater and thought of her. Lore. She glided through his mind as though she, too, rode the currents of air. That woman... how could he describe the guilt he felt knowing that he'd left her behind?

She could be in all manner of trouble and he'd never have a warning. And knowing Lore, she had almost certainly gotten herself into trouble while he'd been gone. She didn't have it in her to not get in trouble. The elf sought it out to entertain herself. He would swear to anyone who asked.

Maybe he should go back. He didn't have to meet them at the Fields of Somber, although at these great heights, he could see the damned graves. The mortals always had to put their bodies in the strangest of places, but the Fields were born out of the last war between the creatures and the humans. The war that made the creatures bend a knee all those years ago.

It was rumored to be haunted. He'd heard many stories of magical creatures who went to visit the unmarked graves in the hopes an ancestor might hear them. They rarely returned without a story to tell.

If the King's half brother still lived there, he had no idea how the boy had survived. Considering his bloodline, the ghosts in that place should have torn him apart by now.

Glinting light in the castle caught his eye. Not because the ruins were sparkling, though there were still bits of glass and shattered windows that sparkled in the sunlight. He noticed because of how the light had a rather magical signature that surprised him. Magic shouldn't have hung around this long, even in a place like Umanor Esari.

Changing directions, Abraxas weaved through the air and then tucked his wings tight against his sides. He gracefully descended toward the castle, long tail whipping behind him to slow his pace. By the time he landed in the old courtyard, the ground didn't even shake.

His old teacher would have been proud. Abraxas had a horrible habit when he was a young dragon of landing so hard the very earth trembled. He'd thought it delightful that he could cause a mini earthquake just by touching down too heavy. The older dragon had been less than enthused by his enjoyment.

His claws clicked on the old stones as he picked his way through the rubble toward where he was certain there had been a light. Long neck craned, he tried to see around a flattened tower, but the rubble was too high.

He hated crawling on his belly. His wings weren't meant to grapple onto stones and move them out of the way, but he wasn't changing back into that other form. He was free for now, and free he would remain.

So he slithered, like a snake, over the rocks and cracked timber that had once been beams. And there, right in the center of the entire castle, he could see the floor had shattered upon some impact. That wasn't the important part, though.

The cracked floor had revealed a second hidden one underneath. And that looked like a mosaic.

Elves, he thought to himself, chuckling as he reached a wing toward one of the larger chunks that remained over the covered message. They were always so good at hiding what they didn't want others to see.

Perhaps he should head back to Lore first, but Abraxas found himself curious to know what these elves had hidden. Using his mouth and wings, he spent the entire afternoon moving rock by rock to reveal the artwork beneath the false floor.

It was ridiculous behavior for a dragon. He pawed through the rubble like a thief in broad daylight, but it felt good to use his body in a way that wasn't killing someone. He could work his muscles, his scales, and his wings for something other than death or destruction.

"There," he muttered, placing the last stone on the ground and stretching his wings wide. He'd done it. He'd managed all on his own, without having to change into his mortal form.

Now, the only thing left was to see what the devious elves had been trying to hide all this time.

Clacking over the mosaic, he started from the top, as the elves always did. They wrote their messages as if they were writing on a scroll. Top to bottom.

At the very top of the mosaic was the war between the creatures. He'd seen that coming. The elves would have been the first to realize that the mortals would enslave them. He still winced at the sight of elves with chains around their throats.

He traced a nail over one of the blonde elves, who stood unchained in defiance. Some things never changed, it seemed.

He followed the story down, frowning a bit now as a cloaked figure appeared to hold the map of Umbra in the palm of his hand. That could easily be Zander, he supposed, or Zander's father. But the sparks of magic around the map made him think perhaps this was a very specific person and not a king. The cloak covered head wore no crown.

"A warlock?" he muttered, peering closer at the obsidian chips that depicted the man. "What are you doing here? Unless you're the one involved with the King, I cannot imagine who you might be."

He'd never heard of a warlock, other than the man who had created the Umbral Knights, of course. But that hadn't been a black magic user. It had been the King's trusted magician, and that man had been dead for centuries.

Or so he thought.

Further down the mural was a very familiar sight. Lore. Or at least, a depiction of a woman like her. Standing tall above a king with a sword lifted above her head. The spirals of silver magic around her could only mean that was Lore. No other elf would have moon magic like that.

Except... Well, the mural made her seem much stronger than she was. He knew how the elves depicted power in murals. He'd seen their drawings more times than he could count. The surrounding orbs were far too many for what she had shown him thus far.

She was powerful, his elf, but not godly.

"What were you all getting at?" he muttered, moving lower down the mural.

The moment he tried to look at the bottom portion, a cloud blotted out the sky. Darkness descended over the castle and Abraxas watched as his breath puffed in frosted air. What madness was this? What magic prevented him from seeing the truth of what this soothsayer had seen?

The elves thought this important enough to memorialize forever. Now, he intended to read that message.

A figure shimmered in front of his vision. He tried to narrow his gaze upon it, in hopes of understanding what the elves had conjured. He had to know. There was something here, something about Lore that was so important he couldn't leave.

He snapped at the gleaming light that tried to cover up the mural. His teeth sliced through the vision, turning it into little more than glowing mist. It needed to move. He only had so much time before the sunlight would appear again and the darkness felt intentional. Like he had to see the last bit in the darkness or it would never make sense.

The light fluttered again. All the smoke joined together to reveal a figure that was not elf like at all. Not even remotely.

The figure before him wore the familiar form of a dwarf who had come to their side when he was necessary. Goliath's eyes were wide and his face scrunched in concentration. He held his hands in a strange symbol, fingers lifted and palms pressed together.

Abraxas had never seen dwarven magic before, and he was surprised to see how technical it was.

Though the way his face had furrowed didn't hide the worry lines around his mouth or the frantic look in his eyes.

"Abraxas?" Goliath asked. "Can you hear me?"

"I'm a little busy right now, Goliath." He peered down at the mural, then back up at the sky. The clouds had almost moved. He'd lose his chance to see the last piece.

What a hard choice.

"Is this urgent?" Abraxas asked. "I found something that I believe will be integral to our journey, but I cannot read it and listen to you at the same time. Can this wait?"

"No, it cannot." Goliath's image wavered, as though he were already losing his ability to hold on to the illusion. "I can't keep this magic up for very long. I'm not... I'm not good at it."

The choice was difficult to make, but he hoped he could return to Umanor Esari. Perhaps the magic didn't require a single use and he might see the mural again later. Given time.

"What happened?" he asked.

Goliath's image shifted as though someone had blown a wind through him. His voice warbled with the sudden gust, and all Abraxas could make out were single words. "Forest... Scream... Lore."

The last word sent shivers down his spine. The frills along the side of his head and neck lifted. "Lore? What happened to Lore?"

Damn the dwarf and his weak magic. Abraxas could see the fool talking but couldn't hear a word that he said. Letting out a growl of rage, he slashed his claws through the image as though that might help.

Surprisingly, it did. Maybe it forced Goliath to redo the spell, or maybe it cleared away any lingering power from the elves. Either way, he could hear Goliath as he screamed through the illusion.

"There was someone following us in the woods! Lore is gone."

Lore is gone.

The words repeated in his mind.

Gone? She couldn't be gone. She wasn't that foolish. If someone followed them, then Lore would have investigated. But she was a fighter. She'd even fought against Zander and nearly won. That meant she was good with weapons and hand to hand combat. Zander had almost beaten Abraxas a few times in sparring, and that should have been impossible.

"No," he muttered. "Where did she run off to?"

"She didn't!" Goliath shouted the words again, as though yelling was the only way to get it through Abraxas's head. "Whatever or whoever it was stole her, Abraxas. We have no way of finding her. We need you to come back."

But she couldn't be gone. He'd just... no. No.

Anger rose through his belly, pressing against his lips until they rose in a snarl. Fangs on full display, he fluttered his wings, spreading them wide and ready to fly. "Where?"

The dwarf rattled off information about how long they had traveled, how many days they had walked through the forest. Apparently, they had no way of knowing where they were in the woods, and that would make it very difficult for Abraxas to pinpoint where they were. The fools. They should have been more aware of where they were traveling, especially if they planned on calling a dragon to their rescue.

He growled. "I'll find her, Goliath. Stay put wherever you are. This might take a while."

He didn't tell the dwarf that if it took him longer than a few heartbeats to catch her scent in the forest, then he would burn the whole thing to the ground. Damn the ancient forest. Damn the Stygian Peaks and all who lived at its base. He cared very little for any hidden or secret creatures who called that place their home.

If a single one of them dared to touch a hair on her head, then he would roast them slowly, starting at their limbs and taking months for their death. He would rip trees from their roots, tear branches from trunks, set ablaze the entire forest until it turned from a sea of emerald to ruby.

None of them would stand between him and Lore. He would find her.

With one last scream of rage blasted into the sky, Abraxas took flight and speared through the clouds. He would find her.

He had to.

CHAPTER 19

Grit stung her eyes. They felt a little too grainy to be anything other than what gathered during sleep, but that wasn't right. The moment she shifted her head, a spike of pain bloomed on the back of her skull. As though someone had struck her with a blunt object. She was sitting upright as well, at least she thought she was.

She couldn't quite remember...

Ah. There was the memory.

She'd been in the forest and there had been a shadow following her. The darkness had lingered in the trees, but she'd seen it. She'd tried to defend her friends against the creature, but then the shadow had revealed itself to be something horrible. Something that shouldn't exist at all.

Blinking her dry eyes open, Lore sought out any details. She was in a cave; she thought. Stalactites hung from the ceiling and drips of water echoed in her ears. A single torch illuminated a figure, and she fixed her gaze on the darkness that crouched in front of her.

"Deepmonger," she growled. "Your kind is supposed to be dead."

The man braced himself with one knee on the ground. His dark skin was black as night, glistening with red streaks in the torchlight. It was a stark contrast to the white plume of hair brushed back from his face and the pale eyebrows. Icy. Cold. Matching eyes glared at her, chips of sapphire in the gaze of an abyss.

He wore clothing made from deer leather. Some of the fur still decorated the edges of his shirt, but everything on his body was surprisingly well made. The hand stitched seams rivaled what she'd seen in the castle, and the meticulous beadwork created a scaled pattern over the leather and up to his neck.

He was someone who shouldn't exist. The Ashen Deep clan of elves had long ago gone underground. As far as the other elves knew, they had all died in a horrific cave in that had taken the most talented of their blacksmiths, silversmiths, and jewelers. Of course, she knew that now to be a lie.

The Ashen Deep were still alive. They survived in the caverns underground, and they had lied to everyone for centuries.

His mouth split in a slight grin, although it wasn't a kind one at all. "And you shouldn't be in this forest. These are our lands, no one else's."

"There are no territories any longer." She spat at him, letting the wad of fluid land near his feet, though that was all she dared do. No one would outright attack a deepmonger. They were more dangerous than most.

This one appeared to be alone, however. Lore thought maybe she could fight him if she could just get her hand into her pocket where she'd kept that secret little...

Her hands didn't move.

Quickly, she glanced down to see that he had tied all her limbs to the chair that he'd placed her in. The heavy tangle of rope had been expertly knotted so she couldn't wiggle out of her bonds.

The deepmonger snapped his fingers, forcing her attention back to him. "What are you doing in my forest, elf?"

"I'm traveling through it with my companions. We're heading to the Fields of Somber." She didn't want to tell him anything, but recognized she had little choice in the matter. He'd make her talk if he wanted to know the truth.

"Ah." He nodded, then gave her a look that said he thought she was lying. "You're making a pilgrimage to seek your ancestors. Is that what you want me to believe? I've heard it before."

"What reason would I have to lie?"

"You're tied to a chair in an unknown place with a ghost talking to you. What reason don't you have to lie?"

Touché. She forgot what it was like dealing with others of her kind. They always had something to say in response, always some kind of retort or smartass remark. Was this what it felt like to deal with herself?

Huffing out a breath, she twisted her wrists in the restraints. "Why don't you take these off me and I'll tell you the whole truth?"

"I'm not taking anything off of you until you give me a reason why one of the last Silverfell elves thought it was smart to walk through Ashen Deep territory." He tilted his head to the side, and she saw the smooth coif of his hair didn't hide his ears at all. They were abnormally long, pointed at the ends just like her own.

Her ears had never been that long, and that should have been enough for him to realize that she wasn't entirely an elf. Perhaps he hadn't noticed yet, although that seemed unlikely.

"You don't get out much, do you?" she asked.

His eyes widened, revealing that no, he didn't. He hadn't left this cave in years, she would guess, and that meant he didn't know Silverfell elves had long ears, too. He could have taken one look at her and realized who or what she was.

This deepmonger thought he was sneaky enough to hide from her. Too bad. She planned to walk all over him now.

"That has nothing to do with my question," he snarled.

"It has everything to do with it. I'm not talking to someone who has no power among your people. Clearly, I am here for a reason, and that is not one I'm willing to share. Go get someone who has a little more knowledge of the world, deepmonger. I will not speak with you."

Lore tried very hard to sound like she was older than she was. If he thought he was being lectured by an elder, then he might be more likely to leap up to his feet.

He stood. She saw the initial reaction flash across his features, the same response she would have given to being scolded by someone much older than her. They were taught from a young age not to question those with more knowledge than themselves.

But then he stopped himself. Muscles bunching and gathering underneath all that glistening skin, he glared at her with something akin to hatred in his eyes. "It is my task to understand why you are here. Not anyone else's."

"I will only say this one more time. I will not talk to you." What she needed was to figure out a way out of these bindings.

Lore twisted her wrists, trying to find a weakness, but the man knew

200

what he was doing. He'd tied her up better than most and frustrated her to no end.

"You can struggle all you like, but you won't free yourself from the ropes," he said.

"You can't know that unless you try," she muttered. Twisting this way and that didn't help, however. "One hand, then. We'll make a deal. You release one of my hands and I'll tell you everything."

He narrowed his gaze, perhaps to try to figure out if she was planning on tricking him. She was, of course, but Lore tried not to let that show across her features. She needed to get at least a single limb free. Then she could grab onto the grimdag she still had strapped to her thigh.

Though, the blade had been suspiciously quiet now that they were in the caverns. She had no idea what that meant.

"Fine," the deepmonger snarled. He strode up to her side and sliced through the cords holding onto her wrist. "If you try something, I will kill you."

"I'm not going to try anything," she muttered. "You have trust issues. Has anyone ever told you that?"

The second he looked away from her, she reached for the blade. It would only take two heartbeats, and then her fingers wrapped around the hilt. She would draw the sharp edge through the cord entangling her other wrist. Then she would lunge for him. She could grab onto him after releasing her legs. All it would take was a single nick to his skin and his soul would flee his physical form.

The grimdag remained quiet. Silent. Not a word, even as she touched it, which should have been her first warning.

Almost in a blur, the deepmonger spun on her. His hand grabbed onto her wrist, stilling the blade against her thigh. He stared down at the black metal, then looked back up at her with a horrified expression.

"Where did you get that?" he hissed.

Lore's mouth dropped open. She had no idea how he'd moved so fast, or how he had caught the dagger before she could even lift it. But now she was stuck. She couldn't lie to him. She couldn't tell him the truth because he'd never let her out of this cave.

The sudden realization of her impending doom rendered her speechless.

His fingers tightened on her hand, squeezing until her bones creaked. She couldn't hold on to the grimdag any longer, and so she had to let it drop to the stone floor with a clatter.

He took his time. The damned deepmonger wanted her to watch him pick up the instrument that could lead to her death. He leisurely lifted it, holding it with very little care. Almost as though he didn't worry that it might take his soul.

He spun it around and held the blade to her throat. "I don't enjoy repeating myself, Silverfell."

"My name is Lorelei." She tried to appeal to any of his emotions. Let him pity her, connect with another elf, something. Anything that would get him to remove that damned blade from her pulse.

"I don't care," he snarled.

The grimdag pressed against her skin until even a swallow would make it slice through her neck. That was when she heard the traitorous weapon once again.

"I always knew I would feast on your soul," it whispered. "Now the time has come to pay."

"Please don't," she begged the deepmonger. "I don't want to die like this. At least let me die fighting."

He twisted the blade just slightly, though it was enough room to let her swallow. "Talk faster, Silverfell. The dagger wants to feast."

She opened her mouth and let all the information spill out. She told him why they were going to the Fields of Somber. She told him everything about the war so that he would at least understand that it was a desperate need that drove them. Lore didn't know if any of this was getting through to the terrible being in front of her, but it didn't matter. At least her soul would be purged for when her death met her.

Though, she'd admit, she had expected him to grow angry. Instead, his eyes widened further and further before he pressed the blade against her neck again. "You aren't lying to me?"

"No," she croaked.

He looked more than a little conflicted. At least that would benefit her. She had made him pity her, and that was a good start.

What she didn't expect was for him to cut through the ties around her wrist and legs, then gesture with the knife. "Stand up."

"Why?" She remained still.

"I'm not going to kill you," he snapped. "But you need to speak with the Matriarch. If all you say is true, then this is something she needs to know. This is beyond me."

Why was he so nervous suddenly? He held the grimdag up in front of him like a shield, but eyed her as though she'd told him she was a saint. She hadn't seen any visions or made any journeys as elven prophets tended to have. But he almost seemed as though he... knew her?

She stood, holding her hands up so he wouldn't attack her. "Lead the way."

"You first." He jerked his head to the right, down into the darkness of the cavern. "Pick up the torch and walk down that tunnel. I'll tell you when to stop."

That had to mean they were close to the entrance then? Perhaps the Ashen Deep clan lived deeper in the earth, but they only brought people to interrogate here. The closer to the surface she was, the more likely she could return and find her way out.

Lorelei steeled herself for whatever would come next. She leaned down, picked up the torch, and turned to face the dark tunnel.

The sharp point of the knife pressed against her spine. "Walk forward, at a normal pace. If you run, I will throw this dagger through your back. Don't think it's likely that I'll miss, either. I'm not interested in playing games with you."

"Point taken." She bit out the reply with a significant amount of acid in her tone.

Lorelei strode through the cavern for a while before she realized the stone underneath her feet had flattened into a smooth polish. And then they walked through a small opening and into what certainly couldn't be real.

The mirrored floor reflected the long columns holding up the ceiling. They were impossibly high. So tall that the light from her torch never reached their tips. They lurked around her in blackened, dark forms. A hundred columns, perhaps, all in neat rows that went on forever to her right, left, and ahead.

"What is this place?" she asked, and her voice echoed through the grand hall.

"Home."

"You live here?" She couldn't imagine living in such a malignant place. All the smooth, mirrored edges were beautiful, yes, but they weren't welcoming or kind. The light from the torch bounced off the columns and made it seem like a hundred people followed them.

"Many of us live here." He reached forward and grabbed her arm, dragging her with him now that they were out of the cavern. "Your kind had forgotten us very quickly. We did not argue when others questioned whether we were alive. The Ashen Deep faded so that we would be ready when the time came."

She shook her head in confusion. "Time came? What are you talking about?"

He didn't answer, and for once, she was glad he didn't.

Lore heard the whispers long before she saw the podiums. The stands were made like the surrounding columns, although much smaller and arranged in a circle. Each podium had a flat top that housed a single glass case. Within those cases were more grimdags than she had ever hoped to see in her life.

A few remained empty, and that was where the deepmonger led her. He hesitated only briefly before he lifted the nearest case and put the grimdag inside it. She swore that some of the other daggers screamed before he dropped the lid back down. It sealed with a burning light around the edges before it faded.

"There," he muttered. "Back where you belong."

"Why are you keeping them like that?" The hairs on her arms raised with the blast of sudden magic he'd used. "I didn't think... Or, I didn't know..."

Another voice interrupted her. Feminine and roughened, as though she'd spent years screaming. "You know why, little mongrel. And you should not be here."

CHAPTER 20

He'd never flown so hard in his life. His wings ached with every flap, but it didn't matter. He would fly himself into the ground if it meant he caught her fast enough. His heart thundered in his chest with the fear that he'd lost her. All because he was the fool who'd left.

Abraxas knew he should have suffered through the mental anguish. The physical form of a man wasn't so bad that he was incapable of surviving it, and she needed him to stay in that form for a time. For at least long enough so that he could help her free her people.

She'd needed him to help her, and selfishly he'd told her no.

The wind whistled in his ears and he swore he heard it mocking him. He hadn't been the person she needed, and that would forever be the story of Abraxas the Crimson Dragon.

Never enough.

He caught her scent a half day's flight from the castle. It was faint, but it was there. He soared through the forest, trying to find the right place where she must have hidden. Or where someone might have dragged her away. But he couldn't pinpoint the exact spot where he'd smelled her. So he did the only thing he could think of.

He changed back.

Abraxas let the scales and muscles ripple away from him as though he were a snake shedding his skin. He plummeted through the air at the tops of the trees, grabbing onto branches even as they smacked his more fragile form. Baring his teeth in a snarl, he endured the pain until he landed on the ground with a harsh slap.

Wounds would heal, but finding his woman couldn't wait.

He straightened, lifting his nose and trying to scent her. Dragons weren't as good at tracking as werewolves, but any animal that had to track its prey would know how to use smell. And dragons were efficient hunters.

Where was she?

She'd stood about ten paces from him recently. The brine and salt of her hair still lingered, almost as though it clung to the bark of the tree. Had she touched it?

That was it, he realized. She'd leaned against this tree and her hair had tangled in the bark. There were still a few pale blonde strands clinging onto the trunk as though she'd left him a trail of breadcrumbs to follow.

He wrapped the strand around his thumb, staring down at his only lifeline. "Good girl," he muttered. "Now, where did you run off to?"

Snapping branches behind him had him whirling. Abraxas lifted his fists, ready to break through whatever or whoever stood between him and Lorelei. The roar in his chest should have terrified whomever dared to provoke the dragon.

But it was not an enemy. Instead, Beauty stepped out of the brush with her hands raised. "Just me, I'm afraid. You've got quite the nose on you to have tracked her here."

He did not care what a mortal girl thought of his ability to track. What he wanted to know was why they were both still standing here when they could be figuring out where Lorelei was.

"Where is she?" he snarled.

"If I knew, don't you think I'd be going after her? We don't know where that thing in the forest took her, Abraxas. We thought you might be able to help with that."

Beauty kept her hands lifted in the air. Perhaps she didn't trust him not to lose his mind just yet, and that was a smart choice on her part. He didn't feel quite himself. Usually, this form would dampen the needs of the dragon, at least a little. He found it easier to concentrate on smaller things when he was in this mortal body. Apparently, that was no longer the truth.

The mere thought of Lorelei being in pain or being hunted made him want to scratch out his eyes. He paced in front of Beauty like a caged animal, his feet drawing him away from the tree and then back into a wall of her scent that only worsened his anger.

"What have you done to track her?" he snarled. "Tell me everything that happened."

"We don't know. Goliath was back at camp with her when she said she saw a shadow moving in the forest. She told him to keep talking, so it sounded like they were still unaware that someone was watching them. Then she went into the woods. Goliath said he heard nothing after that until she screamed his name and shouted at him to run."

Abraxas squeezed his eyes shut. She wouldn't have told the others to run if there wasn't serious danger. What could live in this forest that would make a woman like her afraid?

He thought of stone giants. Creatures who pulled their roots up from the earth and reached for her with gnarled hands. But no, none of those monsters had survived the last war. They'd all died out, and he would know if any of them had remained.

Those were not the monsters he had to worry about in the forest. They did not linger in the shadows.

"What else?" he snarled.

Beauty's eyes widened as though she had nothing else to tell him, but realized how dangerous that could be. "Um..." she stuttered. "Goliath then said we'd need you to help find Lorelei, because neither of us are very good at tracking. He had a bit of dwarf magic that he remembered how to use, so he used that to contact you. Then we waited until you got here."

"I told him not to wait for me," Abraxas snarled. "I told him to find her. That I would search as well."

"Then what led you here?" she asked, her voice pitched low so she wouldn't anger him any further.

"What do you think, Beauty? I didn't come here for you." The growled words snapped through the air like a whip and she took a visible step back from him, her eyes squeezed shut in pain.

He wanted to be kind to this woman who had earned such honor.

The snarling, growling monster in front of her was not who she deserved to see. He should be an honorable man for her, and all he had managed to be was a loyal dog to Lorelei.

"I'm sorry," he muttered, waving a hand in the air as if dashing away his previous words. "That was callous of me and I should never have spoken to you in such a way. This is... Not easy for me."

"Do you think it's easy for me?" she asked, her eyes wide with unshed tears. "She's my friend too, you know."

The bushes rustled and Goliath stepped out of them with a ridiculous amount of twigs in his hair. "If the both of you would stop arguing for a few minutes, we could talk about how we plan on finding her."

Abraxas stiffened at the tone, but realized that the dwarf was right. They were stuck in this forest with little help if they couldn't work together. The dwarf had already admitted neither he nor the human were good at tracking, but Abraxas would find himself very limited if he tried to search with them. He needed their eyes, their ears, and everything that they could tell him from the ground, while he soared through the air.

"I can smell her," he informed the dwarf. "But not from the air. I can search from the skies, but the forest is very thick. I wouldn't be able to see her even if I tried very hard to, so there has to be another way for all of us to hunt for her together."

"Take a breath, friend." The dwarf then had the audacity to sit down on a fallen log and pop his chin onto a fist. "If we think about this, perhaps we can figure out what we're up against. That should tell us where to look first."

He had thought his anger was under control. He felt bad for snapping at Beauty, and the young woman still appeared wounded by his words. The dragon did not have a talent for fine words, not when he had to think like a man to find the woman he...

The words faded from his mind and fury took its place. A bright heat flushed through his face and he snarled, "Sit? You want us to sit when she could be out there dying?"

"Rushing into any circumstance doesn't help anyone involved," Goliath replied.

"I'm not going to stand around here and wait for you to make a decision when there is an entire forest to search before nightfall." Abraxas turned to march away, so he didn't char the dwarf into a tasty snack.

Beauty's voice stopped him in his tracks as she shouted, "The rebellion is more important than her life, Abraxas!" And when he glared at her with fire in his eyes, she gulped and added, "So are your dragon eggs."

Oh, those were foolish words to say to him. She was just a child, he reminded himself. So young compared to him and Lore and even that dwarf, he'd imagine. Beauty had no idea that she'd told a dragon that he could not collect an item from his hoard. That he couldn't search for the treasure that had been taken from him.

His feet moved before he could stop himself. Hissing like a serpent, he approached her until their noses almost touched.

She was brave, this one. Beauty didn't back down from him this time. Instead, she glared back at him with the same amount of venom.

She'd fear him soon enough.

He opened his mouth, the low growl echoing from his throat, one of an ancient beast. "Let me make this very clear. If you lose her, then you lose me. Make no mistake, child, I am only here because of her. I care for two things in life. Those eggs. And that woman."

The silence between them grew tense and strained. She tried to hold his gaze, but she'd never be able to summon a similar rage to the one that burned inside him. She had never lost someone like Lore.

Goliath heaved a sigh and hopped off his log. "You think you can do this alone?"

"I do," Abraxas replied, never breaking his glare with Beauty.

"Do it, then." Goliath stood just outside his field of vision, so close to Abraxas that he could feel the wind tunneling between their arms. "You think you can find her without us, then find her. You think you can get those eggs without us? Then do it. But I think we're very aware that you need help right now. I understand dragons are prideful, but damn it, I didn't know they were morons as well."

The words at least burst a bubble of clarity in Abraxas's head. He needed these two people to help him find Lore. And if he wasn't so frantic, then he might see their use a little easier.

He took a long, stuttering inhale to calm himself, then glanced to the side at the dwarf. "It's like I can hear her screaming in my head. She's begging me to find her, and I don't know where she is."

"Then you shouldn't have left in the first place, my friend." Goliath took the risk and patted him on the shoulder. "We'll find her, though. Together. That's what friends are for. Now stand down, dragon. Take a deep breath and perhaps we will find out what attacked her. Eh?"

A deep breath. He could do that.

Abraxas sucked in air through his nose and then released it out of his mouth. Another. Deeper this time. The dwarf was right. He couldn't tear the world down for her and find her at the same time. He needed to calm down.

Finally, he could breathe again. He could focus on something other than the rage running through his very soul, and that was when he smelled it.

"What is that?" he muttered, turning his head and sniffing the air. "That's... Not possible."

"What isn't possible?" Goliath asked.

Abraxas tried very hard not to be distracted by the way Beauty sagged as he turned away from her. He'd feel guilty about that later, long after he figured out what made that brimstone smell.

No, it wasn't brimstone. He approached the tree again, but the scent wasn't quite where Lore had stood. It lingered, though. Like smoke and ash and... mold?

He tilted his head to the side, shaking it slightly at the impossible thought that burst to life in his mind. "It cannot be."

"I've come to realize a great many things are beyond my reach and knowledge. What do you smell?" Goliath stood beside him, hands on his hips and glaring at the shadows. "I thought for a moment it was the King but... I suppose I still have enough hope that it's not."

"It wasn't Zander," he muttered, stomping through the forest and trailing after that illusive scent. "Zander always smelled like alcohol and sweat."

Beauty let out a little snort and started after them. "Maybe that's why none of the women liked him very much."

"I think there were more reasons than that." Abraxas paused and looked down at the dirt. There were long lines in the earth, deep furrows where someone had clutched the mossy ground.

She'd been dragged away from here. Someone had grabbed onto Lore's legs and dragged her away from the camp.

He bared his teeth once again, crouching down to trace the lines with his fingertips. "Dwarf, I assume you are not so incompetent that you don't know where we are. Even just an idea of it?"

Goliath took off his pack and set it on the ground. From within the recesses of the leather, he yanked out a map and brandished it before him. "We're here," he said, pointing to the base of the Stygian Peaks. "The Fields of Somber are but a day's walk."

Oh, Abraxas could wring this little fool's neck. His hands shook as he reached out and turned the map counter clockwise in the dwarf's grip. Then he tapped it, forcing himself not to plunge a finger through the vellum. "Do you see a forest on that side of the Stygian Peaks? We're in the Gloaming, you fool."

Even Goliath's hands shook. "We're... what? No, that's not possible."

"You read the map wrong and you brought her into the Gloaming?" He stood and could no longer control his voice. In a thunderous rage, he shouted, "You brought a Silverfell elf into the Gloaming! You idiot!"

Goliath shook so hard he rattled the vellum and he looked for all the world like he'd accidentally murdered Lorelei. He certainly could have.

"Why's that a bad thing?" Beauty asked, her own voice shaking.

Save him from the idiocy of young mortals and even younger dwarves. Abraxas pinched his nose and replied as calmly as he could. "The Ashen Deep rule these woods. They were no friend to Silverfell elves." He let his hands drop and met Beauty's worried stare. "And they kill half elves on sight."

CHAPTER 21

S he knew she was in deep trouble when more elves stepped out of the shadows. Lore noted that these elves were dressed much nicer than the one who'd brought her in here.

The dark woman who glared at Lore, clearly their leader, wore a dress made of spider silk. It clung to her curves, large holes in the sides revealing smooth skin that glistened while she walked. The long tangle of her pale hair mimicked the material and weaved through the spider silk until it was almost impossible to tell where her locks began and where the dress ended.

She moved with a lithe grace. Predatory, almost. The mere sight of her made a shiver dance down Lore's spine as every hair on her body stood. She knew when she was in danger of dying, and this woman wouldn't hesitate to kill her.

Swallowing hard, she glanced over at the grimdags. If she could break through a glass case, then she could grab one, and might survive this ordeal.

"Don't even look at them," the woman said, her voice carrying through the darkness like a clap of thunder. "They are not for you."

"None of this is for me, now is it?" She shouldn't argue. Lore told herself time and time again that provoking the angry woman was a terrible idea. But her mouth ran away from her control. "You've all been hidden for a long time, Matriarch. I assume that's what I'm meant to call you?"

"You will call me nothing. You will not speak unless you are spoken to." She stepped closer into the light and Lore saw that her eyes were completely white.

No colors. No iris. Nothing but a blank wash of pale that moved in the socket. She'd never seen eyes like that before, but she knew what they suggested.

The Matriarch was blind. And yet, somehow, the woman could still see.

Lore took a step away, but the deepmonger put his hand on her back. Stopping her from moving with a twist of his wrist. The cold press of a real knife rested against the base of her spine. It wasn't a killing blow. But it would make it so that she'd never walk again if he sank the sharpened tip into her skin.

Right. She wasn't supposed to speak, to exist, to live. Not right now, at least.

She gulped again and nodded at the Matriarch. She learned quick, hopefully that would give her a few more seconds to live.

The Matriarch glided across the floor to the grimdags. Her mission was obvious. The grimdag Lorelei had held for almost a month now still pulsed in the glowing chamber, as though it wanted attention. The Matriarch tapped her fingers on the glass and tilted her head to the side, listening to what the knife had to say.

Could they speak of what they'd done? Lore had never thought to ask the blade any questions other than if it could kill Umbral Knights. She hadn't wanted to hear the extent of its dark deeds.

Now she found herself curious. Just what would it have to say? Would it have whispered that the Ashen Deep clan was still alive, and that she should fear them? Or would it tell her that there was something wrong in the forest long before the deepmonger had attacked her?

No. Grimdags weren't helpful, nor were they supposed to be. They tore and ripped at the world and others so that they could devour souls and condemn them to a life of purgatory. That was the sole purpose of their existence.

Lore squared her shoulders, narrowed her eyes, and watched the Matriarch trace patterns on the glass. She didn't let her eyes flick over the other three deepmongers who had walked out of the shadows with her. Those three men were even larger than the one behind her. The twists of their braids hugged tight to their heads, and the blackened leather armor they wore radiated with dark magic.

The Matriarch diverted her attention from the glass and narrowed her eyes on Lorelei. "You are here because you think you can change the very fabric of time?"

"I know that I can." The words flew out of her mouth before she could stop them. "But like I told your friend behind me, I am here only to pay my respects to those who live within the Fields of Somber."

It wasn't technically a lie. No one lived in the Fields, other than the King's half brother. But many people would confuse her words with someone who wanted to speak with their ancestors.

Lore should have known she couldn't trick this woman. The Matriarch was smarter than that.

The other woman scoffed. "You lie worse than you fight, half blood."

Surprisingly, the man behind her stiffened. The blade pressed more dangerously against her spine as he leaned around her to ask. "Half blood?"

Were they related? Lore didn't know any other reason the Matriarch would measure such a censoring look upon him. Her disappointment in the young man behind her was evident.

Lore flicked her gaze to the other three men and noticed they all wore expressions of either humor or frustration as well. And come to think of it, they all looked alike. Each one of them had the same nose, very similar mouths, and a matching scowl that could blister the skin right off of a person's hide.

Strange. She'd thought there would be more deepmongers, but now she wondered if it were just this family left.

She drew her attention back to the Matriarch, who hissed, "Look at her ears, Draven. How did you miss something so obvious?"

Lore could hear him swallow behind her and then felt the burn of his gaze on her exposed ears. "I thought Silverfell elves were... lacking in that quality."

"No elf is lacking unless their blood has been ruined by the touch of a mortal." The Matriarch slashed her hand through the air. "Her blood is tainted."

"My mother didn't have a choice in the matter." She refused to let anyone speak ill of the woman who had done whatever she could with what she was given. Lore lifted her chin and glared at the Matriarch. "But you wouldn't understand that, now would you? Instead of going to the camps with the others, instead of being shuffled into a mold covered ruin of a city where mortal men looked at you with hunger in their eyes, you lingered here in the shadows. Hiding while the rest of your kin bore the brunt of the punishment."

She shouldn't know any of that. Not really. Her mother had told her too much of the time before, when the elves had flourished, and then Lore had been curious about why the time of the elves had ended. The truth of their history was worse than any nightmare or story her mind could have conjured. They had suffered.

The deepmongers hadn't.

Even the Matriarch's hatred flickered for a moment at Lore's outburst. One would have to be completely heartless to not understand that Lore had been a product of unwilling partners and an unlikely pair, who had never tried to see each other again.

But her father was from an old family. Her mother hadn't wanted to fall out of grace. They'd tried for the sake of the child and then everything had fallen apart. Her father had run. Her mother had died. And Lore had been on her own for far too long.

She tried not to look at the others. At the men who now pitied her while they still thought she was less than them.

Half elf.

Half human.

Neither of those species wanted her.

She'd come to terms with it long ago, but that acceptance didn't make this any easier. At least the knife at her back slid away from her skin. The deepmonger behind her had more of a heart than his mother.

And she was certain the Matriarch was his mother now.

The other woman at least had the decency to soften her tone. "We did not hide. We endured the darkness and the rot so that someone would still be alive when all this came to an end. And yet here you are. A half blood who thinks she can fulfill an ancient prophecy. As though the elves of old would have ever whispered about someone like you."

She had no idea what the woman was talking about.

Nor did she care. A flame of anger licked her throat and Lore spat, "I don't care about prophecies, and I don't believe in them. The ravings of a mad elf twisted into some fanatical belief have no effect on my life or the choices I make. I do what is right and what our people need. Nothing more, nothing less."

The deepmonger made a sound of clear disbelief. They obviously were all caught up on some prophecy that an Ashen Deep seer had muttered centuries ago.

He leaned forward and muttered in her ear, "Mother will never believe that."

"I knew she was your mother," she hissed back. "But I've seen more impressive visions smoking elfweed than any of your prophets, so let's get things straight. Whatever they saw in a drug induced haze? Those prophecies mean nothing other than the strain was good."

"Silence." The Matriarch shouted. "Whether you believe in prophecies or not, I will not have you mucking up the future with your very existence. We will keep you here until all the cards are revealed."

Keep her here?

"What?" Lore looked around them, trying to find a way out. "No, you can't do that. You have to understand, the King is still alive. He wants to murder everyone like us, and we've pissed him off enough to try. So you cannot think to keep me here when I might be of some help to the—"

"Rebellion?" the Matriarch finished for her, interrupting Lore's spurt of words. "Yes, the grimdag told me all about that. You believe that you can stop the spin of the world, little girl? But you must understand that everything happens for a reason and if you are so dead set on changing it, then the world will fight back against you. You'll stay with us."

A single nod at her captor was the only other response Lore got. The three men stepped forward to help, and all four grabbed onto her arms with the speed of the wind. They dragged her down the mirrored halls, ignoring every shout she let fly.

"Stop! Listen to me. This is the wrong thing to do. I can't stay here. I have to help them, and if I don't, then something horrible might happen to all the other elves."

None of them were listening to her. She focused her attention on the youngest, the one who had found her in the first place.

"You don't want to do this. I'm just like you, don't you see? You couldn't even tell my ears were too short. I swear, I'm not doing anything other than trying to save our people. And they are our people. Don't let anyone tell you otherwise."

He kept his gaze ahead, refusing to look at her. "Stop talking, halfbreed."

"I'm not going to stop talking, just like I won't stop trying to save those of us who are left. Did you know there's an entire world out there that you haven't seen? A world full of magical creatures who have been struggling to survive. We could change that."

Damn it, she sounded like her mother. She tried planting her feet against the floor to stop them, but they just lifted her up so high her feet didn't touch the ground.

How they could see anything in such bitter darkness made little sense to her. She couldn't even see them any longer. They seemed to disappear until they threw her across the floor and she landed hard on her hands and knees. The ground was still smooth, and at least she'd come up against a wall.

Holding her hands out, Lorelei was horrified to realize she couldn't even see her palms. They were going to leave her in complete darkness.

She stumbled back the way she'd fallen, striking her knee against something that felt like a cot and her arm against something hanging from the ceiling. She kept lurching forward until she struck the bars of the cell. And of course they'd put her in a cell. Of course, they had locked her up.

"You can't leave me here!" she screamed. Her voice echoed, mocking her fear. "I can't see!"

No one responded. She couldn't even hear the sounds of their footsteps as they walked away.

Lore had no idea how long she sat in that cell. There was no way to tell how much time had passed. She counted the sounds of dripping water on the floor until she forgot the numbers. She waved her hand in front of her face whenever the darkness grew too deep, but that didn't help. The shadows seemed to cling to her face. She could see nothing. Her mind wandered through memories and then made shapes in the shadows. She saw people, monsters, even a dragon. All of it couldn't be real, but Lore had a difficult time convincing herself otherwise.

Madness crept into the corners of her mind. It whispered that many people had succumbed to this horrible experience. Others had tried to survive the dungeons of the Ashen Deep and they had failed.

She recognized the voice when she was most lucid. It was the same voice of the grimdag who had wanted her to kill. To destroy. It didn't care who it feasted upon, but now apparently it wanted her soul.

There was no winning in this situation. No way to crawl out of the darkness toward some semblance of light.

Moonlight.

Lore took a deep breath and settled herself. She remembered now that she was a Silverfell elf, and the moon lived inside her skin. She didn't have to hide herself or her magic any longer. And though there was only a small amount of moon magic in her, she could use it to beat the darkness into submission.

From then on, whenever the darkness threatened to overwhelm her, she lifted a hand and let the moon glow from her skin. Just a bit. Only a pale glow, so she wouldn't go mad.

And then, one day, a plume of light approached her. It burned her eyes to look at, but she couldn't refuse the feast it presented. She stumbled toward the bars and gripped them, watching as the copper flame merrily danced in the hands of a very familiar man.

Lore would not beg.

She would not bend so far as to plead with a deepmonger.

Lorelei bared her teeth in a snarl that would have made Abraxas proud. "Hello, Draven. What are you doing here?"

He ignored her question, and instead, he placed a plate full of food and the candle in his hand on the floor. He then crossed his legs and sat down just out of reach. "What do you mean there's a whole world out there that I don't know?"

Oh, that feral grin spread wider on her face. She knew it did.

But the young man had no idea he'd already bent to her will. Now she would make him break.

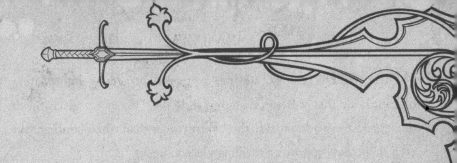

CHAPTER 22

Lore had never thought she'd be in a dungeon staring at a deepmonger who wanted something from her. The Ashen Deep weren't even supposed to be alive. Yet, they appeared to be thriving in the darkness, away from all other elves.

Here she was. Watching this young man and hoping he knew what he asked of her was impossible. But also hoping that he never realized just how much she was going to get out of this interaction.

"Excuse me?" she asked, still a little unsure she'd heard him right.

"You said there was another world out there while we were dragging you down here. I need to know if you were telling the truth." He nudged the plate closer to her. "It's been almost a day since we've brought you down here. You must be hungry."

"Are you trying to bribe me with food?"

"Maybe." He grinned, and the expression turned his intimidating face into one that was surprisingly handsome. "I've never given much thought to the world outside this cavern, other than when hunting. But even then, the forest isn't a thrilling place to be."

She shouldn't smile at him. She shouldn't do anything other than glare at this young man. He'd dragged her down here with his brothers. He'd been the one to lock her up into the darkness for who knows how long. He claimed it had only been a day, but she swore it was a week.

"We call it the Gloaming," she muttered while still staring at the food. "The forest is dangerous and dark. Apparently, we were traveling through the wrong place. My companions and I weren't even supposed to end up here. I wasn't lying when I said we were headed to the Fields of Somber."

That was the last time she'd give Goliath the map, that was for sure. He'd been confident in his skills to direct them where they all needed to go. Obviously, the dwarf had overestimated his abilities.

"The Gloaming." Draven tasted out the word on his tongue, head tilted. "I like it."

"I'm glad," she replied, although she wasn't so sure how honest the words were. It wasn't as though she wanted to be here, and she didn't want to create any kind of relationship with this young man.

But if he could get her out of the dungeon, then she had to try. He'd need to admire her more than his mother did, that much she was certain of. And if that required that she tell him more about where she was from, then Lore could do that.

Her only chance was to beguile him, as Beauty might say. That would be more than a little difficult. They were so different. His people thought half breeds like herself were less than human. Not even good enough to be a mortal, and definitely not good enough to be an elf.

It would be pure luck if she could get this young man to pay her any mind at all, but she supposed she had to try.

Lore shifted so her hair covered the points of her shorter ears and then gestured to the food he'd laid out. "Is that for me, then?"

"If you answer some of my questions. Yes."

She wasn't sure how useful her answers would be. Although, she knew that the deepmonger before her wanted to know about the world above. The world he'd never been allowed to see. It was her choice to tell him the good or the bad.

Lore gave him a nod and hoped that would be enough.

He gestured toward the food on the other side of her bars. "Take some, then. Whatever you desire, it is yours."

She eyed the meal then, surveying what he'd thought to bring her. The strawberries were rather shriveled and small. They were clearly from a garden that didn't see the sun as often as it needed to. And then the bread looked like it had been baked a few days ago, perhaps the best he could get from the kitchens without someone noticing that there was food missing. The jug farthest from her was filled with crystal clear water.

The latter made her dry throat ache. She'd give anything for a taste of cool water.

Reaching her arm through the bars, Lore hesitantly ghosted her fingers over the food before she grasped the jug's handle.

Like a snake, his hand darted out and grabbed onto her. He wrapped his fingers around her wrist, his grip too tight to wiggle free from. Of course, he wouldn't let her take something she needed that easily. They were elves. She knew better.

But instead of cutting through her wrist like she'd expected, he turned her fingers over in his grasp. Carefully, he traced the lines of her palm with the very tips of his fingers.

"These hands don't look any different from mine," he muttered. He stared intently at the white moons of her nails and the dirt underneath them. "My mother would have me believe you are only a common animal. Chattel to be used as we see fit."

"Many share that opinion," Lore ground out through her teeth. She didn't yank her hand away from him, even though she wished to.

"So you said."

"I have known little else from the elves. Half breeds like myself are never to be loved, befriended, or even touched." She curled her fingers into fists. "There are some elven clans who would cut off the hand that touched me, you know."

He looked up at her then, eyes wide with what didn't look like fear, but amusement. "Do you think my mother would cut off my hands for touching you?"

Damn it. He didn't have to look so handsome when he was breaking elven law. There was a certain levity about him that was rather contagious. His brilliant smile lit up the darkness, even in the slightest amounts.

"I think your mother follows the old ways, and the thought of her son touching me would make her blood boil. If she doesn't cut off your hand, then she will cut off mine."

He tilted his head to the side, narrowing his eyes. Worse, he tightened his grip on her. Just enough so that she could feel he had no intent of letting her go any time soon. "I've already touched you, half breed. When I brought you through the caverns. Even my brothers have touched you."

She looked at the way their hands were joined, how he still traced the lifeline of her palm. "You know this isn't the same."

Her skin burned where he'd lingered. She shouldn't have let him touch her at all. The thought of Abraxas seeing this moment made her stomach turn. But then again, he'd had to seduce the hag for their cause. Was this any different?

If this deepmonger asked for more from her, more of her flesh, in return for freedom... What would she do? Would she deny him when it was her only means of escape?

She would.

Lore's soul revolted against the mere thought of anyone touching her like that. Abraxas was the only man who set her heart on fire and this deepmonger would have to do better than seduction if he wanted the truth out of her.

Twisting her wrist, she flipped her hand and grabbed the handle of the jug. Quickly, she snatched the water back into her cell.

But she was a woman of her word first. She set the jug down next to her, no matter how great a temptation it was, and then gave him a single nod. "Ask your question, deepmonger. In return, I will take a drink."

He lifted his brows and withdrew his hands. "Bravo. I didn't know you could move that fast."

"Your question."

"Ah, I suppose I asked for such curtness. You claimed that the world out there is different from here. Tell me how."

She supposed that was easy enough to answer, although it would take a long time. They both had nothing but time in this dungeon, however.

Lore saluted him with the jug of water and drank deeply of the cool liquid. She gulped until her throat was coated with fluid, so she could better tell him everything he desired. And when she finished, she wiped her mouth on the back of her arm and then began.

Telling him about Tenebrous was easy enough. The muck and the mire painted a picture of tragedy and terror. It didn't take much to convince him that her homeland was grim and that the elves there lived in squalor. She laid on the circumstances a little thick, perhaps, but she didn't exaggerate the atrocities the King had committed. Or the crimes that her people had endured for centuries.

"Why stay?" he asked when she finished. "It sounds like a prison more than it does a home."

"Where else is there for us to go?" She laughed, but the sound held no mirth.

"Anywhere!" He lifted his hands into the air and gestured all around them. "There is an entire kingdom to hide in. Just as the Ashen Deep have done for so many years."

Sweet, innocent thing. "There is nowhere mortals do not rule any longer, Draven. We are fighting every day to the death, hoping they might understand we are people. But elves are little more than pretty baubles to them. We work, make elegant clothing, dress them in jewels that were meant for our ancestors so they won't hunt us in our sleep. And if we're found on the streets by those who lead, then we will be killed on the spot."

His eyes widened with every word she said. It was terrifying, she'd admit. The life the elves had to live was one of hardship and discomfort. But he needed to know just how horrible it was out there for them. He had to understand why she needed to help their people.

He'd quieted. Draven's expression warped into something contemplative but also sad. "Are there other clans of elves out there? If the Silverfell elves won't come to your aid, then there must be someone else out there who wants to help."

That was enough questions answered for a snack, at the very least. She reached for the loaf of bread. Carefully, slowly, she ripped off the smallest piece so she wouldn't shove the entire thing in her mouth.

It took her a while to answer as she chewed the sliver of bread until it was little more than mush. "The clans don't have any say any longer. They are only myths these days. Perhaps some use the clan names as an excuse to hate each other, but the old days are long gone. The elves do not have power. We haven't for a very long time."

He leaned away from her, wincing at the mere thought. And yes, it was a horrible, downright awful way to live. None of the elves wanted to admit how hard it was for them. Perhaps because the other magical creatures had it even worse. At least the elves could hide in plain sight.

He took a deep breath and shoved the last bit of the food in her direction. "It seems to me that you are in the unique situation of understanding the elves more than my people. You have been denied your right as an elf, and now you understand that the rest of the elves have been denied their rights to be a person."

"You'd think that would give me some satisfaction," she muttered, grabbing the rest of the food.

"Does it?" he asked, his eyes dark and wide.

She thought about the question, mulling it over in her mind. Did it? Did it make her happy to know that the other elves were suffering exactly as they'd made her suffer for such a long time?

"No," she replied. "It doesn't."

He stood and dusted off his backside, then bent down to pick up the tray he'd left behind. "You've given me much to think about. I did not realize how little I understood about the world. Or perhaps how much those details would interest me."

She'd done something wrong. He didn't want to help her escape at all, but at least she'd gotten food out of it. Lorelei gestured at him with the bread in her hands. "Thanks for filling my belly."

"Thank you for the interesting conversation." Draven bent his head in an almost bow. "You are not what my mother claimed you to be."

"I take that as a compliment."

He winked, and that bright grin flashed in the shadows again. "It was meant as one."

CHAPTER 23

Following Lore's scent proved more difficult than he'd thought. The Ashen Deep had a talent for slipping through the world unseen. They snuck through the shadows and air; it seemed. But he was a dragon and no one would stand in his way.

Five days. That's how long it took him, and his heart stuttered in his chest the entire journey. He was certain that he'd be too late. That they would find the hovel of those monsters and discover her dead.

Yet, there was no way for any of them to know if they had made it in time. He stood in the forest with Beauty and Goliath, staring at the opening that sliced through the earth.

"It doesn't look like a cave," Goliath muttered as he scratched his beard. "Looks like someone took a knife and wiggled it around."

"Someone?" Beauty repeated with a soft snort. "You mean a giant, surely."

That's exactly how the crack in the ground appeared. Abraxas knew magical environments well, and the Ashen Deep were notorious for cutting through the earth to get into their underground lairs. At least, they had been. Long ago.

He tilted his head back, annoyed that his hair had gotten in his way, and took another steadying breath. Moss, rot, and that horrible scent of mildew permeated the surrounding air. This was the right place.

"It's here," he muttered. "That's where they've taken her."

All three of them had hidden as best they could. Goliath had it easiest. He'd ducked alongside a bush. Beauty had her back pressed against a tree, her hands wrapped around the hilt of a wicked-looking blade. The long sword could cleave the head off a man, although he wasn't sure she'd want to.

They were not the team he'd hoped to bring. Though he considered them good people, they were untested as far as battle. He didn't want to lose anyone because he was foolish enough to throw them into the waiting spikes of deepmonger blades.

Looking over at his companions again, his chest tightened at the thought of losing them. They were... dear to him. More than he wanted to admit. He couldn't see them leave when they were so new to his life. He rarely had the opportunity or the luxury of calling anyone friends. He couldn't risk them like this, not when he knew no one measured up to the Ashen Deep.

Abraxas found he didn't want to let that luxury go.

"I'll get her," he grumbled. "You two will stay here. I'm not interested in a battle today."

Goliath's hands tightened around the knives in his hands. "We can take them. You don't have to worry about us, dragon. We've fought worse."

They hadn't. No one had fought the Ashen Deep since the last major war between the magical creatures and the mortals. He remembered the last devastating battle when the Ashen Deep had destroyed an entire army on their own. Only fifteen of those talented warriors had killed hundreds. And then they had told the other elves that they would not continue to live like this. They would retreat, and the other elves were on their own. It was the beginning of the end.

He had hoped... Well. There was no hope left for any of them without the Ashen Deep.

"You have never fought warriors like this, dwarf." He quirked a brow. "Although I have no doubt you would frighten them, I find myself growing impatient once again. They will answer to me for taking what is mine."

He couldn't give them any time to argue.

Abraxas let the magic swell throughout his body. His bones broke and his flesh tore. The dragon ripped his body apart again, though it was too soon since the last time he'd changed. It hurt worse. It always hurt worse the second time.

With a snarl, he unfurled his wings and allowed them to stretch through the trees. Two of the smaller oaks fell as his sides pressed against them and flattened the trunks to the mossy undergrowth. It wasn't enough, but it would let the Ashen Deep know he was here.

Though they were talented warriors and skilled in many kinds of magic, he didn't worry about them fighting him. After all, very few creatures in this realm could harm a dragon.

"Abraxas!" Beauty shouted. "We can do this without death!"

No.

They couldn't.

He lunged toward the sliced opening in the ground and stretched out his neck to peer into it. A single warrior hid in the shadows, cloaked in magic that should have made him impossible to see. But a dragon's slitted eye saw through almost every spell.

He could only imagine what the man had seen. The warrior's eyes bulged. Likely he'd been under the impression there were no dragons left. Abraxas assumed that was the rumor among their kind, considering the dragons hadn't fought in the wars, nor were there many of them left at that point.

With a rather evil grin, he dropped his jaw open and let the fires of his chest spill out. He watched as those terrible flames licked at the ground. The deepmonger barely had time to run, with the fires licking at his heels. Abraxas exhaled again. He let heat pour from his chest, spilling through the earth and tearing at everything that stood in its way.

He would burn this entire forest down if they didn't give her to him.

Over and over again, for long breaths and long minutes, he burned their home. He knew the flames would seek out all they could. The air grew hot around him already. The earth had boiled at the top of the tunnel that led into their homes. The moss crisped with heat. Soon, all the deepmongers would sweat in their hovels. The cool air they so loved would sear their lungs and lack the oxygen they needed.

He could do this for days if they wanted to test his might. But he already knew there was movement in those mice holes. Whoever was the ruler of the Ashen Deep wouldn't allow him to kill everyone just to keep her prize.

Ah, yes, there it was. The earth farther out at the edge of the forest crumbled. It shifted and roiled like something living underneath it. There was something living beneath that earth, though it likely was a foolish amount of elves who thought they could fight a dragon.

Abraxas let the flames die out of his chest and patiently waited for the deepmongers to arrive. They crawled out of the pit they'd created. The extra tunnel likely existed only for escapes like this. Three women, six men. All just as he remembered the Ashen Deep. Dark with sparks of white hair and streaks of pale brows.

The woman in the front clearly ruled the others. She held out her hand for them to pause behind her and glared at him with hatred. "Dragon," she spat.

Oh, it pleased him to know even she was surprised. The Matriarch couldn't hide the widening of her eyes or the horror on her face. She had thought all the dragons were dead, and that was the first mistake they made. He was not dead, and he would take back what was his.

"You have something of mine," he snarled. "I will take it back."

"We have stolen nothing of the sort." The Matriarch, for she must be the Matriarch, strode toward him as though she weren't afraid to be boiled alive in her own skin. "My men and women do not steal from above. If one of them did, then I assure you, we will happily give back your gold."

"Gold," he repeated, letting the word drip from his tongue. "You think I desire gold?"

"Your kind is rather fond of it. Is it not? I assume if you are here darkening our doorstep, then you lost a piece of your treasure." She took a deep breath, and he could smell the fear on her exhalation. "Whatever treasure one of my children took, I will return it with more in fold. Perhaps we have something in our collection you might desire more."

They thought he was little more than some mountain dragon whose hoard had been disturbed. Was that what others assumed of dragons in the end of times? Had they felt his people to be animals that only cared about what foolish trinket they could find next?

The thought angered him almost as much as losing Lore.

He reared back, arching his neck imperiously over her head. "Think, Matriarch." At her startled flinch, he grinned wide enough to show all his teeth. "Yes, I recognize your position. I met your great-great grandmother long ago, and trust me when I say this, she was far more terrifying than you could ever hope to be. Now I need you to consider what you might have stolen from me."

Her thoughts spun over her mind, and Abraxas heard Goliath hiss out a low breath.

They were taking too long. Abraxas had taunted the elves for more time than his companions were comfortable with. They wanted to get Lore and leave this cursed forest.

So did he. But first, he would make sure that the Ashen Deep never touched what was his again.

The Matriarch licked her lips. "There was a wanderer in these woods. She brought with her an artifact of my people. If it is the knife you speak of, then I'm afraid that is the one treasure we cannot part with."

Was it so far from this woman's mind to realize that he might want Lore? Not the knife?

"I care little for baubles of magic," he snarled. "Perhaps you should consider the wanderer instead. The woman your warrior attacked without honor and then dragged deep into the darkness. She is mine. And I will have her back."

Silence rang through the clearing. Far too powerful and filled with hatred.

When the Matriarch spoke, it was with more venom than even a green dragon could spit. "You want that mongrel?" the Matriarch hissed. "That half breed who fouls the line of elves?"

"Careful what you say about her," he snarled in response. "I would sooner burn you alive than I would allow you to insult her again."

"Fine, then I will only speak the truth." The Matriarch pointed at him with a long fingered nail. "That barren abomination will never give you what you want. She should not exist, and now that she does, the entire world may fall at her feet. You play with things you cannot know, dragon. The prophecies have always been very clear. No half breed shall ever lead us into the light."

He should have argued. He should have burned her where she stood and then sent Goliath into the darkness to find Lore.

But he waited, because he knew that was what Lore would want him to do. She'd want him to give these people a chance because no matter how much they hated her, no matter how many of their bitter words filled the air, Lore would give them the opportunity to prove themselves.

With one more glare, the Matriarch snapped her fingers and one of the young men stepped forward. "Bring the girl," she snarled. "Throw her to the dragon and let us hope that he feasts upon her bones."

He'd never been more shocked in his life.

It worked.

He watched the young deepmonger disappear back into the darkness before baring his teeth at the Matriarch once again. "If he brings her out to be dead, then I will burn your home to ash. And the rest of your clan will earn their namesake."

"We've already earned our namesake, dragon. Many times over." She waved an imperious hand in the air. "We have no fear of death in this house."

Save him from the dramatics of elves.

Abraxas kept his throat burning with flames that licked between his teeth and escaped out his nose. At least, he did until they brought out Lore.

She was covered in dirt and grime, and wore an expression on her face of pure hatred. But she was alive. They hadn't killed her, a small miracle considering what he knew about their kind and how they viewed people like Lore.

The young man held his arm around her waist and a knife to her throat. The grimdag screamed revenge, but Abraxas knew they wouldn't kill her. Not while so many of them were out of their tunnels.

The Matriarch lifted her hand, and the grimdag stopped screaming. "We'll give her back to you, dragon. But before we toss this barren mongrel at your feet, you will promise us to leave this place. I don't care how you leave. I don't care what reasoning you give yourself. But if you step foot in this forest again, I will have not just her head, but your own."

He'd like to see her try. There wasn't a chance in the world that she'd kill him, but he would give her ego that small boost.

"You have my word," he snarled. "Now let her go."

The young man hesitated only for a moment before he threw her out of his arms. Lore hardly stumbled. She launched herself into movement, racing across the bubbling ground as though it didn't even burn her feet.

Maybe it didn't. All he knew was that she was safe, and she had survived and he had saved her in time.

The dragon form melted away from him faster than it ever had before. By the time Lore had reached him, Abraxas wrapped his arms around her waist and yanked her against his body.

He ran a hand down her back, the other frantically touching whatever he could to make sure she was well. That she was alive.

"You're okay?" he whispered into her hair, still stroking the length of her spine to that dip in her waist that he adored. "They didn't hurt you?"

"I'm fine," she said against his throat. "I'm fine. Why did you come for me? I could have... I would have..."

Lore couldn't finish the sentence and he knew it was because even she didn't believe the words. She wouldn't have survived, not in the way that she thought. But he'd come for her and that meant everything would be all right.

He would make sure of it.

Abraxas caught the gaze of the Matriarch, the last of the Ashen Deep, as they returned to their horrible secret hovel.

"You owe me a debt, dragon," she called across the clearing. "If I see you, that dwarf or mortal, or any other of your companions, I will drink wine from your skulls."

CHAPTER 24

H ad she heard him right?

Lore was certain that she had heard the Matriarch correctly. Yet she could only hope that Abraxas wasn't so mad to agree to what the woman had said.

He owed her a debt. The Matriarch. The Ashen Deep always collected their debts, and he knew such a thing. Abraxas was no fool. He'd lived longer than she had and that could only mean that he understood the implications of what the Matriarch had yelled to him.

Had he even said anything in return? She could only hope the answer was no. He shouldn't have said a word when that dastardly creature flung her terms for returning Lore to him. Although she had little chance to ask Abraxas.

He rushed her toward the bushes where she noted Goliath and

Beauty were hiding. They didn't get the time to have any sort of reunion before Abraxas grabbed all of them by the shoulders and threw them forward.

"If you thought we were moving fast before," he snarled, "you are about to be very surprised."

And she was. She hated that he was right because all of a sudden, they were sprinting through the forest with Abraxas's deep voice shouting after them.

Move faster.

Watch that log.

Beauty, if you keep slowing down, I will carry you.

His words rang in her ears and Lore heard the thudding footsteps of Ashen Deep racing after them. She could almost feel their power and hear the whispers of the grimdags as they were hunted. The deepmongers would ensure that the trespassers left their forest.

Now she understood why so few ever tried to cross through the Gloaming. And how so many people went missing and never came back when they stepped past the treeline.

It took them a very long time to race through the undergrowth and out into the marshes they'd originally walked through. Lore's lungs ached, but her body was thrilled with the sprint through the trees. Her very soul screamed that such activity was exactly what they were meant to be doing. She deserved to dash through the forests and feel the cool air running its tendrils through her hair.

She stumbled to a stop on the road that led toward Tenebrous, although the city was at least half a day's walk away. Lore fisted her hands on her hips and dragged in slower, much deeper breaths. Goliath ended up on his hands and knees on the ground. His breathing sounded just as ragged as Beauty's, who had bent at the waist and gagged.

"Never again," the dwarf wheezed.

"Never," Beauty agreed, shaking her head and spitting out a wad of phlegm. "That was terrible. And now we have even longer to go. Maybe we should get horses."

"No horses," Abraxas snapped from behind them. He strode toward them while looking as though he'd only taken a leisurely stroll. "The lot of you need to be tougher than this if you want to fight the King."

He had no right to insult her friends like that.

Lore whirled around, still breathing hard and slick with sweat. "We managed the first time, didn't we?"

"With another person's army behind you and no. You didn't succeed." He tapped her chin with a finger. "This time, you have me on your side. Which means that we will kill the bastard, but I refuse to make any more mistakes than necessary. We're going to work on your lungs."

She jerked her head away from his touch. "Oh, that's rich coming from you. The dragon who made a debt with the Matriarch of the Ashen Deep. Did you really think I wouldn't hear that part?"

"I had hoped you were so pleased to see me that you would faint into my arms and not realize what she said." He crossed those arms firmly over his chest. "Of course I knew you'd hear, Lore. But I had to get you out of there somehow, and I wasn't about to start burning their home again when they'd given us a chance to leave."

"You should have done exactly that! Now we don't know what they're going to ask you to do." She pointed at his face, knowing that he hated it when she did that, but not knowing what else to do. "You just got out of that situation. Where someone ordered you around because you owed them a debt. Why are you so willing to jump back into the exact same circumstance?"

"Don't you accuse me of that."

She took a step closer to him, anger burning so hot in her chest that she couldn't breathe. "That's exactly what I'm doing. I refuse to allow you to make such foolish mistakes again. It's like you don't know how to take care of yourself!"

"Ah!" he scoffed. "You're going to tell me that when you're the one who ran off into the woods after a deepmonger and then thought she would get out of their dungeon on her own? Oh yes, I'm certain you were locked up in there. They wouldn't let a half breed out of their sight."

She flinched at the word. He had to know how much she hated the term and yet, here he was. Using it like it didn't matter what he said to her any longer.

She hissed out a long breath and dropped her hand. "Heard that part, did you?"

"I heard all of it." Something flickered in his gaze. She really hoped it wasn't pity.

She swallowed hard and glanced away from him. "Then I should at least admit that they didn't lie. It's all true. I'll own up to that."

The truth specifically surrounded that one word the Matriarch liked throwing around when it came to Lore.

Barren.

That was what they said about half breeds, at least. It was why a lot of her kind ended up in brothels. She'd never heard of a half elf ever spawning children. The magic of the elves might not completely desert them, but it certainly didn't let them procreate.

All that anger in him just... stopped. He froze. Chest heaving, the fury drained from his body. Instead, he looked at her with that heated expression she hated and loved at the same time.

Goliath cleared his throat. "Beauty and I have decided to set up camp a little way down the road here. I think you two need some time alone. Yeah?"

Her gaze hardly even flicked in his direction. They could roll out the bed rolls. She trusted them to do that much. It didn't matter if they wanted to start walking toward the Fields of Somber again. She would catch up to the two of them.

Her eyes were locked on the dragon, who looked like his entire world had shattered in front of him. Just because she was barren? He couldn't have thought they would ever have children together if he wanted to be with her. After all, elves didn't lay eggs.

It wasn't that, then. She didn't know why he was so crestfallen on her behalf. But she needed him to stop looking at her like that or she'd also fall apart at the seams and they couldn't do that. She couldn't do that.

"Abraxas," she muttered. "Stop looking at me like I'm broken."

"They made you feel like you were broken," he rasped. "They put you in that dungeon and they reminded you just how little the other elves respect you."

Was it hot all of a sudden? Lore poked a hand underneath the collar of her shirt and muttered, "I'm going to find a fairly clear pool of water to clean off. You can come with me if you want to keep talking about this, but I might not reply."

She turned away from him and made no plans to turn back. He could stand there looking like a love struck idiot if he wanted to, but she couldn't handle this. Not when all those old emotions bubbled up to the surface.

The Ashen Deep weren't correct in the way they viewed the world.

They saw everyone who wasn't a pureblooded elf as a problem and a detriment to the bloodline of elves. They spent years of their lives convincing others that their way of thinking was the only way of thinking. It had worked, too. Even the Silverfell elves hadn't liked her when they first met her. They'd thought her mother was dirty, even though it hadn't been her choice to have a child.

Once her mother died, everyone had turned away from her. The clan of elves who should have supported her eventually died out. And all others were even less likely to put up with a begging half breed.

Her feet sank into the muck of the marshes and Lore let out a sound of disgust. "Gross," she muttered, shaking a foot and slogging through the wet weeds until she found a spot deep enough to at least dunk her clothing into.

She reeked, and that only made her feel less like an elf. Elves didn't sweat. They were perfect creatures through and through. Their long run would have slightly winded a real elf. Like Abraxas. But her? She had too much mortal in her.

Reaching behind her head, Lore whipped her shirt off. The thin undershirt beneath it clung to her chest, slick with sweat and hugging tight to the gaunt lines of her ribs.

She angrily dunked the cloth into the water, muttering the entire time about elves and their foolish ways. They didn't make her any less of a person because they all shared an opinion that she wasn't a real elf. She was angry at herself for letting them get under her skin.

"Lore."

"Please don't," she snapped. "The last thing I want from you is to hear more arguments. I don't have it in me to fight anymore, Abraxas. Just leave me alone."

But he wouldn't leave her alone. The damned dragon refused to relent to any of her requests, no matter how much she wanted him to.

Large hands clamped down on her shoulders, gently lifting her up from the bog and into his arms. He didn't spin her around. He must have known she wouldn't want him to see her face, because the iron bands of his forearms wrapped around her chest and belly. He pressed her back to his chest and held her close to his warmth.

"I thought I lost you," he murmured in her ear, his grip tightening. "I smelled that deepmonger on the wind and I thought they would have your head rather than keep you in a dungeon. I don't know how I can explain that feeling to you, Lore."

She'd felt it before. The moment those acid balls had rained in through the Great Hall, she'd known what it would feel like to lose him, and she hated the feeling. Hated that she'd fallen so deeply underneath this dragon's spell.

"We can't feel like this," she whispered. "I was fine. The deepmongers seem to be more than we originally thought."

His chin touched the top of her head. "Tell me."

"The Matriarch's son took care of me in the prison. She wanted me to be in the dark, alone, perhaps to see if my mind would crack and the work would be done for them. But I still had some magic left." She lifted a hand, noting how mortal her skin looked now. "I used it all up, and then he came to visit with a candle and a question about the world above. I think he's curious. If he was given the chance, he'd likely leave that underground realm and join us above."

"It would be a start." His hand splayed over her ribs, thumb gently stroking the overheated skin there. "You said they put you in a dungeon?"

"Dark. That's all I remember about it. There wasn't anyone else in there with me, if that's what you were planning on asking. I shouted for hours. No one responded."

"They'd have put charms on the cells, anyway. Old magic would force prisoners to think they were alone in the dark. It's a dangerous game to play, but I don't think they mind overly much if their prisoner goes mad while under their watch." His hand tightened against her ribs and again he muttered, "I thought I'd lost you."

She felt the relief melting through his body. His shoulders eased, his breathing slowed, he even swayed slightly from side to side, as though they were dancing.

Lore licked her lips and stared out over the marsh. Fireflies had woken to dance over the cat tails. "Would it really be all that bad? You'd be free from all this. You could do whatever you wanted."

"It would be a nightmare to lose you." His head tilted and she felt the heat of his lips against the side of her head. "I'd be alone. Again."

A shuddering breath rocked through her entire body.

Goliath had been right. She was part of the dragon's hoard now, whether she wanted to be or not. Abraxas would stop at nothing to keep her around him, and that had nothing to do with how he felt about her.

A dragon collected things. People. Precious items that might only be valuable to the dragon himself. And knowing that they might never collect those eggs had only made his attachment to her stronger.

It meant she couldn't ever trust his feelings for her. He would forever war between his emotions and his need to put her in a cave somewhere and never let her see the light of day.

Sighing, she ran her fingers over his arm. "You're the only reason the rebellion is still standing, Abraxas. If you don't fight, then we lose."

He stiffened again. Slightly, but enough for her to notice. "If you die,

Lore, then I will not step foot in that castle. The rebellion's cause is not one that I care overly much about. I've seen this happen before, long ago, and I'm certain that I will see it happen again in my lifetime. Mortals and magical creatures have always fought each other for power."

A spike of anxiety struck her in the chest so hard she felt as though someone had stabbed her. "Don't say that. You can't put that on me. Don't make it sound like all their lives rest on my shoulders if I don't keep you entertained."

"You don't have to entertain me. You just have to stay alive."

He said it so matter-of-factly. Like it was an easy thing to do in this day and age.

"No." She wrestled herself out of his arms, stumbling into the muck and mire of the swamp. Spinning around on him in anger. "You are so important to this cause, Abraxas. You can't do this for me and you can't say that you're only here because of me. Putting all that pressure on my shoulders is... is..."

He arched a brow. "Like saying the only reason the rebellion could succeed is because of my loyalty?"

"That's not fair," she growled.

"Isn't it? You're doing the same thing to me, Lore. You're putting the entire fate of the rebellion on my shoulders and whether or not I stay here with you. We're both villains." He pointed to her feet. "You're going to soak your boots and then tomorrow's journey will be hell for you. I'm taking the map this time. Otherwise, Goliath will turn us all around again. You really picked a winner, inviting that one to come along with us."

He stomped away from her, but Lore felt like her heart had left with him. That man had no right to turn this around on her. No right!

She spun and kicked the water, launching a clod of dirt ten paces away from herself.

CHAPTER 25

Abraxas made certain they were going in the right way this time. He kept the map in that stupid pack of his and grumbled constantly about his own foolishness for not noticing that they'd gone in the wrong direction.

He'd flown over them! He should have looked back and seen that they were walking toward the Gloaming, but he'd been so focused on flying and reveling in the luxury of being a dragon. Abraxas had shirked his duties and then bad things had happened. He wouldn't make that mistake again.

Of course, that also meant that the others were ready to tie rocks to the bottom of his boots and sink him into the marsh.

Beauty jumped over a deep puddle and huffed out an angry breath. "We can't keep walking all day, Abraxas. You know the water will blister our feet. We have to stop eventually. This pace is too brutal."

And then it sounded like she muttered something about her thighs chafing, but he refused to ask what that meant.

Here was as good a place as any to stop for the night, he supposed. There wasn't a suitable resting spot in any of the marshes they'd traveled through. And yes, Goliath had been an idiot bringing them through a forest when there was no forest on the map between Tenebrous and the Fields of Somber.

Abraxas still hadn't talked to the dwarf, although tonight might as well be as good as any. He watched as Lore dragged a log toward a relatively dry place and Beauty gathered an armful of sticks.

"You don't have to gather those," he mumbled, then took what she held.

"We need a fire. Some of us lack flames that burn inside our chests." She looked like she was about to topple over, poor thing.

He patted her shoulder and then shoved her toward the log Lore had set down. "A dragon flame doesn't need any tinder, and I assure you, it is just as warm as the fire you could build otherwise."

Abraxas had been reluctant to light such a flame. They were difficult to put out and when they were in the forest, such a fire could get out of hand. Now that they were in the bogs, he could only imagine the flame would summon creatures who wanted to fight.

But tonight, his weary companions needed something to entertain them. Something to keep them going.

A minor risk would be worth the reward of their happiness.

"Sit down," he told them all. "Warm your bones and I will get us food for the night."

"There's nothing to eat in the bogs," Goliath grumbled, but he still sat down with the two women. "We've been hunting for many evenings now, and not a single thing has poked its head out of those cursed cat tails."

Abraxas spat out a ball of flames into his palms. He held the tiny sprite tightly, working it in his hands as though it were clay that needed to be rolled. Then he set it down on the bed of tinder that it would appreciate but would devour quickly. "You stay here," he muttered. "Keep them warm until I get back."

When he glanced over his shoulder, all three of his companions were staring at the fire sprite with jaws dropped open. Perhaps none of them had heard of dragon magic before.

Good, he enjoyed surprising them.

With a single wink directed at Lore, he melted into the shadows and set off to hunt. Goliath was right. There were few animals that survived in the bogs, and most of the ones that were here weren't edible. He'd not eat a lizard. It didn't matter how hungry he was.

They'd walked by what smelled like a burrow of rabbits and that would satisfy the others. It took him a while to track them down again, and they were so spread out he had significant difficulty getting his hands on them. But he managed by blowing more fire into their warrens and then digging them up after they'd roasted.

Abraxas couldn't decide if this would have been easier as a dragon or more difficult. Either way, he was grumpy by the time he'd made it back to the camp with four rabbits. One for each of them.

"Here," he grumbled, thrusting them out for someone to take. "Dinner."

Maybe it had all been worth it for the expression on Lore's face. Her eyes widened, and he swore he saw her throat work in a swallow as she salivated.

"Rabbit?" she asked, taking them from him and handing the others off to their companions.

"What else would they be?" He shouldn't be so rude. "Swamp rabbit. I can't promise they'll taste as good as what you're used to, but they ought to keep us going for another day."

He hadn't finished the sentence before they had all dug into their respective dinners. Goliath ate like an animal, not caring that meat was stuck in his beard or that there was a bone hanging from his bottom lip. Beauty and Lore at least were a little more delicate, although they ate with a startling speed he hadn't expected from the two women.

Abraxas needed less food than the rest of them. He would feast in his dragon form when he was ready, but most serpents could go a longer amount of time without eating. So he meandered, finding another log to put on the opposite side of the fire, then picked at his rabbit as delicately as possible.

He gnawed each bone white and glistening, then he'd flick it to the fire sprite. The ball of flame eagerly gobbled up anything that was given to it, part of the reason he liked them so much. He always knew whatever he put in those flames would disappear. He didn't have to worry about someone else finding it.

Finally, the others devoured enough to satisfy their rumbling bellies. Goliath sank onto the ground with his back against the log, picking through his beard for any morsels he might have dropped into the tangled mass.

Looking over all their satisfied expressions and the relaxation that had come over them, he was left with his own sense of peace. He'd done something good in hunting those rabbits. He'd made his companions happier, healthier. And therefore, they would be more prepared to fight or defend themselves if necessary.

He didn't know what to call the warm feeling fluttering in his chest, but it pleased him all the same.

"Bravo, dragon," Goliath said after cleaning himself. He balanced laced fingers atop his belly and let his head rest back against the log. "Warm fire. Full bellies. What else could a person want?"

"A bed," Beauty replied without hesitation. "A down bed with fluffy pillows and cool air blowing in from the window. You wouldn't happen to have a couple of those out there in the marsh, would you, Abraxas?"

He almost bristled at the words, but recognized the teasing in her tone. She appreciated his effort too, even though it felt as though everyone was ribbing him.

Maybe this was what it meant to have friends. They teased, he took their teasing, and then fired it right back. Unfortunately, he had little experience with these kinds of interactions. So instead, he shook his head and smiled.

"Easy there," Lore replied. "You keep saying things like that and I'll start believing the rumors of the elderman's daughter who likes the finer things in life."

"I do." Beauty laid down on the log, taking up the space behind Goliath until their heads nearly touched. "I very much enjoy luxury. You would too if you grew up with goose down and gold."

"I always knew you were the spoiled one. Out of all the other brides, you appeared to be the one who really hated getting dirty." Lore grinned at the jab, and Abraxas watched as they went at it.

Their words were hurtful and yet clearly meant with loving intent. He didn't quite understand it, but he'd admit it was entertaining to watch them grow more and more escalated with their barbed tongues.

"Oh sure," Beauty sat up with a triumphant expression. "You're the elf who is convinced that elfweed saves every situation when, honestly, it's illegal for a reason."

"Said by someone who has never smoked elfweed."

That last bit roused Goliath enough for him to harrumph and add, "She's right on that. If you'd ever smoked elfweed, then you wouldn't be saying that. The stuff is divine."

Beauty pressed a hand to her chest. "I'm offended you'd offer! I don't touch illegal substances."

"Maybe you should," Goliath snickered.

The three of them were so comfortable with each other. Even when they appeared angry.

Goliath and Beauty touched each other with an ease that spoke of a friendship years in the making. He didn't mind it when she scratched his head without asking, and she didn't mind when he leaned against her leg to stare into the fire. They were adorable. Kind to each other.

Even Lore didn't mind sitting so close to them and her eyes didn't linger on their movements. She was at peace. Completely at ease without worrying about what they would think of her.

He wished he knew how to do that. Abraxas couldn't remember the last time he'd had a friend, let alone someone he could trust as they did each other. Dragons were solitary or loyal to one other. Not... like this.

Lore's gaze met his over the sprite's merry flame. "You all right, Abraxas?"

Were his thoughts so obvious? He nodded and ran a hand over his head. "I'm fine. Just thinking about tomorrow. We should reach the Fields by then."

"Ah." She crossed her legs and leaned back on her hands, the picture of grace in the middle of this horrible swamp. "Have you ever been to the Fields?"

He didn't want to reply. Everyone knew of them, of course. But at this point, he'd heard so many stories that he didn't have the faintest idea of what to expect.

He shifted closer to the fire, knowing the glow would cast his angular features into harsh shadows. "Should I expect ghosts?"

The other two stilled and looked over at Lore as though expecting a terrifying story to start. The elf refused to give them what they were hoping for. She tilted her head back and let out a short, barking laugh. "No, thankfully. I haven't ever seen a ghost there. Most of those stories are old wives' tales."

Beauty groaned with disappointment. "Come on, you could have at least lied to us."

"Do you want me to tell you there are spirits walking those lands?" Lore frowned. "Although, I suppose there are the wights. We will all need to figure out a way around them because no one wants to fight the wights. Trust me."

That sounded worrisome. Abraxas asked, "Wights?"

"The living dead," Lore replied. Then rolled her eyes when Goliath made an "oo" sound. "Oh stop it. You know they're real, and they're just as dangerous as the legends claim. Keep your dwarf mouth shut."

Goliath hooked a thumb back at her while grinning at Abraxas. "Lore here is petrified of the wights. She says they eat people if they can catch them."

"They do!" she exclaimed.

Oh, his poor little elf. He didn't think he'd ever see the day where she was frightened of something, but here they were. She couldn't even think of the wights without a shudder moving her shoulders.

The dwarf saw his reaction. The other man waved a greasy hand at him. "Look at that, right there. Lorelei of Silverfell, you have a dragon tailing you like a lost puppy. Do you believe a wight will try to attack you with him standing behind you?"

"I don't expect a wight to be smart enough to care about what it's attacking," she grumbled, shoulders lifting to her chin. "I think they fight whatever is living around them, hoping they can feast on mortal flesh and regrow it on their own shambling bodies."

She wouldn't sleep a wink if she kept talking like that.

Abraxas chuckled and lifted an arm, making a space underneath it for her. "Come here, elf. I'll keep you safe from wights tonight."

It was the first time he'd been so outwardly affectionate toward her, at least around others. Their companions held their breath and stared at Lore with wide eyes. Beauty kept flicking her gaze between the two of them. Waiting for the fairytale moment to happen.

Lore blinked a few times, her gaze never straying from his lifted arm. "What do you want?"

"Come here," he repeated, lifting his arm even higher. "We all need to rest tonight. Without nightmares, about half dead men stumbling after you."

Now it was time for her jaw to loosen, dropping in shock.

Sure, he knew it was a little surprising to see that he'd come around this far. But if she left him hanging, he wasn't sure what he'd do. Or if he'd survive it. The embarrassment of having her deny him in front of her companions would send him to an early grave. He knew it was hard to kill a dragon, but this sure seemed like a great way to do it.

Goliath grunted. "Oh, Lore. Would you just get over there? If you don't take the offer, I will."

His elf scrambled to her feet and rushed around the fire to slam down on the log beside him. Gone was the grace he'd equated to her moments ago in his mind. She looked rather stunned as he dropped his arm over her shoulders and tucked her against his side.

Poor thing didn't know how to process this. But he noted how she eased up to him, her muscles becoming liquid as she remembered that a dragon could keep her safe.

"Goliath," he started. "I overheard that you worked with Margaret for a long time. Why don't you tell me about her? I'll admit, I don't trust her."

He talked with the other man long enough to feel Lore relax completely against his side. And Beauty very quickly succumbed to staring into the flames with a rather lax expression on her face until her eyes drifted shut.

Finally, he grinned at Goliath. "I think that's a job well done for the two of us, wouldn't you agree?"

"And here I was thinking the two of them would never stop talking." The dwarf lifted his arms over his head and yawned. "Keep that one safe overnight for me, will you? She's rather special."

Abraxas glanced down at her head on his chest and shifted her until he knew her neck wouldn't be sore in the morning. "That she is. Quite special indeed."

CHAPTER 26

The fog surrounding the Fields of Somber weaved through her legs. Lore knew it wasn't natural. No mist did that without someone commanding it.

Although, knowing the history of this place, she could only assume the person directing said vapor was already dead. It merely continued its master's bidding. The thick mist lingered over unmarked graves, weaving through the headstones and pooling over the burial sites. Graves, she could only hope, that would stay the final resting place for their inhabitants.

Her mother had told her about the wights when she was very little. A group of elves had decided to visit the Fields, hoping their ancestors would tell them how to battle the mortals. Lore would never forget her mother's sneer and how she'd spoken to the others about creatures made of rotting flesh and rattling bones that would tear their hair from their scalps.

She shook herself out of such horrible thoughts. They were here for a reason, and now they had finally arrived. Which meant she had to pay more attention to their surroundings and less to her own damned fear.

Goliath paused beside her, his hands already filled with knives. "I never thought I'd see this place in my lifetime."

"I never wanted to see it," she replied.

"None of us do. It's a reminder that we failed once." The mist gathered around them, rising on a gust of wind into the vague shape of a person.

Lorelei watched as shoulders appeared, half of a face, and a helm that had once been used in battle by her own people. She'd seen drawings of warriors like this before, but never thought she'd meet one face to face.

Another gust of wind blew through the figure and it disappeared back into the mist. Suddenly, she feared the mist wasn't mist at all. What if this unexplained fog were the spirits of countless souls that had lost their lives here?

"Was that a ghost?" Beauty asked from behind them.

"No." Lore swallowed hard and shook her head. "Ghosts wouldn't linger here where they failed. They would only exist in torment if they remained on this land. That... That was a figment of our imagination."

Goliath snorted. "All of our imaginations?"

Well, she refused to believe that it could be anything other than that. Spirits were real, of course, and she'd assumed that they would exist somewhere in this realm, but she didn't think that she'd ever see them. Why would an elven warrior present himself to her, anyhow? She was the half blooded daughter of an elf that had forsaken her own kind long ago.

No one wanted to speak with Lore.

Shaking her head, she slogged through the mist toward the center of the Fields of Somber. "Get your wits about you. Ghosts or no, we need to find this royal and see what he can do for us. If we don't find him, then all of this was for nothing."

Heavier footsteps followed her first. The ever brave dragon would always be the one to rush after her. That did not surprise her in the slightest. The other two footsteps took a while, though. Likely, both Beauty and Goliath had to gather their wits. She didn't know what they were feeling, but she had a sneaky suspicion it was very similar to what she felt in this moment.

Fear. Gut wrenching fear that twisted through her stomach and rattled her very bones.

"Steady now," Abraxas grumbled, his voice deep and low. "There are things in these fields that can smell your emotions."

"Things?" She didn't want to know. Not really. If there were rotting corpses that were about to shamble after them, then she wanted to fight and not wait for them to attack. "What are you sensing?"

He shook his head, glaring out into the fog as though he could see through the thick blanket of white. "I'm not sure. I've never... It's new to me if there are beings out there. The mist is full of magic, old and new. It's hard to tell what is actually out there and what isn't."

Shit, well, that sounded bad. That sounded like they were all royally fucked.

She stopped walking through the Fields and waited for them all to gather around her. "All right, we need a better way of dealing with this. If you were the half brother of the King, where would you hide?"

Goliath stroked his beard. "Here? There aren't a lot of places to hide unless he's been burying himself every night."

Beauty hummed low underneath her breath. "Not to mention the wights you talked about. Wouldn't they have grabbed him by now if they were around?"

"Um." Lore didn't know. They were all looking at her like she had the answers, but she didn't. She knew nothing about where they were or how they should go about finding the half brother. All she knew was that they had made it.

She hadn't thought much farther than that.

Abraxas must have seen the panic in her gaze, or perhaps he smelled it. He interjected into the conversation with a very calming voice. "There's a lot of land to cover, and I don't think we should split up. I also don't think we should spend the night in the Fields. So, I would propose that we try to circle the area first, staying close to the outside just in case something attacks us. Then we can make trips deeper into the Fields of Somber in a few days. If you're all amenable to that."

She blew out a long breath. Yes. Perfect. He knew the safest plan that wouldn't risk everyone's lives. She could do this.

"Right," she replied with a sharp crack of her voice. "That sounds perfect to me. What about you two?"

Goliath's eyebrows had drawn down tight and furrowed. "I think you're not thinking about this the way you normally would. Are you still afraid of those wights?"

No. She wouldn't let him goad her into admitting that this place shook her. "We saw a ghost, Goliath. What do you think has me on edge?"

"I think you're afraid to turn around and see a dead person looking right at you." He lifted his hands in the air and wiggled his fingers. "Ooo, the great half elf who's fought countless men fears a myth!"

"You don't know they aren't real, Goliath. Besides, I'm not afraid of them. I just want us all to be very aware that there is something in the fog and that we aren't alone." She sniffed. "There are more important things to talk about right now than my fear of the walking dead."

"Really? Well, you wouldn't mind going around that tombstone on your own then." He crossed his arms over his chest and eyed her with a grin.

Lore knew he was goading her. She knew he just wanted to see her scream when she walked around the marker and then come running back to them. But damn it if her pride didn't sting.

Whipping around, she stalked toward the tombstone that was larger than she was tall.

Abraxas called out behind her, "You don't have to do this, Lore. We should stick together."

"I'm not even out of eyesight," she grumbled. "Yet." Then she steeled herself and walked around the tombstone, just out of their vision.

A man stood on the other side of the stone. He had his forehead pressed against the mossy surface, and his hands twitched at his sides. He looked very much like any man they might have seen before, and she thought he was mourning the loss of someone who was buried there. His lips moved in silence, as though lost in prayer.

They hadn't been alone, after all. Though her heart jumped in her chest at the sight of him, she also realized they had been rude. This wasn't the haunted place they all thought of it as. For some, this was the only remaining area where they could mourn the loss of their family.

"I'm so sorry to interrupt," she breathed, taking a step back with her hands up to show she meant no harm. "We weren't aware there was anyone else here."

The man turned his head to look at her with a sharp movement. One of his eyes was missing. The bottom half of his jaw had been torn clear off and his tongue hung out of the maw left behind. He had no hair on that side of his head, and the white gleam of bone poked shimmered in the dim light. His jolting movements continued as he lifted an arm toward her and she saw his hand lacked several important fingers.

"Wight," she croaked. "It's a wight."

Somewhere nearby, she heard Goliath laugh. "Oh right. Sure! Get on with it, Lore. Just get back here, would you?"

She took a single step back, but it wasn't far enough. Her vision had already gotten hazy in the corners and was she breathing? She didn't think she was. Maybe she was holding her breath as the creature took another step toward her, dragging his right foot behind him.

"Lore?" That was the voice she wanted to hear. The deep, guttural tones of a dragon who hated seeing her in any kind of pain.

A hissed curse echoed in her ear before she felt Abraxas's arm around her waist. He jerked her out of the wight's way and physically carried her back to the others.

"Actual wight," he gritted between his teeth. "Get your weapons out."

Lore pressed a hand to her chest and wondered why her heart wasn't thundering as it should be. She couldn't even feel the dreaded organ beating and did that mean she was dead? Had she taken one look at that cursed creature and died?

Abraxas stepped into her line of vision and she focused on his worried expression. "Breathe, Lore."

She was.

"Lore, I need you to breathe. That creature is quite slow, so we have some time here. But I cannot imagine that there aren't more where that came from. We have to get moving."

She wanted to argue with him that she was breathing, and him
yelling at her wasn't making it better. Then she tried to take a deep breath
and realized she couldn't inhale any more. She'd already filled her lungs.
She just wasn't exhaling.

Releasing all the air seemed to help a little. She then gasped in a full
lungful of air at his slight nod.

"There we go," Abraxas said. "Keep doing that while I get the others
ready to run. Can you do that? Can I leave you for a moment?"

She had no idea. What would happen when he left? Would she sink
back into that horrible panic attack that had threatened to swell over her
head?

Lore looked down at her hand and realized it was latched on his
arm. Abraxas placed his hands over hers, twining their fingers together
and then lifting her hand to his lips. "Keep breathing, all right? You're
stronger than this."

Stronger. She could be stronger.

Inhale, exhale. Inhale, exhale. Her fingers released their claw-like
hold on his arm and he disappeared from view. Unfortunately, that left
her staring at the wight that took one stumbling step after another. It
didn't mind how fast the process was. Instead, it just kept going. Step by
horrible step.

"Breathe," she whispered, her voice stilted and shaking. "Keep breathing."

Except, more shadows appeared out of the mist behind the other
wight. Skeletal figures with flesh hanging off them like ripped clothing.
An army of people awash with dull grays and darkened reds. An army of
the dead shambled toward them and Lore knew deep in her belly that
they would never survive this.

"Lore!" Goliath shouted. "Run!"

Hadn't she just said that to him?

As though his words were a whip crack, she spun and ran toward them. Her lungs worked just fine now as adrenaline surged through her body with a vengeance. She reached out a hand to Abraxas, and he threw her a knife. The blade landed in her palm and sliced through the flesh, but it didn't matter.

Except the moment her fumbling attempt to catch the knife resulted in blood, she heard an answering howl rise through the fog. The sound was one of a human in pain. A screech of anguish and... and...

Hunger.

Eyes wide, she kept pace with Abraxas behind the other two. Goliath was arguably the slowest of them, but Beauty was only a mortal. If she was caught with those creatures, she would fall first. Magic was necessary in this fight.

"Can you cast anything?" Abraxas shouted, then added, "Not that way! Left!"

Another wave of the dead appeared from the direction they'd been running. As they all turned, Lore replied, "I haven't had a chance to recharge! We've been stuck in the mists for days now. I need the moon."

He cursed, and the sound made her entire body hurt. She knew just how important it was to fight right now, and all they had was a dragon.

"Can you burn them?" she called out. "In this form?"

"Not as a man." His worried glance didn't help. "It's harder as a dragon to keep track of everyone. The fires are not as controlled as you might think. If I'm not human, I cannot look after them as well."

She heard the unsaid words. He would only care about her, and the others would fall to the wayside. He would burn anything and everything he could, but she would be the only one tucked underneath his wing.

Damn it. They didn't have a choice, now did they?

"Right!" she screamed. Lore grabbed onto Beauty's arm and threw her away from a wight that had appeared out of the earth. It narrowly missed grabbing Beauty's ankle with bony claws.

They all ran and Lore threw caution to the wind. "Turn into the dragon, Abraxas! I'll watch over the other two."

He gave her a sidelong glance, but wasted no time. Thank all the gods in the realm that he trusted her, or they all would have died.

His skin melted away and suddenly there was a massive dragon standing in the clearing with them. She'd forgotten how huge he was. His eyes were almost the same size as she was tall, and he turned his attention to the wights with singular intent.

Lore threw herself at Goliath and Beauty, forcing them all to crouch on the ground beneath the flames that spurted above them. She'd seen those flames before. They had rendered her mother to ash in a matter of moments.

Shaking, she held her two dearest friends close. "We're going to be all right," she repeated over and over.

Beauty's trembles shook through her, or maybe it was her own shaking that shuddered through the two companions she had her arms wrapped around. Whatever it was, she couldn't afford to feel like this.

Lore lifted her head and shouted, "Abraxas! To the right!"

He turned his head, and the flames spilled out of his mouth. But it wasn't enough. There were more wights, all yanking themselves out of the ground and rushing toward them.

"Behind!" she screamed.

He turned again, and she feared it wouldn't matter. No matter how many times he turned around, eventually the wights would reach them. They didn't feel fear or care in the slightest that he was burning others of their kind. They walked through the ashes as though nothing had happened.

"Abraxas!" Lore stumbled to her feet, dragging the other two with her until she stood between his front claws. "I don't think it's going to work."

She could hear them now. The rattling of their leg bones as they drew ever nearer. The cracks of their jaws as they gnashed their teeth, ready to feast upon flesh when they hadn't been so satisfied in a very long time. Were they growling? Or groaning? She couldn't tell.

Lore placed her palm against Abraxas's side, feeling the heat of the scales underneath her touch. "We tried."

Damn it. They had come so far.

Light gleamed to her right. Lore turned her attention to the sudden brilliance and realized the light came from a flaming sword. So hot it burned bright blue, the sword sliced through the necks of the wights in front of it. Their heads slid to the side and revealed a young man.

His dark hair stuck out in every direction and his eyes were wild. For a moment, she thought she was looking at Zander. Until she realized this young man was rather skinny in comparison, and his eyes were bright green.

"Follow me!" he shouted. "And make that dragon small or I'm leaving him out here!"

Lore met the stunned gazes of her companions and shrugged. "Run!"

CHAPTER 27

He wouldn't have chosen to trust the random man who appeared out of the mist, but apparently that's what they were doing. Abraxas thundered after them, sending spurts of fire at every group of wights that tried to stop them. He figured it couldn't hurt to keep burning them all to a crisp.

Really, how many dead things were in these fields? They kept coming, no matter how many he burned.

Thousands.

An army.

Ah, he realized. So the Fields of Somber weren't just a grave, they were cursed lands. The greatest battle in history had taken place here, and while the souls had likely fled, their bodies had remained. Some magician had played with these corpses and then cursed the very ground itself.

Then, of course, Lore had said magical creatures liked to come here to visit their ancestors. He could only guess the first king he'd served had something to do with this. Two birds, one stone, so to speak. He'd let the terrible warlock play with his magic and found a new way to kill off the magical creatures without it appearing like he'd been outwardly attacking them.

The old man had always been too smart for his own good. But this was dastardly, even for him.

He spread out his wings and launched into the air, following his companions as best he could while looking ahead. Their path was soon ringed with fire as he sent more and more balls of flames out into the massive amounts of the dead that trailed them. He hoped this newcomer wasn't about to lead them to their death or throw them into the waiting arms of a much more dangerous foe.

The man with the flaming blue sword gestured up ahead of their wild flight, pointing at what looked like an old crypt. Abraxas had seen the buildings before. The mortals liked to store their dead in them when the winter months were too cold to bury those who had died.

Great. A crypt. What could go wrong?

Abraxas sank down through the wind and landed hard on the ground. The entire earth shook with his impact, just as he'd intended. Though his companions stumbled, so did the wights behind them. The creatures weren't as limber as his friends, and it would take the wights a few moments more to stand.

He let the scales disappear from his body, the horrible cracking feeling of changing back into the mortal form slicing through his spine. The pain from this change was worse than before. He'd used the magic too much, and if he did it again without rest, he feared he wouldn't even be able to stand as the man.

No dragon was meant to be in this form for more than a few days. And they weren't meant to change into it every single day. He was a dragon before he was anything else.

Wheezing out a breath, he ran up to the others and tried hard not to show the pain on his face. "What now?"

The man with the sword had already turned away from them. He sprinted toward the crypt, leaving them no option but to follow.

Lore reached for his hand, and Abraxas felt his heart swell in his chest. At least she feared for his safety as well as the others. Although, now he was concerned that she could sense how weak he'd become. He wanted her to know that he'd hold all the wights back for her if she asked. Even if that led to his end.

She helped him race to the crypt, ignoring the stranger as he waved his arm dramatically for them all to plunge into the darkness. And yet again, they all trusted this man they didn't know. They raced through the open door of the crypt without even looking behind them. No hesitation. Just sprinting into the unknown.

Trust, he supposed, was a very strange thing. One either had to earn it, or the circumstances must be dire enough that it no longer mattered.

Lore's hand slipped out of his as she ran after her friends and that left Abraxas no option. He ran through as well, with the unknown man breathing down his neck.

"Help me!" the man shouted, throwing his shoulder against the stone door.

As the largest person in their company, Abraxas immediately turned to help. He caught sight of the wave of dead that had followed after them. Countless wights. Waving their arms and stumbling toward them with unhinged jaws and eyes wide with the desperate need to feed.

Abraxas set his back to the stone and shoved hard. The sound it made as it screeched across the floor of the crypt was horrible, and his ears ached as he continued to shove.

"Close, damn it," he ground out. Hands reached through the doorway, but then with a final heave, the door shut.

The sudden darkness flooded in, blinding him. But he heard the wet sounds of flesh hitting the ground where the hands had been severed off the arms of the wights. Their growls beyond the stone door grew muffled, yet it was impossible not to hear their slaps against the stone walls.

"There," the man beside him said. "That was a job well done, I'd say. Let me find the light now, you lot. Give me a moment."

Rummaging in the darkness. The sound of a pin hitting the stone floor. Or perhaps that was a flint? The briefest curse as the young man searched for what he'd dropped, and then the triumphant exclamation as he found it.

Who was it that saved them?

A bright flash burned in the darkness as the young man lit a match and then illuminated a candle. He was far too close to Abraxas, but in that light, Abraxas lost all his breath.

"Zander?" he asked, stunned.

The man who stood before him could not be the King. Abraxas knew that without question. He'd helped to save them, first of all. And Zander would rather save his own skin than that of others. But the young man looked so much like his brother.

Abraxas cleared his throat and took a step away from the other man before he did something foolish. Like punch him in the face for looking like the man they all hated.

Though, something must have shown on his expression as the other man stepped away from him, too. Flinched away from him, really, as if expecting Abraxas to attack him.

"Apologies," Abraxas stammered. "I didn't... I know you're not..."

The young man's surprised expression cleared. He stuck out his hand and made sure the candlelight illuminated the offered appendage. "My name is Zeph, if you were wondering. Short for Zephyr. My mother always said I looked like the spitting image of my father, and I suppose you proved her right."

"You're clearly in the line of royals." Abraxas hesitantly took the offered hand and shook it. "I used to work with your brother."

"I'm sorry for that." Zeph tried a smile, although it didn't reach his eyes. "I've heard he isn't a good man."

"No, he isn't."

"I also heard my father wasn't a good one either." Zeph's fingers stiffened, then dropped his hold. "I try every day not to be like the two of them, if that's any consolation."

He wished he could say it was, but that bloodline always erred toward darkness.

Abraxas hadn't thought about what it would feel like to see another man who looked like the King. He looked at this young man and felt years of suffering weighing on his shoulders.

He'd thought that pain would be easier to manage. Abraxas had hoped in looking at Zeph that he'd be able to see the mother, rather than the father. But he didn't. He couldn't see anything other than the younger brother, who had never been on the throne, but likely would have caused just as much pain.

Zeph must have seen that written all over his face. It wasn't as if

Abraxas had ever tried to hide his emotions, not even from Zander. He'd just been ignored for so many years that it didn't matter what his features said.

"Ah." Zeph backed away from him as well and scratched the back of his neck. "I see there is bad blood between the two of you."

"Quite." The word came out more as a growl than any mortal sound.

Lorelei stepped into view, and he had the utmost pleasure of watching the boy turn beet red in her presence. He wasn't surprised. The boy had likely never seen an elf before, and it was always startling the first time.

"We've been looking for you," she said. "I take it you are the King's half brother?"

"I am." He set the candle down on a nearby stone casket, then started searching around. Abraxas could only assume the boy was looking for another to light. "Not that many people know that, and I'd be much appreciative if you could keep it between the... uh... well, five of us, I suppose."

Zeph appeared to freeze for a moment as he realized just how many knew that secret now. Another person was easier to control, but five?

Abraxas knew the boy's mind already raced through all the ways they could tell anyone he was here. His hands shook as they skated over the stone casket, still half-heartedly trying to find another candle for them.

None of them knew what to say as the boy panicked. Abraxas wished this were an easy fix, but Zeph didn't want anyone to know who he was. If Abraxas were Zander's family, he wouldn't either.

It was Beauty who rescued them. She walked over to the young man, picked up a candle just out of his reach, and handed it to him. "I wish I could say we didn't plan on telling anyone, but we need your help."

He froze, stunned as he stared into Beauty's lovely eyes. Abraxas knew what that felt like. Beauty had a way of making people feel seen. She smiled, and the entire world glowed.

The boy's face turned a darker shade of red, and he tousled his already spiky hair. "Yes, well... I don't know what I can do to help you. Not really. You see, I've lived here my whole life. I can't go out there and change anything."

Beauty made her smile even brighter. "You'd be surprised how much a single person can change everything."

Right, well, she was going to make the poor man's heart burst if she kept on like that. Zeph stared at her with moon eyes and she looked back at him all bashful that she'd said such a thing to a prince.

And he was a prince. Make no mistake about that, Zander's half brother should be recognized in the royal line. Maid for a mother or no.

He didn't want to be the one to interrupt this meeting of two rather surprising people, but he knew that he'd have to be. Goliath had already clasped his hands over his heart and looked like a proud father at a wedding. Even Lorelei cast a narrowed glance at Abraxas, as if warning him not to step in.

Of course, he had to be the bad guy. Send the dragon in when you need something done.

"Listen," he started, interrupting the two of them while they still stared at each other. "We need to know that you're actually Zander's brother, and I have to know how you've stayed hidden all these years. Otherwise, I will assume you are a mad man who thought living in the Fields of Somber would keep you away from the Umbral Knights."

Zeph returned his attention to arguably the most dangerous person in the room. "Umbral Knights?"

"The shadow creatures that are yours to command." Abraxas

shrugged. "Or perhaps not if your brother is still alive. We're not sure how that magic works, if I'm being honest."

"I... Well." Zeph cleared his throat. "Listen, I think we'd all be more comfortable talking about this from the living quarters, if you don't mind. I, for one, could use a drink. And it looks as though the rest of you might be in desperate need of something to eat and somewhere to rest?"

Oh, no, he didn't. He would not get around answering Abraxas's question while dangling food they all needed. That wasn't how this was going to go.

He grabbed the boy's shoulder as he tried to walk past Abraxas. "I don't think so. Who are you? Who was your mother?"

"My mother?" Zeph's eyes flashed. "She was a maid in the castle where your fool of a king ruled. She didn't want a child, because she was too young to have one. She brought me here so I wouldn't end up like him. So I'd have to become a good man on my own. And I am. You don't have to worry about me attacking you here."

"Don't we?" Abraxas snarled. "I don't trust anyone because they say I should trust them."

"I wouldn't have saved you from the wights if I wasn't trustworthy."

"Or you might have wanted to kill us yourself," he argued. "There are many reasons to save people, boy, and not all of them are good."

There it was. That darkness he'd always seen in Zander's eyes when someone did something he didn't like.

Zeph reached up and wrapped a hand around Abraxas's wrist and snarled, "Have experience with that kind of saving, do you?"

Lore interrupted them both with an exasperated sigh. "Enough, you two. Abraxas, if he wants to offer us food and lodging, then we'll figure out a way to protect ourselves. Zeph, I don't think any of us can question whose son you are. I'm sorry you've been greeted so poorly by my companions, but I can only offer my apologies in the slightest of ways. We've been on a long journey to get here, and what we have to talk to you about is very important. And probably not pleasant."

She always had a way of speaking like she'd slapped someone. He released the boy with a little shake, just enough to remind him that Abraxas had turned into a dragon only moments ago and he would do so again. Even if that meant caving in this entire crypt around their head.

Zeph shook out the fabric of his shirt and nodded. "Right. Welcome then, I suppose."

Abraxas refused to feel guilty when Beauty shot him a look of disapproval. Yes, he understood that they needed Zeph to be on their side and, of course, he also understood there were plenty of hurdles that he'd thrown in their way. However, he refused to let any of them be at risk because no one had the thought of pushing this young man.

The candle bobbed in Zeph's hand as he strode down the long lines of caskets. For the first time, Abraxas realized they were in a rather clean crypt. He'd been expecting cobwebs and skeletons grinning from the wall. But this place was spotless.

Sure, there were still plenty of stone coffins, but for the most part, it could have been someone's house.

Zeph led them toward stairs that went even deeper into the ground, and Abraxas spared one last look at the stone holding out the army of the dead.

A firm hand grabbed his arm. "Come on, dragon. I don't think we have to worry about that for a while, yet."

"Are you so sure?" He hoped Lore saw the apprehension on his face. He didn't know how to say the words.

"We're going to be all right," she replied, tugging him deeper into the earth. "It's just like a cave, isn't it? We're safe here."

He didn't know if he'd ever feel safe again. Not when it was her life on the line.

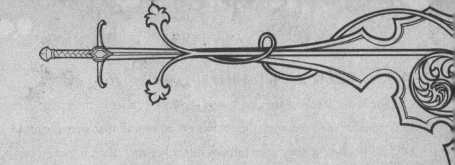

CHAPTER 28

L ore trailed along behind the rather odd man and was stunned that they'd found the King's half brother. This young man was not the person she'd expected, but no one could deny he looked like the spitting image of his sibling.

Even in the dim candlelight as they walked down the stairs, she thought they were following Zander. It didn't matter if she saw him from the front or the back. Lore had flashing visions of the man who had kicked her in the face after defeating her in a fight. She'd never wanted to see him again, and certainly not like this.

But all that barely contained rage in Zander's movements wasn't in this young man. Zeph walked with a light gait on the tips of his toes. His jaunty behaviors were of a person who had a brightness in his soul. Of a man who knew what happiness tasted like.

Even when he lived in the heart of a graveyard.

The lower levels of the crypt were spotless, similar to the upper part. Lore couldn't quite get over the shelves on every wall that were meant to hold bodies before they were buried. But other than that, it looked very similar to any other home.

Zeph had a table with chairs set up in the back corner, near what appeared to be a small fireplace, although there was nothing in it. No coals, no wood. A few cots were to their right, though one had not been slept in for some time.

"Sorry for the mess," he blustered as he raced ahead of them,

The mess was a single cup and plate that he'd left out. He almost dropped both items, stumbling over what seemed like air.

Beauty rushed forward with her hands outstretched. "Let me take those. Please. I know we're intruding on your space, and I don't mind. Just tell me where they go."

She'd missed something between the two of them, she thought. Zeph looked at Beauty with a rather stunned expression on his face, dark curls obscuring his vision in tangled clumps. Those were lovesick eyes if she'd ever seen them, and she was surprised.

The young man might never have seen a woman other than his mother. At least, that's what it seemed like. But the interest in his gaze was more than that.

Lore cleared her throat, coughing into her fist. "Zeph, do you mind if I ask a personal question?"

His eyes flicked to her, worry filling those bright green eyes. "Uh, I suppose."

Lore figured it was best to rip the bandaid off now rather than to soften what she had to ask. "Have you ever left the Fields of Somber? Or did your mother keep you here your whole life?"

He bristled, but she already knew the answer. He made it so obvious. His shoulders curved in on himself and his fingers flicked at his sides. Nervous ticks. The boy was about to lie.

"Of course. I had to leave for food." He twitched again, his left eye blinked a little faster than the right.

"Ah, of course." She nodded her head, clasping her hands at her waist in what she hoped looked unassuming and nonthreatening. "I apologize for assuming otherwise. I just know that if I were your mother, I would want you to stay hidden from the world in case your brother searched for you. That would likely include making sure you stayed here. No one comes to the Fields of Somber, and if they do, they are not looking for the half brother of the King."

His throat bobbed in a heavy swallow. "No, they aren't usually expecting to find anyone here at all. And we need to leave to get food, as you can tell."

"And your mother didn't have any contacts to send food for the both of you?"

This time, his left eye twitched on its own. He glanced over at Beauty as though he didn't want her to hear all this, before he bowed his head and stared down at his hands. "My mother did while she was alive, ma'am. She had friends who still worked in the castle who wanted to make sure the two of us survived."

So it was a small band of servants who had made all the difference in this world. Lore vowed to find out who those brave individuals were so she could compensate them for what they'd done. The smallest choice of a kind hearted individual had sent ripples through fate itself. Perhaps those people would never know they were heroes, but they had changed the very fabric of time by keeping this man alive.

She pressed a hand to her chest, fists closed, a symbol of honor among the elves. "They were honorable to take care of you like that. How often did you see them?"

The question caught Zeph off guard, and it was the first thing to make him slip. "My mother always got the food from them. That way, no one actually saw that I was alive."

"Right." She nodded, eyebrows drawn down as if she were concentrating on his words. "And after her death?"

"The food stopped coming. I'm not sure if they knew she died or if they also died. I've been stealing from caravans that pass by." He scratched the back of his neck. "But even those caravans give this place a wide berth as of late. I've gotten good at shooting rabbits, though."

"We don't need to eat your food, then." She nodded at him with a smile. "Just a place to sleep."

He seemed to catch up with everything he'd revealed to her. With a heavy inhale, he frowned and continued messing with his hair. "Right. Mother always wanted me to be polite and... well."

Lore looked over at Beauty and gestured for her to jump in. Apparently, the young prince was most comfortable with her dear friend, and Lore would use that to their advantage. Even if it meant exploiting that connection a little.

Beauty didn't care. "Your mother was very kind, but I think it's all right if you've never entertained before. We'll figure out the best way to invade your space without making it too hard on you. Perhaps a good night's sleep would be best for all of us."

"Yes, a good night's sleep. Um." Zeph looked over at the two cots, clearly in pain about some decision he had to make. "I don't have a lot of beds."

Lore dropped her pack onto the ground with a loud thump. Everyone in the room stared at her, but she just shrugged and pulled out her bed roll. "Good thing we have these. I'm perfectly happy to sleep on the floor if you don't mind us all piling in here. A night without worrying about what might find us will do me some good. I might actually rest deeply for once."

"I don't mind if you sleep in here," Zeph blurted.

"Good." She busied herself with getting her bed roll all settled. The bag needed to be emptied of half the things she'd brought. She needed to clean her knives as well.

The rest of her company didn't waste time. Goliath walked over to the farthest corner, set all his things down, and laid back with his head on his pack. No bed roll required for that one. She'd seen him sleep on the edge of a cliff. He didn't care at all where he slept.

Beauty quietly talked more with Zeph, her cheeks turning a pretty shade of pink. Lore noticed how she angled her body a certain way so she'd look smaller from Zeph's perspective.

She'd have to talk with that girl. The young man had realized what she looked like while they all sprinted away from the gnashing dead, and he had seen her size while they were all standing around talking. She didn't have to hide her appearance. His eyes were so wide when he watched her, he obviously wanted to take in all of her form without missing a single detail. And, if she wasn't mistaken, the interest in his eyes hadn't faded one bit in being able to see all of her with no pressing distractions.

Hiding a smile, she fiddled with a couple of her knives and then pulled them out. The others would sleep. She'd sharpen these quietly and get them cleaned. They were trapped underneath the walking dead. They would have to fight their way out. She had no misconceptions about that.

Though the others might be able to relax without thinking of the future, she could not.

Halfway through cleaning her second knife, Zeph appeared with an armful of blankets. "I forgot my mother had knit these."

The tower in his arms wobbled and Beauty leapt forward. She grabbed a few blankets off the top and grinned at him. "Let me help."

"You seem very good at catching things I drop." His cheeks turned that tomato color again.

Lore rolled her eyes but took the offered warmth. "Thank you, Zeph."

"There's another bed if someone, uh... If someone wants it." He looked at Beauty, but then forcefully returned his attention back to Lore and Abraxas.

As the only two people still awake, she figured she had to be the one to say something. Lore looked at Abraxas, trying so hard not to roll her eyes. "We'll take our chances on the floor. Beauty, get some rest. You've been begging for a proper bed this whole trip."

If it were anyone else, she'd worry that a talk might be necessary before sending the two of them off toward the makeshift bedroom together. But she doubted Zeph was capable of making any sort of move in that direction, and Beauty had no idea what she was doing. They would stay up all night, listening to each other breathe, but that was better than the alternative.

Shaking her head, she looked back down at the knife she'd somehow sharpened way too much and sighed. At least someone knew what they wanted.

Heavy footsteps approached, and Abraxas crouched down in front of her. "You keep sharpening that blade and you're going to chip it."

"I've sharpened blades before."

He held out his hand. "Allow me."

She couldn't tell him no, now could she? The man had seen a thousand more blades in his life than her. With a huff, she set the knife's hilt in his hand and gave him the cloth meant to clean it. The sharpening stone, however, she kept in her hand.

He arched a heavy brow. "Aren't you going to give me that so I can fix what you did?"

"It's sharp enough. And no, it's not weak." She nodded at the knife. "That is elven made. It can take a sharper edge than you'd expect."

"As you were then."

Abraxas sat down, crossed his legs, and put all his focus on the knife in his hands. For a bit, she let her mind wander through tomorrow's adventures, but then her attention caught on his fingers.

He had nice hands. The strength in his forearms helped him ease the cloth over the blade with measured gestures. Veins stood out on the backs, leading her eyes down to those long fingers. A painter's fingers, she thought, or perhaps those of a musician. He handled the blade so delicately, as though it were made of glass. Back and forth he drew the cloth, dancing his touch up and down the dangerous edges.

Oh, those were perilous thoughts. She swallowed hard. Going down that path wouldn't end well, and they were in a room full of people. But she couldn't stop thinking about those hands.

He moved with such careful regard to detail. And Lore knew, without a doubt, that he'd pay similar consideration to every string he plucked on her body and every chord he hit just right.

Releasing a shuddering breath, she looked away from his hands. At anything else. But there was nothing to look at in this barren, though oddly clean, room.

Damn it. She couldn't look at Goliath. That made her stomach turn. Staring at Beauty and Zeph made her seem like some overbearing aunt surveying their every move so... so...

Her eyes found his damned hands again, and she felt her heart catch in her chest. No, she couldn't look at him. Couldn't feel like this. Not when there was a legion of dead people above her head and they had to convince a social recluse to leave his hovel.

Lore could argue with herself all she wanted, but her mind always strayed back to him. This dragon who might have burned the Fields of Somber to the ground for daring to attack him. And instead, he sat crossed legged in front of her and focused on taking care of her weapons. So she could protect herself properly.

Her heart did that weird flip in her chest again, and she almost groaned. Oh, no. She was in so much trouble.

"I think it's clean enough," she croaked. "We should head to bed."

He set the knife on the ground, still not looking back at her. "Probably a good idea. We have our work cut out for us in the morning."

Now what?

Lore didn't know what she was supposed to do, so she just rolled onto her too thin cushion and laid down on her back. She stared up at the ceiling and crossed her hands over her heart. That was normal, right? She didn't look suspicious doing that, did she?

Abraxas sighed, and she thought that would be the end of it. He'd go to his side of the room and they would both lie there, watching the night go by, until the morning hit.

But he didn't go over to his corner of the room where he should have been. Instead, he crouched next to her again, sat down on his hip, and then palmed her side. "Roll over and make room."

"Excuse me?" she muttered, though she rolled without even thinking. "What are you doing?"

"Getting warm for the night. In case you didn't notice, this is a crypt, and it's freezing." He fluttered the blankets through the air, two of them, and tucked the edges around her shoulders.

Lore noticed that he tucked in the blankets, but then left his arm around her waist. Her dragon held her close to his heart. Not a single inch of him apparently planning to apologize for such a thing.

"Lore," he said. "Would you relax?"

"I just don't understand what's happening."

"You're safe," he whispered in her ear. "I promise. Lorelei, Lady of Starlight, I will keep you safe."

How had he known she still feared the creatures above them? That she hadn't wanted to sleep for fear of what nightmares would plague her dreams?

As he settled down, resting his head just above hers, she felt all the anxiety in her chest disappear. Sinking into his arms was wrong, but she did it. She let him take the weight of her body and set her hand on top of his. Just over her ribs so he could feel her breathing.

"Good night, Abraxas," she said.

"I'll keep your dreams at bay, Lore. Rest well."

And for the first time in her life, she truly felt like she was safe.

CHAPTER 29

Abraxas crossed his arms over his chest and looked at the ragtag group of people he was supposed to keep alive. They'd all gathered around the very small table to eat a breakfast that he still wasn't sure how Zeph had provided. The young man didn't have any magical abilities, so the large amount of bacon, bread, and fruits was surprising to say the least.

Goliath had taken over cooking the bacon while a tiny fire sprite gave them enough heat to make the bacon crispy. He'd claimed dwarves knew how to cook, and proceeded to produce copious amounts of smoke.

Though he was certain they would all die from smoke inhalation, the smog hadn't stayed in the room. Somehow, that fireplace did feed to the outside.

Abraxas thought it was more likely that the chimney had been enchanted rather than it leading to fresh air. Otherwise, wouldn't the wights have crawled through the hole and down to attack them in their sleep?

The table was arranged as though they were in a very formal dinner. Beauty, with all her talents, knew exactly how to make place settings out of nothing. Even Lore had pulled the cots close so they all would have somewhere to sit. Not just in the two chairs that she'd placed at opposite ends of the table.

They were all bound and determined to make this seem like a proper meal together. A real family gathering, if he wanted to think that.

Although, he was acting as the strange family member who lingered in the back while all the others enjoyed themselves. He watched them with a small smile on his face, staying out of the way until they were ready.

Lore's eyes continued to drift to where he stood, though. He'd noticed how flustered she had gotten when he cleaned her knives for her. Who knew the elf could be seduced and all he had to do was make her weapons look pretty?

Actually, he should have guessed that. Now that he thought about it, Abraxas was rather disappointed he'd taken so long to figure it out.

She'd felt so wonderful in his arms. He had barely slept just so he would remember this moment. He'd branded every tiny detail into his brain as thoroughly as he could. The way her hair smelled. How she sighed in her sleep and held his arm a little tighter around her waist. Her dreams had remained pleasant as well. He'd kept his promise that he would chase all her nightmares away.

"And we're ready," Beauty said, clapping her hands together with glee. "This looks rather lovely, don't you think? We really did something grand with very little."

He was glad she thought so. Abraxas pushed off the door frame and joined the others, sitting down carefully in one of the chairs while hoping it didn't break under his weight. Human creations were fragile, in his experience. And a giant dragon couldn't make himself smaller. Even in mortal form.

He reached for the single fork and waited patiently while Goliath loaded everyone's plates with more food than they could eat.

The dwarf arched a brow at his gesture to stop putting food on his plate. "You're a dragon. You need to eat."

"I eat mostly in that dragon form."

"And you haven't eaten in a very long time. So let's make this very clear. We might not get food like this in a while. You will enjoy it, and you will eat whatever I give you." He slammed a hunk of bread down on Abraxas's plate. "I slaved over it."

"I highly doubt that," he replied with a sardonic grin. At least now he knew when the dwarf was teasing him and when the man meant business.

He noticed Zeph's wide-eyed stare at their words. The young man would have to get used to them ribbing each other. Abraxas remembered how strange it was for him when they really got going. The others were still more gentle with him.

When everyone had settled and dug into their food at least a little, Lore cleared her throat. "Listen, Zeph. I think it's time we tell you why we're here."

She expected to have this conversation over food? He supposed that might be a smart idea, but it could also be a terrible one. Zeph wasn't comfortable with them yet, although he had to be aware they couldn't stay in this crypt forever.

Beauty's eyes widened as well, and she leaned forward to hiss, "Are you sure this is the right time for that?"

"No time like the present." Lore wiped her mouth on the back of her hand and pointed her fork at Zeph. "How much do you know about your brother?"

"Very little. My mother never met him, but she talked about my father often." He set his fork down, the conversation apparently not agreeing with the food. "I know my father was not a good man. She hated him."

Lore nodded, still chewing her food. "Well, at least your mother was sane. Your brother was very much like his father. A mad man who wanted everyone to bend a knee to his whims. The problem is that we're all speaking about him like he isn't still alive, but he is. You're sitting in a room with the people who tried to kill him. We failed, unfortunately, but I don't intend to let him continue walking this realm without trying to kill him again."

He could have cut through the silence with the fork in his hand. Damn it, Lore. She had the subtlety of a hammer sometimes.

Apparently, it would take a dragon to explain the situation they were all in without it sounding like they were hunting down this bloodline and intending on killing them all.

He cleared his throat and began, "If I may? I worked very closely with your brother his entire life. Your father passed down my loyalty to his son. So you might say, I know both of them as well as I would my own family. I know you must have questions."

Maybe it wasn't the right thing to say. Zeph looked at him like he'd grown two heads and spoke in tongues. "Questions?"

"Lorelei threw out a lot of information at you all at once. Your brother was a monster. We tried to kill him. We failed. And now we want you to help us in some way, shape, or form, and all of that feels rather overwhelming." He steepled his fingers and pressed them against his mouth. "Does that about sum it up?"

Zeph nodded.

"I'm giving you a chance to ask whatever you want before my companions give you even more information that's going to make your head spin worse than it is right now. I'm letting you know that there is a choice here. You can control this information and how you receive it." Abraxas tried to smile, although it wasn't a natural expression on his face. "I know you have questions."

"I do." Zeph stared down at the table, then looked at Abraxas with determination in his eyes. "But I think the greatest question is what you want with me."

Ah, well. Of course, the boy would ask the most difficult question to answer. And the only answer that none of them wanted to admit.

Abraxas looked at Lore. She wasn't the best person to handle that question, but she wasn't the worst either. If Zeph shared a similar perspective that it was best to face the worst, then Lore was the only person who should answer this question.

She hummed low under her breath, then licked her teeth. Obviously, the right words were hard to find. Especially considering she'd already scared the boy.

But she found the one thing she wanted to say. She always did.

"Your brother committed many atrocities, but none so awful as continuing your father's work. I'm sure you heard that the King's line is the only one who controls the last dragon?" She eyed Zeph with a critical look until he nodded. "Right, well, that man sitting there is the last dragon."

"I figured." Zeph's cheeks turned bright red. "He was a little hard to miss on the battlefield, what with all the flaming breath."

"Good. So you remember that. Abraxas never wanted to kill anyone on behalf of the King, and he didn't want to be a slave to a mortal. But your brother held three dragon eggs in a cursed box that only the blood of the King can open." She splayed her hands wide on the table. "He left with that box after we thought he was dead. Our intent in coming here was to find you, then find the box, and open it."

There was that silence again.

Zeph's shocked expression had never left his face and Abraxas worried the boy might never recover from this shock. They'd pushed him too far, too hard. He needed some time to think.

Or breathe. If he would inhale, that might help a bit.

Finally, the man exhaled long and low. The gust of wind that he expelled would have set sail a ship, but he was nodding with a ferocity that terrified Abraxas. "Right, okay. So my brother was just like our father. He trapped three dragon eggs, and now you want me to release those dragons on the world so that they can do whatever they want."

"Two dragon eggs," Abraxas replied.

Zeph pointed at Lore. "She just said three. Which is it?"

"Your brother killed one of the eggs in front of me. A crimson dragon like myself, who was likely ready to protect the only female dragon we have left." Abraxas pressed a hand to his heart and hoped that his plea would be enough. "There is only one of me now. I know I cannot ask a mortal to understand the longing that comes with that knowledge, but I hope you can understand why I will fight for this until my last breath. I could gain a family again after all this, Zeph. All the pain and death I have caused would not be for nothing if I can bring my kind back to Umbra."

The young man swallowed hard again. His left eye ticked and Abraxas knew his fingers were twitching underneath the table. It was too much. They shouldn't have pushed him this far, and did they really think they could trust the boy with all this information? He was a child.

And a hermit, at best. They had come into his home with noise and color and magic and he'd done well enough until this moment.

Abraxas sighed, though it might have sounded like a growl. "We've asked too much of you."

"Too much of me?" Zeph waved a hand in the air, although he wasn't making eye contact with any of them. "No, no. I understand. You want your people to live and you want life to return to normal after what my family has done to you. I'd be a fool to not see that. I just... uh..."

His chair screeched across the floor. Zeph stood, breathing heavily and staring down at the table.

Then nothing. He kept staring at the ground and Abraxas was quite certain they'd not only asked too much, but that they may have broken the man.

He looked over at Lore, who shrugged helplessly. If she didn't know what to do, then how were any of them supposed to act?

Abraxas sighed and asked, "Are you all right?"

The words seemed to break Zeph out of whatever fugue state he was in. The young man flinched and then muttered, "I need some air. I'll be right back. Please don't leave."

And then he was gone.

He'd sprinted away from the table as though he'd grown wings and ran up the stairs so quickly that Abraxas only had to blink to lose him.

Beauty glared at Lore. "You scared him off. Great idea."

"Oh, this was my fault?" she snarled. "Someone had to tell him why we were here. It's not like any of you were going to do it."

"We didn't have to tell him the first day we got here! We could have taken the time to get to know him, to let him get to know us!" Beauty stood as well, planting her hands on her hips and staring at where Zeph had run. "I'd be terrified too if a bunch of magical creatures had walked into my home and said they needed me to help kill my brother."

"Would you rather I have let us all sit and get to know each other while hundreds if not thousands of wights wander over our heads?" Lore hadn't stood, but her voice thundered so loudly she might as well have towered over Beauty. "This place might have kept him and his mother safe for a time, but the wights only had two meals below their feet. Not five."

Beauty quieted down at the horrible truth they all knew. This place was a death trap. They didn't have to worry about if the wights got in. They had to worry about when.

Abraxas sighed. "Well, someone has to go after the boy. Might as well be me."

The dwarf hopped up from his chair as well, wringing his hands. "Do you think that is wise? I'll admit, Lore was a little heavy handed with her words. But out of all of us... you're the worst."

He had a point, but Abraxas could be delicate. He nodded and replied, "I spent many years in the courts, and I never once had to duel a single person. I'd beg you to give me a little more credit than that, Goliath."

No one tried to stop him as he walked away from the group. Abraxas made his way up the stairwell that led all the way to the stone door.

Zeph sat on top of a stone coffin, staring at the door with an intensity that rivaled the gaze of dragons. Who knew what went through that young man's head at this moment? A thousand possibilities floated between them.

"You're not required to help us," Abraxas said. "I know it's a lot to ask of anyone. My apologies for putting any responsibility or guilt on your shoulders."

Zeph's shoulders curved in on himself. "My older brother and my father..." He cleared his throat. "I'm glad I didn't know them. I'm glad my mother brought us here, even if the price was her life. I heard everything that happened, what my brother has done... I can feel it. We have a connection, he and I. And he's not right. I can feel that much."

"And I'm sorry to hear that." He made his way around the other coffin and sat down on top of it as well. The stone groaned underneath his weight, but at least it held. "Do you mind if I sit with you for a while? We don't have to talk."

They both stared at the stone door that protected them all, even though they could still hear the slapping sounds of wight hands hitting the surface.

Zeph gulped. "Yeah. That would be all right."

CHAPTER 30

Lore had been disappointed when Abraxas returned without the young man who was supposed to be their savior. The dragon grimaced at her expression before shaking his head.

"He went out to scope the land," Abraxas had said. "He told me to wait three days and if he didn't come back, then we should probably leave as well."

Three days.

Three whole days where they raided Zeph's food supply and sat in the dark gloom of a crypt.

Goliath and Beauty kept each other entertained with card games from a stack they'd found next to Zeph's bed. Although Lore would have to be blind to not see the angry looks Beauty kept sending over to her. The young woman was furious that Lore had scared off the only person who could help them, and Lore would admit she was a little angry at herself as well.

But their reality was three days in the dark, and hopefully that would change the moment Zeph returned. And she had to believe Zeph would return.

By the morning of the fourth day, she wasn't so sure that she'd guessed correctly. The boy still hadn't shown himself, and he'd told them to leave. She couldn't keep anyone here hoping that he might return, when he was likely waiting until his home was vacant again.

"I guess that's it," she muttered as she watched Goliath and Beauty set up another game of cards. "We should head out now."

Beauty looked up at her, eyes wide and jaw tight. "But he's not back yet."

"I know." She pushed herself off the wall and walked over to their table. "He said to leave, though, and I don't want to stay any longer than we're welcome."

"He's the only one who can help us," Beauty whispered, staring down at the cards. "We can't just give up now."

"We're not giving up. We're going to look for another option and then we're going to do whatever it takes to find the eggs. At the very least, we can have them in our possession while we try to figure out the next step. Right?" Lore searched for Abraxas and realized he was nowhere to be found.

Likely the dragon had headed out to see if they could leave the premises. He always was one step ahead of her, so she wasn't all that surprised to notice his disappearance. He'd come back, eventually.

Beauty shook her head. "I don't want to go, Lore. I think we should wait for him. To make sure those wights didn't get him, or something worse."

Zeph interrupted them, sounding exhausted. "No wights got me. You don't have to worry about that at least."

Surprise surprise, the half brother had returned. Lore lifted her brows to see Abraxas standing behind the boy with his hands tucked into his pockets. As though he'd known Zeph would return the whole time. He'd just been waiting for the right moment to let him back in.

Abraxas met her gaze and shrugged with a slight smile on his face.

Clearing his throat, Zeph stepped into the room while balling his fists at his sides. "Sorry to worry you all. I just had to go get a few things from other crypts around the Fields. I've decided to go with you, even though my mother's ghost is likely rolling in her grave right now."

If he had walked in and shot an arrow at her head, Lore would have been less surprised. She opened her mouth, closed it, then opened it again to say, "You're coming with us?"

"I plan to. I know it's probably not what you were expecting, but it's the right thing to do. If my bloodline was the one to cause all this trouble, then... well, I suppose it's up to me to fix it."

That was all rather mature of him, and Lore hadn't expected that. She had thought he would leave them all in the dust the first moment he had the opportunity to run. She was pleased that he wanted to help, but now she wanted to know why.

"What changed?" she asked, walking up to him with narrowed eyes. "You'll have to excuse my curiosity, Your Highness, but you didn't seem interested in helping us at all just a few days ago."

He gulped, his throat working as he stared at her approaching him. "Well, I had a good long chat with Abraxas and he reminded me that the world can change if we're the ones to help do it, so I thought... You know. He was right."

"When did you talk with Abraxas?"

"The day I left." Again he gulped. Was the boy that intimidated by her? "He's very convincing, and he's right. If we want to see change in the world, then someone has to do something. Why can't I be the person who makes the difference?"

"There's no reason in the world why you can't be." She put her hand on his shoulder. "I'm glad you're going to work with us. Please don't mistake my tone for anything other than confusion. We're going to change the world, all of us. I'm just surprised you would want to help us."

"Why?" Zeph met her gaze head on.

"Humans don't care about magical creatures. People like you think my kind are lesser. That's been the way of things for a very long time and I know you want to make an impact, but it will be a very slow change."

He nodded. "I don't care how slow it is. I want that change to happen and I want to be part of it. My mother hid me here for my entire life, and she wouldn't want me to cower before adversity. She wanted me to be someone good, and I think the only way to do that is to help you."

Zeph put his hand on top of hers, and Lore could feel his conviction through the touch. He wanted to help. And he didn't think she was a monster or an animal because they weren't the same.

A sudden thought struck her, a horrible one that whispered she shouldn't drag this poor young man into her fight. He had no idea what she was asking him to do, and he would be horrified when he realized the weight of responsibility she had placed on his shoulders.

If she did this, was she any better than Margaret?

Her heart thundered in her throat again and she couldn't breathe. What if she was becoming just like the Darkveil elf? She'd see the worst side of herself and that wasn't what Lore had ever wanted out of her life.

Damn that woman for putting her on this path. Damn the King for all he'd done that had broken their people for years.

Lore removed her hand from his shoulder before he felt her shake. "I'm glad you're coming with us, then. One couldn't hope for a better partner in all that is to come. I can only hope you are not ruined by it all."

"Ruined?" Zeph asked.

Beauty launched out of her chair and joyously interrupted them. "We'll have to pack! You said you gathered things from other crypts?"

His attention fractured between the strange and intimidating elf before him, and the warm, kind-hearted young woman, who appeared so excited to speak with him. Zeph chose the right person to focus on.

"I did." He turned toward Beauty. "There are so many magical artifacts that were left behind by all the great warriors who once lived here. My sword is one of them. But I brought gifts for everyone here. I thought... Well, I thought they might be useful."

Abraxas held out a large sack, and Lore realized he must have been hiding that the entire time. She glared at him when he shrugged at her again. Was he in on this with Zeph? Had the two of them conspired to make this grand entrance for the young man?

"Gifts?" Beauty said, her eyes even wider. "Oh, how thoughtful."

Lore needed to get out of this room or she'd start rolling her eyes at the two love-struck children who couldn't take their eyes off each other. "Everyone pack. We'll talk about those gifts later," she said, trying very hard not to grumble. "We've got a long journey ahead of us and still have to figure out where the eggs are."

"Where are we off to this time?" Goliath asked, stretching his arms over his head.

Well, she hadn't thought about it. Lore hadn't expected them to get this far.

Now they had the even more arduous task of figuring out where the eggs were. And how to get them. Or steal them. Or where they even were in the first place.

Damn it, she had no idea what to say now. The idea that they now had to figure out what to do next made all the blood drain from her head. She looked over at Abraxas, hoping he might have something to say, only to see that he, too, was just as stunned.

"Home, I guess." She met each of their gazes, taking time to ensure that her own eyes weren't too wide or horrified. "There has to be someone close to the King that we can speak with. Someone who would know where he would go. Where he would have hidden the eggs."

Goliath shrugged. "It's as good an idea as any. I'm sure there are plenty of people in Tenebrous who still sympathize with him, considering the reaction when all the magical creatures were out celebrating. We'll find someone. Maybe the Madame knows more that she didn't tell us."

They weren't going back to that wicked woman. Even Abraxas paled at the thought, then he gestured for her to come stand by him.

Lore wasted no time. She rushed to his side and stood with her arms crossed, watching the others get ready when she'd been packed for days now. "Do you have any idea where he went?"

"Not even the faintest idea. Zander would not tell me where his secret hideout was. Information like that would give me far too much power." He rolled his shoulders back, stretching his spine. "Are you all right?"

The question startled her so much that she snapped her neck, looking at him. With a wince, she rubbed at the sore spot. "I'm fine. Why do you ask?"

"You looked a little off when you were welcoming him into our crew."

He nodded at Zeph as the young man laughed at something Beauty said. "You know you're not dragging him to his doom. He's a grown man, he can make his own decisions."

"He has no idea what waits for him," she murmured. "Zeph thinks we're going on a wonderful adventure and I don't even know if he's going to come back alive."

The words finally gave a meaning to the weight that laid heavy on her shoulders. None of these people might return, and she'd known that from the beginning. But now the pressure of keeping them alive had become real. The wights were her first concern. Not even the Ashen Deep scared her as much as those monsters.

Abraxas's hand slipped to her back, out of sight from anyone else in the room. He gently rubbed small circles over the tense muscles. "It's not your job to keep them alive. They know what they got into when they signed up to kill the King."

"Not that boy."

"That boy is a young man who has been locked up his entire life. He's jumping at the chance to leave this place, and now he has people to help introduce him to the world. Not just strangers who would likely take advantage of him and then leave him in a ditch after robbing every item he carried." Abraxas leaned down, so she had to look him in the eyes. "Listen to me when I tell you this, Lore. You will help them in any way you can, but their lives are not your responsibility."

She wanted to shout at him that he was wrong. They all looked at her to make decisions, and that meant they thought she led them. What if she led them into a battle they could not win? A battle where all her friends died, and she was the last?

"Breathe," he whispered. "You have to breathe, Lore."

She sucked in a deep breath as Goliath walked up to them. He'd already strapped his bag to his shoulders and the jaunty expression on his face was one she'd only seen when he was feeling the most adventurous.

"I'm going to check outside for any lingering wights," he said with a wink. "Zeph said there weren't any when he came in, but one can never be too careful. We'll be ready in a few moments, Lore."

"Right." Her voice wobbled a bit when she said that. "I'll be ready as well."

She waited until she couldn't hear his footsteps anymore before she forced herself to breathe in that deep, unnatural inhalation.

"Lore," Abraxas said. "You're going to be all right."

"How?" She looked at him with wide, panicked eyes. "How can I be all right when I might lose them all?"

He opened his mouth like he had an answer, but no words came out. Abraxas merely closed his lips again, sighed, and then looked away from her. Together, they watched as Zeph and Beauty rummaged through all his things, putting together a pack that would be too heavy for either of them to carry. Abraxas never stopped rubbing her back. Not for a second.

It took the two younger members of her companions forever to get their things ready. Or maybe it was only a few heartbeats. But they finally looked at her with pride that Zeph wasn't falling over any more.

He gave her a sharp nod and said, "Ready."

"Are you?" She'd be the one to inspect him, and Lore wasn't easy to please.

She strode forward, away from the comforting touch of a warm handed dragon. Without pausing, she lifted the strap on Zeph's shoulder and let it fall down hard. He shifted with the weight, already a bad sign. She pulled at him from behind, just a little, but he lurched backward with the movement.

Lore rounded his body and stood in front of him with a single lifted brow.

"It's a little heavy," he admitted. "But I think I'll be all right."

"We're traveling a long way."

"Then I'll likely get real strong on the journey." He raised his chin, clearly ready for an argument.

Lore might have given him that too, if there weren't echoing clatters as Goliath sprinted down the stairs. She whirled around just in time to see the dwarf trip down the last few, his beard flying behind him with the speed at which he traveled.

"What happened?" she asked, reaching for knives that she hadn't yet strapped to her thighs.

"We've got a problem," Goliath hissed as he struggled to his feet. "A big one."

"More wights?"

"Worse." His eyes widened and his beard trembled. "There's about a hundred Umbral Knights covering the Field, and those were the only ones I could see. I assume that means there are more. Everywhere."

Umbral Knights?

Lore frowned and shook her head. "The Knights don't come here. The Fields of Somber are a place of peace."

"Not anymore." Goliath cleared his throat and hesitantly glanced at Zeph. "The King is here. He knows we came to find his brother."

It all clicked into place in her mind. Of course he was here. Of course he had hunted them down because he knew what the smartest next step would be.

Her hands curled into fists and she snarled, "He's not a king anymore."

CHAPTER 31

The name of the King sent a shiver down his spine. Abraxas knew he had no allegiance to Zander any longer. Those eggs were so far beyond his reach, it didn't matter if the King was here. Right now, he had to focus on the family right in front of him. The people who had made such a vast impact on his life.

However, he still felt that zing of fear after hearing that Zander was near them.

And then he could feel it. The oil slick dark magic that always slithered around his very heart and squeezed whenever Zander was near. He could feel the King and all the Umbral Knights that whispered in the dark shadows.

His stomach twisted. He should have felt them long before this.

The blood drained from Lorelei's face, and he vividly remembered finding her in the dungeon after Zander had his way with her. He'd always known that Zander was a cruel man, but the sight of her with bruises and cuts all over her face... The way the King had fought her, breaking bones and shattering through her skin as though she wasn't even a person... That had been the moment Abraxas realized he couldn't stand by and watch as all this happened.

Of course, he'd thought about it before, but it had never been a reality before her. Lorelei had given him the gift of freedom and the clarity of seeing the world as it really was. He would never forget that.

Everyone remained still in the crypt, staring at both him and Lorelei. They waited for some kind of order, some direction of what to do. But he knew that his lovely elf had frozen in fear because her worst dread had come to life.

The King could kill all of them. And he would, gladly. They were the reason he lost his throne, and the reason he had to go into hiding. If Zander caught any of them, he would kill them slowly and with his bare hands.

Oh Lore, he thought. All your nightmares are coming to life.

Abraxas couldn't let her deal with this on her own. Not when he knew how hard she'd worked to keep them all safe.

"Zeph," he barked. "Did those gifts of yours happen to be weapons?"

The young man blinked a couple times, then nodded. He dropped the bag off his shoulders and dumped the contents out onto the floor. "They are, actually."

What spilled out of the boy's bag was a surprising amount of weapons, enchanted and otherwise. Knives, swords, a bow, throwing daggers, the list went on and on.

Abraxas couldn't stop the surprise from showing on his face. He gruffly said, "Well, that'll do."

He hoped, at least. The bow would go to Lore. She could take out most of the Umbral Knights on her own, although he didn't know how many were out there. He snatched up the well-oiled oak weapon and held it out to her.

"Take this," Abraxas said while pawing through the rest of the weapons.

She took the bow, and that seemed to startle something out of her. Her expression hardened, and she shook the fear off her shoulders. Suddenly, his Lore was back.

She pointed at Beauty. "I know you're good with a sword, and you have your own, but would you like a second?"

"I've always wanted to fight with two," the young woman replied, but then she nodded at a heavy looking broadsword. "I think that'll suit me. My father used to have one in his house that I played with as a little girl. I would wave it around and the damn thing could cleave a small tree in half when I swung it."

"Perfect," Abraxas said. He scooped up the broadsword. It was heavier than he expected, although she heaved it from his grip with no hesitation.

Though, the moment she saw Zeph looking at her with an expression of surprise, she curved in on herself. "I'm stronger than I look," she replied, shifting her feet.

"I can see that." Zeph looked far too impressed by that, and Abraxas had no idea how the two of them were still feeling that emotion when the King and all his army stood above their heads.

Goliath shifted forward and picked out all the knives. One by one, he strapped them to himself until he was covered in at least thirty.

He shrugged when he caught Abraxas's eye. "I throw them. A lot of them, actually. Run by the bodies, pick 'em up on the way. It works best for me."

Well, Abraxas would enjoy seeing that spectacle. He'd never seen a dwarf fighting, even though he'd had hundreds of years to see that sight. The dwarves rarely got involved, although the myths always claimed everyone wanted a dwarf on their side in battle.

There. Now everyone was armed to the teeth other than Zeph. He looked the boy over and arched a brow. "I don't know your fighting style, but did you grab anything you know how to use?"

Zeph scoffed. "I don't need any of these weapons, friend. Have you forgotten what I wielded to save you?"

Right, the flaming sword. Abraxas almost didn't want to know what curse was on that weapon. Or spell. But generally speaking, weapons always had curses.

Now that they were all armed to the teeth, he felt a little better. Until Zeph scuffed his foot on the ground and asked, "What weapon are you bringing?"

Abraxas bared his teeth in a snarl. "I am the weapon."

The boy's eyes widened, and then he looked away from the dragon. Apparently, it was all too easy for him to forget that Abraxas was a dragon hiding in the skin of a man.

He looked around at the small amount of people they had and realized he was all right with this. They could fight their way through the massive amounts of Umbral Knights. They could get away. All they needed was a plan.

He met Lorelei's horrified gaze and knew that would be on him. And he was all right with that, too.

"I know Zander better than anyone here," he started. "He'll make a mistake. He's running on nothing but anger now, and that's the worst way to walk into a battle. We can outwit him."

Beauty lifted her hand in the air and watched him expectantly.

He looked at Lore and asked, "What is she doing?"

"She didn't want to interrupt but has a question," Lore replied, chewing the inside of her lip while poorly hiding a smile.

"Right." He nodded at Beauty. "Go ahead. You're free to interrupt me whenever you want, Beauty."

She dropped her hand and balanced both of them on the pommel of her sword. "What about the Umbral Knights? Goliath said there are a ton of them, and we don't know how he's controlling them all. Should we assume that we can fight all of them?"

Well, that would be an issue. But he would not let them fight too many of the Umbral Knights. Even a few of them were dangerous enough, and every additional one threatened their wellbeing even further.

"We won't fight many. I want you all to get out of the way as soon as there is room. I will change back into the dragon and you'll all have to climb on top of me. There won't be a lot of time for any of this to happen. I'm sure the Knights followed Goliath back and they are most certainly lying in wait. You'll have to ensure that you kill the ones you can, but then run. As fast as you can."

It was the only thing he could think of. Abraxas would love to battle with Zander. He'd love to burn the King to a crisp and make sure he was dead for good. But he had to take care of these people first. He had to make sure they were all safe before he could return and destroy the man who had tried so hard to ruin him.

The people who stood in front of him hardened before his eyes. They all prepared for battle, ready to fight for and to ensure the others remained breathing as well.

They were good people. Good friends.

He just hoped he didn't lose any of them today.

"Get ready at the door," he grumbled, pointing for them to leave. "I'll join you in a moment."

They all scrambled, but he put his arm out as Lore tried to move past him. He wanted a few moments alone with the elf before the battle broke out and he might never see her again.

Heart thundering in his chest, he waited until the others were out of earshot before he focused his attention on Lore.

Her eyes were wide with fear and anxiety. Her shoulders were squared though, and her hands clutched the bow with a strength he knew would propel her through the battle unharmed. She would survive, because that was what she did. After all these years, she had always survived, no matter what the cost.

"Don't take any chances," he said. "Do you understand me?"

"You know I don't take any chances that aren't necessary," she replied. Lore tried to shoulder past him, but he wasn't letting her go that easily. Not until she confirmed she wouldn't let herself die for another.

"Listen. There are a lot of things unsaid between the two of us. If I thought the King would catch up to us this quickly, I would have said them already."

She met his gaze, and the fires burning in them called out to the dragon that lived underneath his skin. "The same words you were going to say in the forest after we first thought we'd killed the King? Those words?"

The very same. The ones that were branded against his heart, but the ones that he couldn't seem to let slip off his tongue. Not right now. He didn't want her to remember this as a desperate attempt for her to see what he felt before something terrible happened to them.

When he said those words, he wanted her to remember the moment forever. He wanted her to feel how much he loved her and that there wasn't a specific reason for him saying it other than his heart yearned for her.

So instead of saying the words, he nodded. "The same words. I just feel them even stronger now."

Lore placed her hand over his heart. The heat of her palm sank through the thin shirt he wore and he knew she felt the same. She had to. After everything they had been through together, there was very little they didn't feel for the other.

Anger, guilt, pain, and love. All of it wrapped up in one confusing bundle of emotion every time he looked at her.

"I won't take any risks," she promised. "I will look out for the others when they need it, but I promise I will make it to you in time for all of us to fly off together. We'll be safe."

He didn't know if she could promise that, but it made him feel better all the same.

"Good." Then he let her go.

Abraxas had the thought of kissing her. One final kiss just in case one of them died. But he wasn't sure he would ever release her if he got her in his arms, and it looked like she didn't trust herself, either. They had to go.

It felt as though there was never enough time for the two of them, and that tore him apart sometimes.

Together, they walked up the stairs to the battle they both knew would be difficult. The others waited for them. Weapons at the ready.

"Shall we?" Abraxas said. He cracked his knuckles and then walked toward the stone door. "Just remember to give me space to change. The magic is a bit more powerful than anyone accounts for, and it will knock you on your back if you're too close. The Umbral Knights will make quick work of you if you're in that delicate of a position."

"Understood," Zeph replied, walking up to the door with him. "Sprint out when I open it, then, would you? We've already planned a sort of pattern to spread out to make sure these Knights are sparse when we get out with you."

Lore's voice interrupted them. "I can take care of any Knights near him. I will need some arrows, though."

Zeph chuckled before replying, "It's an enchanted bow, Lorelei. Pull back on the string and you'll have an arrow. That's how it works."

"Ah." She looked down at the bow with appreciation. "That'll be fun. I'll take care of the Knights in the immediate area. Just let Abraxas run and I promise, nothing will touch him before he changes."

For the first time in his life, Abraxas had no worries about a partner in battle. If she said no one would touch him, then not a single one would.

He balled his hands into fists, then gave Zeph a nod. "I'm ready."

The young man rolled the door open, and Abraxas sprinted out into the daylight. His eyes seared with the sudden light, but he didn't stop running. He had to get far away from the crypt so he could change.

An arrow whirred by his ear and he heard the solid thunk as it hit metal armor. Then another, and another. A veritable rain of arrows that zinged through the air and thudded against their targets. Over and over. He never heard a single one strike anything but metal and he knew that Lore was keeping her promise.

Once he was certain he'd gone far enough, Abraxas let the change rip through him.

It hurt. More than it ever had. The dragon tore through his mortal form, shredding muscle and bone so quickly he almost lost himself in the sudden movement. He'd never experienced such a thing in his life, but he knew this was the last time he could afford to become a human again for a while. He needed time to heal, to be the dragon where his mind could focus on what he was. Who he was. Right now, he'd changed so many times that he wasn't even sure how to use his wings again.

But he had to. His mind had to take control over his body or they would all die.

Stretching his head up, he felt the muscles in his neck working as he let out a roar that shattered the very air. His wings spread wide, he knocked aside any of the Umbral Knights that were behind him. Abraxas lashed his tail and felt the crumbling bits of old tombstones smashing into the Knights in his way.

That should clear them enough room.

He tilted his head and watched as the tiny figures of his people ran toward him. Goliath reached him first, clambering up his scales to the ridges along his back. Then Zeph. Then Beauty.

Just as Lore was about to climb atop him, they heard the King's voice.

"Lorelei!" Zander shouted, his voice carrying through the mist. "I have what you want!"

He saw the look in her eyes. And he knew what she was going to say long before she said it.

Lore patted his leg and looked up at him. "I can't leave. You know I can't."

"Lore," he growled.

"I hate to break my promise to you, but I am going to take this risk." She reached up with both hands for him. "If I can make him tell us where the eggs are, then we're so much farther ahead than we are now. I have to try, Abraxas. You know I do."

He did. That didn't make saying goodbye to her any easier.

Abraxas spread a wing around them, then lowered his head down into her waiting arms. She pressed her forehead against his nose and he knew she was only saying goodbye, just in case.

It still broke his heart.

"Stay alive," she whispered. "And keep them safe."

"I called you Fire Heart once, but now I think your name is Bright Heart." He lifted his head and slammed his wings through the air, sending Umbral Knights flying back. "Your bravery and soul shine much brighter than any flame."

Abraxas took off, knowing that he left a piece of himself behind with her.

CHAPTER 32

Lorelei watched as everyone dear to her flew away. Abraxas would take care of them. She knew he would. He wouldn't let them die without putting up a fight that would shake the very earth.

Goliath clung to the spikes down Abraxas's spine, but he stared back at her with horror in his eyes. Beauty had tears streaming down her cheeks and an arm outstretched for Lore to take, even as they lifted off the ground.

Only the King's half brother watched her with understanding. He knew what she was doing, and likely the boy realized her plan. He was smart, for all that his bloodline was filled with monsters.

They took off for safety and a numb feeling occupied her chest. She wasn't angry that the King had interrupted everything. Honestly, there was a hint of relief in what she felt. At least now she knew where Zander was. She knew he hadn't died, and that the rumors were true. He had survived, and there were more battles for them to fight.

She turned toward the sea of Umbral Knights, and that was when the anger hit her. Like a fist to the belly, it bloomed hot and burned in her chest. She wanted to scream at the world for allowing such darkness to brew right under her nose. She wanted to cut through everyone who stood in her way. The King would feel the wicked edge of her blade today, even if that meant she had to die.

The first Umbral Knight ran at her with wild abandon. That was its first mistake. They had been around for centuries. Shouldn't they know how to fight better by now? She drew her bow and pulled back while an arrow appeared. Her elven birthright slithered out of her hands in ropes of bright moon magic and clung to the arrow as she released the string. The glowing tip sank into the eyehole of the armor, straight through the shadows.

Before, she'd have expected only to hear a solid thunk and the suit of armor to continue moving. Instead, the arrow exploded in the darkness and she heard a screech of anger, then all that smoke funneled out of the Umbral Knight. Banished by the light of the moon.

She pulled back again. Another glowing arrow sliced through the air. Again and again she let them fly until she'd cut a small space around herself. The Umbral Knights hesitated now. They realized they were in the presence of someone who would not be easy to kill.

Lore lowered her bow and a cool wind flicked through her hair. The lash of her ponytail snapped behind her. She reached to her sides and pulled out the two daggers she always kept with her.

Her dragon had cleaned these. He'd sharpened them with hands that belonged to her, hands that wouldn't rest until he'd felt them touching her skin again. She would not die today.

Brandishing her blades, she tilted her head and grinned. "Come on. What are you bastards waiting for?"

Four of them rushed her at the same time. They all sprinted forward, swords at the ready, but they were too slow in those heavy armored suits. Lore dropped low, whipping out one of her legs to trip the first one. She came back up in an arc, bringing her now glowing daggers up through the slit just below the chest plate of the next. The blade of another struck down, but she'd already swung her arms up in time to parry the blow.

Double knives gave her more leeway than the single blade of a sword. She used both of her arms to throw the third Knight off balance, in time to catch the next attack of the last. They fought like that for a while. The two of them would swing and she would catch them, over and over, until her arms shook.

Lore waited for the opportunity to present itself and there it was. At the last moment. The perfect chance for her to plunge her blade through the eye of the third, swing his body around to parry the last strike, and then throw him at the other. She leapt upon the tangled mass of bodies and sank a dagger into the eye of the remaining Umbral Knight.

Breathing hard, she stood. Ready for the next battle. But the glowing smoke had already identified its weakness, apparently. As she watched the black mist exit the armored suits, it found other hosts.

Her heart stopped when the first hand clawed its way out of the ground. The skeletal fingers gripped the soft earth and pulled itself out of the shallow grave. Smoke swirled in its empty sockets and the clacking jaw shuddered with hunger.

The Umbral Knights had possessed the wights.

All she could hear was the echoing of her own breath in her ears.

The ragged sound of her lungs as she realized that she'd never be able to keep up fighting like this. They would tackle her to the ground and they would feast on her flesh.

The first wight shambled toward her, arms outstretched. This one had once been a woman. Her skirts tangled in her legs. That was why she moved so slowly. She'd lost half her face to time, the other half remained covered by the long tangle of her dark hair.

Lore stepped to the side and slashed the woman's throat, but she kept coming. With a spike of fear, Lore leapt out of the way of her dirt smeared fingers.

They didn't die, she remembered. They couldn't because they were already dead.

Horrified, she backed away from the incoming army that once again wanted to devour her. But then she realized there were Umbral Knights behind her as well. The armored kind that were easier to kill but no less deadly.

He'd trapped her. The King had known this was how the battle would end, and he had ensured she would remain cornered against the crypt. Right where he wanted her.

Lore flexed her fingers on the hilts of her daggers and lifted them again. She would fight whatever he wanted to throw at her, and she would win. She had no other choice.

The Umbral Knights parted and down the long hallway their armor created, she saw him again. He didn't look like the Zander she remembered, nor had his beauty remained after the attempted murder.

Zander had once been a handsome man, but the dark magic that kept him alive already ate away at the mask he'd worn.

The silver stripes of hair above his ears had stretched higher and his cheeks had grown gaunt. The darkness in his eyes was familiar. Hatred burned in them. She grew lost in those shadows, almost so much that she missed the wound at his neck.

The wound she'd created had extended over his throat and split open the skin. She knew she'd cut deep into his flesh, and that should have been enough to stop him from moving. But instead of blood leaking out of the parted muscles, shadows swirled. Keeping death at bay.

For now.

He lifted his hands and clapped at her performance. "Bravo, Lorelei." Zander grinned at her, and she noticed his sparkling white smile had turned gray. "You always were one to watch, and now I think you were hiding so much more from me than I originally thought."

"You're supposed to be dead," she snarled.

"I know. You tried your best."

That patronizing, pitying tone grated on every inch of her soul.

She gripped the daggers a little tighter in each of her hands. "I don't know what dark magic you used to avoid death. I'll be honest, though; I am curious."

Keep him talking, she told herself. He always liked to talk about his own accomplishments and he would be the first to talk himself into a corner. If she could distract him for a little while longer, she might not have to fight him. She might be able to get out of this situation with her head still attached.

Zander stopped clapping and lifted his hands in the air. "Hell if I know, darling. This wasn't my magic, but the magic of my ancestors. My father made sure people like you couldn't kill me. I'm the last of the line, after all. Don't you think they would do anything they could to preserve it?"

He wasn't, though.

He didn't know about his half brother, or he wanted her to think that he didn't know about him. Lore would keep that in her pocket for a later time. When he was less aware that she had inched another step closer to the crypt. If she could get inside again, she could wait for Abraxas to return. He'd come back for her and burn everyone to the ground.

"Ah, ah, ah," Zander tsked. "Do you think I'd let you get away that easily? My darling elf, you're too smart to think that."

"I think you know less of the world than you think, and perhaps that curse keeping you alive has sunk into your mind." That was a weak argument, even to her own ears.

Zander walked toward her, the picture of relaxation and a man who had nothing to fear. "There are a hundred Umbral Knights on all sides of you. That crypt won't save you."

"I said nothing about a crypt."

"You all thought you were being so smart, hiding away in that dank cave like I wouldn't find you." His head jerked to the side, as though the words caused him pain. The movement revealed more of that horrible open wound. "I always know where you are, Lore. The magic that made me like this also let me know where to find the person who tried to kill me. I'm quite sure that if I return the favor, it might change me back to myself. So I will hunt you through this entire realm if I must."

She blinked, and suddenly he wasn't ten paces away from her. He was right in front of her. Zander's hand snapped out like the mouth of a snake and closed around her throat.

Gasping, she held onto his wrist with one hand and slapped at his chest with the other. Scrabbling for some purchase, anything that would stop the vise from stealing any more of her air.

He held her tight, enough to make it difficult to breathe but not cutting off all air. Zander darted them back toward the crypt until her spine struck the hard stone with a sharp sound of broken ribs and a flash of pain.

"You tried to kill me," he snarled. "You took away all that I valued in this life. I'm going to cut you up into tiny little pieces so you can feel what I do."

She searched the edges of his armor, trying to find a crack, anything that would allow her to get closer to his skin.

With a sound of disappointment, he grabbed onto her wandering hand and bent her fingers back. Lore let out a small whimper. Her gaze flew up toward the gray sky as though her body couldn't look at the pain he caused.

"I'm going to cut these off first," he murmured, holding her hand so he could look at it with her pointer finger bent so far she couldn't even focus on his words. "I think I'll cut them off one by one and let them heal, so you can look at the deformity every day and think of me. Just like I think of you."

The sound of her finger breaking echoed in her ears while the pain zinged through her body like lightning. She screamed, or tried, but the sound that came out of her mouth was a choked, horrible wheeze. The tap of her finger on the back of her hand felt unnatural.

Zander tightened his grip around her neck and lifted her from the ground. She kicked her feet, trying to connect with his torso, but even when her boot struck his ribs, he didn't flinch.

He was like the wights staggering behind him, creating a never ending field of dead bodies that stared at her with empty eyes. Soulless. Desolate.

"Even now, you think you're going to escape, don't you?" His fingers squeezed so hard she thought he would tear through her throat. "You think you're going to go home."

Home. What did that even mean for someone like her? Was it the memory of her mother's death at the order of this man? Or was it the cold, dusty attic where she had lived alone for many years?

Lore didn't have a home. And that was all because of this man who had thought it would be easy to trap magical creatures and force them to live like slaves. It was his fault she didn't have that warm feeling in her chest when he mentioned the word. All she felt when someone said home was a longing and an anger that she'd never experienced it before.

The flash of rage sank into her skin and the last bit of her magic blasted into her hand that gripped his wrist. The bright light burned her eyes, and then she felt her hand sinking into his skin. As though she melted away bits of his flesh.

With a curse, he released his hold and dropped her to the ground. She landed hard on her hands and knees. Coughing, she tried to roll away from the boot she remembered so well, connecting with her ribs.

Except that boot never came. A swell of Umbral Knights yanked the King away from her at the exact same moment she heard the sounds of metal striking metal. Armor toppled and hit the ground.

But what she focused on most were the evil whispers that sang through the air.

"Feast," they hissed as they approached the Umbral Knights. "We hunger."

A hand grabbed her shoulder and yanked her upright. She listed to the side, grabbing onto the person who had stood her up only to gape at the glistening dark skin and obsidian chip eyes.

"You," she whispered.

The deepmonger who had brought her food flashed her a bright grin before slicing his blade through the air behind her. The grimdag screamed in victory as it fed upon the soul of the wight who had tried to attack her. The body dropped to the ground, empty and finally resting.

"I thought you knew my name is Draven," he replied, pulling the blade close to himself once more. "You may call me that if you like."

"Considering you've saved my life, you may call me Lorelei." She pressed her hand against her throat, but her broken finger made her pause.

Lore's entire world tilted to the side again as she stared at the pointer finger, still pinned in the wrong place. It shouldn't do that. No fingers should do that.

Draven noticed it at the same time as she did. He let out a hiss of sympathy and then grabbed onto her hand. "It's better if I do it now, but you'll have to heal it later."

She gave him a nod and then screamed as he pulled the finger back into place.

"It's done," he muttered, repeating himself a few times as though he had to soothe his own nerves. "It's done, Lorelei. Now I need you to run. Go to the edge of the forest, away from this place. We'll handle the Umbral Knights."

She held her hand to her chest, the ache making it hard to focus. "Why?"

Yet again, he answered with a grin. "Not all of us want to remain hidden. You're very convincing when you want to be. Now go! We'll hold them off. Get to that dragon of yours."

She didn't have to be told twice. Lore ran through the waves of Umbral Knights and it seemed like every time one of them tried to attack her, a deepmonger was there to kill it. The hissing sweep of grimdags echoed in her ears long after she'd sprinted out of the Fields of Somber toward the forests at the base of the Stygian Peaks.

CHAPTER 33

Wings spread wide, he glided out of the clouds and down to the base of the Stygian Peaks. Abraxas had difficulty breathing through the fear of what Lore would endure. His chest already glowed with flames ready to release upon the hordes of enemies that had descended upon her.

It took too long for him to find a safe place to land. He opted to slam through the trees and damned if some branches cut through the thin membranes of his wings. He would get through the barrier of woods and leaves, and then he would return for the elf that was his.

Abraxas landed hard on the ground and shook himself to dislodge the people clinging onto his back. They needed to get off of him so he could leave.

He had to go.

He had to find them.

He needed to...

Beauty slid off his back too quickly and landed hard on her leg. Her sharp cry echoed around them, and he squeezed his eyes shut at the sound.

He needed to go, but he couldn't leave her without knowing the extent of her injury. Not when Lore would kill him if anything happened to her dear friend. And in truth, he couldn't move himself if Beauty was hurt. She had become dear to him as well.

Lowering his head to the ground, he set his chin on the moss and stone, eyeing her. "Are you all right?"

"No, I..." she hissed out an angry breath, hands clutching her leg. "I rolled my ankle on the way down and I think something's wrong with it."

"Can you stand?"

She bit her lip and nodded, although her expression was not one of confidence.

To his surprise, Zeph stepped up to her without even the slightest bit of hesitation. He crouched beside her and notched his shoulder under her armpit. "Here, lean on me."

"I don't think you can lift me," she muttered, obviously upset to mention such a thing. "I'm not light."

"And I'm not weak. Have a little faith, would you?"

Zeph lifted and Beauty struggled to stand up with him. Abraxas helped as he could, setting his giant head next to her so she could grab onto his scales for handholds to lift herself up. They got her upright, but putting any weight on that leg would not happen. The moment she tried, she fell once again with the pain.

"So stupid," she kept muttering. "So silly to break something now of all times. I'm so sorry, everyone. I just... I didn't..."

"It's not your fault," Abraxas replied. Although a slight flare of anger still burned in his chest. He didn't have time for this. "Few have ridden a dragon in their lives, and it's not the same as jumping off a horse."

What could he do? He had to make sure they were all safe before he left them. That's what Lore had told him to do. And yes, he realized he was following orders a little too precisely, but that was what he'd been created to do. Following orders was literally in the very essence of what made a crimson dragon.

Growling, he looked through the forest back toward the Fields of Somber. Though he couldn't see Lore, he knew she was there. Waiting for him.

"Find a splint," he said, his voice thundering. "Something straight."

Goliath patted his side. "You need to go find her, my friend. We can handle it from here."

"Find a splint," he repeated. "I cannot return to my mortal form yet. This is... difficult for me. I have to make a choice I don't want to make, but I will see to it that Beauty is well before I return to Lore."

Zeph helped Beauty limp to a fallen stump where she could sit down, but Goliath still lingered at Abraxas's side.

The dwarf cleared his throat and said, "You know, my friend, telling you to look after us wasn't an order. She needed you to leave, so she did what she had to. You can make your own choices."

He searched for the right answer, knowing that his words could be misconstrued. Abraxas didn't have the talent for speech or a gift for convincing others of how he felt. He'd never had to do this before.

Finally, he looked down at the dwarf and gruffly replied, "It's a hard choice for me, too. Not because of the order, but because you are all my friends. I don't wish to see you harmed any more than Lore."

Tears welled in Goliath's eyes, and a single one dripped down his cheek like a diamond. It fell into the hidden parts of the dwarf's beard, and then he cleared his throat. "I'll go find a splint. You can't change for a while, you said?"

"It would cause me immense pain." He didn't know what it would do to his dragon, either. He hadn't changed this often in a long time. The King rarely made him choose between forms and didn't mind when Abraxas disappeared for days on end to heal within his pools of gold.

This was uncharted territory.

"Then don't change." Goliath patted his leg one more time before turning toward the forest. "We've all been through enough pain lately."

He hated how true the statement was.

Abraxas lifted his wings, stretching them wide for a powerful thrust that would propel him out through the trees again. But then he heard it. The sound of footsteps sprinting, thudding across the forest floor and racing straight at them.

With a snarl, he turned to the sound. Fire licked from his nostrils, ready to burn whoever dared attack them while they were weak.

Lore burst out of the underbrush, holding her arm against her chest and red streaks circling her throat. She ran as though someone were following her, staggering over fallen limbs as she never would have done before. But she was alive. She had found them, and he stopped thinking.

The change rushed through him, blistering his skin and ripping fire through his lungs. It didn't matter. The pain didn't stop him as he raced toward her, likely staggering himself as though he'd been through battle.

He struck her too hard. Though she only reacted with a small oof of breath and then they clung to each other. He held her against his chest, feeling her ribs expand with horrible rattles of air.

"You're alive," he breathed into her hair. "I'm so sorry I didn't come find you."

"There wasn't time," she muttered. "He wouldn't have given us any chance. You did what you had to do."

"I should have stayed with you." It ate him up, knowing that he hadn't protected her. That was his job. His only function in life. He protected what was his and who he served.

Lore drew back in his arms, staring up at him with a frown on her face. "I can take care of myself. They couldn't."

They might have been fine. The King didn't care about a dwarf, a bride he'd forgotten about, or a young man overlooked by a kingdom. Abraxas knew his captor well, however. Lore had left a mark on Zander that the King would never forget.

His eyes trailed to her throat, and he touched a single finger to the swollen welts there. He counted each mark. Five individual places where the King's fingers had been while he strangled her. "How did you get away?"

"He's not himself," she replied, ignoring his question. "I thought he was evil before, but the magic that made the Umbral Knights has consumed him. I don't think he can die, Abraxas."

"Anything can die."

"I don't think he can anymore." Her worry had sunk deep into her skin. He saw it in the wrinkles around her eyes and the set of her jaw.

She watched him as though he had the answer. He didn't know how to kill Zander, and he certainly had never heard of a creature who could evade death. It wasn't possible. He knew that to be true.

"Lore?" Goliath's voice cut through their conversation. "Are you all right?"

351

He was forced to release her, because no matter what they did, he always had to let her go.

But then she took two steps out of his arms, stumbled, and went to her knees. Abraxas caught her and swung her up into his arms.

"You aren't all right," he grumbled as he strode toward the others. "What happened?"

"It's nothing," she muttered, lying through her teeth. "He broke my finger, is all. I just didn't think it would hurt so much."

"He what?" Anger made his vision turn red. He wanted nothing more than to rip Zander's spine out through his back.

Goliath's shoulder shoved at his hip. "Let me see her hand. I can help."

Abraxas ignored the dwarf. "Lore, show me."

She looked up at him with those big ocean eyes, and he knew she wouldn't show him. Instead, she clutched her hand closer to her chest and shook her head. "I don't believe you're thinking straight right now. Goliath should look at it."

"Show me," he snarled.

He couldn't make her show him the wound, nor could he get rid of the anger in his chest. A small voice whispered in the back of his mind that maybe he was going mad. All this changing back and forth between man and beast had brought his mind too close to the brink of an animal. His ability to calm himself, to think clearly, had disappeared in the wake of fury that made him want to rip and tear even in this form.

Arms shaking, he led her over to the log where Beauty sat and deposited Lore beside her. Carefully. Oh so carefully. He brushed his fingers over the top of her head, tracing the outline of her now ragged ponytail. He couldn't touch enough of her even as the calluses on his hands pulled at the delicate strands.

"Step aside, dragon." Goliath shouldered his way in front of Abraxas, then reached for Lore's hands.

He forced himself to take a few steps back. The dwarf needed air to breathe and room to work, and none of that was possible if Abraxas loomed over him. But damned if that wasn't the hardest thing he'd ever done.

Every wince she made, every softly drawn breath, made him want to break something. He wanted to put his fist through a tree and listen to it tear the forest apart as it fell.

Zeph stepped up beside him, crossing his arms over his chest. "They'll be all right. Both of them."

"They better be," he snarled.

Goliath took the better part of the afternoon to bind both of the women's broken bones. He took forever, and Abraxas had paced a path through the forest floor by the time the sun had set.

Finally, the dwarf stood up, brushed his hands off at his sides, and nodded. "That'll have to do. I have nothing to cast a spell and heal the two of you, so you'll have to do that on your own for a bit."

Abraxas grunted. "Didn't we bring healing potions?"

"Not something that'll help set bones." Goliath gave him a censoring look. "Or do you want to test out the potions yourself?"

"I think we've been traveling a long time and all of us have forgotten a great many things."

"Are you accusing me of something, dragon?"

Lore heaved a sigh and then shouted with surprising strength, "Enough!"

They both flinched and looked at her.

She glared at them with more than enough anger to be intimidating. "You two will stop fighting. Immediately. I need you to listen to what I saw in the Fields of Somber, and then we will decide what to do from there."

Of course, no one wanted to hear the horror story from the Fields. They all had to endure, however. The entire crew of them gathered around her and they all listened to what seemed like an impossible tale.

"The Ashen Deep intervened?" he asked, though the words felt wrong on his tongue. "They never do that."

"They do now," Lore replied. He could see she didn't believe it herself. "He said not all of them want to hide any longer, and that I should run."

A thought ran down his spine, sending chills dancing across this mortal flesh. "He told you to run?"

"To the Stygian Peaks, and to find you." She nodded at Abraxas and, for the very first time, he saw her cheeks turn red with a blush. "He said to find the dragon and that you would protect me."

His gut reaction was to remind her that he would. Forever. No matter where they went or how far she ran, he would protect her with every breath in his body. But the Ashen Deep did not give warnings without reason.

Abraxas looked out into the forest, his eyes searching for any movement and his ears listening for any heartbeat that might linger in the shadows. "We're not safe here," he breathed.

The dwarf stood, hand on his belt and in between the many knives he still had strapped onto himself. "What do you hear?"

"Nothing yet. But if that deepmonger wanted us to run, then I don't think we've run far enough for comfort." Abraxas knew Zander well. Attacking in the middle of the night, when everyone else was asleep, was a plan the King favored.

Zander didn't want to fight fair. He feared he would lose. He'd rather attack his enemy when they least expected it and cut their throat without battle.

Lore planted her hand on the log and pushed herself up, her face pale with pain. "I agree. I don't think we're safe here, but finding anywhere safe in this forest would be difficult. Zeph? Do you know of any place we might seek refuge?"

The young man shook his head. "No. I've never been this far from the Fields."

Beauty spoke for the first time since they'd all sat down. Though her own face was pale with pain, and she clearly didn't want to move, she pointed up at the mountains. "I think there's only one way to go. And that's up."

Lore tsked. "Don't be foolish. You aren't in any shape to climb a mountain."

"Neither are you," Beauty snapped. "We should look for a cave. Or anywhere that we can hide for a while before the King finds us sitting out here like we've been waiting for him to kill us."

In mere moments, they would devolve into an argument again. He already knew their tones well. They were like two sisters squabbling about who was right.

"I know a place," he said, his voice cutting through the dispute. "An abandoned elven castle, high on the mountaintops. I flew past it on my way here."

They all stared at him with hope in their eyes. Other than the dwarf, who inspected him with no small amount of worry. "Can you change again? So soon?"

No.

He still felt the madness clawing at him. Any swing of dark emotion ripped at the barrier he'd put in place. It was only a matter of time before that beast he'd held at bay swallowed him whole.

Abraxas shook his head. "I guess we'll have to climb."

CHAPTER 34

The higher up the mountain they climbed, the worse the weather got. Lorelei paused, holding onto the scraggly trunk of a tree that was thinner than her arm, and glanced back over the ground they'd covered. They were so high up.

The valley below appeared so small from up here. She could see the marshes of the Fields of Somber, stretching all the way to the cliff's edge, where the sea spread out beyond her sight. If she squinted, she could make out the tiny speck of Tenebrous to their right. And, of course, the forests from which the Ashen Deep had come.

A shiver shook her shoulders, and she turned her attention back to the snow-covered peaks. They had a long way to go yet, or so she could only assume.

Abraxas had claimed the old elven stronghold would give them shelter for the night, but she feared there wouldn't be enough time to get there. Beauty's leg had held them up. She hobbled the best she could, with an arm wrapped around Zeph's shoulders, and she hadn't complained even once.

But her breathing had gotten heavier in the past couple of hours. So much so that Lore worried she would pass out. Zeph paused whenever he could to give her a chance, but then they would have to keep up with the others.

Lore had started making excuses about her own injury. She didn't need the hand all that often, other than fighting, and no one would follow them up the grueling goat trails that led to the summit. Still, she didn't want Beauty to be the only one hurting. And Beauty shouldn't blame herself for their slow pace.

Even Lore felt the effects of exhaustion. She and Goliath were made for this kind of journey. The dwarves could walk for ages and Lore glided over the snow and stones. But this was a long trek.

Abraxas had disappeared over the ridgeline a bit ago. He still hadn't come back.

She could only assume that meant they were getting closer, and that he knew where to go. Or maybe he was searching ahead for a better path so that Beauty wouldn't have to be dragged the rest of the way.

Goliath paused, waiting for her to catch up to him.

"We can't keep going like this," he said as she reached his side. "Beauty can't do it."

"I know. We have to be close." Or at least, she hoped they were. "Abraxas wouldn't lead us in the wrong direction."

"Finding a place in the air is a lot easier than it is on land." He looked at the ridge where Abraxas had disappeared. "I hope he knows where we're going and isn't about to come back and tell us to change paths."

She could see that happening. He'd return with a frustrated expression on his face and then point to another peak where their shelter actually was. She'd look back at Beauty, already pale with pain and exhaustion. And then she'd have to tell him to look for a cave for the night. They would huddle around the fire and try to stay alive until morning.

Her breath frosted in the air as she spoke. "We'll endure. That's what we do best."

"Is it?" Goliath sighed, and she heard his weariness in the sound. "Do we endure because we are good at it, or because there's never been another choice?"

She didn't know the answer to that question. Lore wasn't sure she wanted to think about it.

Through the dimming light at the top of the peak, Abraxas appeared. He stood tall and strong, not affected at all by their journey. He didn't even look tired, although she knew he had to be.

Abraxas lifted an arm and waved for them to join him. She could only hope that meant he'd found the castle.

Picking up her pace, she sprinted over the stones and pushed every muscle in her body to get to his side. Breathing faster than before, she asked, "Are we nearly there?"

"We made it," he said, his expression softening as he looked at her.

Did she appear tired? She shouldn't. Elves could travel for days on end without having to stop and yet... She was exhausted. She needed to sleep and think and plan for whatever might come at them tomorrow.

Lore had fought the King again, and she hadn't realized how much that would affect her.

Abraxas slung an arm around her shoulders and tugged her against his side. "Just a bit longer, Lore, and then we'll see what is left of this castle. I have a feeling you'll be more useful than I when we arrive."

Considering that most elves knew how to hide their precious belongings, she supposed he was right.

They waited for the others to catch up to them before they pushed forward the last bit. The remaining length of their long hike ended with snow. She watched the tiny delicate flakes fall from the sky, each one more lovely and perfect. But every time they touched her cheeks, an icy chill fractured through her body.

And then they walked into what felt like a dream.

She'd never seen a place like this before. The elves who'd made this haven had taken special time to cast wards that shimmered as they passed through them. Lore had the strange sensation that she'd walked through a bubble. Magic popped against her skin, and then the cold disappeared.

Even now. After all these years and after the ruin of their home, the magic remained. Strong and powerful as the day it was cast.

Zeph and Beauty walked through the wards and both gasped at the sudden rush of warm air. Though Lore couldn't tell if they were surprised at the magic or the remains of the glass castle.

"Where are we?" Beauty asked, her eyes dancing over every detail she could see.

Lore tried to look at the ruins through the gaze of a mortal. Sharp, jagged spires cut up to the sky like knives made of ice. The shattered remnants of windows would radiate with colors with the right light, but now, all they could see were the terrifying shadows that looked like teeth along the once beautiful floor.

There was a mural on the ground, she noticed. Bits and pieces of the stone floor had been pulled up recently. And as she looked even closer, she noted a few gouges that could easily be the marks of dragon claws.

Even Lore hadn't heard of this place, although she had heard little of elven lore. It wasn't like her mother wanted to talk about the people who had cast her aside. And then she hadn't had a lot of contact with other elves after her mother's death. They wanted nothing to do with a half blood.

Abraxas stepped up to her side and gestured with an arm. "This is Umanor Esari. One of the last and greatest strongholds of the elves. Or at least, what is left of it."

She knew she should be honored to be where other elves had lived, but it left a rather hollow feeling in her chest. All that remained of the history and beauty of her kind were the broken remnants of a building that had once been astounding.

Swallowing hard, she took a few more steps on the same path that so many others had walked. "You said there was something I needed to do here?"

"I had hoped you could feel the spells the other elves had left. There usually is some kind of safe house, or a hidden door where others could hide in case the castle was attacked. Not all the elves were warriors." Abraxas paused, then chuckled. "Although most of them were."

Children, she imagined, were likely the ones who needed shelter in case of an attack.

She looked up at the moon and felt its light filling up her chest. She took the beams and wrapped them around her wrists, using them as the power she needed to seek out the magic that should be nearby. If there was a safe house, then she would find it.

Breathing out a long breath, she released her silver power until it hit against something that wasn't supposed to be there. A spell that made an entire building invisible to the naked eye.

"It's in the back right corner," she whispered. "I don't know how big it is or if there's any food in there."

"Good enough," Abraxas said. "How do we remove the magic?"

A real elf could have muttered a few words and the curse would lift without a problem. But she wasn't a real elf, and the magic wanted to fight back against her being here.

Lore sighed and started over to the hidden door. "Blood," she said. "It wants my blood."

Resigned to a little more pain, she walked to the barrier, and the spell made her mind wander. It whispered in her ear that she had seen nothing. That she didn't want to come over to this corner of the castle and she wanted to go to the other side. Didn't that make more sense?

Magic was always so compelling, and she'd heard the words before.

Lore lifted her hand and touched the very edge of the barrier. It sliced through her palm as though someone held a knife out to her. A splatter of blood struck the air, the red sparkling like rubies before dripping down the revealed glass wall of the safe house. An elf had built this with the intent that everything would remain secret, even when the wards were broken.

The interior was hazy to the naked eye. It blended in with the background, and she couldn't quite focus on it.

Abraxas reached out a hand and touched the glass. His fingers left a small imprint of dirt behind. "That'll do. Now, let's get everyone inside."

Could they all fit inside? Inside what? There was nothing here and she should search elsewhere for shelter.

Lore shook the magic off again and gestured for the others. "Quickly. I can already feel the wards coming back. This won't last very long."

Her companions rushed past her, each one pausing until she knocked them forward and through the magic. They didn't want to go into this building anymore than she did. A small voice in her head wondered if there was a reason for all of their hesitation. Perhaps the magic wasn't meant to hide it from prying eyes, but was meant to hide it forever. What curse had been laid on this place?

They didn't have a choice, though. Already the skies had darkened with a storm that could freeze them all in the night. They had to go inside.

She slipped through the magic as the wards burst back into life. She had the distinct impression of all her friends and the haziness of the building disappearing before she stepped into the interior of the glass safe house with the rest of them.

Someone had set this place up so that it would always be secure for anyone who entered it. Long shelves to her right contained jars full of spelled water that would remain cold and fresh. Food that was obviously still good enough to eat, bread, fruit, even a few cured meats that somehow had remained fresh and well. She'd seen nothing like it in her life.

The other side of the small glass house had exactly five cots and trunks for each of them to put their things in. The light blue blankets looked warm and comfortable. A fire burned at the end of the room in a glass fireplace, crackling merrily and warm.

"Strange," she muttered. "I didn't think to find any of this in here."

"Neither did I," Abraxas replied, then he cracked his neck with a sigh. "Why don't we look at that hand now, shall we?"

"I think we should focus on making sure Beauty is comfortable." She wasn't sure she could handle someone trying to take care of her right now. She'd fold into his arms and never want to crawl out of them.

Abraxas looked over at Beauty and Zeph, who had already made their way to the farthest cots and sat down across from each other. Zeph held Beauty's hands in his own, rubbing them to get some heat back in them while he asked her how her leg was feeling.

Even Goliath looked a little put out, but he dropped his bags onto the trunk at the foot of the middle cot and sighed. "Fine. It's fine. I can take this one. Everyone go off with your respective partners, would you?"

"Poor man," she said with a slight chuckle. "He always likes to be dramatic about these things, but I know he'd never look at another woman the way he looked at..."

She wasn't supposed to say anything about that, though. Was she?

Abraxas's lips twitched with a smile. Then he nodded toward the cot closest to them. "Just sit down, would you? I'd like to take a look, if that's all right with you."

It wasn't.

It was.

She didn't want him to see how ugly her hand looked and besides, he couldn't heal it. Dragons didn't know how to heal, and the wound was already too far gone for any magic to fix it. She had to heal it the old fashioned way, and that was fine.

But she wanted to be near him. She wanted to feel his hands on her arms and for him to tell her that everything was going to be all right. This journey wasn't wasted. They could still find the eggs and continue forward with this plan of theirs.

And yet...

Damn it, her feet were already walking over to the cot and then she slammed down onto it with a heavy sigh. She was so tired of all of this. She was tired of figuring out what to do next and how to go about saving the rest of her people.

She was tired. And Lore thought maybe, just maybe, she might have earned some time to breathe.

Abraxas walked over beside her and sat down on the other cot. He reached for her hand, gently holding it by the wrist so he could look over the finger that Draven had roughly jerked back into place.

He turned her hand, rotating it with so much care it almost brought tears to her eyes. She didn't deserve that kind of touch, and yet, he always held onto her as though she were breakable.

"He didn't do this right," he muttered. "We'll have to reset your finger when we get to a healer."

"It'll already be healed wrong by then."

"Well, then we'll have to break it again." He looked up at her with a ferocious anger in his gaze. "You won't be able to bend it if it heals like this. And then how will you fight?"

With every ounce of her being. Like she always had.

Lore lifted her injured hand and placed it on his cheek. She held onto the sharp outline of his jaw, forcing him to meet her gaze. "I'm going to be fine, Abraxas. It's just a broken finger. I've had worse."

"You never should have experienced such pain," he hissed. "Any of it."

And then it all hit her all at once. This man had stuck with her through more than he ever should have. He didn't care that she'd never given him much hope or reason to stay around her. He stayed because he wanted to, or for some other unfathomable purpose that she couldn't piece together.

Lore licked her lips and asked, "Why are you still here? Is it because you think I'll find those eggs or for something else?"

He met her gaze, and she saw the answer in his eyes. "You know why

I'm here, Lore. There is no pressure in those words, and no expectations on my part. I am here. I will be here. For you and only you."

Lore swallowed hard, her throat working around emotions that stuck in the center of her body. She couldn't... She didn't...

He leaned into her touch, then tilted his head to press a gentle kiss to her palm. "It'll be all right. We have time, Lore. We have plenty of time."

But what if they didn't have as much time as they thought?

CHAPTER 35

They stayed in the glass safe house for the better part of a week. Abraxas was ashamed to admit that this was largely his fault. He'd needed to change into his dragon form and stay that way. So he'd left rather than subject the others to the overly sized scaley beast.

But damn, it felt good to be back to himself. He soared through the skies, splitting clouds in half while he searched for the King in every nearby hiding place he could seek out. Zander was sneaky, however, and Abraxas hadn't found him in his hunts. The King had disappeared.

Then again, so had the Ashen Deep.

He could find no trace of the deepmongers, not even above the Fields of Somber as he glided over the ruins. Not even their scent lingered. Though it should have, considering how long they must have fought.

And they had fought a great deal. Nothing remained of the wights that he could tell as he flew above them. The Fields of Somber were eerily quiet and empty. Just as a graveyard should be.

The madness of his dragon propelled him forward, away from the Fields and to the sea where he hunted for prey that was more difficult to find. He plunged beneath the waves, lungs burning as he searched for anything that would fight him. He took his time with the sharks that swarmed his strange form. Toying with them. Playing with the creatures who thought they were predators until he could feast upon their flesh.

The hunt drove away any remaining madness that lingered in his mind. And though he wasn't certain he'd been gone for a week, that was about the time when he returned. He landed outside the safe house and waited until Lore opened the door. That was when he slipped back into his mortal form, although the creature inside his chest groaned with disappointment.

He didn't want to return to that weakened state, either. He would have preferred to continue as the clawed, toothy version of himself who frightened all. But he knew that time would come again. It just wasn't right now.

Abraxas stepped through the wards into the elven safe house and found himself surprised by how angry the others were.

Lore stood near the door, glaring at the others as though they had personally insulted her. Zeph remained apart, apparently cataloging their food while he ignored that an argument was even happening. Goliath and Beauty faced off with their arms crossed and both panting with rage.

"I take it I came at a bad time?" he asked, ducking the rest of the way through the door and closing it behind him.

Beauty pointed at the dwarf. "This one refuses to see reason, so thank all the gods in the heavens that you're here, Abraxas. Maybe you can pick him up and dunk his head in the snow, so he stops being an idiot."

"Oh, that's rich," Goliath snarled. "The little princess wants to go home and live in comfort when she knows damned well we cannot trust the powers at large. She just doesn't want to wander around on a sprained ankle!"

"You know that's not why I want to return to the castle! We have nowhere to go other than this frozen wasteland. We have no idea what to do next. The King is hunting us." Beauty ticked off her fingers with each part of her list. "Do you need more reasons than that?"

"I do!" Goliath turned to Abraxas while pointing at the woman now behind him. "Would you please tell her to see reason?"

He flicked his gaze between the two of them, then looked at Lore for help. "Do I want to get involved in this?"

"Probably not," she muttered. "But we're going to have to get involved. We were talking about our next steps before you got here. Beauty thinks we should go back to the Umbral Castle and ask Margaret for her assistance. Goliath thinks we should continue forward the way we've been going. He doesn't trust any Darkveil elves, apparently."

Interesting. Abraxas arched his brow and looked at the dwarf.

Goliath grumbled, "You wouldn't trust her either if you had seen what she does with those shadows. Unnatural magic, that. She reminds me of the Umbral Knights sometimes, and I don't believe she's trustworthy."

Neither did he. Abraxas had dealt with the woman enough to know a snake in the grass when he saw one. Margaret would do what she wanted and only what suited her. If others had to fall along the way, then so be it. She would step over their dead bodies and never look back.

Beauty shook her head with a sharp movement. "You don't know her like I do. She wants what is best for this kingdom and for the creatures who don't have anyone else to speak for them. I'll admit, her methods aren't as kind as some, but she doesn't want to hurt anyone."

"That's a beautiful notion," Abraxas replied. "But in practice, I don't think I believe it. She's going about this in the only way she knows how. I understand that. But I don't think it's the only way."

He didn't think it was possible to make Beauty any more furious than she already was. He'd been wrong. Her face turned red as a tomato, and she balled her hands into fists. She looked like she was going to pop, actually.

What had he said? He'd been truthful. He answered her question. Why was she angry at him now?

"What is going on?" he asked. "Someone make her stop doing that."

"I think I'll let her work through that emotion on her own." Lore walked away from him toward the fire, where they had pulled out a few chairs.

Where had those come from?

He hadn't given it much thought that the entire safe house had been perfectly set up for them, as though it had known they were coming. But the magic in this building had created a cozy little nook for them. He supposed he shouldn't question comfort when it was provided freely.

Abraxas trailed along behind Lore and sat down beside her. The warmth of the fire sank through his bones, easing the tension in his muscles. "So, we're trying to figure out our next steps?" he asked. "And the only option so far is to return to Margaret or... not?"

Lore gave him an unimpressed stare. "We obviously hadn't gotten that far into the conversation before you got here. You have impeccable timing."

"Indeed I do." He hooked an arm over the back of the chair and craned his neck to see the others. "Would you three join us, please? I don't care that you're angry, Beauty. And Zeph, you can stop pretending to survey the food quantities. I think the magic in this house will keep the stocks full."

The young man's face paled, and he walked over while biting his lip, waiting for the next person to start yelling. Abraxas noted that Zeph even sat down next to him. As if the dragon would be the one to take care of him. Or provide a better shield.

Abraxas leaned over and whispered, "They fight because they're family. Took me a while to get used to it, too."

"They get so loud," Zeph muttered.

"It's overwhelming, isn't it?" He then slapped the boy between his shoulder blades. "You'll be fine. Now, I think we first need to figure out what our plan is. Do we want to regroup and talk through options? Or do we want to find the eggs? Perhaps we should find Zander? There are many paths and if we don't pick one, then I'm sure it'll start to get confusing real fast. We need one goal in mind while we work on this. Together."

The others stared at him in stunned silence, so he could only guess no one had suggested that.

Lore licked her lips, the movement rather distracting, before nodding her head. "Right. Well, for me, I think it's most important that we find those eggs first. I don't care if Zander is alive."

Immediately, Beauty spoke up. "I don't think Margaret would agree with that. We left to get those eggs, sure. But having Zeph in the mix makes everything more complicated. What if Zander attacked us because we'd found someone who could overthrow him? We shouldn't disregard the power of a rival to the throne. Keeping Zeph with us is threatening his life much more than if he were in the castle with the rebellion's army."

It was a fair point and not one he'd given much thought. Abraxas had given up on trying to understand the reasoning for Zander's decisions a long time ago. The King rarely made any choices with logic and instead, let his emotions rule.

Which meant it could be likely that he'd found out about Zeph as well and wanted to have the boy killed.

Lore replied, "You don't have to worry about that. He was there for me."

Silence was her response as everyone in the room stared at her. Even Abraxas couldn't imagine why, although a thought bloomed at the same time, she confirmed his fears.

"I maimed him," she said. "Now he wants me to suffer the same way he is."

He would kill that bastard with his own hands, no matter how long it took. Abraxas would enjoy feasting upon that blackened, cursed flesh. He would rip the King apart bit by bit if he ever hurt Lore again.

He'd do it now if he could find the slippery eel of a man who called himself King.

Beauty's face had paled. "Ah, well. We need not fear that the King wants to kill Zeph, then."

"We don't," Lore replied. "So I suppose now we're back to finding the eggs. Does anyone else have any other ideas?"

Apparently Beauty wasn't quite done yet. "I still think we should return to the castle and introduce Zeph to Margaret. She'll want to know who he is and how he can help us. If we don't at least introduce him, then she'll have no idea who can help her."

Zeph lifted his hand tentatively, as though he wasn't all that certain he was allowed to speak. At Lore's nod, he dropped the hand and said, "Well, I don't know about you, but I think finding out whatever my brother is hiding might be a little more important. Don't you think?"

Lore tilted her head to the side, surveying the boy who had surprised them all.

Truly, Abraxas had thought Zeph would side with Beauty, who'd given him more attention than he'd likely ever had in his brief years. The young man was head over heels for a young woman who had also charmed a dragon. To hear that he had differing opinions from her? That boded well for his life outside of the crypt.

Abraxas had to ask, "What do you think your brother is hiding?"

"Well, if my mother's experience with my father is anything to consider, then I assume those eggs." Zeph shifted in his seat, rocking forward and back. "They could be awfully powerful if in the wrong hands, and I'm sure that my brother would want to hatch them. He already lost one dragon."

So they had returned to the same plan. Find the eggs. Do whatever it took to find them, even though no one had a clue where they were.

Abraxas slumped in his chair, staring into the flames as though they might hold the answers. "Right. Easy choice, then. Find the eggs that were stolen by a man currently kept alive by black magic cast by a long dead warlock. If we can find anything else there, those eggs will be the easiest. Though I don't think they'll be easy to find."

He could have cut the silence with a knife. They all realized how difficult a task this was, but none of them had any idea how to get to the next step. Or even where to find a clue to start them off in the right direction.

Goliath coughed into his hand. "Did you say dead warlock?"

"I did." If he could have shot fire out of his eyes, he would have. "What do you know, dwarf?"

"Not much more than superstition and rumor. There used to be a warlock who lived in these mountains. Dangerous ruin now, but I knew a couple people who got in once. They stole some black magic jars and got out but... Maybe that's what you're looking for?"

Abraxas saw his own emotions mirrored in Lore's eyes. It was more than a start. It was the perfect opportunity for them to stay out of Margaret's clutches.

She leaned forward and braced her forearms on her knees. "That'll more than do. Black magic jars, you said? What was in them?"

Goliath shrugged and made a face. "I wouldn't know. They only claimed they'd done it, but no one can know for sure. Seemed like a true story, though. They said the tower was the only one on the entire mountain and grew out of the stone like a living building. Shadows spread out from the base and tinged the very stone with darkness. Seems like a warlock's home to me."

"Or a witch," Abraxas interjected. "Either would have spelled the entire building. Who knows what might happen if we wander in there alone?"

The dwarf shrugged again. "I wouldn't know. They survived, although they said they only stuck their head in, grabbed the first thing they could, and then ran down the mountain like ghosts were chasing them."

Perhaps they had been chased by ghosts. No dragon would ever put it past a warlock to ensure all his spells terrified those who dared enter his home. He knew very well the dangers they were facing in walking into a place like that.

He looked over at Lore and asked, "Do you think that's a place

Zander would hide the eggs?"

"If it's the very same warlock who made him immortal? Where else would he hide them?" Although her expression was one of fear and worry.

Good. At least she understood how stupid they were being for even entertaining this thought.

"That's one way of looking at it." This was the only lead they had and if that could get them a little closer to finding the eggs? It was worth the risk they would have to take.

Lore reached over and grabbed his hand. She laced their fingers together tightly. "Even if the eggs aren't there, then at least we might get a few hints at how Zander is the way he is now. If nothing else, perhaps we will discover a way to kill him. Really kill him this time."

He sighed and squeezed her hand. "You're right. I won't risk anyone else, though. This will be dangerous enough with the two of us."

Beauty squawked, "What? You aren't going alone!"

Abraxas let go of Lore's hand and laced his hands behind his neck. Leaning in the chair, he winked at Zeph as if to tell the boy to enjoy the argument that was about to happen.

And it did, of course. But he could listen to these ridiculous fools argue for hours. They were his fools, after all.

CHAPTER 36

L ore stood next to the giant wall of the dragon and tried to still the thundering beat of her heart. Was she doing this? She'd never thought in her life that she would ride a dragon, let alone soar through the air as high as the clouds. And yet, the others had already done it. Could it be that dangerous?

Goliath walked over with her pack in his arms, grinning far too wide. "Just don't fall off, and you'll be fine."

"Thank you for the reminder," she snarled. Lore wrenched the bag out of his grip and heaved it over her back. "For a second there, I forgot I would be at cloud height for the foreseeable future."

She hadn't given much thought about if she feared heights, but now she was quite certain that she did. After all, if she fell, then she would almost certainly die. And she was supposed to just hang onto those spikes on his back? They weren't easy to hold on to.

Lore looked up into Abraxas's amused expression and muttered, "Maybe we should consider straps. Or a saddle. Something that would give me more than those slippery spines to prevent plummeting to my death."

He rolled his giant eyes and shook his head. The spines moved a little with that movement, and she knew better than to assume that meant they would be sturdy in the air.

His throat swayed with a deep chuckle. "You aren't going to fall off. Your ancestors used to do this all the time."

"No one rode dragons."

"Actually, your ancestors did. Remember how I used to say we would steal elves when we were lonely?" He stretched out a wing for her to step up and clamber onto his back. "They also rode with us through the clouds. If I remember right, there were a few Silverfell elves among the older ones there who had been riding my family for centuries. They were quite good at it."

"You're not making me feel better," she grumbled. But Lore stepped on the leathery appendages and clambered her way up his back. If other elves had done this before, then she could as well.

The climb was made easier by the scales that shifted every time she touched them. The texture was already roughened by his age and wind, like someone had run sandpaper over the surface. She stepped up onto what she assumed was his shoulder bone and paused when she realized how high up she was.

Dragons had always seemed to be such prideful creatures in the stories everyone told. They hoarded wealth and power, but allowed themselves to be ridden like any other animal?

Sure. She'd believe it when she saw a mural from the ancient times depicting such an activity.

Lore grabbed onto the spines of his back and hauled her leg over the ridges. The seat between the spines was surprisingly comfortable. She tested out, moving a little and realized she could lean against the bone behind her and it would support her. She'd still have to hang on tight with her thighs, but this wouldn't be as uncomfortable a ride as she'd thought.

Grabbing onto the spine in front of her, she measured that it ended at her breastbone. She'd be able to lean forward if she had to. There was enough room between each one, and they got shorter up the length of his neck.

Crimson scales underneath her legs warmed at her touch. The comforting sensation eased a bit of the tension in her chest, but not quite enough that she didn't shriek when he stood.

Lore stared wide-eyed at the ground. "On second thought, I think we should hike to wherever this tower is. We can find it on foot."

"That would take months," Abraxas said, still chuckling. Again he shook his head and his entire neck rattled with the movement.

She was forced to shift along with him and hold on tightly as he stretched out his wings. Damn, they were big. She felt like they went on for miles as he readied them for the long trip.

"Goliath!" she called out. "Make sure you take care of Beauty. You know how to get in touch with me if you have to run."

"We're in a safe house, Lore. Stop worrying about us and enjoy the ride." He waved at her as though she were a beloved child headed off to war. He even wiped a fake tear away from his face. "Enjoy the journey! They grow up too fast."

"I hate you!" she shouted, as Abraxas beat his wings for the first time.

The thunderous wind slapped against her ears and dust kicked up in all directions. On the second pulse of his wings, snow blasted her in the face. Her hair blew back and the blistering cold made her shiver. She squeezed her eyes shut and tried to breathe through the sensation of her stomach dropping out of her torso.

Oh, she was going to be sick. She'd throw up all over him and then he would never let her ride him again.

Good. She didn't want to do this again. Flying was horrible and it would serve him right for insisting that they travel like this. Every inch of her body screamed this was unnatural to be so far from the ground.

He tilted to the side, and she swore she almost fell off. Squeezing her eyes closed even more tightly, she hugged his spine to her chest and squeezed her legs so tight she thought she'd leave dents. This was dreadful. Her head felt like it was going to fall off and she feared they were going to turn upside down and she'd slide right off of him.

He shifted again, this time evening them out, so she didn't have to hold on to him as hard. But it was difficult to pull her fingers out of the fists that frantically clutched onto him.

"Lore," Abraxas chuckled, the wind bringing his voice back to her. "You can open your eyes now."

"I'd prefer to keep them closed for the entire journey, please. You can find the tower on your own. Just drop me off when we're done."

"I think you'll want to see this," he replied. "You'd be angry at yourself if you missed this view."

She wouldn't. She'd live just fine without ever knowing what this looked like, but... Well. He'd been right before and she didn't want him to think her weak.

Lore peeled her eyes open even though it made her want to puke. She first saw him looking back over his shoulder. That strange face that looked so familiar and yet wasn't at the same time. His mouth had opened in a broad grin and he clearly was quite pleased with himself.

Then she noticed what was behind him and her jaw fell open in surprise. The clouds rolled out in front of them like a carpet. Fluffy and bright, they created a sense of a floor even though she knew she couldn't stand on them. The rolling sea of white foam and mist was tinged with sunlight until they sparkled with diamond dust. The brilliant blue sky stretched out overhead so far she could almost see the pink of a sunrise beyond their reach.

"Oh," she whispered. "This is beautiful."

Though her words were likely caught by the wind and dashed away from his ears, Abraxas clearly understood what she meant. He turned his attention back to the sky and beat his wings again.

They must have been gliding, she realized. She hadn't felt the powerful flex of his muscles beneath her thighs until now. He moved with a natural grace and an ease that belayed many years of practice.

Each wing flap was timed, so they continued to glide along the current of air. And though it was cold, the sun beating on her back warmed her skin. She realized he was also keeping her warm. Somehow, the crimson of his scales had heated enough so that his flames spread into her body without ever burning.

She hated to admit it, but he was very right. She would have been so disappointed to have never seen this in her life.

"Have you finished panicking?" he asked, still very amused by her reaction.

"I think so. This isn't all that scary anymore," she shouted.

"Good. Let's see how you do with this, then!"

He tucked his wings against his sides and suddenly they were plummeting out of the sky. Lore screamed and held on for dear life again. They were going to die. He was going to run them directly into the ground, which was right underneath the clouds.

They plunged into the mist and she couldn't see anything. All she could feel was the wind in her hair and the way it blasted against her eyes, making tears stream over her cheeks.

Then they cleared the cloud cover. He snapped out his wings again, and they halted in their wild fall from the sky. He beat his wings a couple times, muscles flexing all around her, and then they were gliding right underneath the clouds. The entirety of Umbra spread out underneath her. So beautiful and so out of reach.

She could see the emerald rolling hills of the north and the marshes from whence she came. The mountain peaks that looked tiny from up here. Even the southern reaches of the kingdom where the sands were golden and the shores bright blue.

The second scream she'd worked up died in her throat.

"Touch the clouds," Abraxas said. "I know you've been dying to."

She thought they might feel soft against her hands. But to touch them, she'd have to let go of his spines.

"Be brave, Lady of Starlight," he said. "You've got more metal in you than this."

Lore took her shaking hands off his back and lifted them up into the air. The icy chill of the clouds surprised her. She couldn't feel them at all, not really, just the sensation of coldness. But when she brought her hands back down, they were covered in glacial water.

A bubble of laughter burst out of her mouth. "I didn't think they'd be cold."

"I didn't either on my first flight." He chuckled, and the sound reverberated underneath her. "I tried to eat them."

"Of course you did. Do they taste good?"

"They taste like nothing. But I told my friends that I'd eaten the sky." He looked over his shoulder and she could see the laughter in his eyes. "They thought I was very terrifying."

"A nightmare of a dragon." She leaned on the spine behind her, trying to at least relax a little. "Truly terrifying in your magnificence and bravery."

He bared his teeth that were each the length of her arm. "Indeed."

Oh, damn it. Her heart did that thing again. It flipped in her chest, then squeezed so hard she could barely breathe. He was...

Perfect.

A voice whispered the word in her head and she refused to think it true, but it was. He was perfect in every sense of the word. A terrifying beast who would hunt beside her and track down anyone who tried to harm her. A monster made for others to fear. Yet, he would take her into the sky, far away from all of that, and let her drift among the clouds.

Swallowing hard, she ripped her gaze from him and cast it down upon the Stygian Peaks. "Where do you think this tower is?"

He seemed to frown in the corner of her eye. "The Stygian range is lengthy, and there are many hidden mountaintops. Goliath didn't mention how long his dwarven friends had traveled."

"Perhaps a long way."

"Then we may be looking for a while."

She smoothed her hand along his back, fingers finding the ridges of scales as big as dinner plates. "Are you all right to fly that distance?"

Apparently, she'd insulted him. "I can fly for hours, little elf. Among other things."

She was thankful for the cold air to chill the flush that spread all the way down her neck. What did he mean by that? Of course she had an idea, but that couldn't be what he...

Abraxas tucked his wings again and suddenly they were careening through the sky as he brought them closer to the Stygian Peaks. She had to hold on for dear life and count every single heartbeat to keep herself from screaming. But every time he did it, flying got a little easier.

They spent the better part of the day searching for that tower. She even learned how to relax on top of him. She leaned back against his spine and told him stories of when she was little.

"I learned how to sprint across those rooftops to avoid the Umbral Knights. They never could catch me, and I knew if I was fast enough, they never would!" She slapped a hand to her thigh. "Of course, there were many times I got too close. I thought once they were going to catch me. That was when I started covering my ears."

"How did you get away from them?"

"I threw a basket of apples at their heads and got lucky. A couple of the helmets were blocked by the fruit because the apples had stuck in the eye holes." It was still one of her favorite memories. That was the first time she'd seen the Umbral Knights as something other than terrifying monsters who wanted to kill her.

Abraxas chuckled. "My, my, how you surprise me."

She could remind him that she'd surprised everyone her entire life, but that was when she saw it. The black spiral rose out of the mist and shone like it was made of crystals. The capped peak had a hole in it where the weather had worn away at the magic. But even looking at it, she could see the pulse of power. Of wizardry.

"Look!" she called out, pointing at it. "That has to be a warlock's tower."

Her dragon looked where she pointed and she felt the catch of his breath. "That's definitely it."

Abraxas brought them lower to an adjacent peak where he could land. There wasn't much room around the tower. A small wooden bridge, rickety and swaying in the breeze, waited for them.

As he scrabbled for a hold on the rocks, Lore slipped off his back and took a few steps to the rope bridge. "We did it," she breathed. "We found it."

The sound of his change erupted and the blast of air that always happened nearly sent her toppling over the edge. But she held onto the bridge and then spun toward him.

He stood tall and strong, his long hair touching his shoulders now. The worried expression on his face didn't match what she felt. They'd done it! Didn't he understand that? They were so close and the eggs might be in those walls.

Energy bounced underneath her skin. She wanted to take him by the face and force him to understand this was their moment! They'd been waiting for this. Everything they had endured had brought them to this place.

Oh, she couldn't take it anymore.

Lore lunged for him, grabbing him by the cheeks and drawing him down to her mouth. She kissed him with every ounce of excitement, worry, and fear that coursed through her veins.

He stilled, surprised at her reaction, but then something in him snapped. She felt the moment everything in him released. His arm banded around her waist and he drew her into him with a sharp hiss.

The kiss quickly turned from innocent and pleasurable to a coiling fire that built in her belly. He nipped at her lips with his teeth, then delved his tongue into the depths of her mouth. Abraxas kissed her like a starving man. Or perhaps, a bit like the beast he was.

When he'd consumed her, he pushed her away from him. He wiped his mouth with the back of his hand, eyeing her through the black locks of his hair. "We'll return to that later," he snarled, pointing at her. "First, we deal with the dark magic here, and then you and I will have time together. Alone."

A shiver of fear or anticipation trailed down her spine. "Agreed." She'd never wanted anything more in her life.

CHAPTER 37

Abraxas reeled, unable to focus on the task at hand. How was he supposed to look for dark magic in this place when she'd kissed him? Willingly? Without him having to ask or beg for a shred of her attention?

A man had his limits. He dragged his mind through the haze of surprise and lust before taking note of where they were.

Warlocks, magicians, witches, and their ilk were more likely to trap visitors than they were to welcome them. This bridge would not be easy to cross. Nor should they even attempt to do so without using the proper precautions.

But damn it, her lips were bright red from their kiss and her eyes were still heated with the possibilities of what they might do later. He'd been waiting for this moment. For her to realize that she could come to him of her own accord.

And now he had to ruin it with the reality of their situation.

Abraxas forced himself to shake off the lingering memories of their kiss and turn his attention to the bridge. "We should assume everything here is cursed."

She blinked at him a few times before seeming to realize that he wasn't talking about their kiss. "Of course." Lore cleared her throat. "I can check to see if there are any spells left on the ropes or boards. If that's helpful?"

Why were they speaking to each other in formalities? He needed to snap out of it, but she was already walking away from him with her hands raised.

The moment she stepped a single foot onto the bridge, her palms flared bright white. The magic inside her burst out and a shield appeared just in time to stop a small black orb that would have struck her in the chest.

Lore froze, and a slight whine erupted from her mouth. "Apparently, we cannot go inside yet."

"Yes, I can see that." He walked up behind her, close enough that he pressed his front against her back. "If you drop the shield, will that orb attack you?"

"If I'm still on the bridge, absolutely."

"Right. Well, step off the bridge then, elf."

"I intend to, if you would get out of the way," she snarled.

Together, they backed up, giving the orb more space to sink into whatever hiding place it had lurked within. Lore lowered her hands, although he noted she kept them ready to throw up the shield again in case the magic returned.

He watched the bridge for any other movement, but that was all the warlock appeared to have done. An orb. Not that an orb couldn't do a significant amount of damage, but at least they weren't dealing with a cave troll.

Lore swallowed hard, then peered up at him. "Should we wait until nightfall? Maybe it's a particular time that we're allowed to enter?"

Or they were out of luck and would battle with whatever the warlock had left either way.

He looked back at the bridge and asked, "Can you hold the shield while we walk across?"

"Not likely. I've never been very good at magic like that. I can hold it while I'm not moving, but walking would be too difficult. It was searching for gaps in the shield, like it knew what kind of magic it had come up against and that it needed to wiggle underneath." She shuddered. "Just the touch of that power was revolting."

Waiting was their best shot, then. He looked up at the sun, tracking how far it had to go until dark. "Only a few hours if we want to wait. Nighttime is our strongest option, I suppose. Then we'll figure something else out."

He set to work getting a fire going. The tiny sprite he brought to life in his palm was all too happy to warm them. It cheerfully crackled while he drew Lore into his arms and clasped her to his chest. Her shivers worried him, although he knew they wouldn't last for long.

Soon, they would need to face whatever terrors waited for them in that warlock's tower. And though his mind wanted to wander through all the possibilities, he forced himself to focus on the now.

Squeezing his arms around her, he asked, "When did you learn how to cast spells? You made it seem like they weren't possible."

"When did I make it seem like that?"

"Back in the castle. When we first met. You avoided magic like the plague." He remembered how fierce she still was, even then. Lore hadn't needed spells to threaten enemies, although she seemed to use it with ease now.

Lore shrugged. "I've always used magic. I've just hidden it. If anyone caught me performing even the most simple of spells, then I would have had my head removed from my body. Or ended up like my mother. I wanted to avoid both of those fates, so I didn't use it."

There it was again, that familiar ache of guilt. It ate at him, knowing that he'd killed her mother.

He'd apologized a hundred times for it. In the way she wanted him to apologize and in the way of his people. He'd done everything he could to make up for that horrible day, and Abraxas knew he had to let that go. He had to be satisfied that he'd apologized. Just because he desired her forgiveness didn't mean he'd earned it.

"So, who taught you to use magic, then?" He placed his chin on top of her head and watched the sunset.

The sky turned bright red as she chuckled. "I guess it comes naturally to us elves. Every time I want to use it, the magic is there. It takes practice, of course. I'm not as good as I could be. But magic never leaves the children of the forest. And the moon is much more giving than other magical mistresses."

Of course it was. The silvery rays of its light danced out of the sky and traced the outline of Lore's skin. He could see it lingering on the edges of her fingers and the smooth planes of her cheeks. The moon loved her, just as he did.

Damn. It hurt to admit that to himself, and he couldn't imagine what it would feel like to say to her. Probably that he'd ripped out his own heart and held it out to her, hoping she'd take care of it. That she wouldn't rip it from his hands and crush it.

Swallowing hard, he resolved to remain quiet until they were in complete darkness.

The night came too quickly. Soon she was pulling out of his arms and stretching her own over her head. Lore then cracked her neck, side to side, then stared at the bridge. "What if we can't get across it?"

"We'll find another way." He hoped.

She lifted her hands and the rays of the moon gathered around her palms. "All right. Let's try again."

They walked up to the bridge, apprehension staining the air with the familiar scent of fear. But this time, when Lore put a foot on the swaying planks, no orb appeared. They were allowed to walk upon the ancient boards.

"Do you think it's safe?" she called out.

"Not at all."

The bridge beneath her next step creaked ominously. Lore looked over her shoulder at him, eyes wide with hesitation. He lunged and grabbed onto her arm just as the board snapped and shards exploded around them.

He thrust her forward with a quick shout. "Run!"

She sprinted over the boards, not caring that they shattered underneath each of her feet. He barely managed to sprint after her. Every heavy footstep was on the very edge of a wooden piece falling, but he propelled himself after her by holding onto the ropes and throwing himself forward.

They both hit the end of the bridge at the same time. He grabbed onto her and toppled both of them over. Rolling, they landed hard on the doorstep of the warlock's castle, both breathing far too rapidly and staring at each other with wide eyes.

Somehow, Lore had ended up in his arms again. He could only assume he'd snagged her before she fell and then pivoted them midair, so he took the brunt of the pain. He'd pat himself on the back later for being a gentleman, even in grave danger.

"Are you all right?" he asked.

"Still in one piece. Not cursed yet. Are you all right?"

He had assumed at least one of them would be spitting blood by now. Yet they were both in one piece. That horrible little orb hadn't reached them, and they hadn't fallen off the exploding bridge.

"Still breathing," he replied. "Do you think we should open the door?"

"After that, I'm not all that sure we'll survive." She craned her neck to look up at said door and grimaced. "Not like we have a lot of choice, though. Might as well give it a try."

His fearless little elf then reached up, jiggled the handle, and shoved it open while they both lay on the front step.

He half expected a warlock to stand in the doorway, glaring down at them both with significant disappointment. If someone was going to raid a warlock, he was sure they were usually more dangerous in appearance than the two of them at this moment. But no one stood at the entrance at all. Instead, all that escaped through the opening was a plume of dust and rays of moonlight through broken windows.

Lore leaned over him, slithered forward on her belly, and looked into the room from the floor. "I don't think anyone lives here."

"Warlocks are sneaky like that." He palmed her waist and lifted her up. "Keep your wits about you."

She scrambled to her feet, ignoring that she'd almost stepped on his fingers, and stood in the doorway. Dust gathered around her like tiny will-o'-the-wisps. "I don't think anyone has lived here for a very long time."

What was she going on about now? Abraxas rolled to standing, trying to ignore the ache in his back, and then peered into the small room with her.

Like many of the towers he'd seen before, this warlock's home was a single room with stairs at the end. Likely, whoever had lived here wanted to design a space that was useful while remaining tall. This room had been his workshop. Strange that he'd put it so low in the tower.

Tables bracketed the walls, carved so that they didn't interrupt the natural circle of the tower. Glass vials were piled up on many of the tables, while glass tubes connected with others. There were small burn marks on most of the wood. He could only assume from fire to keep the potions bubbling.

But, as Lore had said, the place looked almost completely abandoned. There were spiderwebs underneath all the tables, and the large scuttling creatures had been affected by magic. The spiders were as broad as his hand. A fine layer of dust covered all the jars and vials.

"I don't think I've ever heard of a warlock abandoning his home," he muttered.

"I thought they all had cleaning spells on their houses," Lore said as she took another hesitant step inside. "The few witches I know always had spells like that. They lasted for centuries after the death of the witch, too. People love buying their old places."

"Even with the curses?"

Lore waved a hand in the air. "Curses can be dealt with. Sometimes it is worth enough to endure a curse just, so one doesn't have to deal with cleaning."

He wanted to warn her to be careful, but recognized that was only worry on his part. She knew better than he did how to walk through a home like this. Lore stepped carefully, looking where she would place her feet before she did.

Finally, she reached the nearest table and then picked up a jar.

"Lore," he snarled, warning her with his tone to be more careful.

"It's just a jar of silkworms." She smoothed her hand over the surface, cleaning away the dust and showing him the husks. "They've been dead a long time. What warlock doesn't spell his ingredients, either?"

"A bad one?" That didn't bode well.

"Or one who dabbled in magic darker than he had a right to." She put the jar back onto the table. "What if he was connecting all his magic to his life force? Dark magic has a way of pulling at a person, but if he connected his life to it, then maybe... Maybe all the spells disappeared when he died?"

Abraxas supposed that made sense, but he knew very little about magic or spells. "Do you think he's dead?"

Lore frowned. "I don't know. There's something wrong here, though. Can't you feel it?"

Not really. No more than any other magical building he'd been in.

One of the spiders crawled out from underneath the table and stretched a hairy leg out to touch Lore's leg. She flinched, jerking away from the arachnid before letting out a frustrated noise. "Don't touch me, please. I'm thinking."

He'd expected her to crush the cursed creature. "Do you want me to get rid of it?"

Both she and the spider looked at him in shock.

Of all the strange things... "Why are you looking at me like that?" he asked.

She pointed at the spider. "Don't touch the cursed creatures, Abraxas. I thought we were both very clear that we would not anger any of the spells in here."

"That's a spider."

"It's a creature who is now filled with magic. It doesn't matter that you're uncomfortable with its appearance." She looked down at the beast and muttered, "I apologize for him. Go under the table again, please. At least until we're gone."

It scuttled back to the horrible web it had made, and Abraxas let out a shudder of revulsion. "I can't believe you're talking to that thing."

"There's probably larger ones upstairs. That one is just a baby, so you should get over that fear."

There better not be, or he would break the rule they'd made and kill a couple of cursed creatures. Or all of them. Maybe he'd burn the entire tower to the ground.

Spiders shouldn't be that unnaturally large. They just shouldn't.

Lore lifted her hands that had already glowed. "I think there's a spirit in here still, but I can't tell if that's the spirit of the warlock or someone else. Or maybe not even a spirit at all. It... lingers. I thought I could try to talk with it. Maybe a summoning circle would work."

"A what?"

A small circle brightened around her, bright as the light of the moon. "Don't interrupt me when I'm casting a complicated spell, Abraxas."

Well, she was bossy today.

He froze as a scream echoed over their heads. It continued on and on, as if someone were being murdered.

"Was that upstairs?" he muttered.

"I think so." Lore let her hands fall back to her sides. "Guess we're going to go see who that was."

CHAPTER 38

She picked her steps even more carefully after the scream. Though Lore couldn't sense any other curses in this room, she also knew that this building didn't want an elf in it. Warlocks envied her kind with their natural talent for magic.

Elves didn't have to rip at the world to obtain an ounce of power. While mortal men had to tear at the very fabric of time to eek out what they wanted. Spiders scurried upside down across the ceiling, traveling with her as she stepped toward the stairs that would bring them to the next level of the tower.

She paused at the base of the winding steps that followed the structure of the building. "Do you think there's something waiting for us up there?" she asked.

"Considering it already screamed, I would guess so." Abraxas laid a hand on her spine, warm and comforting. "We have each other, Lore. I'll watch your back, and you'll watch mine."

Did he not realize there was very little she could do against an angry spirit? Particularly one of an ancient warlock who had found a way to cheat death? Most spirits were furious for a reason. They hadn't wanted to die, but that wasn't the way of the world. They could either stay or go once their mortal form had expired. Most of them didn't know that staying would mean they watched everyone else continue on without them. And they could no longer influence anything.

Swallowing hard, she put a foot on the stairs and began the ascent.

The second level of the tower appeared to be a place of research. Countless books and scrolls had been forgotten here. No one ever came to steal the knowledge that this single man had acquired. And it had to be a man.

The mess he'd left behind was enough for her to think that. But also warlocks were notorious for living alone and out in the wilds. Witches stayed near villages hoping they might still help someone, even though they were universally despised.

She knew it was dangerous, but Lore still picked up a scroll that had fallen off one of the bookshelves. She peered at the inscription on the surface and her stomach twisted as she realized it looked a lot like an elven ruin.

Words written on the edges caught her eye.

Appears to be some sort of prophecy.

An elf? Perhaps bringing about the end of the world. Will have to investigate further.

Abraxas set his hand on top of the scroll and tugged it out of her grasp. "I thought we said we would not touch anything?"

"I don't think a scroll will cause the entire building to crumble around our ears." She reached for it again, but paused when he held it out of her reach. "Why don't you want me to see that?"

"I've already seen the prophecy, and it's on the mountaintop where we left the others. You can look at the real thing for yourself when we're finished here. Without knowing what an idiotic warlock said about his findings." He put the scroll on the highest shelf of the bookcase near them. "Right now, we need to get through this cursed building without losing our heads."

She wanted to ask him why he didn't want her to see it. Considering it was a prophecy about elves, one might think she would need to look at such a thing.

Memories flickered in the back of her mind. Hadn't the Matriarch mentioned something to her that sounded very similar to this situation? Odd phrases about a young elf thinking she could change the fabric of time, or perhaps that she was trying to change the world? Lore couldn't remember right now. The sound of spider legs on the ceiling distracted her thoughts.

If she could just think, then maybe...

Another scream echoed overhead. This time, it didn't sound like the person was in pain. No. It sounded like they were angry.

The entire tower rumbled with the noise and a large piece of the ceiling came loose. Abraxas yanked her out of the way before the slab of plaster struck her in the shoulder. She narrowly missed a very painful injury.

Breathing hard, she leaned against the broad expanse of his chest. "Thank you. Again."

"I don't think it wants us here," he muttered. "It seems to me that whatever spirit inhabits this place would prefer to remain alone."

"I think that's a safe enough guess."

She wouldn't mind leaving it alone, but the longer they were in this building, the more she felt it likely that the King had hidden the eggs here. There were too many clues. Too many items that revolved around the current circumstances.

Her mind caught on a single thought that should have occurred to her long before they'd made it through the second level. "If the King had brought the eggs here, wouldn't you think there would be footprints?"

Abraxas froze, then looked down at her with a curious expression on his face. "Footprints?"

She pointed to the floor where their prints had remained. "Everything is covered in dust. Everything. If he'd come here for any reason, then someone would have left boot prints. Right?"

If her theory was correct, then they should leave. This haunted place had nothing to do with them, although the scroll made her wonder if she was meant to be here. At this moment in time.

The entire tower had called to her, it seemed. As though a part of her very existence hid in these walls.

Abraxas shook his head, then craned his neck to look up the spiraling stairwell. "Everything to do with that box is magic, Lore. I've seen it appear in impossible places and move without a single person touching it. I think, considering everything we've seen, it's highly likely the warlock who cursed that box lived here. And if the King can summon the box to him, wouldn't it make sense that the warlock could do the same?"

She supposed it did. And if she were giving someone a spell that powerful, she'd also want to make sure she could get it back.

"Up again, then," she whispered.

He glanced at her with worry marring his handsome features. "Stick closer this time. I smell something."

"What do you smell?"

His eyes had already strayed away from her. He stared up at the next level, lifted his nose, and muttered, "Brimstone."

Ah, of course. More dark magic and likely another curse or ward that was going to attack them. All she needed was for that spirit to come barreling down the hallway at them, and then everything would be complete. Just like the horror stories she used to read when she was little.

Lore flexed her fingers at her sides and tried to summon as much of her own power as she could. "I'll do my best to shield you. Take slow steps. I'm going to have to rebuild it every time you move and I don't... Well. I think I've explained already why that's a bad idea."

Abraxas managed a small smile in her direction. "I don't need much of a shield, Lore. I'm a dragon. Very little can hurt me."

"I've seen you get hurt in this mortal form. You aren't covered in scales today." She threw the shield up in front of him and concentrated as hard as she could. "Walk slowly."

It took them a while to get to the third level, but she was glad they didn't rush. The brimstone he'd smelled was indeed from a dark curse, but not from something that would necessarily attack them.

She'd been right about there being larger spiders.

At least twenty of them stood between them and the next door. A few of them were the same size as large dogs, but there were a couple that were as large as ponies, and those were the ones who made Lore nervous. All the walls were covered in a thick layer of webbing. Holes in the nets must have been where the spiders stayed during the day when the sunlight was too bright for them to move. A few of them lingered in those lairs. Others were already wandering around, slow, lethargic. As if they were still tired.

She grabbed onto the back of Abraxas's shirt and forced him to freeze. The great dragon who had sworn he wasn't afraid of anything trembled beneath her touch.

"Don't. Move." she said.

"I figured."

Lore tried to keep her attention on all the spiders. Some of them appeared to be asleep. Their many eyes were closed and their giant legs were all tucked in close to their bodies. The sleeping spiders were backed into the web covered walls.

Three of the spiders, the largest ones, wandered around the circular room. Their enormous eyes peered throughout the room and into the shadows. One lifted a leg and touched a strand of web. It twanged with the movement. Apparently, that was what the spider had hoped for, because it moved on. Its furry mandibles never stopped gnashing at the air.

Perhaps it was hungry. She hoped it wasn't, though.

Lore pressed herself against Abraxas's back and stood on her tiptoes so she could whisper in his ear, "I don't think their eyesight is very good."

"What makes you think that?"

"Just from what I know about other spiders." She prayed she was right this time. "I think, if we avoid the webs and step very slowly, we might walk by them unseen."

"I'm going to scream. Or vomit."

She wanted to slap him, but the sound would alert the spiders to their presence, and she didn't want to take that risk. "You're a dragon."

"And if I were in that form, I would burn this entire building to the ground." He pressed back against her as one of the largest spiders walked by the doorway. The heavy belly dragged along the floor, the rasping sound of bristly hairs on stone turned even her stomach.

"We don't have an option to burn it down, so take a step forward and if they notice us, I will do my best to blind them so we can run."

Although the spiders could follow them upstairs. The only two choices were to leave or remain quiet. Any mistake would get them killed.

Lore tried hard not to think about that.

She walked in front of Abraxas, knowing that she'd have to be the person to keep them moving forward. One foot on the webbing covering the floor, ever so gently, Lore tested out her full amount of weight on the webs. Then she froze and waited to see if the spiders would recognize an unknown presence.

When none of the spiders moved, she took another step. And again. Six steps into the room was where they encountered their first problem.

One of the patrolling spiders stopped in front of her. It appeared to be smelling the air, or at least attempting to do so considering its mandibles kept clacking right in Lore's face.

She knew it couldn't see her. She knew it wasn't doing anything other than what it was supposed to do. Spiders paid attention to what was in their webs. That was how they stayed alive. But then the creature let out a long hiss, and she saw the horrible fangs inside its mouth.

Face screwed up in fear, she lifted her hands and let the bubble of a shield form before them. Abraxas wrapped his arm around her waist and tugged her a little closer to him.

She had the distinct feeling that if the spider reared up onto its back legs, Abraxas would pick her up and heave her over his shoulder as he ran. Or he'd turn into a dragon right in the middle of the building and burn it all down. Long before they could get what they needed to get.

The spider let out one more loud chomp before it moved on.

Lore heaved a sigh of relief and closed her eyes for a second. She needed a few moments to gather her wits. Just a couple seconds behind closed lids, where she wasn't staring at a battlefield of spiders larger than they should ever be.

"Lore," Abraxas breathed in her ear. "Move."

"Why?"

She opened her eyes and looked down to see a spider next to them had woken up. She'd thought all the big ones were out patrolling, but she was wrong. So very wrong.

The beast that hauled itself out of the webs was the size of a horse. Its legs were as long as she was tall and those eyes were too large. Too many. It uncurled its legs, opened its mouth a couple times, and then did something horrible. Something Lore would never forget.

It spoke.

"Why do I smell warm flesh?" it muttered, listlessly shifting from left to right.

Oh.

Oh, no.

Lore swallowed hard and moved. She picked up her pace and perhaps was a little too clumsy with her movements. Just before they reached the stairwell that led up to what she could only hope was the final level of this tower, she stepped on the wrong web.

The loud snapping sound was like she'd fired a bow in the middle of a silent room. All the spiders stopped moving and as one looked over at the intruders. The biggest spider had four dinner plate sized eyes on top of its head. And all of those eyes met Lore's startled gaze.

"Flesh," it muttered. Then they all lunged.

Lore sprinted to the doorway and threw Abraxas past her. Then she spun around and lifted her hands up. A shield wouldn't do. She didn't know what would stop creatures like this other than daylight and she wasn't a creature of the day.

She could no more summon the sun than she could change the seasons, but the silver light of the full moon could be just as blinding. For the moon reflected sunlight even in the darkest of times.

A wall of shimmering light appeared in the stairwell's doorway. It filled the space with a brightness that blinded Lore even as she threw it into existence. The spiders ran up against the wall and then flinched away. They hissed, rearing up on their back legs and flaring out their front appendages. Their jaws snapped and horrible snarls echoed throughout the room.

But not a single one tried to walk through her wall of light.

Blowing out a long breath, Lore took a step away and let one of her hands drop. The brightness remained as she'd intended it to.

"Good enough," she wheezed. "That'll buy us some time."

Abraxas had been surprisingly quiet through all of this. Lore turned around to see that he'd fallen onto his backside on the stairwell. He still watched the spiders with an expression that was equal parts horror and disgust.

Lore eased down on the stairs beside him, bracing her back against the wall and her leg behind his ribs. "I don't think they can come through."

"You sure about that?"

"No." She returned her attention to the angry, cursed creatures. "But it will give us enough time to get through the rest of this tower and then hopefully find the eggs at the top."

"You know, I didn't imagine that this tower would be filled with... those." He gave his head a little shake, but that didn't seem to help the fear that had him pinned to the floor. "If I had realized we'd be fighting giant spiders, I might have sent you on your own. Or better yet, made Goliath come with you instead."

"If I'd known you were afraid of spiders, I would have been less terrified of you when we first met." She patted his shoulder and looked up the stairs. Like all the others, this one was swathed in darkness, dust, and shadows. "Are you ready to see what else waits for us?"

"Do you think it's more spiders?" He peered at her with eyes so wide she wanted to assure that it wouldn't be.

Lore would give anything to ease that terror in his chest. She'd promise him the world if only he'd return to that brave, powerful dragon that she'd grown so fond of. But she supposed it was nice to know that he wasn't perfect.

"It could be," she muttered. Then Lore stood and held her hand out for him to take. "But I doubt they could get any bigger."

"Magic begs to differ," he grumbled. Then he accepted her help to stand. "Let's go find out, I guess. I am going to burn this place to the ground when we're done, though."

"I don't think anyone would blame you for that."

CHAPTER 39

Hope was a dangerous emotion, and it clawed at his chest as they crested the last stairwell. Abraxas knew better than to dream the eggs were here. He'd been disappointed many times in his life.

They had no way of knowing how tall this tower was. The warlock might have spelled the building to have never ending floors that became more dangerous as they climbed higher. Or they may never reach the top. The stairwell could revert them right back to the nightmare with the spiders, no matter how many times they got through them.

But that hope still wriggled underneath his skin. What if they actually were close this time? What if they were going to find those eggs and he would see them again?

Breathless, he walked behind Lore to the next room, only to discover that it had been blown to shreds by someone else already.

"Oh," Lore muttered as she stepped through the rubble. "Perhaps this is how he died."

Considering the wall to their left was no more and the only thing remaining in the room was ash and rocks, that sounded accurate. Half of the next stairwell had crumbled and revealed the stone that had once built the tower.

The clouds outside looked more friendly than what they had gotten in here. The wind blew a little harder than he'd expected and the stars laid out before them like a blanket studded with diamonds.

The beauty he saw through the missing wall grounded him. Abraxas started on this journey for a singular reason and if the eggs weren't there, then they would find another way to get them. He would be all right.

He'd made friends on this journey, something he'd never had before. He cared for these people as though they were his family. And he would continue to care for them regardless of what they found in this tower.

Abraxas turned toward the stairs and then bent down onto a knee. "Use me as a stepping stone, Lore. Let's see what's up there."

"Are you sure?" she asked, her brows furrowed in worry. "I don't mind if you want to go first."

"Go ahead." He grinned up at her. "Let me down easy if you find nothing but dust."

He supposed it was the coward's way out. But looking into that room and seeing only rock and rubble would crush him. Abraxas simply couldn't do it.

As always, his Lore didn't hesitate. She placed her boot on his thigh and launched up to the stairwell that had crumbled away by half. She grabbed onto the soft stone and hauled herself to the top of it. Without even looking back, she disappeared from his sight and he could only hope she would find something good beyond.

Abraxas had to focus on breathing. He couldn't let the dark fears overwhelm him. And so he turned his gaze to the stars again. Just as he had the first night they'd met when he had been so angry. So upset.

And then he'd seen a Lady made of Starlight and he'd known his life would change in that moment. Forever.

Lore had surprised him, just as she'd shocked a lot of people before him. And the longer he was around her, the more he realized what a gem she was. He was lucky to have met her, and he wouldn't waste that opportunity to get to know her more.

He stared into the stars until he heard her whisper, "Abraxas?"

When he turned, he saw her framed in moonlight. She was covered in dust. Likely he was as well. Her eyes were wide and her hair had fallen out of its usual tight ponytail. The short strands created a halo around her head.

She didn't look disappointed. She didn't look sad. Instead, he couldn't quite understand her expression as she held out her hand.

"Jump," she said. "I'll help you up."

He didn't hesitate. The siren at the top of the stairs had called out to him. Abraxas ran toward her and used the stones to bound off. His feet hit heavily onto an already crumbling stone, but he jumped left, right, and then straight up. He caught hold of her outstretched hand and together, they pulled his much heavier body up to her side.

Lore held onto his fingers for a moment longer than necessary and he knew that she had to feel the same way he did. Her eyes sparkled in the stars. That was enough for him to know.

"Well?" he asked, breathless. "What did you find?"

"I think you should look for yourself."

Was that a good or a bad thing? He couldn't breathe through the anxiety of it, but... what if they were there?

He stared down into her beautiful eyes and something in them promised that he could relax. She wasn't afraid, and that meant there was nothing to fear. Nothing at all.

Abraxas let his hand slide from hers and turned around to look into the room beyond. The roof was missing, so he assumed this was the very top of the tower. The moonlight filtered through the exposed ceiling and illuminated a single podium in the center.

It took him a moment to see all the details. First, this area wasn't covered in dust at all. It was pristine and clean, as though no one had ever left it. Second, a box in the middle of the podium perched precariously because it was a little too large for the stand.

The worn wooden edges were worse than he'd seen it last. The clasps had obviously been tampered with, although they were still sealed shut without question. And, of course, the echo of dark magic swarmed the eggs within.

A long, shuddering breath shook through him. Those were his eggs. He could feel them.

And if he looked hard enough, he could see the glow from their souls even inside all that sinister power. They were alive. They were still whole.

Abraxas almost fell to his knees with relief. "They're alive," he whispered. "They're still alive."

"Did you ever doubt for a moment they wouldn't be?" Lore touched his back and the feeling of her hand pressed against him was a blessing. She gave him strength. "I don't know how we're going to get them out of here, but you know where they are now. We both do."

He wasn't leaving this room until he had them in his arms again. Abraxas had to know those eggs were safe and that his reign as sole dragon had ended.

His heart stuttered at the thought. He wasn't the only one, even though he'd come to terms with the possibility that he would end up being the last dragon. He wasn't alone.

That same scream as before echoed, and this time, he knew where it came from. A spirit appeared above the eggs. It glared down at them, though there wasn't much left of its form at all. He thought perhaps it was once a man. The wispy edges of his body had all but disappeared in the years since his death. Now, he was little more than a glowing mist that hovered over the podium.

Lore hissed out a low breath, and Abraxas knew she intended to fight that creature. But he'd seen spirits before and he'd spent centuries among other creatures. This warlock's spirit would not differ from countless others.

"What do you want?" he asked. "What do you want in return for what you guard?"

The warlock's ghostly face split into a dark grin. "You seek to take that which is mine."

"I do not want the box," Abraxas argued. "I care nothing about your magic. I merely want what the box contains for those eggs are mine and mine alone."

The mist of the warlock's body spread over the ceiling, rolling like thunderheads as the spirit grew more solid with rage. "No one can lay claim to the spirits of the unborn. They are untainted and thus cannot be owned."

"I lay claim to them. They are my progeny. They are my children, even though we do not share blood. They are mine," Abraxas fiercely replied. "You will not take them from me."

Lore took a step closer to him, ducking behind his back. "Abraxas, don't make the spirit angry."

He wasn't intending to, but the warlock was lecturing him on what he could lay claim to and damn it, those eggs were his. He'd spent nearly two mortal generations protecting them and even more generations trying to find them. If they belonged to anyone at all, then they belonged to him. He'd given up his life for those eggs!

Without thinking, he took another step forward. "Whatever it is you desire as payment for the eggs, I will pay it. Those are mine, however, and I will take them."

The warlock's form gathered together and his dark voice muttered, "So be it."

Like lightning, the mist plummeted through the air and struck Abraxas in the center of his chest. The sensation of ice cold magic startled him into taking a deep breath and his vision skewed, blinked, then he was blind.

Darkness swallowed everything other than a tiny pin prick of light so far away, he almost didn't notice it. And then it all rushed forward as though someone had turned on the sun.

The warlock stood in front of him. The wavering blueish green of his robes floated around him as though he were underwater.

"You brought the half elf to this place?" the warlock hissed. "Don't you know what the legends say of her kind?"

"There are no legends that would change my mind." Abraxas knew this to be true, and his voice rang with confidence. Control. The warlock had no right to insult her, and he would dash this vision to pieces if he did.

"You would do better to snap her neck now than to let her live." The warlock waved a hand behind him, and the darkness turned into a perfect likeness of the mural Abraxas had seen at the castle. "She will bring about an age of ruin."

The vision revealed the bottom of the mural. It showed an age of war and hardship. Magical creatures rising out of the ashes and battling with mortals on fields across Umbra. It showed how difficult the times would become.

But he didn't see an age of death and destruction like the warlock did. Instead, he saw the magical creatures finally living the way they were meant to. And he saw the image of a blonde elf leading them home. To a real home. One that they had never laid claim to.

"The age of man is coming to an end," he muttered, his voice carrying through the gloom. "Nothing you or I can do will stop that. This ruin you speak of is change. You will not survive it because you were not willing to ride the tides of time. That is not my problem."

"You will see how much death she'll bring," the warlock said. "Kill her now and I will give you the eggs."

Baring his teeth in a snarl, he lunged for the throat of the warlock. He gripped the incorporeal figure in his hands that turned into claws. "Touch her and you will die."

The warlock laughed, however. And the sound echoed in his ears, so he almost didn't hear the sounds of croaking. Nor did he feel the sensation of hands gripping his wrist and another trying to slap at his chest.

A blinding white light blasted in his eyes and suddenly he could see again. His hands weren't wrapped around the warlock's throat at all.

He'd grabbed Lore by the neck and strangled her.

Abraxas released his hold, horrified at the bright red marks on her skin once again. The bruises would be brighter this time, far more prominent than when Zander had choked her. And he was the one who had hurt her.

What had he done?

A crimson dragon was designed to protect that which it loved, and he had harmed the only thing in the world that mattered. Even more than the eggs. Even more than... life itself.

Dropping to his knees, Abraxas wrapped his arms around her waist and pressed his face into her belly. Breathing hard, he whispered against her skin, "I didn't mean... I couldn't see..."

She coughed, heaving in air through her lungs, but she still placed her broken hand on his head. "Dark magic has a way of twisting our minds. I know you didn't mean to."

"Even under a spell, I never thought I'd be capable of that." His hands shook in the folds of her shirt.

He'd always felt it would be impossible for him to hurt her. It should have been. He had bound himself to protect Lore, whether she knew that or not. To realize that he could do what Zander had done?

Abraxas wanted to cut his own hands off. He'd remove them so they could never touch her like that again. Never.

"Enough," she whispered, threading her fingers through his hair. "You can blame yourself for this later, Abraxas. But right now, we need to get those eggs before he comes back. You didn't mean to hurt me."

He forced himself to let go of her and to stand. Although he couldn't meet her gaze. "He said things about you, Lore. Things you should know."

"And we'll have that conversation when there's time for it." She cupped both hands on either side of his jaw and forced him to look at her. "I forgive you, Abraxas. Stop being angry at yourself for a choice you didn't make."

"You're forgiving me too easily."

"I'd forgive you for a great many things, Abraxas. And I would punish you for many more." She drew him closer to her and pressed their foreheads together. "Breathe. We have to figure out how to get the eggs without triggering whatever other trap he's left here."

He wanted to stand there and breathe with her for the rest of his life. Abraxas inhaled when she did, exhaled as she drew all the stress and anger out of his body. She left him feeling more leveled headed and cooled than he had in a long time.

Enough so that he knew what he had to do. There was only one way to get the eggs, after all.

He brought his own hand up and cupped the back of her neck, holding her closer to him. "I'm going to take them."

"We need to know if there's a spell first."

"I don't care if there is. The cursed warlock thinks he can get away with invading my mind and making me attack you? I will take the box from him, and I don't care if this entire tower falls." He breathed her in. "I think it's going to fall. So I need you to run."

She shook her head against his. "No, absolutely not. I won't run while you risk your life."

"You will." He drew back and smiled down at her, then tucked a strand of hair behind her ear. "We all have our time in the sun, but you gave me long moments in starlight. Stay alive for me, Lore. Run, and I will find you again. Because I love you, Lore. My soul and yours were split from each other centuries ago and it took me lifetimes to find you. Trust me when I say I will not lose you again so easily."

He kissed her with all the love in his heart and the exhilaration that she finally knew. He took his time just in case there wasn't another moment like this between them. In case one of them made a foolish mistake and all of this was lost. And then he turned to the chest and felt the dragon inside him awaken. He'd have to be fast. Faster than he'd ever been before.

Lore's footsteps backed toward the door, and then he heard her quietly say, "I love you too, Abraxas. As impossible as that sounds."

She stepped down the stairwell, and he listened to the thundering steps of her sprinting through that demolished room. The screeches of the spiders as she evaded their attack. Paper crunching beneath her booted feet. Rushing footsteps beyond shattered glass and vials that should never have been broken.

Good enough. She'd make it across the bridge next. He focused entirely on the eggs, the children, that were his.

"You're mine again," he whispered to the eggs. "I'll keep you safe. I promised."

A dragon never broke his promises.

CHAPTER 40

She ran, even though it shredded her heart to do so. Leaving him alone in that place, it felt as like she was admitting to being comfortable with his death. Anything could happen without her. He didn't know how to cast any spells or how to avoid dark magic that the warlock had left behind.

But he'd told her to run. And Lore knew if she had stayed, then she would have died in the rubble that tower would become.

They both recognized the warlock had trapped the building. As she leapt over the spiders that tried their best to catch her fleeing form, she knew that was the only logical thought. No one dared rob a warlock, but if they did, then they would find themselves dead sooner than growing rich off their findings.

Abraxas had made the only choice he could. He would be the only person to suffer the consequences if something happened.

She rushed out of the tower and across the tiny bridge. The rickety wood had replaced itself and broke away yet again as she ran across it. More trickery. More curses that shouldn't exist.

Lore wanted to tear it all down herself. The magic in her body desired the same thing. She could feel the anger of the moon at how a single man could pull so much power out of thin air and think it was acceptable for him to do so. Warlocks stole from the very earth they stood on. Blasphemous power deserved to be punished.

Just as she reached the other peak, a rumble started in the tower. She saw the first bricks start to fall. The ceiling ripped off as though some unseen hand had grabbed onto the building and pulled the top off. Some massive child playing with a toy.

She saw Abraxas standing in the center of the madness as stone swirled around him and rubble shook to life. A jagged rock caught his cheek, and she watched the bright spray of blood as it sliced through him. He never hesitated. He never even flinched.

Instead, he kept his focus on that box, reached out, and placed his hands on the sides.

Lore had to drop onto her hands and knees to prevent herself from falling off the ledge. The entire earth shook with the rage of ancient magic that had prevented people from stealing whatever it wanted to protect. Centuries had passed since any had dared to challenge the warlock's spell. It was all too happy to rise to the occasion.

Abraxas had his hands on the box and then he lifted it up and she felt her entire soul take flight with him. He had it! They finally had the eggs after all this time. And as he wasn't seeking to open the box just yet, nothing could lash out at him from that curse.

But then the entire tower tilted. It slid to the right as though someone had cut a wedge out of the base. Abraxas staggered on the top, his legs sliding in all directions, trying to catch his balance.

She pressed her hands to her mouth and tried not to scream. The high peak of the tower seemed to sway in the breeze as the spell upon it sought to destroy the entire construction.

He needed to get off that building. She didn't know how he planned on doing that while holding onto the box. He should have thrown it at her and had her run. But then the first level of the tower folded. Broken glass blasted out of the sandwiched rooms as the second story fell down onto the other. She was certain Abraxas would have to leave the box.

Instead of doing anything that she'd expected, he ran to the very edge of the tower and threw the box out into the wind.

"No!" Lore screamed, stretching out her arm as if she could catch it. She even flung a spell through the air, hoping the dragon eggs would respond to a summoning charm.

Her magic fell away from it, rebounding from the curse and instead sending a rock flying back at her. Lore ducked out of its way just in time to see Abraxas leap after the eggs. He plummeted through the air, still in mortal form, and then he disappeared from her sight.

"No," she whispered. Lore couldn't hear herself over the sound of stone, brick, and wood falling down the mountain side. "Abraxas, what did you do?"

She crouched at the flattest edge of the peak and peered over the edge. Nothing. There were only the clouds that obscured her vision from ever finding the man she loved and that box of eggs which should have changed the world.

Lore refused to believe he was gone. She couldn't imagine that he'd throw himself from the tower without a plan, and that meant he had known what was going to happen. He'd known that there was a chance for him and the eggs to survive. All he had to do was... something. Anything.

Her fingers curled over the sharpened edges of the stone beneath her. "Abraxas," she muttered. "Where are you?"

He had to be all right. She didn't know what she'd do if he wasn't all right, only that it wasn't fair for him to disappear when she'd just discovered her feelings for him. They couldn't say those words to each other and then be ripped apart. Not when she'd never felt so strongly about another person in her entire life.

He had to come back.

She held her breath and then the moonlight caught on the smooth edges of scales. A flash from deep within the clouds, but it was enough. She'd seen him.

The mist parted, and a dragon soared into the silvery light. His wings beat at the air, struggling to lift him up through gusts that wanted to push him down. And then she saw them. The box of eggs clutched in his mouth.

Her heart stuttered, stopped, and then thundered in her chest. He had them! He had the eggs, and they were... free?

Had they done it?

Lore threw her fists into the air and screamed, "Yes!"

They'd done what they had set out to do. What everyone had thought was impossible. Those eggs were theirs and they hadn't died gathering them, although she certainly had the assumed that they might. They'd survived the unthinkable.

She waved her arms frantically at Abraxas and she saw him flash her a dazzling grin as he wheeled over her in the sky. His wings spread wide as the sun poked out over the horizon. A bright streak of pinks, reds, and purples filled the air as he soared overhead with the last of the dragons held safely in his mouth.

Lore lowered her arms and tears pricked her eyes. This was the future she'd hoped for. Dragons flying through the sky without fear of spears cutting through the delicate membranes of their wings. This was the hope that she'd felt when she first saw him fly.

That hope bloomed in her chest. It unfurled great petals that glistened in her mind's eye like honey and wine. They were all right. Everything was going to change for the better.

She sat down on the peak and wrapped her arms around her knees, watching as he meandered through the clouds. He flipped and twirled, graceful as he gave the eggs a flight that they'd never had before. She could almost hear the sounds of their bliss.

Those two souls had no idea how much they were going to transform the world. They didn't know how many people would watch them grow with a hope that control of Umbra would return to the magical creatures. After all this time.

They were more than just a symbol to her people. Each of those eggs was the proof that circumstances could change. That fighting for their rights and for others to see them was possible.

The feeling in her chest grew so powerful that it was almost painful. Lore didn't know what to do with it. She wanted to scream with elation. She wanted to sob with relief.

"Mom," she whispered, letting her words float through the air while hoping her mother's spirit would hear her. "I continued your work. As much as I hated it for taking you away from me, I see now why you did what you did. This was worth all the blood and the tears."

To look at how happy Abraxas was, to know that she'd had a part in it, she understood why her mother had fought so long and so hard.

He wheeled one last time through the clouds before he drifted down on an air current. Abraxas hovered beside her and gently placed the box at her feet.

"I think that went as well as could be expected," he said, the deep dragon voice like thunder.

"Neither of us died," she replied with a soft smile. "And it appears you are not the last dragon anymore."

"Indeed." The scales around his throat pulsed with the light of flames. "They are ours again, Lore. Not just mine. You helped me save them and for that, I will forever be in your debt."

"No." She shook her head. "You owe me nothing. Seeing you with these eggs reminded me why I've been doing all this. It's hope for a better future."

The fires in his throat died, and he gave her a look that only emphasized what he'd said just moments ago. He loved her. She loved him. They'd spoken those words in a moment of fear and worry because they both had thought they might never see each other again.

But now they had. He grabbed onto the rocky peak with his legs and then gripped the edge with the claws at the end of his wings. He stared at her with that knowing look, and Lore hoped perhaps he would turn back into a man for this moment.

Instead, he growled, "I have changed too many times lately, and I cannot return to my mortal form without risking great pain. But I will have you know, Lore. I meant what I said. With every ounce of my being."

"As did I." She leaned down and picked up the box of eggs, holding them carefully in case the magic rebounded again. "I wouldn't have said the words if I didn't mean them."

"Are you going to run from me again?"

She looked at him sharply. Had she run from him before? She'd rather assumed she had managed the relationship between them well enough. Though, the more she thought about it, the more she realized he was correct.

She had been running from this for a very long time. Whether that was fear of her own emotions or fear of connection, she didn't know. But she'd run away from him since the moment they first laid eyes on each other.

"I will not run," she said. "Not this time. I've found you have become too dear to me to ever run again, Abraxas."

"Good." He eyed her a little more thoroughly. "I'll hold you to that. Now, would you like to leave?"

"More than anything." She didn't want to see if those spiders would crawl up from the depths.

Lore feared they may have loosed the creatures upon the mountains, but then she decided that was all right. No one lived here any longer, and the beasts had some level of intelligence that was greater than the average arachnid. If they could find a home in these cliffs, then let them. Who was she to decide that such souls shouldn't live?

Still, she glanced over her shoulder to make sure there weren't any large, furred legs crawling up behind her while they talked.

"Thinking of the spiders?" Abraxas asked. "I'll set them on fire if we see them again."

She looked at that beloved face of his, with the quirky way his dragon lips tilted to the side as he realized she was looking at him. And everything else faded away. She wasn't worried about the spiders or what other thing the warlock might have hidden. She didn't fear the end of this journey and what would happen between them.

All she could think about was him. That the smile on his face had changed forever now. He'd gotten back the eggs, the most important things in his life. He saw her as someone who was trustworthy and who would uphold any promises that she made.

Lore had only wanted to be that for another person. That bone deep desire to have a partner who looked at her with utmost trust had been buried for so long, she'd forgotten it existed.

The last person to look at her like that had been her mother. Her expression had softened while she said goodbye to Lore, for the last time, although she hadn't been aware of it. With a bright smile on her face, her mother had stroked a hand down Lore's face and whispered in her ear that she would love her forever.

She'd forgotten what it felt like. To be loved and to love in return.

But she had to stop staring at him like the dolt she was. He'd think something was wrong and then she'd have to explain that she was fine, just expecting that she might pop with the emotion in her chest and did he remember that she loved him? More than he realized. More than she enjoyed admitting.

Lore was making herself feel sick even thinking about how much he now meant to her and how awful this feeling felt. And wonderful. And horrible. And somehow stronger than anything else she'd experienced.

She cleared her throat and shook her head. "No, don't burn them. If they're wild in the mountains, then perhaps that will give magical creatures a better opportunity to reclaim this land. No human will dare attack spiders that large."

"Let's just hope they don't get even bigger," he replied with a snort. "Are you ready to leave?"

"More than I've ever been." She shifted the box in her hands, wrapping an arm around them so they were tucked against her side. "Are you going to land so I can get on you again?"

He shook his head, and that glint in his eyes burned with mischief. "No, my dear. Bright Heart that you are, you must know there isn't enough room for me to land. You'll have to jump."

"Jump?" she repeated.

Abraxas let go of the stones and wheeled off into the air. He soared, circling around her just underneath the peak until she realized he wanted her to leap onto his back.

A sudden burst of bravery flooded through her veins. She'd defeated the tower of an ancient warlock and ridden on the back of a dragon to get here. She'd battled kings and formed alliances with a rebellion of magical creatures who sought to break the chains that had weighed them down for centuries.

With a loud whoop of euphoria, she ran across the edge of the mountain peak and launched herself into the air. The wind whistled in her ears. Her own scream echoed, and then she hit Abraxas's back.

Wildly, she hooked an arm around a spine and held on for dear life. But he wouldn't let her fall. She didn't question that for a second.

He shook himself, helping her as she wrapped a leg over his sides and heaved herself into a safe seated position. Lore placed the eggs in front of her and never let go of them. Not once as they rode off into the morning light.

And what a picture they must have painted, an elf and her dragons.

CHAPTER 41

He'd seen the look in her eyes back on that mountain cliff. Abraxas knew just how much she wanted him. How she desired to bury her hands in his human hair and rip out strands as she devoured his lips.

They'd desired each other for a while now. She wasn't the only one who shared that desire and if he weren't a dragon, they'd already have discovered what made the other gasp with pleasure or shiver with anticipation. He intended to find time alone with her, no matter what happened between them.

Abraxas had enough of this cat-and-mouse game they'd been playing. He'd heard her finally admit that he meant something to her, and now it was time to find out just how much. How far she was willing to go. And just how much he could push her to discover more about this attraction between them.

He landed next to the glass safe house, his balance faltering for a moment. The flight had been further than he'd traveled in a while. Even though he'd never stayed still for too long in his dragon form, the King had always wanted him near the castle.

The safe house was now in sight, he realized that he was quite tired. His wings shuddered and his legs turned to jelly the moment he no longer had to keep them all secure.

Lore slid from his back, landing hard on the ground before placing her hands on his heaving sides. "Are you all right?"

He nodded, unable to say anything through the great gusts of breath he had to suck in through his mouth.

"Are you sure?" she asked, those beautiful brows furrowed in worry. "You don't seem all right."

"Just tired," he wheezed. "Stand back so I can change."

It was a bad idea. Changing would only mean all of a dragon's exhaustion would hit him in mortal form. But he wanted to hold her. Now that they'd said the words, he craved to wrap around her and tug her close to his heart. To feel her own beating against his chest while he finally, finally kissed her.

"That sounds like a bad idea," she replied.

Again, was.

He still did it, hoping everything would fade once he got the opportunity to be with her. Be near her. Hold her.

The moment all the scales melted away from him, he realized how wrong that decision had been. Abraxas listed to the side. He stumbled, holding out his arms as though there was anything to brace himself on. There wasn't. Not until a loud thump echoed against the stones, and a warm body slipped underneath his arm.

"Easy," she muttered, bracing her legs to hold him up. "I've got you."

She wouldn't in a moment. Already the edges of his vision turned foggy as black and white specks warned he was about to pass out. He hadn't done that since he was a little dragonling.

"You should get Zeph," he wheezed.

"Why's that?"

"They're going to have to drag me into the safe house." Those were the last words he remembered saying as an icy chill consumed his body and his vision went dark.

Abraxas woke after what he could only assume was hours later. His first impression was the quiet sound of a fire crackling nearby and the low murmurs of people who didn't want to disturb the one who was resting.

Him, he suspected.

He wiggled his toes and fingers as memories filtered through his consciousness. They'd gone to the warlock's home. The eggs were safe with Lore. He'd passed out in front of her like a child because he had pushed himself too far to bring them all the way to the tower and back in the span of two days.

He'd made a fool of himself by passing out. Abraxas might never live it down.

"Oh good," Lore's voice broke through his thoughts. "You're awake."

The struggle to peel his eyelids open suggested that she could be wrong. He wasn't awake at all. He was in a nightmare where he could barely feel his body and he wanted that horror to end. Otherwise, he'd throw up on the floor.

"Not awake," he croaked. "I think I might be dead."

"You certainly aren't that. Otherwise, you'd be feeling quite a bit better, I suspect."

He tilted his head to the side, an action which made the entire world spin around him alarmingly, and found her.

Lore sat beside the cot they must have thrown him on. She'd taken her hair down, and it stuck out in all directions. The wind had tangled it into a rather strange dandelion puff on top of her head. Her eyes were bright red and her cheeks were windblown. She had dark circles under her eyes that made her look sickly.

He thought he'd never seen her more beautiful in all his months of knowing her.

Even though he shook, he still reached out and touched the back of a finger to her cheek. "You look lovely," he said.

She caught his hand in hers, smiling at him as though he'd told her she was worth a dragon's trove of treasures. "I don't, but thank you. I thought you'd want to be awake for this."

Awake for what?

He didn't want to sit up, if that's what she was asking him to do. He would throw up and fainting in front of her had been embarrassing enough.

"For what?" he rasped.

"Zeph wants to try opening the box. He isn't sure it's going to work, and we've already set up a couple of spells to make sure it doesn't kill him. But we wanted to wait for you. Just in case he can actually open it."

They were... what?

Abraxas planted his elbows on the bed and shoved himself upright. The entire world spun. What little food was in his stomach pressed against the back of his throat, but he swallowed it down.

They were going to open the box. They were going to see if their theory was correct and if Abraxas no longer had to fear the worst.

What if he could? What if Zeph could open that horrible, weather beaten lid and Abraxas got to see the eggs again?

It had been so long since he'd seen them. Would they even remember him? Of course they would, he scolded himself. Those eggs remembered more than anyone gave them credit for and they knew who had saved them. The babies inside might not yet be able to see, but they recognized energies. They'd recall the feel of his gaze and the whispered words of encouragement that no one else had ever said to them. Not in centuries, at least.

He swallowed again and swung his legs over the edge of the bed. Hands still shaking, he squeezed the wooden frame of the cot and stared at Lore's expression. "I'm all right."

"Are you sure? The last time you said that to me, you then fell on top of me and almost crushed me." Though she said it with a smile, he knew he must have hurt her.

He was a big man to fall on such a small woman. They were both lucky he hadn't broken her ribs.

Perhaps he should be more honest this time.

Abraxas grabbed her hand and laced their fingers together. "I'm not all right. I won't be until we know if he can actually open the box. Until I know if I can see them again."

She understood his fear. Of course she did. Lore had become an extension of himself as they experienced the same hardships repeatedly. She lifted his hand to her mouth and pressed a kiss to his knuckles. "We'll know soon enough."

He forced his eyes to turn away from hers and then surveyed the rest of the room. Beauty and Goliath stood next to each other in the back, both propping up twin mattresses from the other cots. The glistening web of magic had clearly been made of Lore's magic. A shield? Likely the best they could do against the powerful curse that would throw Zeph if the box didn't want to open to him.

And Zeph himself stood in the center of the room with the box. He shook out his hands, as though his fingers already stung with the lightning of wizardry.

The young man made eye contact with Abraxas and flashed him a confident grin. "I know I'm of the same bloodline. I suppose it'll be interesting to know how strongly I resemble my brother."

"It's magic, boy," Abraxas replied. "It cannot be tricked by appearance alone. I don't know what the warlock's rules are. Few have tried to open the box other than the King, even when Zander was a child and his father ruled over what hides within."

"I guess I should be honored to get a chance." Zeph wiggled his fingers again. "How badly will this hurt if I make a mistake?"

"A lot." Abraxas let his gaze wander to the back of the room where there were many odd objects decorating the shelves. "They should have a potion ready for you. Just in case. Lore almost died the last time she tried to open it, though she was lucky I was there to save her."

"I'd almost forgotten about that," she whispered. "Maybe he shouldn't try to touch it."

Zeph gave them both a rather unimpressed look. "I'm going to open it. This is the only reason I'm here, isn't it?"

Abraxas bit his lip, but nodded at the boy. He wasn't wrong. They had only brought him with them to see if he could lift the lid of the box, but what if he couldn't? Then they were right back in the same place they'd been before.

With a quick squeeze of his fingers, Lore replied to the young man, "Go ahead and try. We've done all we can to protect you."

Damn it, he wished he could do more. They all held their breath as Zeph reached out with both hands for the lid. He put his fingers on the top, smoothing his palms over the surface as though taming a wild beast.

Zeph tried to flip the lid, and the magic exploded. The bright whips of power lashed through the air with no one to control them. Abraxas wrapped his arms around Lore and yanked her against his side. The magic struck his arm instead of her face.

Zeph, as expected, flew across the room. He landed heavily against Lore's shield, which shattered upon impact, and then he fell against Beauty and Goliath. The mattresses were a good idea. All three of them tumbled onto the floor with heavy thuds.

The magic retreated into the box and left them all bruised and breathing hard.

Lore peered through her fingers and asked, "Everyone still alive?"

It took a few heartbeats for answering groans to echo across the room.

"Alive!" Beauty replied.

"Barely," Goliath groaned.

Even Zeph sat up, his hair sticking straight up and crackling with electricity. "Alive, but what the hell is in that box?"

No one knew. That was the problem. And the box knew well that Zeph was not Zander, and no matter what they did, that would mean they couldn't get the lid open. Although, Abraxas had to at least note that the magic hadn't been as cruel to the King's half brother as it was to most people who tried to open that lid.

Sighing, he released his hold on Lore and let his hands drop to his side. "I should have known that it wouldn't open. Not for anyone other than Zander."

Beauty shoved the mattress off herself and then stumbled to her feet. Her expression could only be described as determined, and that made Abraxas prepare himself for a fight.

"Don't blame him for this," she said, pointing a finger at Abraxas. "I told you we should have brought everything back to Margaret. She might have some kind of idea what to do from here. It's not like she hasn't been in the trenches for years, trying to prepare us all for this moment."

"Would you stop bringing up Margaret?" he snarled. "You're the only one in here who even remotely trusts her."

"Because she saved my life!" Beauty shouted, and then snapped her jaw shut. She shuffled her feet on the floor before speaking again. "My father would have sold me off to the highest bidder and married me to an old man for money. Margaret gave me a purpose better than that. And gave me the perfect explanation so that I never had to do what my father wanted. I owe her my life."

"You owe her nothing more than the life you gave up," he replied. Abraxas stood on shaky legs, so she knew his words meant something. "She took a future from you that while you might not have liked, but was the future you were meant to have. I don't know what she's planning, but until now, Beauty, you were the only human in the room. Did you think she planned to keep you around for long?"

Beauty's mouth dropped open, but she had nothing to say in response. She'd likely never thought of it in that way, and he hated to be the person who brought it up. But someone had to mention it. Someone had to point out that she was the outlier in the room.

He perhaps felt a little bad at being so abrupt. He didn't want to hurt her, but... What else was he supposed to say?

Zeph patted his hair down and muttered, "We're all arguing about the wrong person, anyway. This Margaret is already in the castle and she's doing whatever she wants to get the magical creatures of this realm in order. That's fine. But my brother is out there getting stronger every moment, and the magic in that box won't let us get the dragon eggs. So what's the plan now?"

If only he knew what to do next. Abraxas hadn't the faintest idea other than knowing they had to stop Zander and they couldn't trust the person who was heading up with all this... effort.

Lore's voice rippled behind them and split through the air as though she were a prophet and they were her subjects.

"What if Zander summons the eggs again?"

The notion wrecked him. Why hadn't they thought of it before? They had the eggs right now because Zander didn't know they had stolen them. But all the King had to do was summon them once more, and they would have to find the eggs all over again.

His stomach twisted and all that hope he'd felt seeped out of his soul.

Surprisingly, Zeph pointed to his pack. "I might be able to help with that."

Silence was the young man's only reply.

Lore narrowed her eyes on him, the first to speak up. "What do you have?"

"Well, I didn't want to bring it up because it might have been stolen from an elven ruin. I thought it might be rude, but... Well, it was meant to be my gift to Abraxas." He marched over the pack and pulled out an amulet.

He had no clue what that amulet would do, but the way Lore's face paled, it must be a powerful one.

447

"Where did you get that?" she whispered, reaching out her hands to take it.

"Mother found it in the crypt when we first arrived." Zeph let it drop into her waiting hands. "She said it negates curses."

"Any curse," Lore said. She cradled the amulet as though it were made of gold. "It will hide the box from even the most powerful of warlock's curses. For a time. They don't last forever."

Abraxas grinned. "Then we'll have to find the King quickly. What's the plan now that this changes everything?"

"We continue on in our own way. We are not the fallen creatures who failed," Lore replied, her words sharp and deep. "We know Margaret will fail because her attention is split too thin. She wants the creatures to take back over, but they are not the threat. Mortal men are not even the threat any longer. We must continue forward and defeat this King who would tear the kingdom apart again. We go our own way."

Beauty pressed a hand to her chest. "Are you saying we don't go back?"

"I'm saying we find other allies. Ones who will put the power back not just in our hands, but in the hands of the magical creatures. We are the ones who have fought for them, after all." Lore looked up and met each one of their gazes. "I convinced the Ashen Deep to leave their haven under the ground. We killed wights and survived an undead King. We can take our homeland back. Not with Margaret, but the right people. The ones we choose and the ones we know will fight by our sides."

The silence in the room was deafening. But Abraxas knew she was right.

He looked over at the others in the room and nodded. "We take this kingdom back together."

One by one, they repeated the words. "Together."

Until they all looked back at Lore, who smiled weakly. "And so we become the few who seek to save the many."

EPILOGUE

L ore had been with everyone while they gathered their things. She stayed right next to their side and never once stopped encouraging them. But the moment they set their gear down outside the forest for the night, the same place they'd camped before entering the Fields of Somber, she slipped out into the darkness.

This time, however, she didn't fear the wights. She didn't fear that the King would still be there, either.

The Ashen Deep were thorough. Even the stories about them were dark and murmured whispers of them coming into a land and wiping out every living thing. They wouldn't have left any wights to shamble the Fields.

She traveled through the night, letting the moonlight guide her feet all the way back to the graves. It took a long time. Long enough that her breath was ragged by the time she stopped. The light of the moon faded in the wake of day.

Lore then spent the next day working hard. Sweat covered her back and slicked down her sides, but she didn't stop. Not once. She continued on through the sun beating on her shoulders, lacking food and water because this was her penance. This was a time for her to purge all the guilt in her chest from so many years, casting aside her history and birthright.

When she finished, she stood staring down at a hole in the ground large enough to fit a body that would never fill it. This was the way of the elves. Her mother had nothing to bury. Not even a necklace or a painting of what she looked like. But Lore could place her memories in the earth where they would be swallowed up for all time. She would lay her mother to rest with all the others of their family who had died on this battlefield.

"Thank you," she whispered, staring into the hole that would never be filled. "For everything that you did for me. I'm sorry I've held onto you for so long. I know you wouldn't have wanted to stay and not be able to go to the ancient fields with your own family."

She should have done this a long time ago. Not letting go of her mother had likely worn on both of them. She'd wanted her mother to be here and her mother's spirit had wished for rest. That push and pull had tormented them both for long enough.

Lore reached into her pocket and pulled out the handful of crushed blue flowers that dotted the Fields of Somber. She'd carried them with her all day, and they weren't much of anything anymore. But the sprinkle of color in the grave made her feel a little better.

At least she hadn't been talking to an entirely empty space.

"Do you have any idea how long I've been tracking your footsteps?" His gravelly voice sent a shiver between her shoulder blades.

She had known he'd find her. The others would wake and they would worry about where she'd gone off to. They were far too close to the Ashen Deep who'd already tried to kill her once. No one trusted that the strange band of elves wouldn't try again.

"Honestly, I'm surprised it took you so long," she said, turning and watching as he strode across the field.

The sunlight had dimmed. Deep shadows spread out from his feet and the nightly mist of the moors sprung up around his thighs. Abraxas had his hands tucked into his pockets and a long jacket draped over his shoulders. Summoned by magic, no doubt. His black hair fluttered in the slight breeze, and the pale streaks of the red and crimson sky hinted at a dusting of scales that hadn't quite left since his last change.

Her dragon meandered to her side, each step measured and slow. He gave her the chance to run, or to tell him to stop. But the time for that was long past. She didn't want to run from him any longer. She wanted him by her side for good.

He joined her at the edge of the grave and looked into the deep hole she'd dug. Lore noticed his hesitation, as though he might actually see a body in there.

"What's this?"

She gestured with a limp hand. "The elves believe a soul cannot rest until they are buried. Even if there's nothing left of them, it's still helpful to have some sort of place to remember them."

His brows furrowed.

Obviously, he didn't understand what she meant, so Lore added, "It's for my mother."

His eyes widened, and she saw the intense discomfort pass over his features. He muttered, "Give me a moment, then."

And he walked away.

She watched him leave, but knew this must be difficult for him. After all, he'd killed the woman Lore had laid to rest throughout the whole day. And knowing Abraxas, he'd probably been watching her for much longer than she realized.

Lore turned back to her mother's grave, wrapped her arms around herself, silently standing vigil until the moon came out once again. Light danced over the hole in the ground and with it, Lore spread her fingers and weaved a spell.

It was harder than anything she'd ever done. Lore knew magical spells others had created, but she'd never created a spell on her own. Not until tonight.

Perhaps hours passed as she worked to make a headstone out of moonlight. When she finished, the only people who would see it were those that walked in the moon's light. But they would read her mother's name and know that someone out there remembered her mother still.

Footsteps crunched behind her as the last light of the spell dimmed.

Lore opened her mouth to say she was ready to leave, but was struck mute as Abraxas knelt beside the grave with an armful of fresh flowers. Flowers she recognized from their journey here, and ones that would have required that he change his form into the dragon once again. The red roses and yellow lilies didn't grow anywhere near the Fields, but somehow he had them.

"A thousand wildflowers would never be enough to thank you for the daughter you left behind," Abraxas growled, his voice deep and low. "I could beg on my knees for your forgiveness for the rest of my life and never expect you to forgive me. But you must know that you have made a beautiful daughter. A wonderful woman. Your child will change this world, and I will stand by her. I will keep her alive, as I could not keep you alive."

Tears pricked her vision. She hadn't expected anything from him. Nothing at all.

And he'd ripped out her heart with his kindness.

"Abraxas," she whispered, reaching out her arms for him.

He stepped into her hug willingly, cupping her face in both his hands and pressing a kiss to her lips that left her breathless. He apologized with reckless abandon and a gentleness that soothed the ache in her soul. Every kiss and whispered apology reminded her how lucky she was to have him in her life. Abraxas told her without words that no apology would ever be enough, but that he would fight every day to be worthy of her love.

And when he pulled away, a sigh on his lips, he pressed their foreheads together as though he couldn't bear to be apart from her for too long. "We have much work to do, Bright Heart."

"That we do." She didn't even want to think about the plan or what they were going to do now. She hadn't given it enough thought, although they were already wandering away from the Stygian Peaks.

Lore didn't know the next steps in their journey. She hadn't the faintest idea how they would find people to fight by their side. Or what she was planning on doing to save their kingdom.

Abraxas smiled down at her, and with that look, she knew he didn't care about any of it. All he cared about was that they were together.

"Lore," he said with a soft growl. "Would you like to rebuild a kingdom with me?"

"I might." She patted his chest a couple of times before tucking her head under his chin. "But I think we have some dragon eggs to hatch first."

The story continues in Brave Heart, preorder today!

ACKNOWLEDGEMENTS

Like the first book, Bego and Nic, you are absolute saviors. Your eyes make sure that this book is at least remotely clean. I don't know what I'd do without the two of you ladies! You are the reason why this book is the way it is.

Big BIG hug to my fiance, my better half, definitely the better looking one in the relationship. Thank you for giving me the space and time needed to really dive into this book. But namely, thank you for giving me the confidence that this story is a good one.

And lastly, this book was dedicated to a very special dog who unfortunately has made his way across the rainbow bridge. Zephyr, I said I would never name a book character after you, but now look at what you made me do. I miss you bud. Every day.

ABOUT THE AUTHOR

Emma Hamm is a small town girl on a blueberry field in Maine. She writes stories that remind her of home, of fairytales, and of myths and legends that make her mind wander.

She can be found by the fireplace with a cup of tea and her two Maine Coon cats dipping their paws into the water without her knowing.

For more updates, join my newsletter!
www.emmahamm.com

CPSIA information can be obtained
at www.ICGtesting.com
Printed in the USA
LVHW090944050422
715332LV00020B/330/J